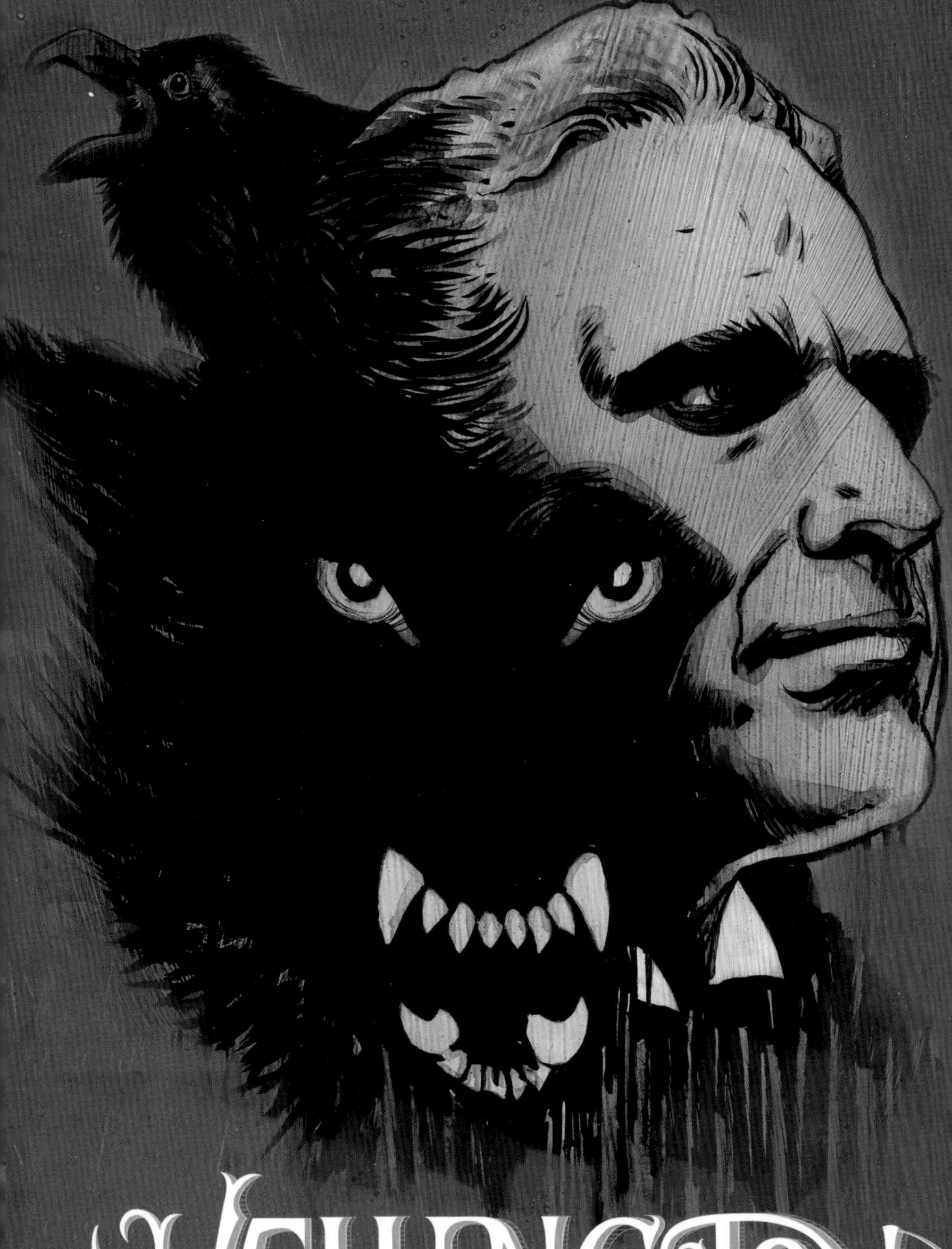

WELLINGTON

IDW

Facebook: **facebook.com/idwpublishing**
Twitter: **@idwpublishing**
YouTube: **youtube.com/idwpublishing**
Tumblr: **tumblr.idwpublishing.com**
Instagram: **instagram.com/idwpublishing**

ISBN: 978-1-68405-689-7   23 22 21 20   1 2 3 4

Cover Artist
Piotr Kowalski

Cover Colorist
Brad Simpson

Series Editorial Assistant
Riley Farmer

Series Editor
Chase Marotz

Collection Editors
Alonzo Simon and **Zac Boone**

Collection Designer
Ron Estevez

Originally published as WELLINGTON issues #1–5.

Chris Ryall, President & Publisher/CCO
Cara Morrison, Chief Financial Officer
Matthew Ruzicka, Chief Accounting Officer
John Barber, Editor-in-Chief
Justin Eisinger, Editorial Director, Graphic Novels and Collections
Scott Dunbier, Director, Special Projects
Jerry Bennington, VP of New Product Development
Lorelei Bunjes, VP of Technology & Information Services
Jud Meyers, Sales Director
Anna Morrow, Marketing Director
Tara McCrillis, Director of Design & Production
Mike Ford, Director of Operations
Shauna Monteforte, Manufacturing Operations Director
Rebekah Cahalin, General Manager

Ted Adams and Robbie Robbins, IDW Founders

Story by Aaron Mahnke & Delilah S. Dawson

Script by Delilah S. Dawson

Art by Piotr Kowalski

Colors by Brad Simpson

Letters by Christa Miesner
and Valeria López

Wellington created by
Aaron Mahnke

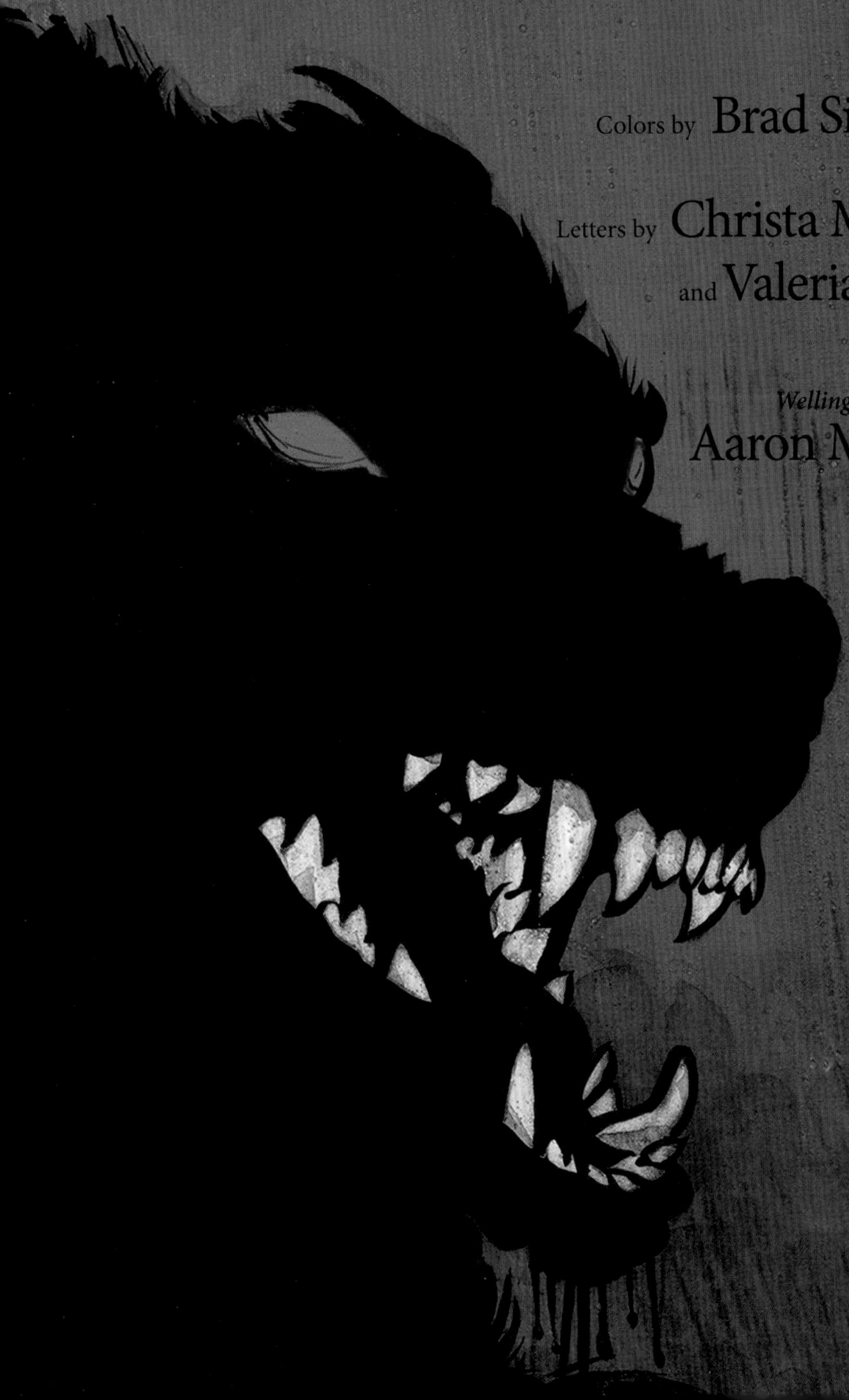

Chapter 1

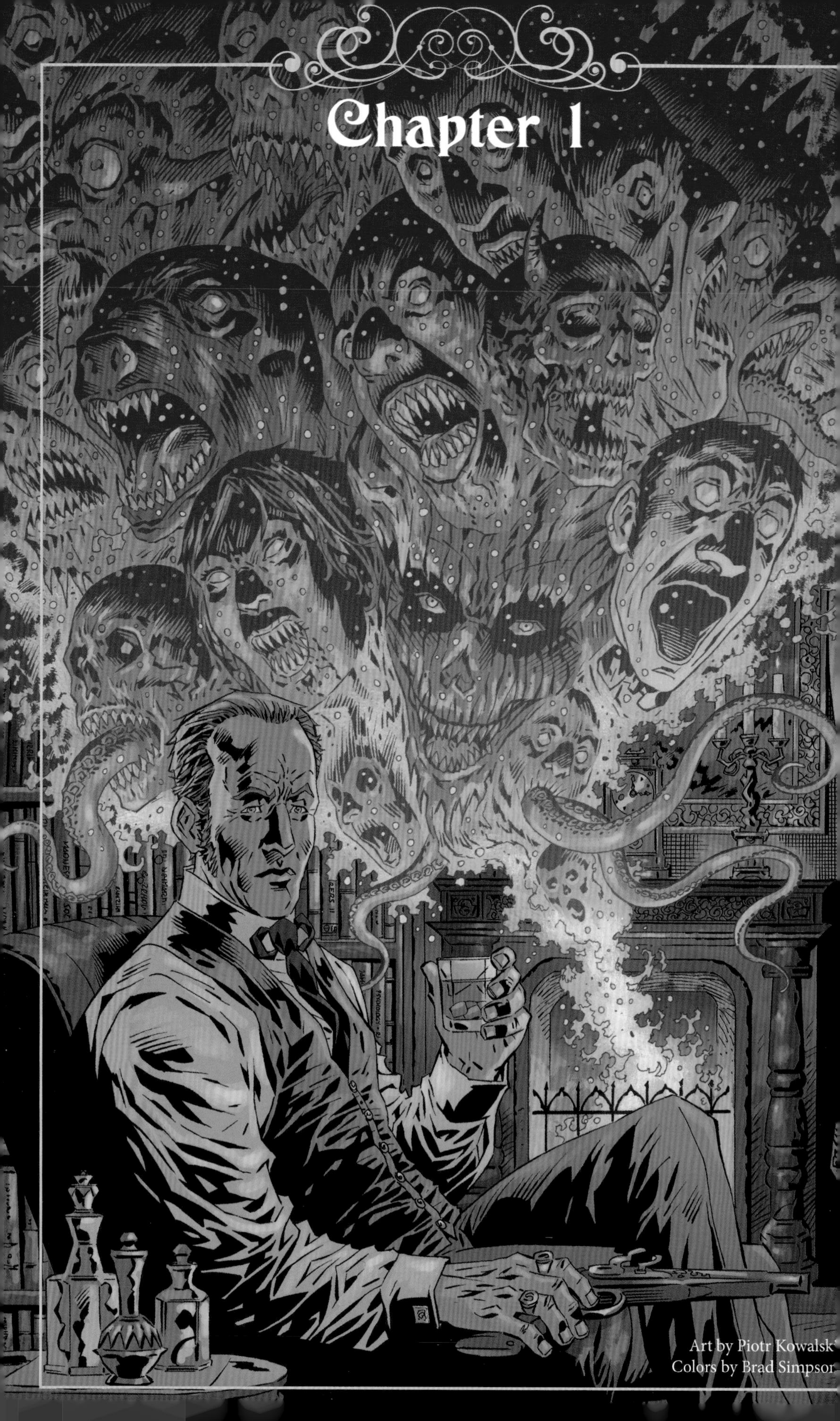

Art by Piotr Kowalsk
Colors by Brad Simpsor

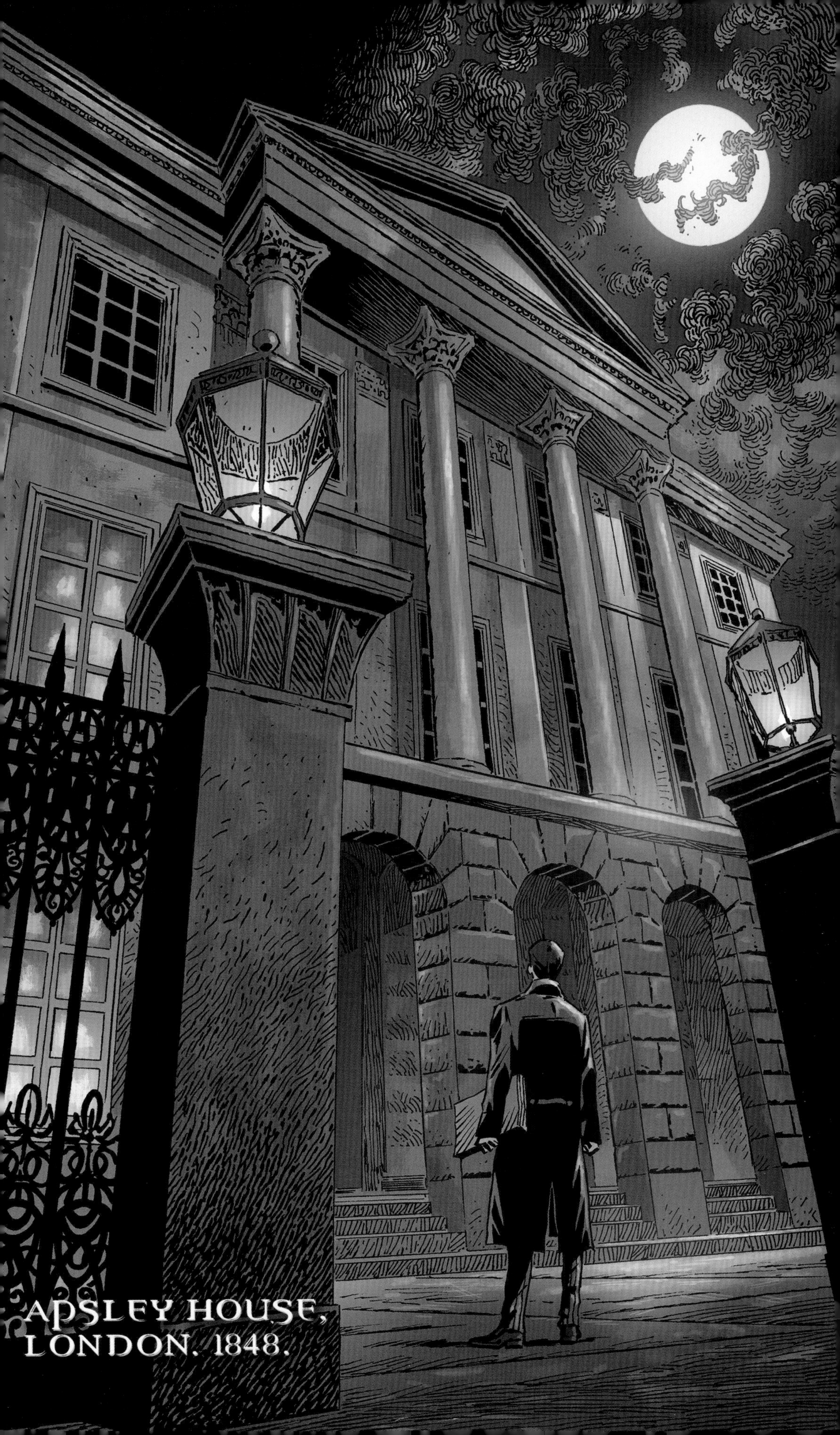
APSLEY HOUSE,
LONDON. 1848.

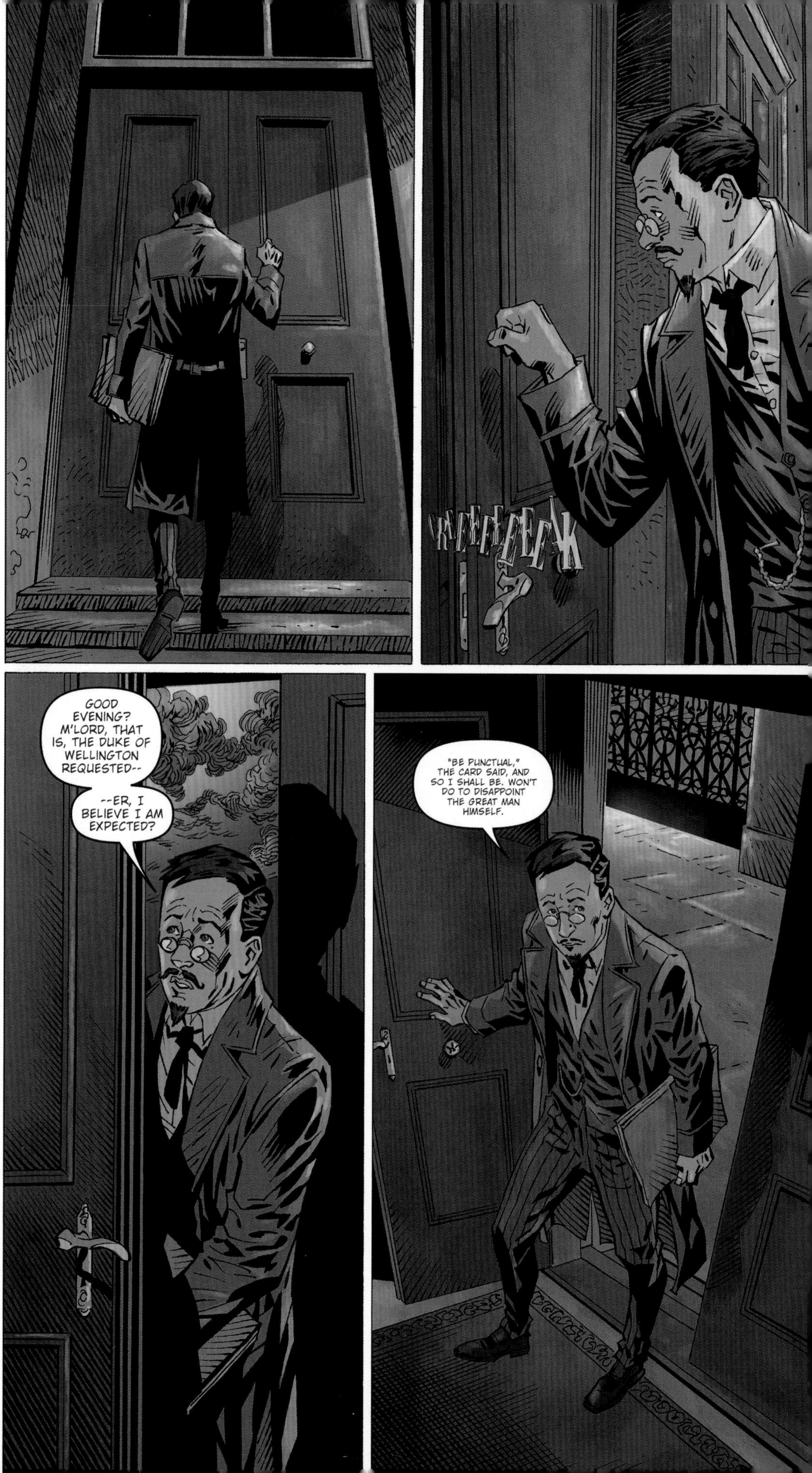
CREEEEEEAK
GOOD EVENING? M'LORD, THAT IS, THE DUKE OF WELLINGTON REQUESTED--
--ER, I BELIEVE I AM EXPECTED?
"BE PUNCTUAL," THE CARD SAID, AND SO I SHALL BE. WON'T DO TO DISAPPOINT THE GREAT MAN HIMSELF.

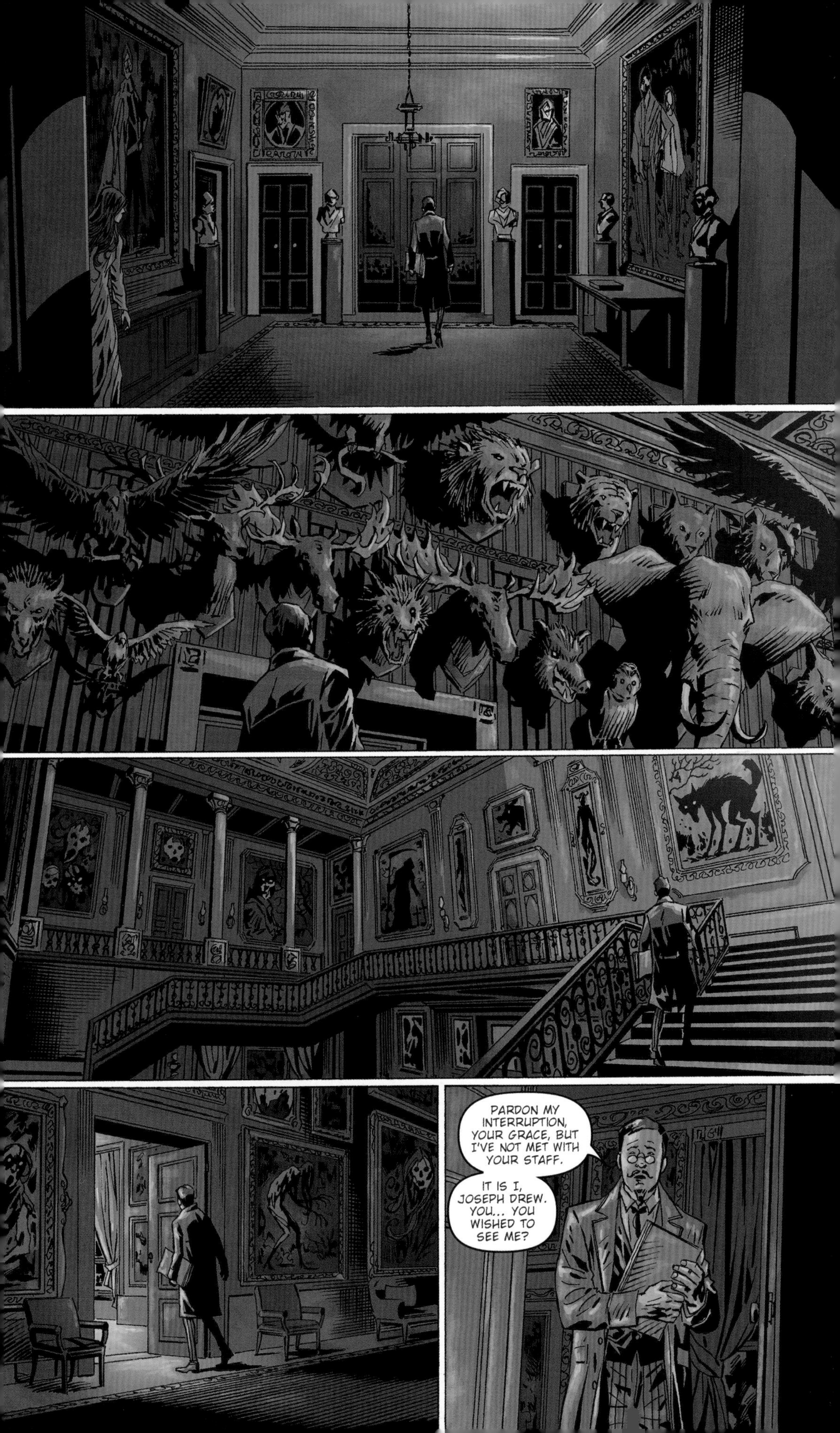
PARDON MY INTERRUPTION, YOUR GRACE, BUT I'VE NOT MET WITH YOUR STAFF.
IT IS I, JOSEPH DREW. YOU... YOU WISHED TO SEE ME?

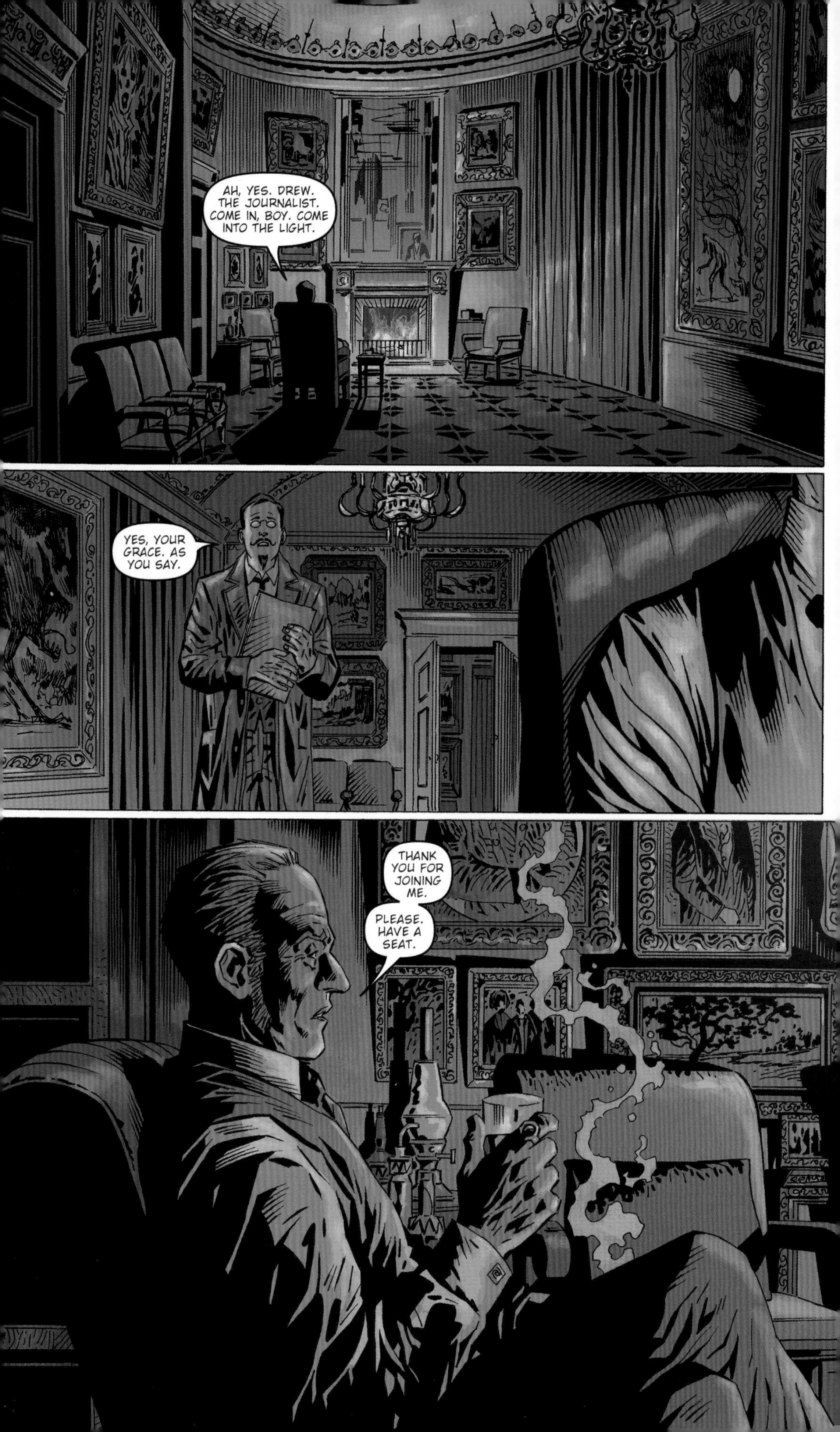
AH, YES. DREW. THE JOURNALIST. COME IN, BOY. COME INTO THE LIGHT.
YES, YOUR GRACE. AS YOU SAY.
THANK YOU FOR JOINING ME.
PLEASE. HAVE A SEAT.

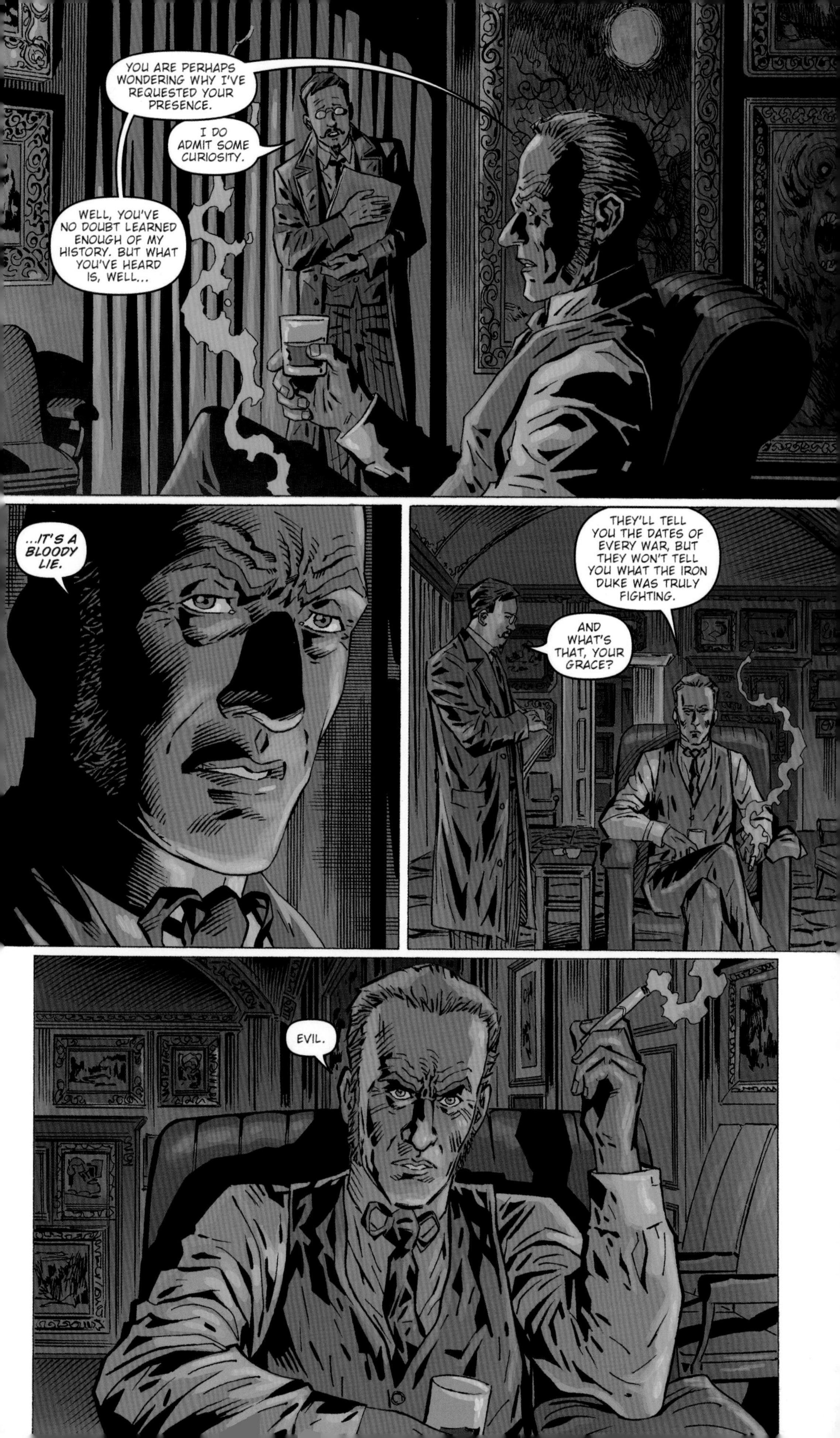
YOU ARE PERHAPS WONDERING WHY I'VE REQUESTED YOUR PRESENCE.
I DO ADMIT SOME CURIOSITY.
WELL, YOU'VE NO DOUBT LEARNED ENOUGH OF MY HISTORY. BUT WHAT YOU'VE HEARD IS, WELL...
...IT'S A BLOODY LIE.
THEY'LL TELL YOU THE DATES OF EVERY WAR, BUT THEY WON'T TELL YOU WHAT THE IRON DUKE WAS TRULY FIGHTING.
AND WHAT'S THAT, YOUR GRACE?
EVIL.

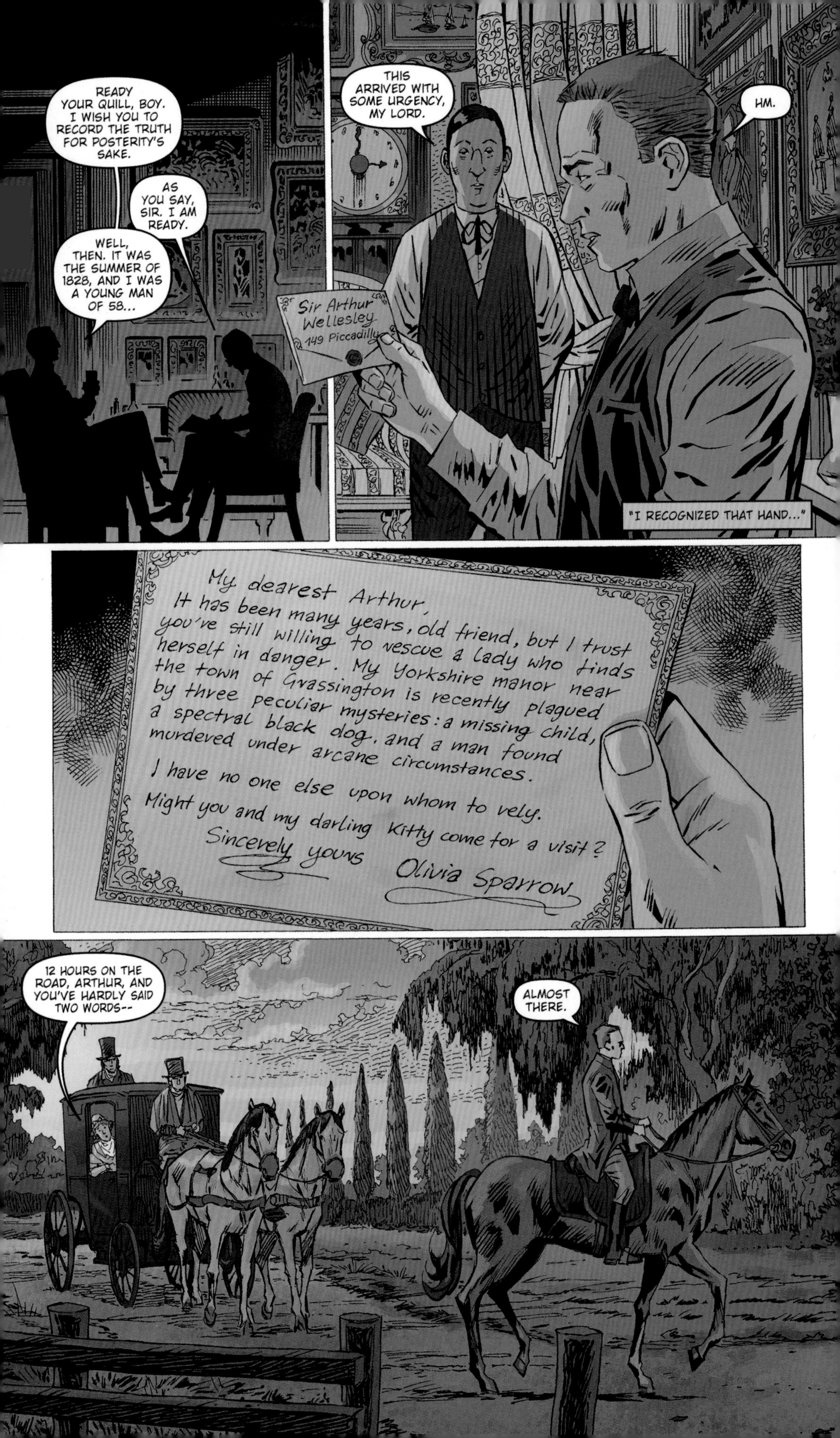
READY YOUR QUILL, BOY. I WISH YOU TO RECORD THE TRUTH FOR POSTERITY'S SAKE.
AS YOU SAY, SIR. I AM READY.
WELL, THEN. IT WAS THE SUMMER OF 1828, AND I WAS A YOUNG MAN OF 58...
THIS ARRIVED WITH SOME URGENCY, MY LORD.
Sir Arthur Wellesley 149 Piccadilly
HM.
"I RECOGNIZED THAT HAND..."
My dearest Arthur,
It has been many years, old friend, but I trust you've still willing to rescue a lady who finds herself in danger. My Yorkshire manor near the town of Grassington is recently plagued by three peculiar mysteries: a missing child, a spectral black dog, and a man found murdered under arcane circumstances.
I have no one else upon whom to rely.
Might you and my darling Kitty come for a visit?
Sincerely yours Olivia Sparrow
12 HOURS ON THE ROAD, ARTHUR, AND YOU'VE HARDLY SAID TWO WORDS--
ALMOST THERE.

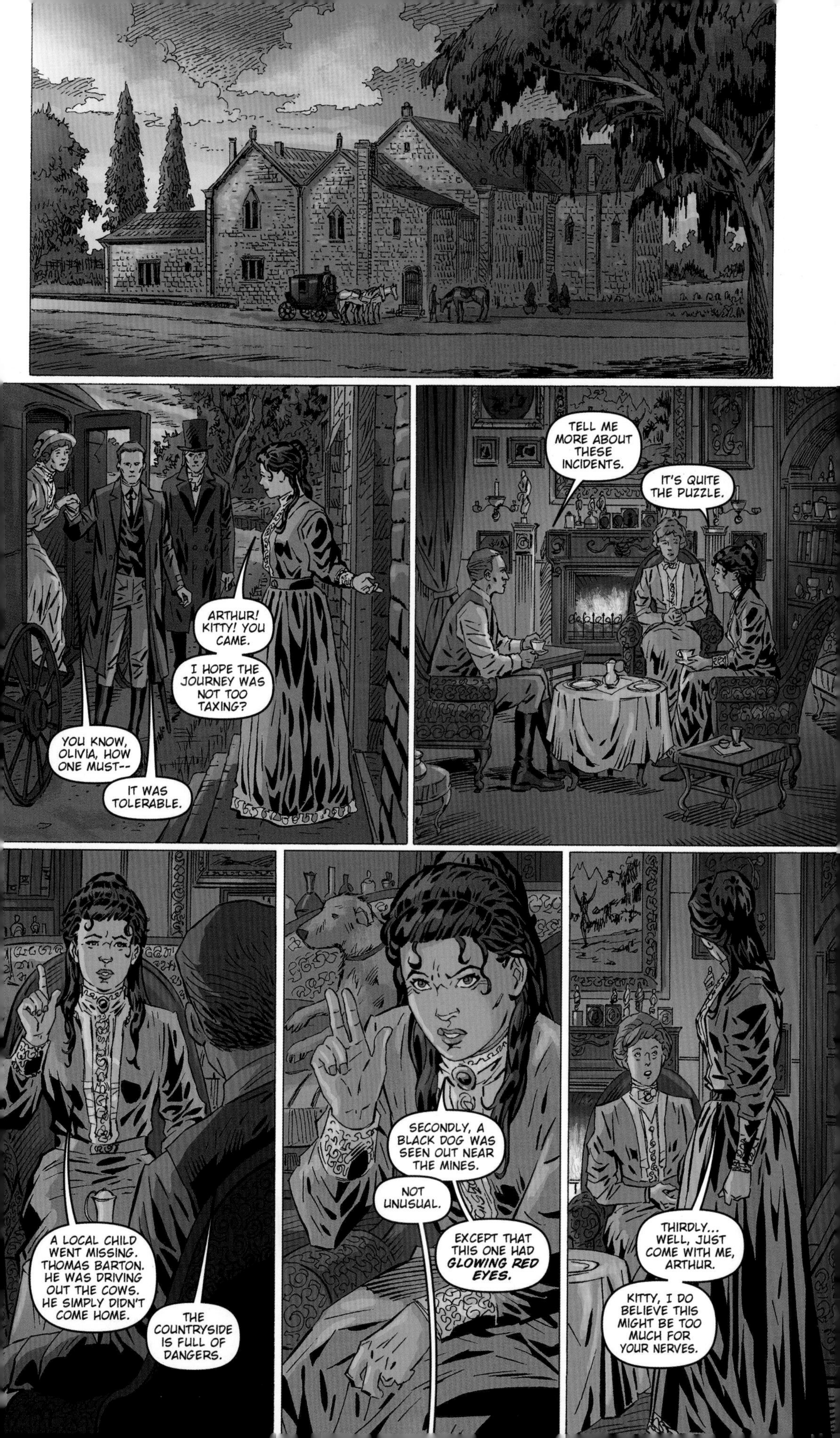
ARTHUR! KITTY! YOU CAME.
I HOPE THE JOURNEY WAS NOT TOO TAXING?
YOU KNOW, OLIVIA, HOW ONE MUST--
IT WAS TOLERABLE.
TELL ME MORE ABOUT THESE INCIDENTS.
IT'S QUITE THE PUZZLE.
A LOCAL CHILD WENT MISSING. THOMAS BARTON. HE WAS DRIVING OUT THE COWS. HE SIMPLY DIDN'T COME HOME.
THE COUNTRYSIDE IS FULL OF DANGERS.
SECONDLY, A BLACK DOG WAS SEEN OUT NEAR THE MINES.
NOT UNUSUAL.
EXCEPT THAT THIS ONE HAD ***GLOWING RED EYES.***
THIRDLY... WELL, JUST COME WITH ME, ARTHUR.
KITTY, I DO BELIEVE THIS MIGHT BE TOO MUCH FOR YOUR NERVES.

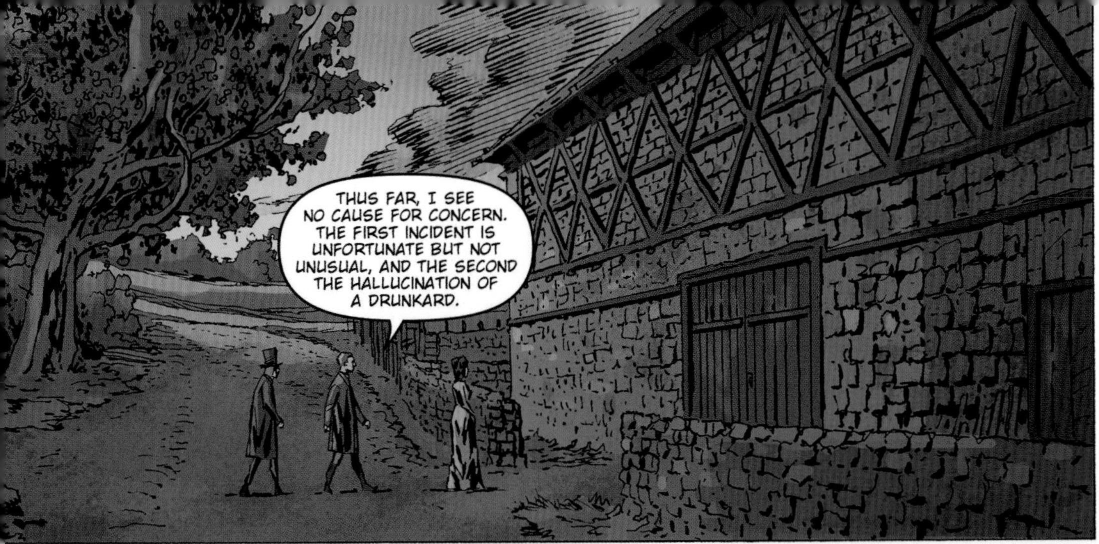
THUS FAR, I SEE NO CAUSE FOR CONCERN. THE FIRST INCIDENT IS UNFORTUNATE BUT NOT UNUSUAL, AND THE SECOND THE HALLUCINATION OF A DRUNKARD.

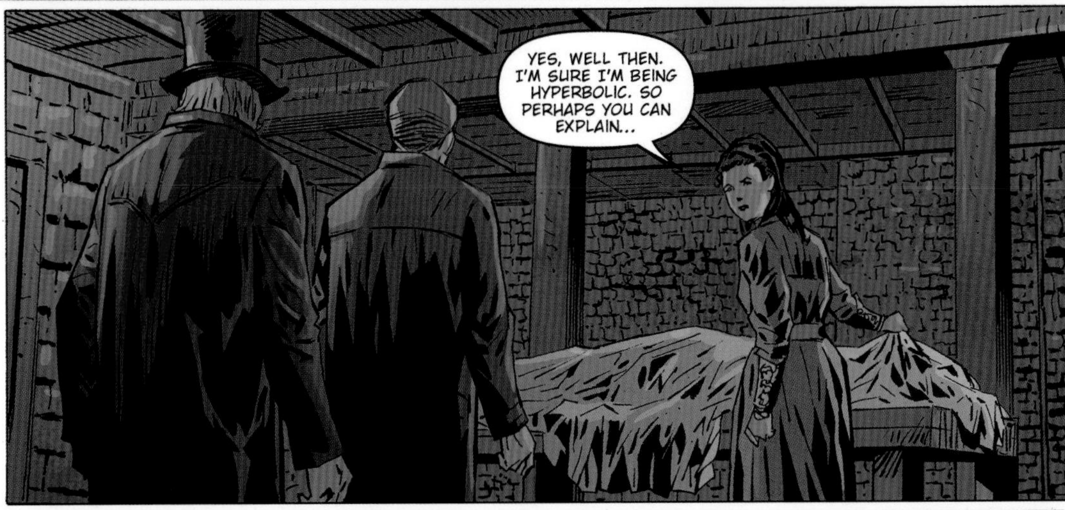
YES, WELL THEN. I'M SURE I'M BEING HYPERBOLIC. SO PERHAPS YOU CAN EXPLAIN...

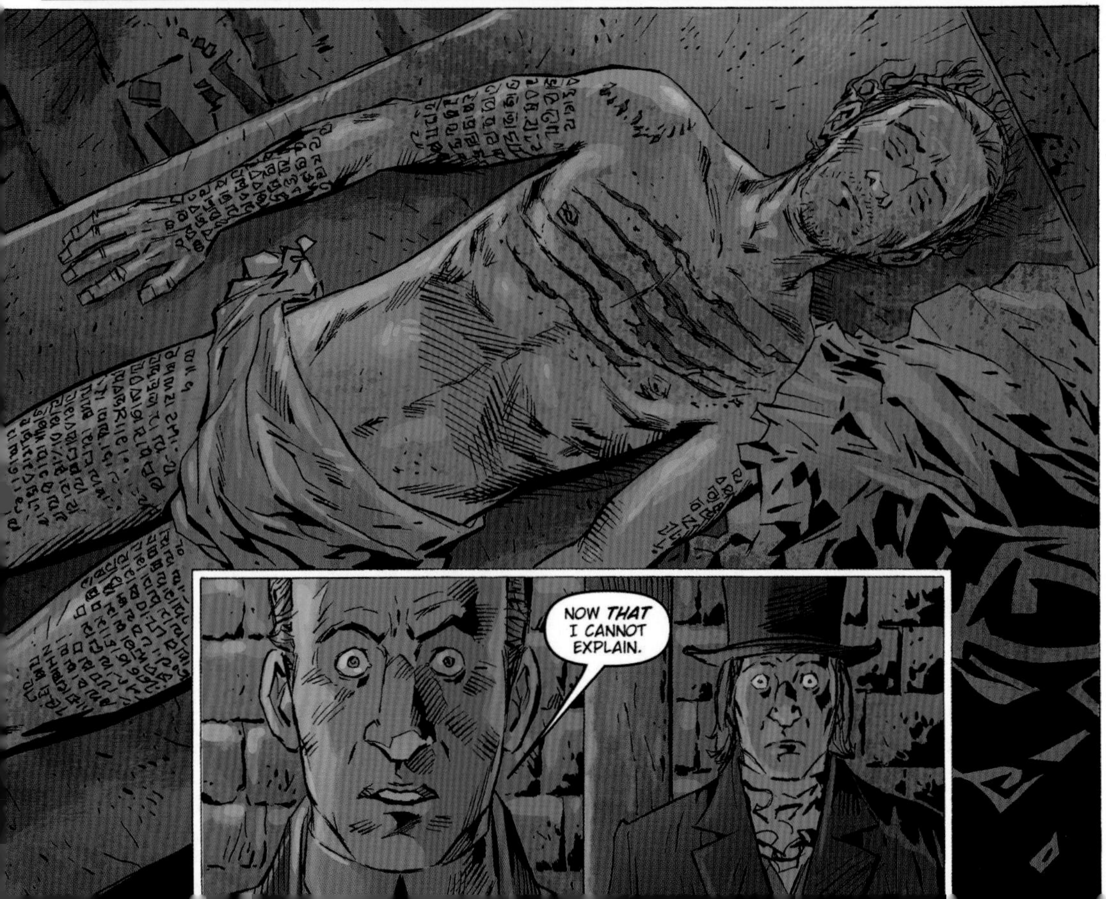
NOW *THAT* I CANNOT EXPLAIN.

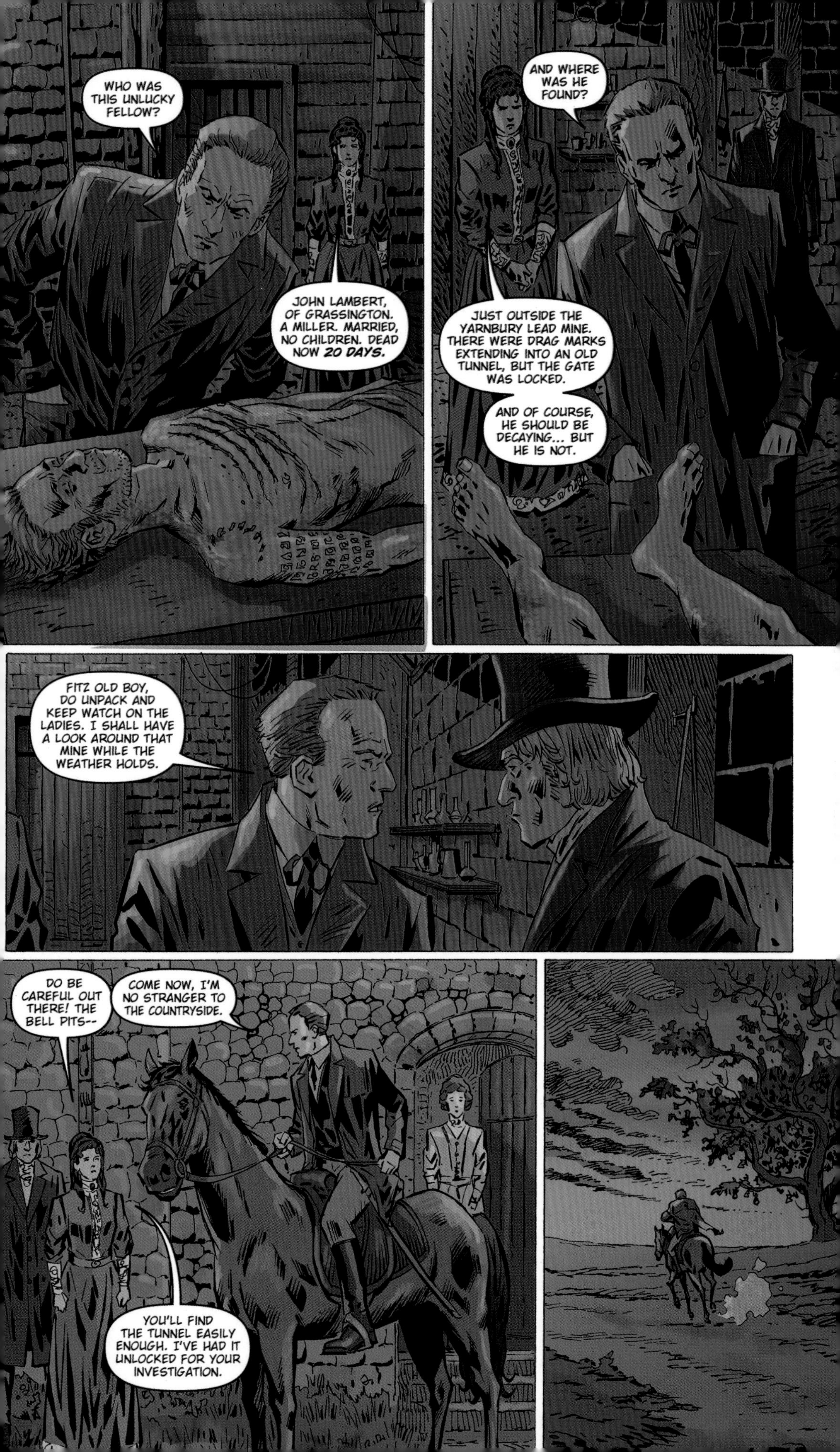
WHO WAS THIS UNLUCKY FELLOW?
JOHN LAMBERT, OF GRASSINGTON. A MILLER. MARRIED, NO CHILDREN. DEAD NOW *20 DAYS.*
AND WHERE WAS HE FOUND?
JUST OUTSIDE THE YARNBURY LEAD MINE. THERE WERE DRAG MARKS EXTENDING INTO AN OLD TUNNEL, BUT THE GATE WAS LOCKED.
AND OF COURSE, HE SHOULD BE DECAYING... BUT HE IS NOT.
FITZ OLD BOY, DO UNPACK AND KEEP WATCH ON THE LADIES. I SHALL HAVE A LOOK AROUND THAT MINE WHILE THE WEATHER HOLDS.
DO BE CAREFUL OUT THERE! THE BELL PITS--
COME NOW, I'M NO STRANGER TO THE COUNTRYSIDE.
YOU'LL FIND THE TUNNEL EASILY ENOUGH. I'VE HAD IT UNLOCKED FOR YOUR INVESTIGATION.

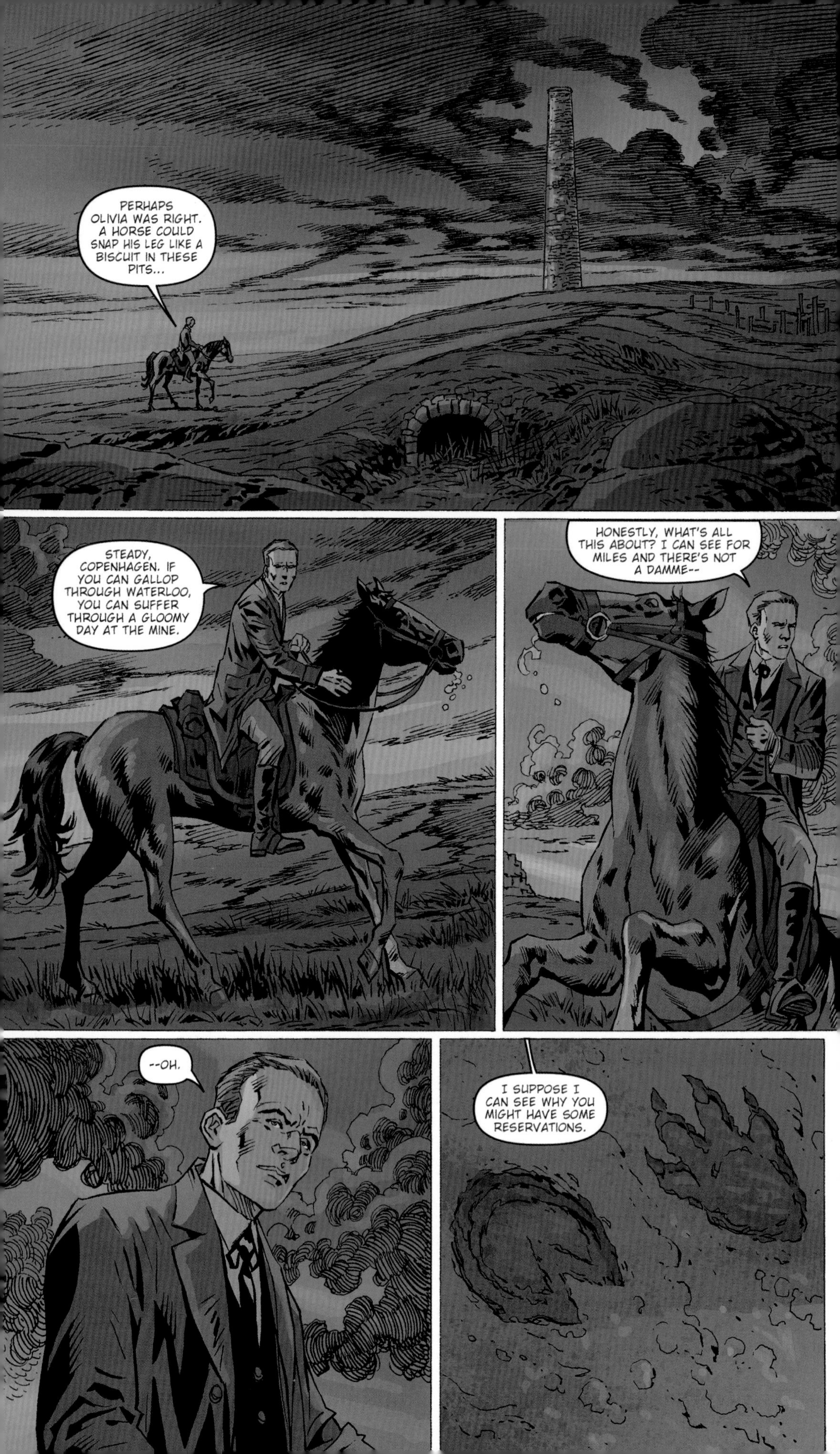
PERHAPS OLIVIA WAS RIGHT. A HORSE COULD SNAP HIS LEG LIKE A BISCUIT IN THESE PITS...
STEADY, COPENHAGEN. IF YOU CAN GALLOP THROUGH WATERLOO, YOU CAN SUFFER THROUGH A GLOOMY DAY AT THE MINE.
HONESTLY, WHAT'S ALL THIS ABOUT? I CAN SEE FOR MILES AND THERE'S NOT A DAMME--
--OH.
I SUPPOSE I CAN SEE WHY YOU MIGHT HAVE SOME RESERVATIONS.

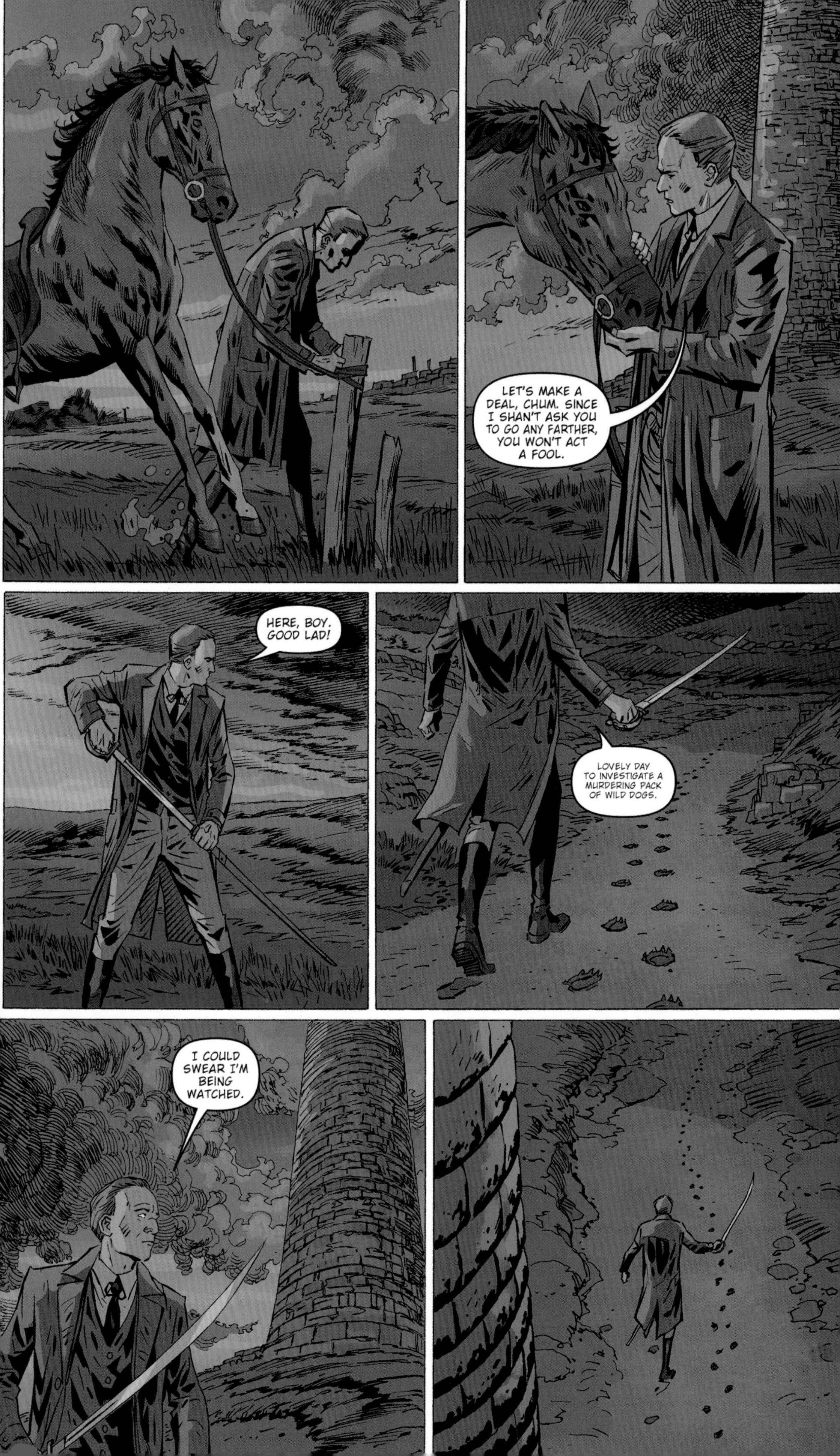
LET'S MAKE A DEAL, CHUM. SINCE I SHAN'T ASK YOU TO GO ANY FARTHER, YOU WON'T ACT A FOOL.
HERE, BOY. GOOD LAD!
LOVELY DAY TO INVESTIGATE A MURDERING PACK OF WILD DOGS.
I COULD SWEAR I'M BEING WATCHED.

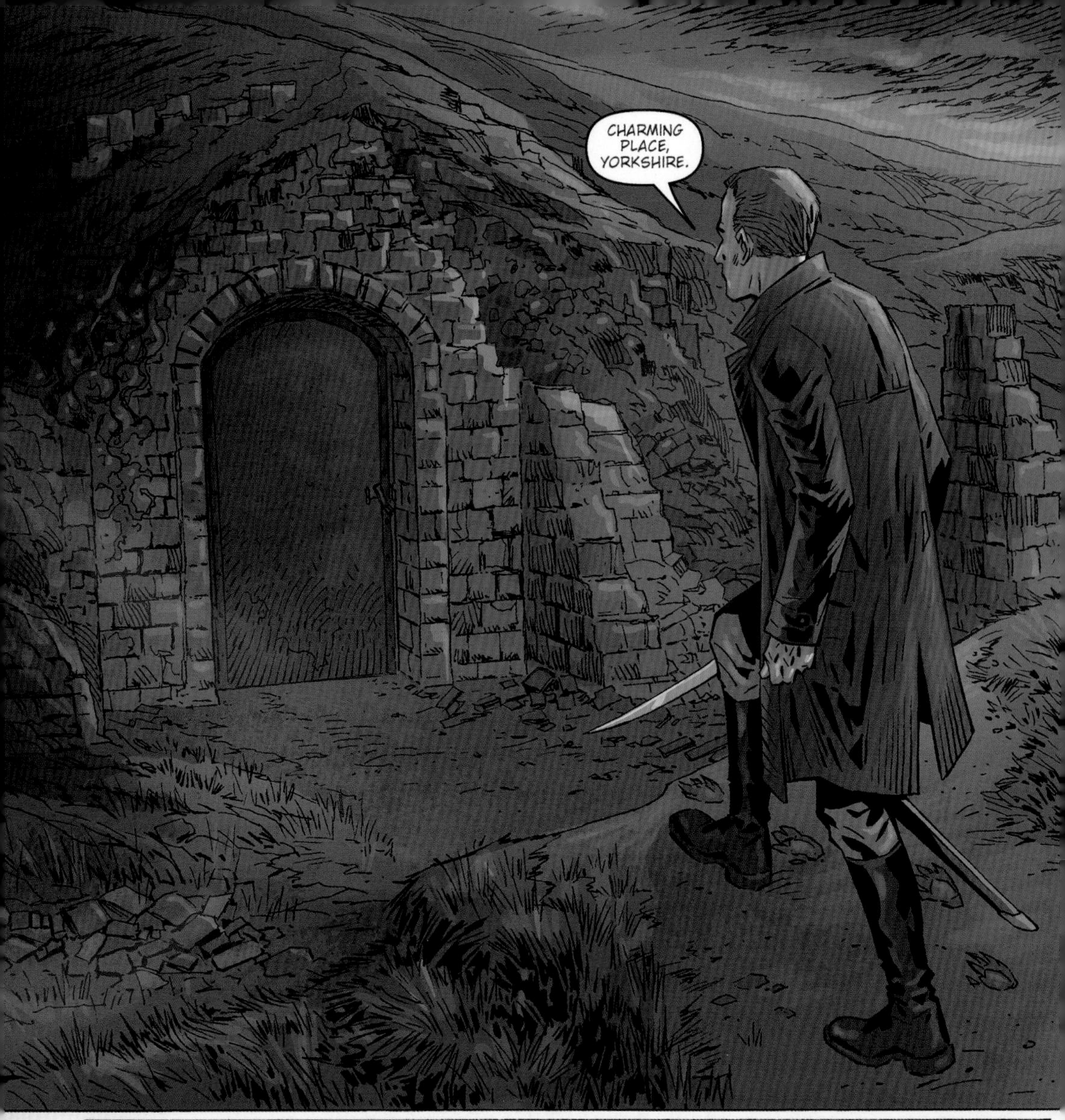
CHARMING PLACE, YORKSHIRE.

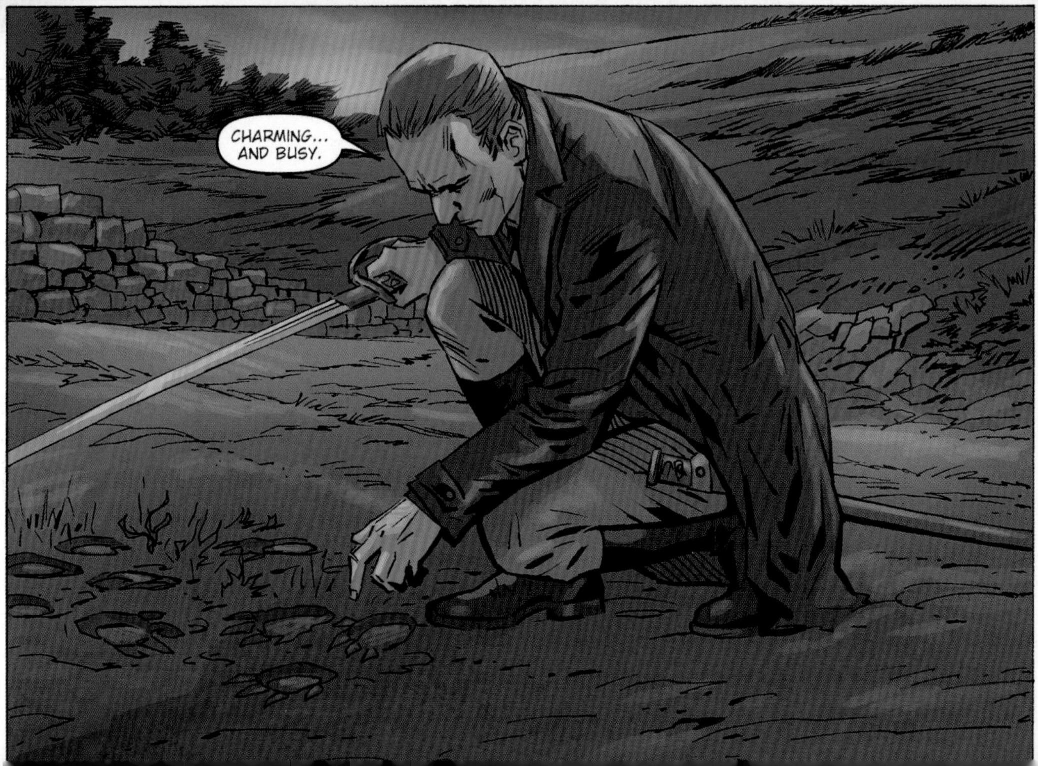
CHARMING... AND BUSY.

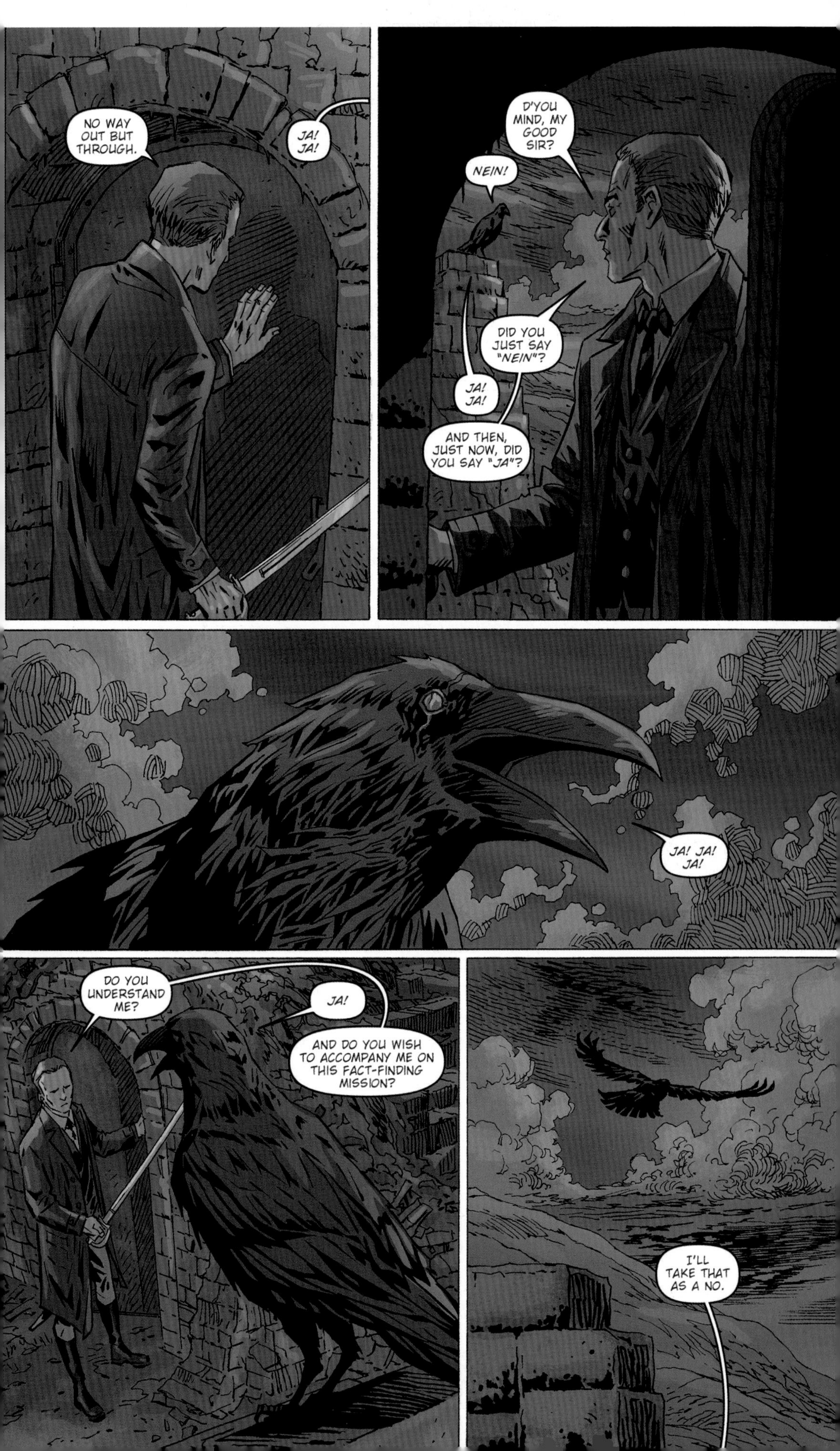
NO WAY OUT BUT THROUGH.
JA! JA!
D'YOU MIND, MY GOOD SIR?
NEIN!
DID YOU JUST SAY "NEIN"?
JA! JA!
AND THEN, JUST NOW, DID YOU SAY "JA"?
JA! JA! JA!
DO YOU UNDERSTAND ME?
JA!
AND DO YOU WISH TO ACCOMPANY ME ON THIS FACT-FINDING MISSION?
I'LL TAKE THAT AS A NO.

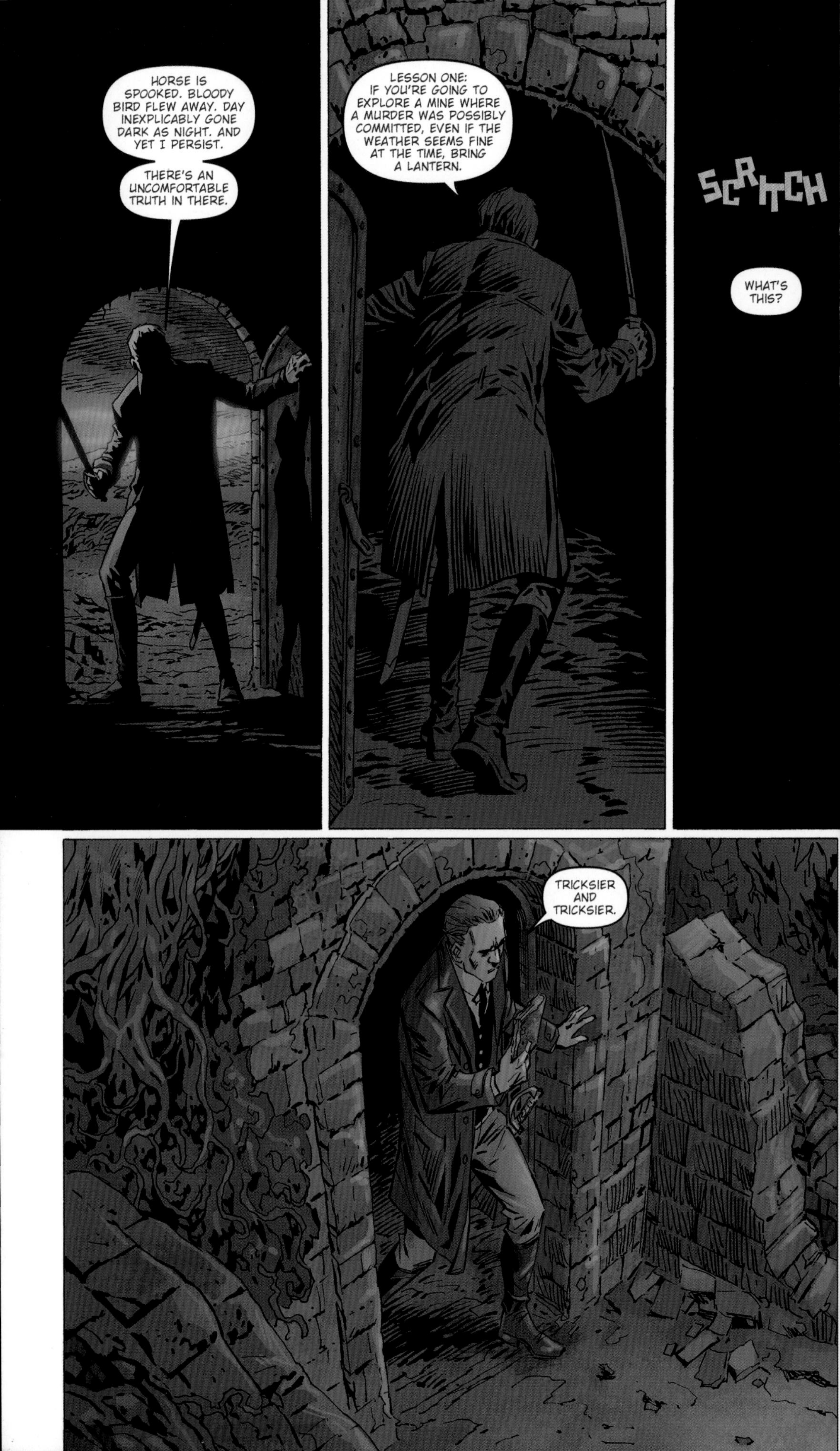
HORSE IS SPOOKED. BLOODY BIRD FLEW AWAY. DAY INEXPLICABLY GONE DARK AS NIGHT. AND YET I PERSIST.
THERE'S AN UNCOMFORTABLE TRUTH IN THERE.
LESSON ONE: IF YOU'RE GOING TO EXPLORE A MINE WHERE A MURDER WAS POSSIBLY COMMITTED, EVEN IF THE WEATHER SEEMS FINE AT THE TIME, BRING A LANTERN.
SCRTCH
WHAT'S THIS?
TRICKSIER AND TRICKSIER.

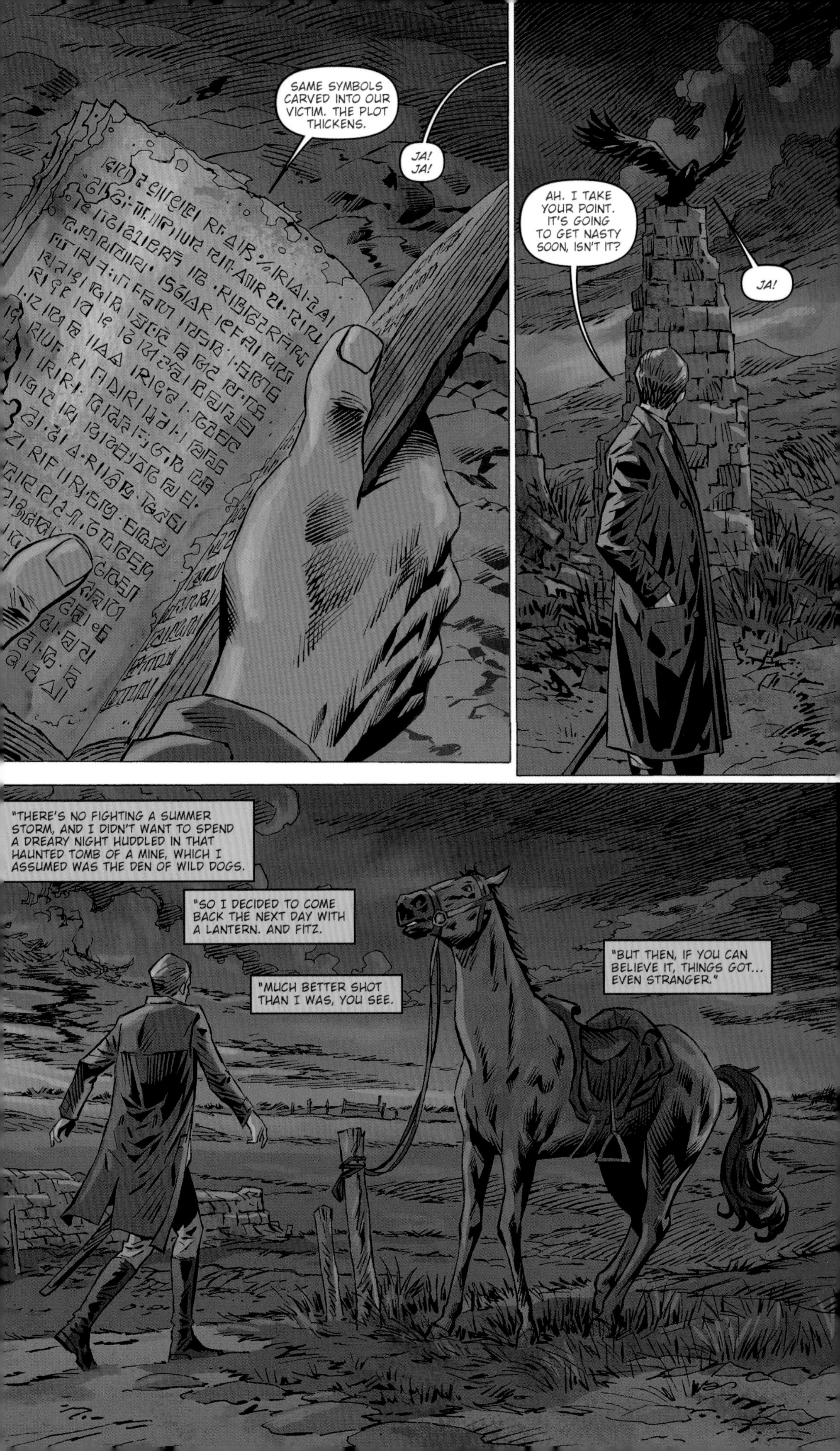
SAME SYMBOLS CARVED INTO OUR VICTIM. THE PLOT THICKENS.
JA! JA!
AH. I TAKE YOUR POINT. IT'S GOING TO GET NASTY SOON, ISN'T IT?
JA!
"THERE'S NO FIGHTING A SUMMER STORM, AND I DIDN'T WANT TO SPEND A DREARY NIGHT HUDDLED IN THAT HAUNTED TOMB OF A MINE, WHICH I ASSUMED WAS THE DEN OF WILD DOGS.
"SO I DECIDED TO COME BACK THE NEXT DAY WITH A LANTERN. AND FITZ.
"MUCH BETTER SHOT THAN I WAS, YOU SEE.
"BUT THEN, IF YOU CAN BELIEVE IT, THINGS GOT... EVEN STRANGER."

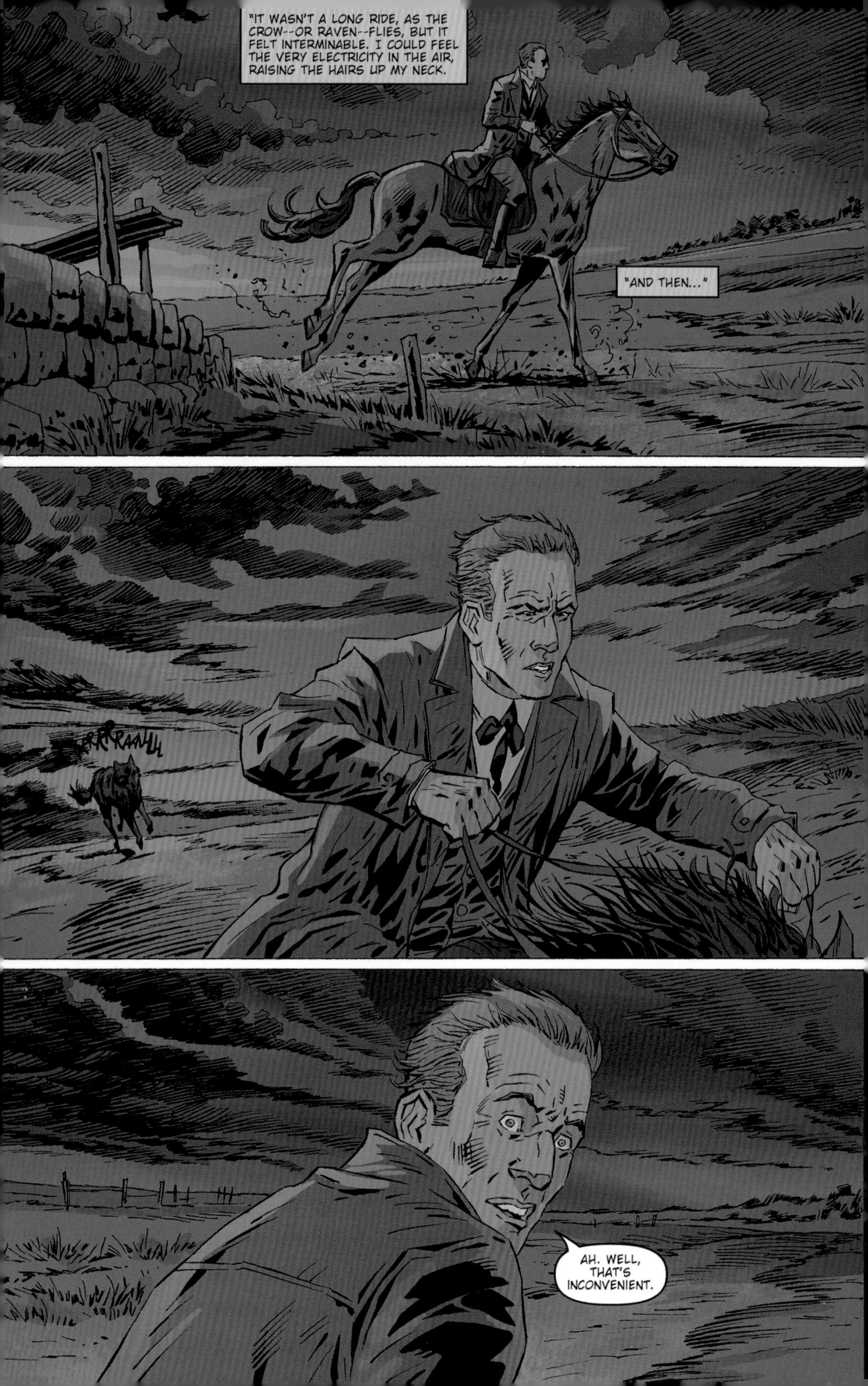
"IT WASN'T A LONG RIDE, AS THE CROW--OR RAVEN--FLIES, BUT IT FELT INTERMINABLE. I COULD FEEL THE VERY ELECTRICITY IN THE AIR, RAISING THE HAIRS UP MY NECK.
"AND THEN..."
RRRAAWLL
AH. WELL, THAT'S INCONVENIENT.

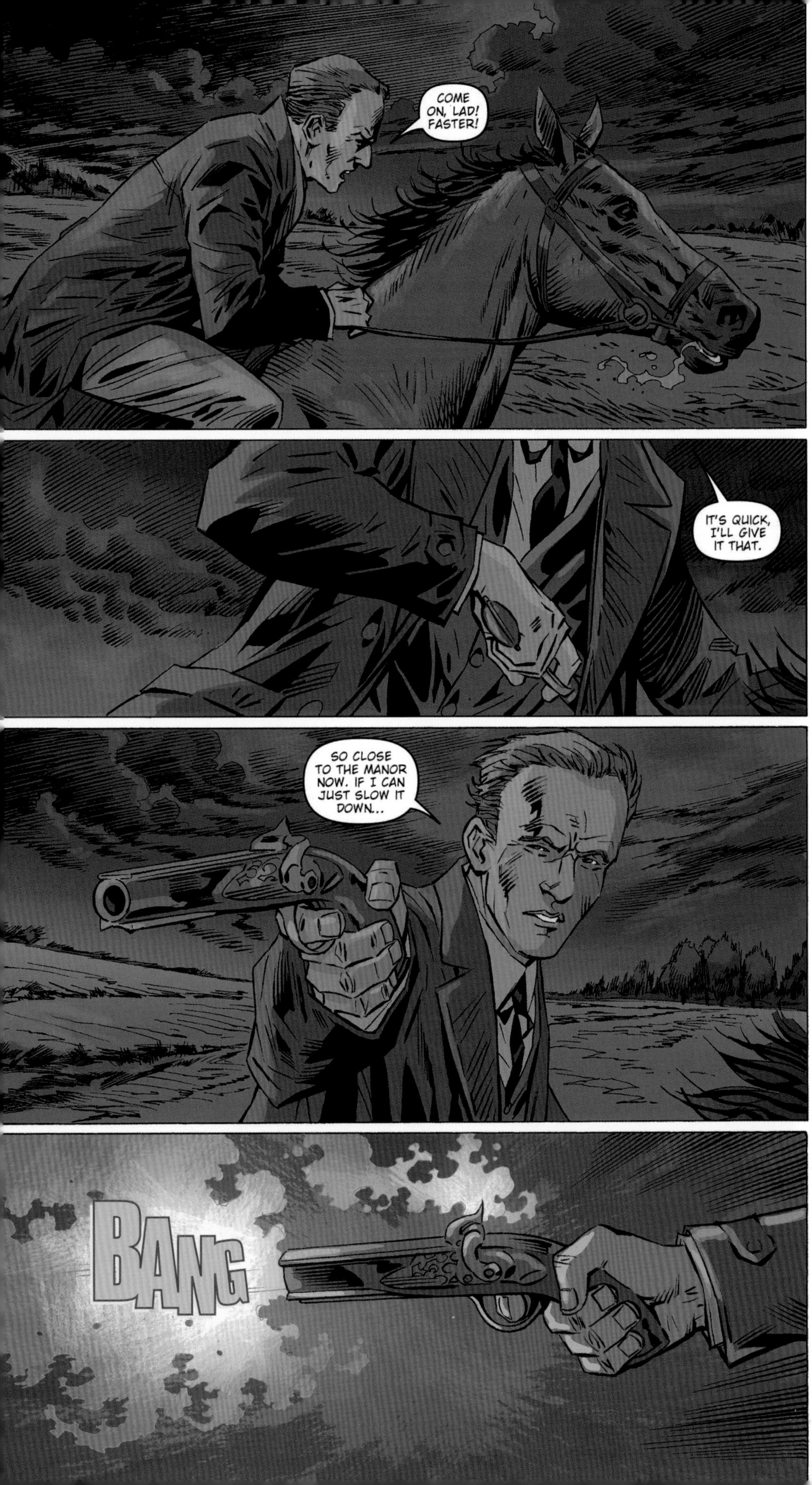
COME ON, LAD! FASTER!
IT'S QUICK, I'LL GIVE IT THAT.
SO CLOSE TO THE MANOR NOW. IF I CAN JUST SLOW IT DOWN...
BANG

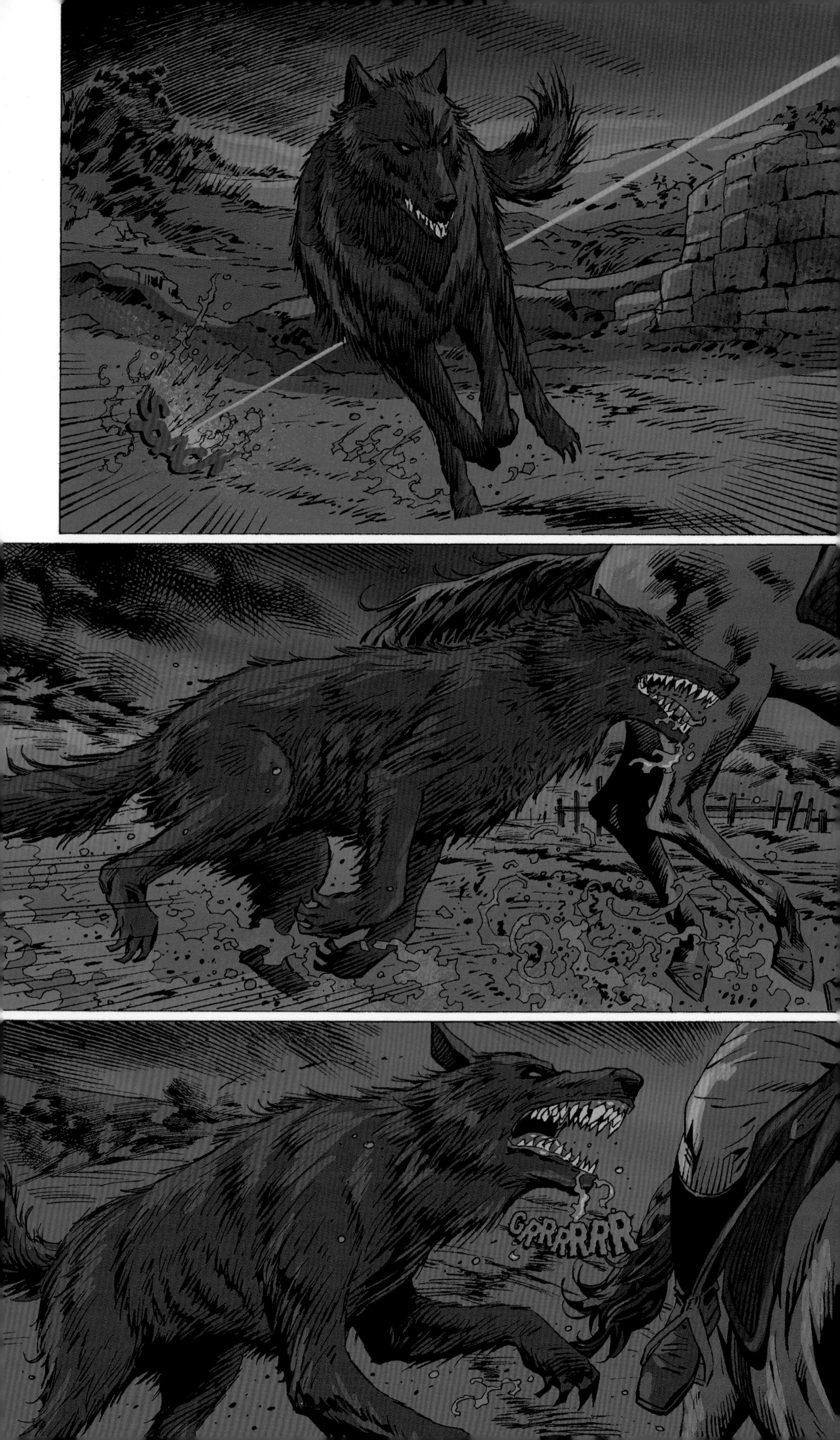
SPACK
GRRRRRR

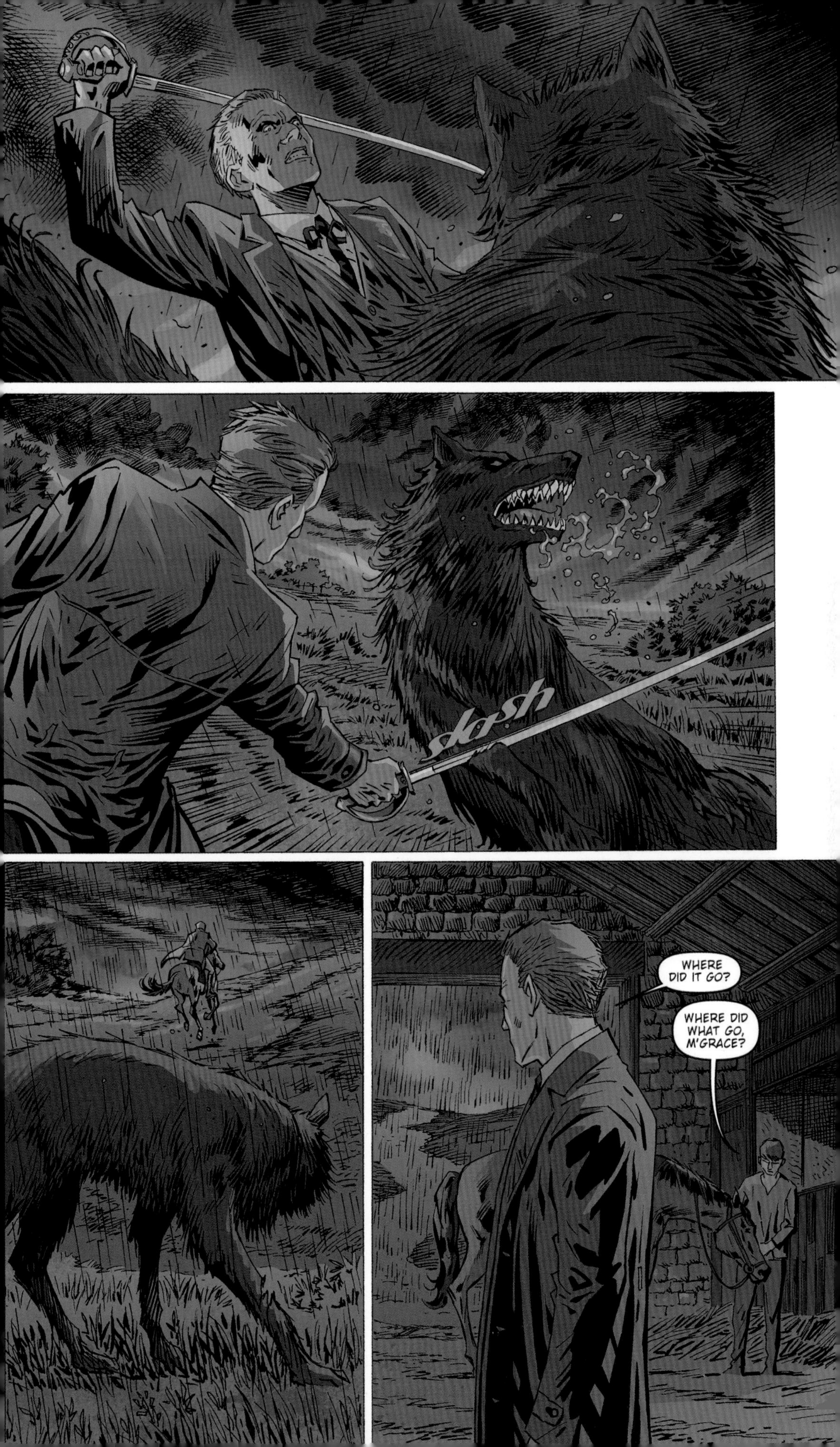

dash
WHERE DID IT GO?
WHERE DID WHAT GO, M'GRACE?

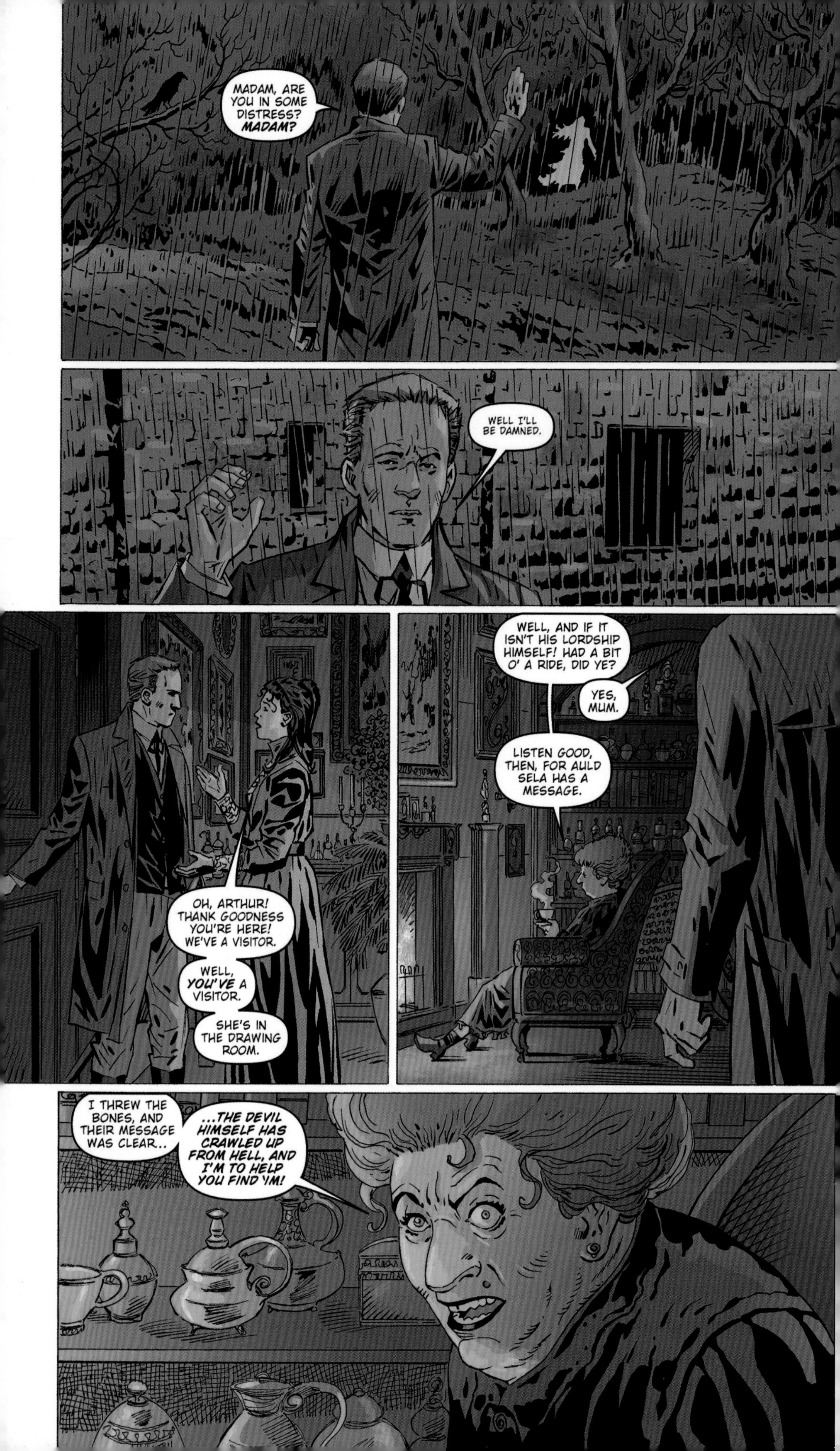
MADAM, ARE YOU IN SOME DISTRESS? MADAM?
WELL I'LL BE DAMNED.
OH, ARTHUR! THANK GOODNESS YOU'RE HERE! WE'VE A VISITOR.
WELL, YOU'VE A VISITOR.
SHE'S IN THE DRAWING ROOM.
WELL, AND IF IT ISN'T HIS LORDSHIP HIMSELF! HAD A BIT O' A RIDE, DID YE?
YES, MUM.
LISTEN GOOD, THEN, FOR AULD SELA HAS A MESSAGE.
I THREW THE BONES, AND THEIR MESSAGE WAS CLEAR...
...THE DEVIL HIMSELF HAS CRAWLED UP FROM HELL, AND I'M TO HELP YOU FIND 'IM!

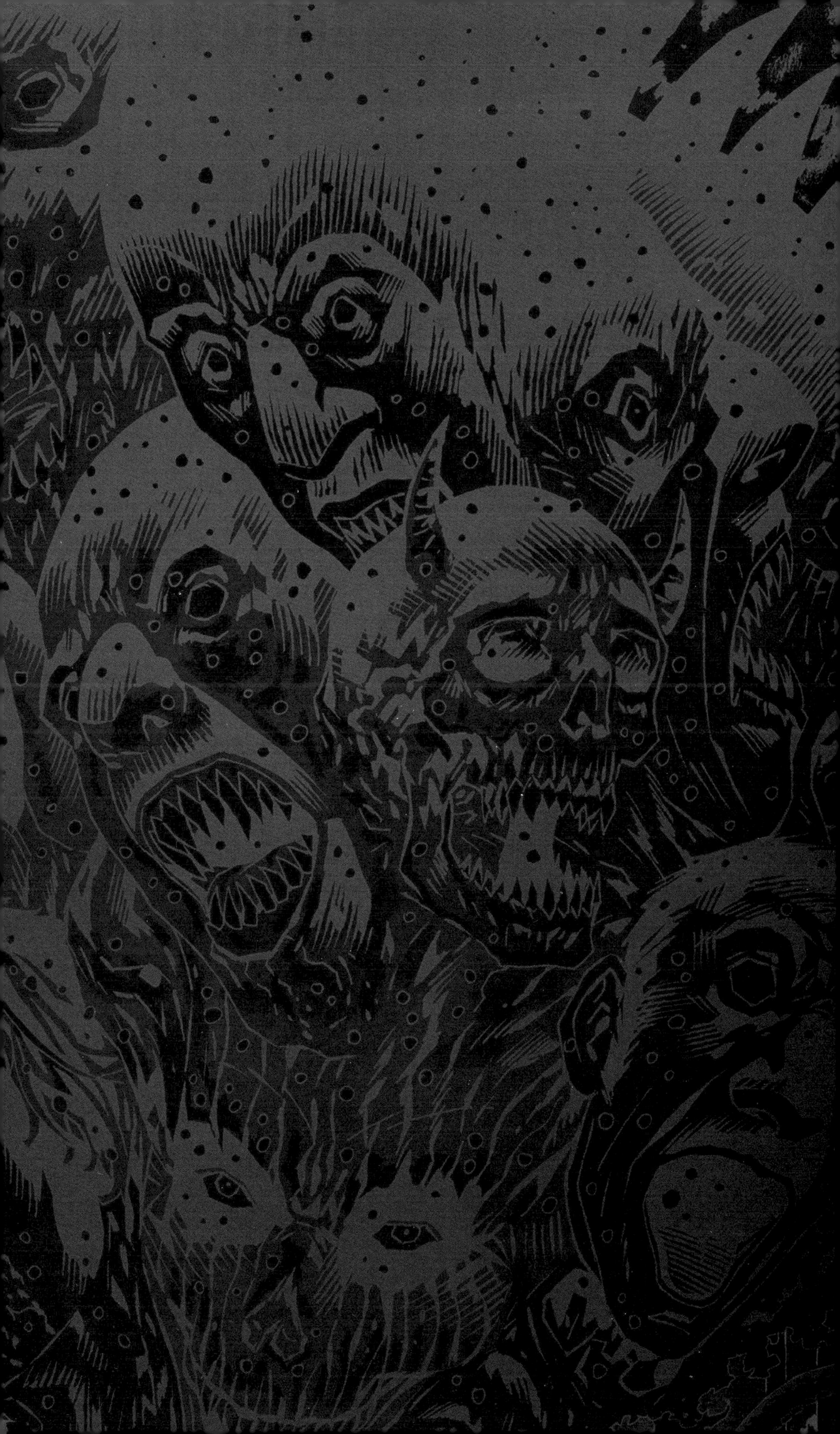

Chapter 2

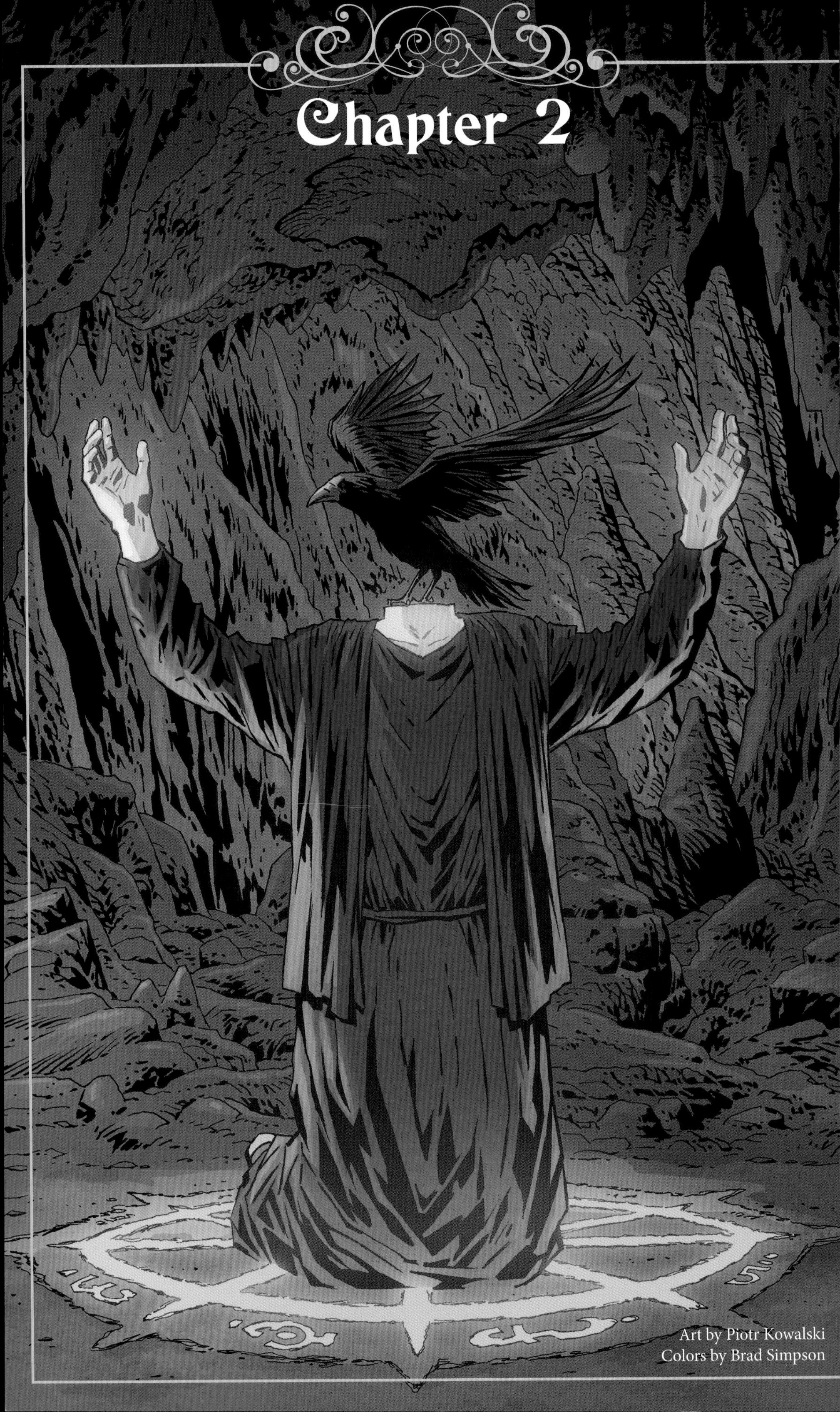
Art by Piotr Kowalski
Colors by Brad Simpson

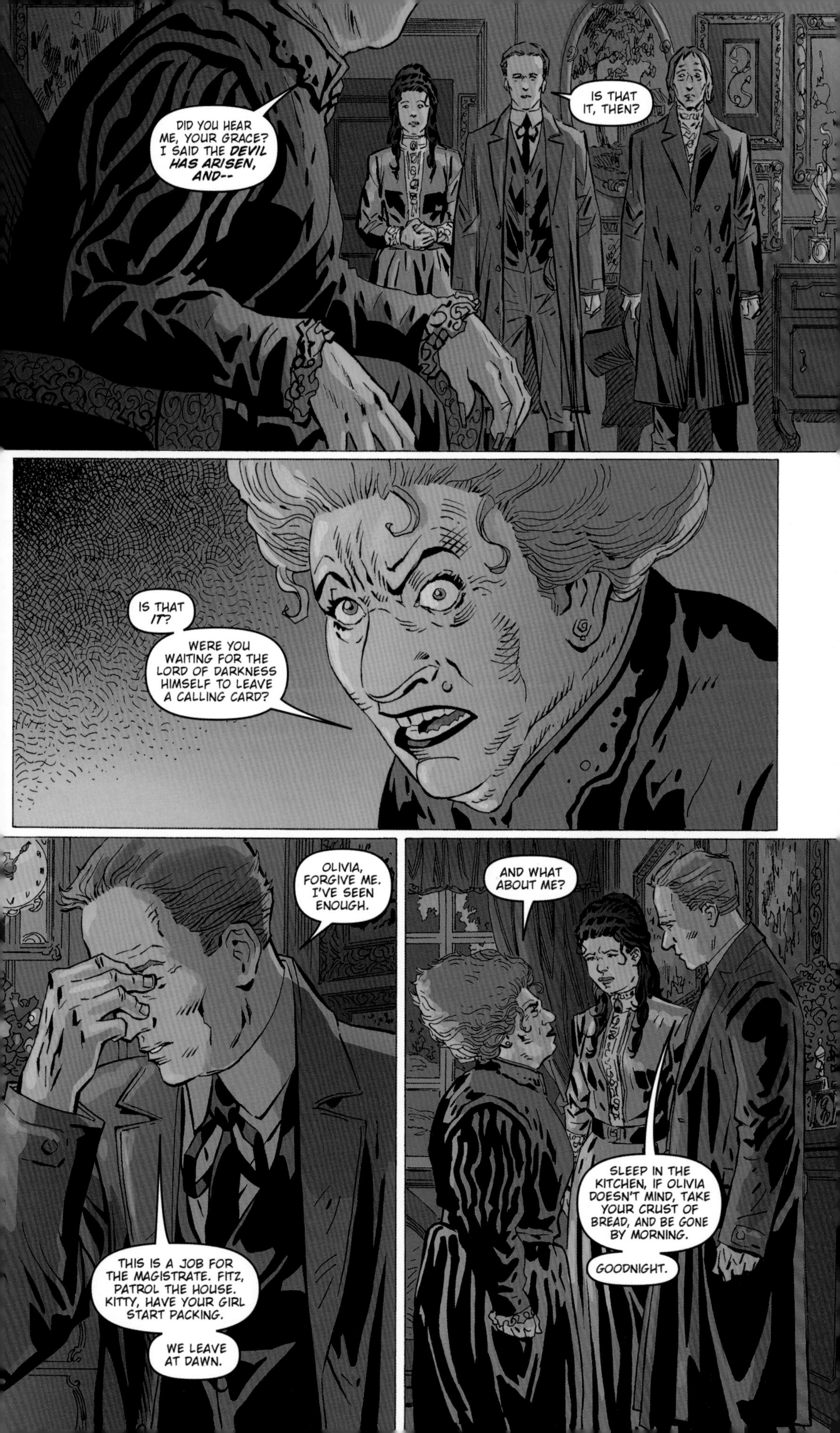
DID YOU HEAR ME, YOUR GRACE? I SAID THE *DEVIL HAS ARISEN*, AND--
IS THAT IT, THEN?
IS THAT *IT*?
WERE YOU WAITING FOR THE LORD OF DARKNESS HIMSELF TO LEAVE A CALLING CARD?
OLIVIA, FORGIVE ME. I'VE SEEN ENOUGH.
THIS IS A JOB FOR THE MAGISTRATE. FITZ, PATROL THE HOUSE. KITTY, HAVE YOUR GIRL START PACKING.
WE LEAVE AT DAWN.
AND WHAT ABOUT ME?
SLEEP IN THE KITCHEN, IF OLIVIA DOESN'T MIND, TAKE YOUR CRUST OF BREAD, AND BE GONE BY MORNING.
GOODNIGHT.

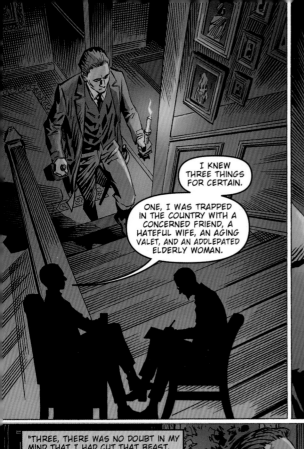

I KNEW THREE THINGS FOR CERTAIN.

ONE, I WAS TRAPPED IN THE COUNTRY WITH A CONCERNED FRIEND, A HATEFUL WIFE, AN AGING VALET, AND AN ADDLEPATED ELDERLY WOMAN.

"TWO, THE EVENTS UNFOLDING MADE VERY LITTLE SENSE TO A SANE MAN."

"THREE, THERE WAS NO DOUBT IN MY MIND THAT I HAD CUT THAT BEAST, AND YET MY BLADE WAS CLEAN, AND THE BEAST HAD DISAPPEARED."

"I ALSO KNEW THAT MEDICINAL BRANDY WAS EXCELLENT FOR CALMING THE NERVES. IT WAS DEEPLY INSULTING, HOW HARD MY HANDS WERE SHAKING.

"AND SO I DID WHAT ANYONE MIGHT: I SOUGHT REFUGE IN SLEEP."

"UNFORTUNATELY, MY DREAMS WERE NO SANCTUARY."

"SLEEP CAME EASILY, BUT WHAT IT BROUGHT... WAS FAR FROM SIMPLE.

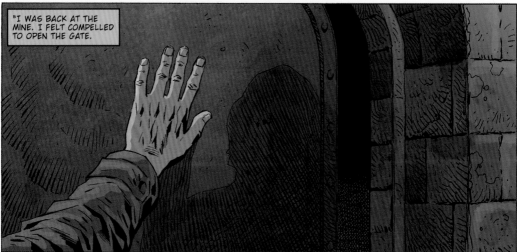

"I WAS BACK AT THE MINE. I FELT COMPELLED TO OPEN THE GATE.

"THE TUNNEL WAS IMPENETRABLY DARK, BUT MY FEET LED ME DEEP WITHIN.

"I SAW A LIGHT UP AHEAD, SOME GHASTLY FIRE BURNING.

"MY GUT ROILED, DREAD BUILDING. WHATEVER WAS UP AHEAD, I WANTED NOTHING TO DO WITH IT.

"AND YET I COULD NOT STOP MYSELF."

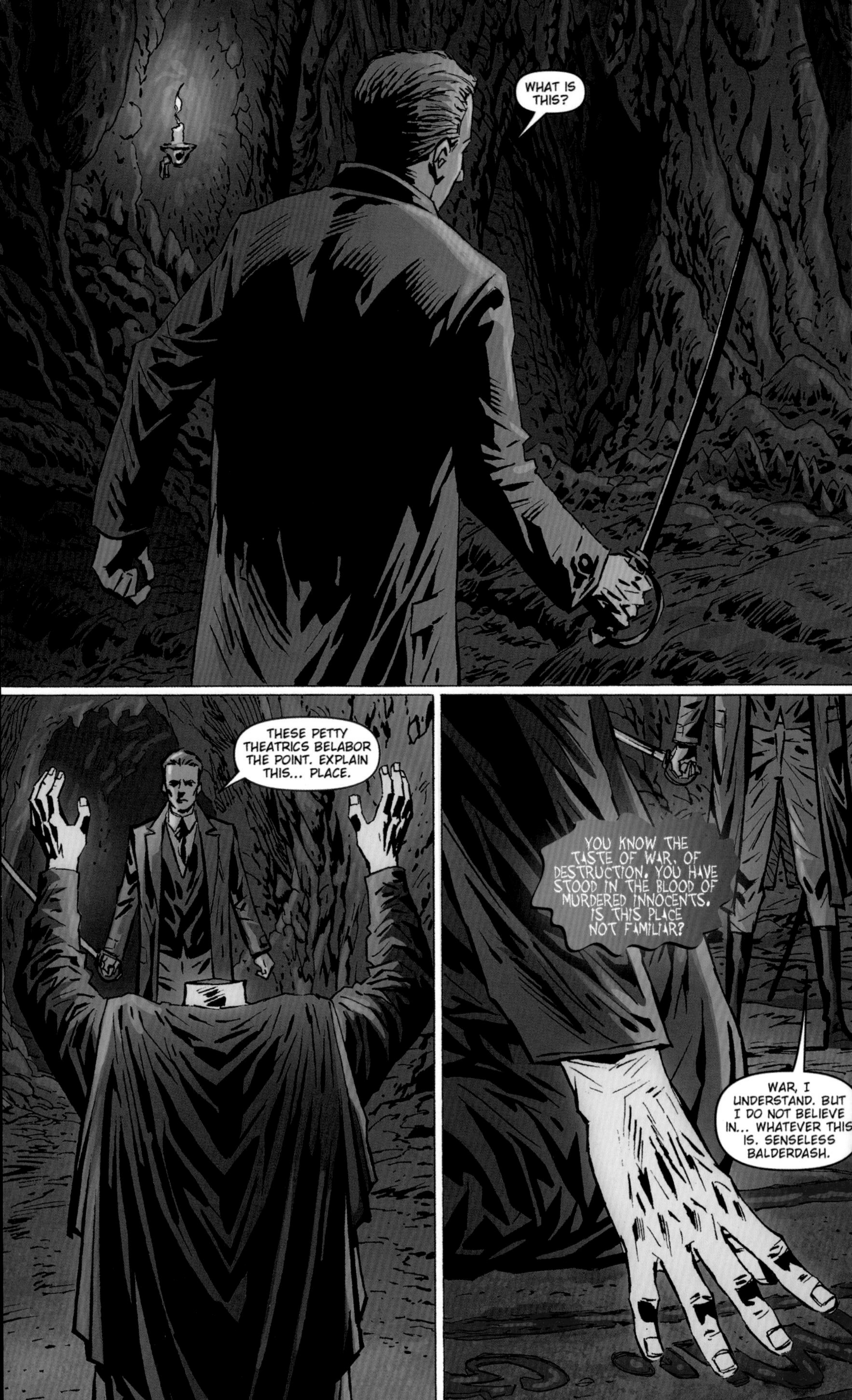
WHAT IS THIS?
THESE PETTY THEATRICS BELABOR THE POINT. EXPLAIN THIS... PLACE.
YOU KNOW THE TASTE OF WAR, OF DESTRUCTION. YOU HAVE STOOD IN THE BLOOD OF MURDERED INNOCENTS. IS THIS PLACE NOT FAMILIAR?
WAR, I UNDERSTAND. BUT I DO NOT BELIEVE IN... WHATEVER THIS IS. SENSELESS BALDERDASH.

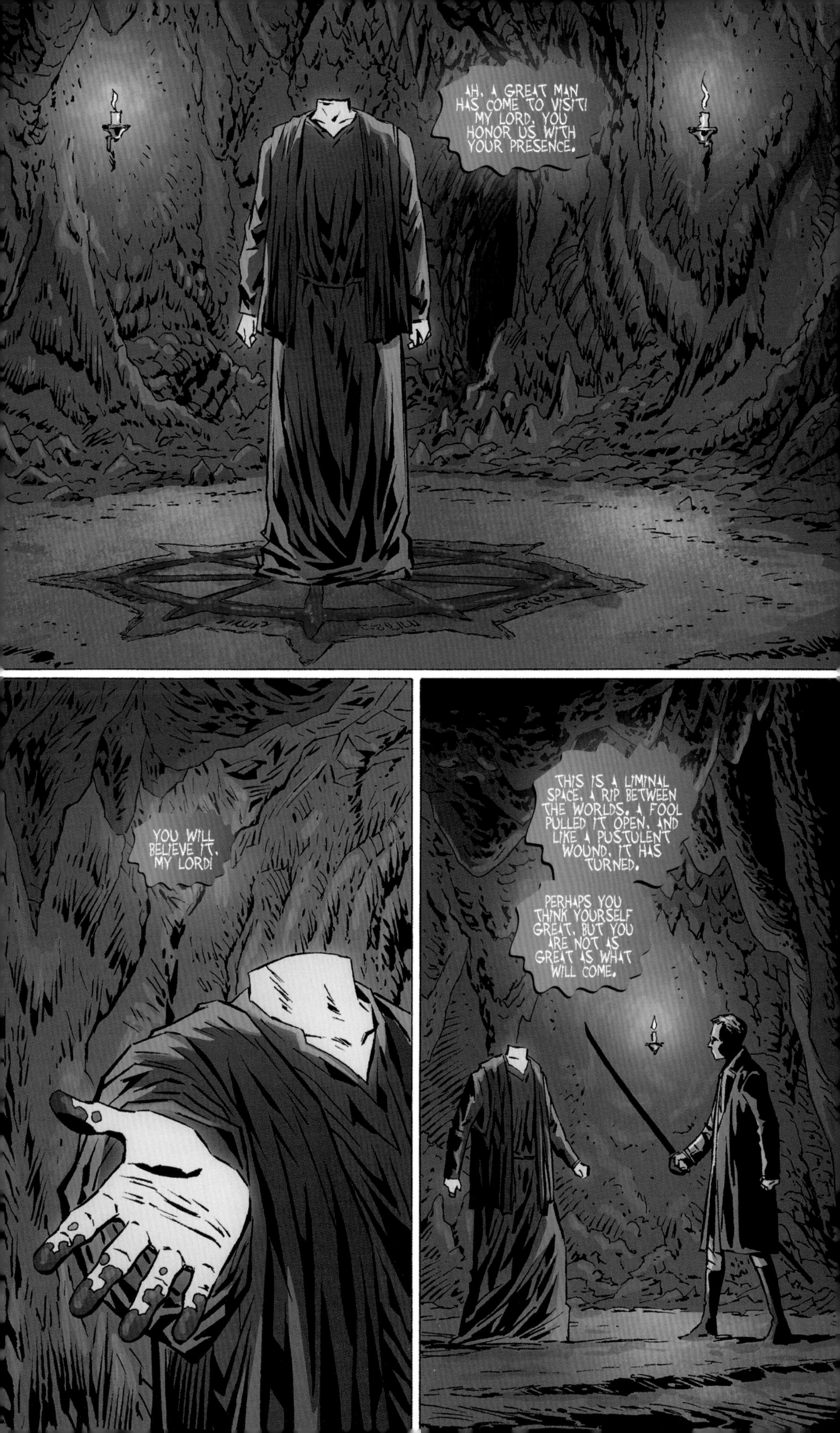
AH, A GREAT MAN HAS COME TO VISIT! MY LORD, YOU HONOR US WITH YOUR PRESENCE.
YOU WILL BELIEVE IT, MY LORD!
THIS IS A LIMINAL SPACE, A RIP BETWEEN THE WORLDS. A FOOL PULLED IT OPEN, AND LIKE A PUSTULENT WOUND, IT HAS TURNED.
PERHAPS YOU THINK YOURSELF GREAT, BUT YOU ARE NOT AS GREAT AS WHAT WILL COME.

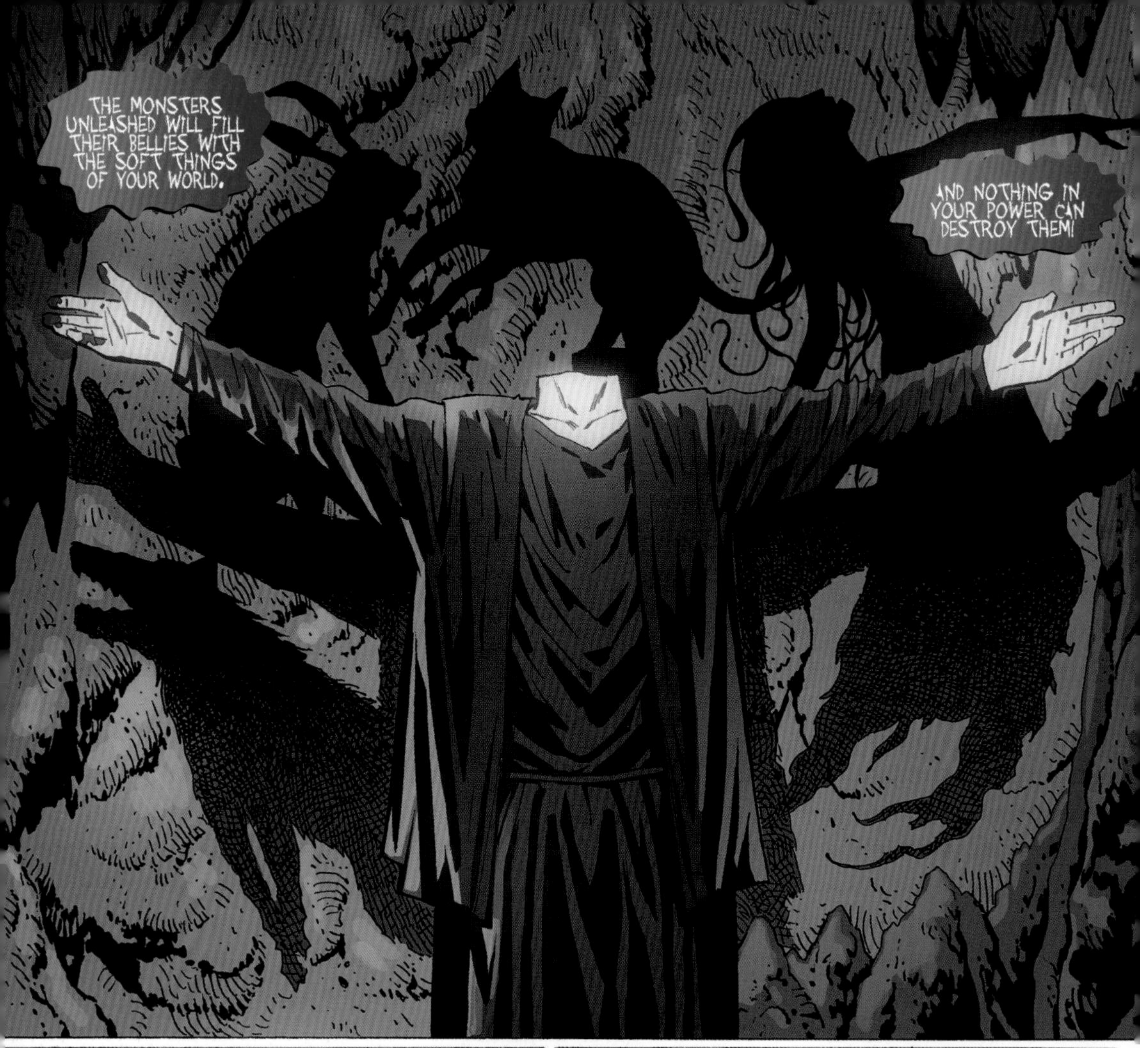
THE MONSTERS UNLEASHED WILL FILL THEIR BELLIES WITH THE SOFT THINGS OF YOUR WORLD.
AND NOTHING IN YOUR POWER CAN DESTROY THEM!

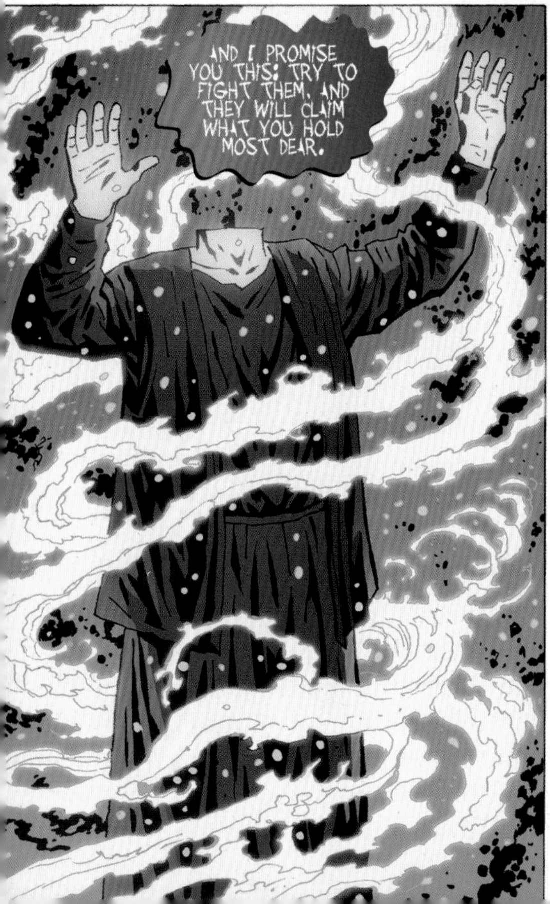
AND I PROMISE YOU THIS: TRY TO FIGHT THEM, AND THEY WILL CLAIM WHAT YOU HOLD MOST DEAR.

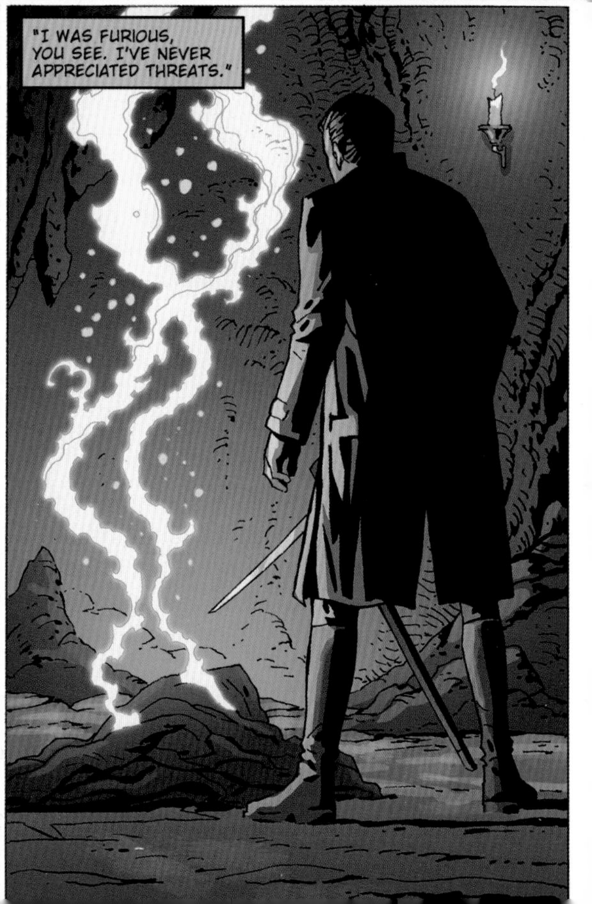
"I WAS FURIOUS, YOU SEE. I'VE NEVER APPRECIATED THREATS."

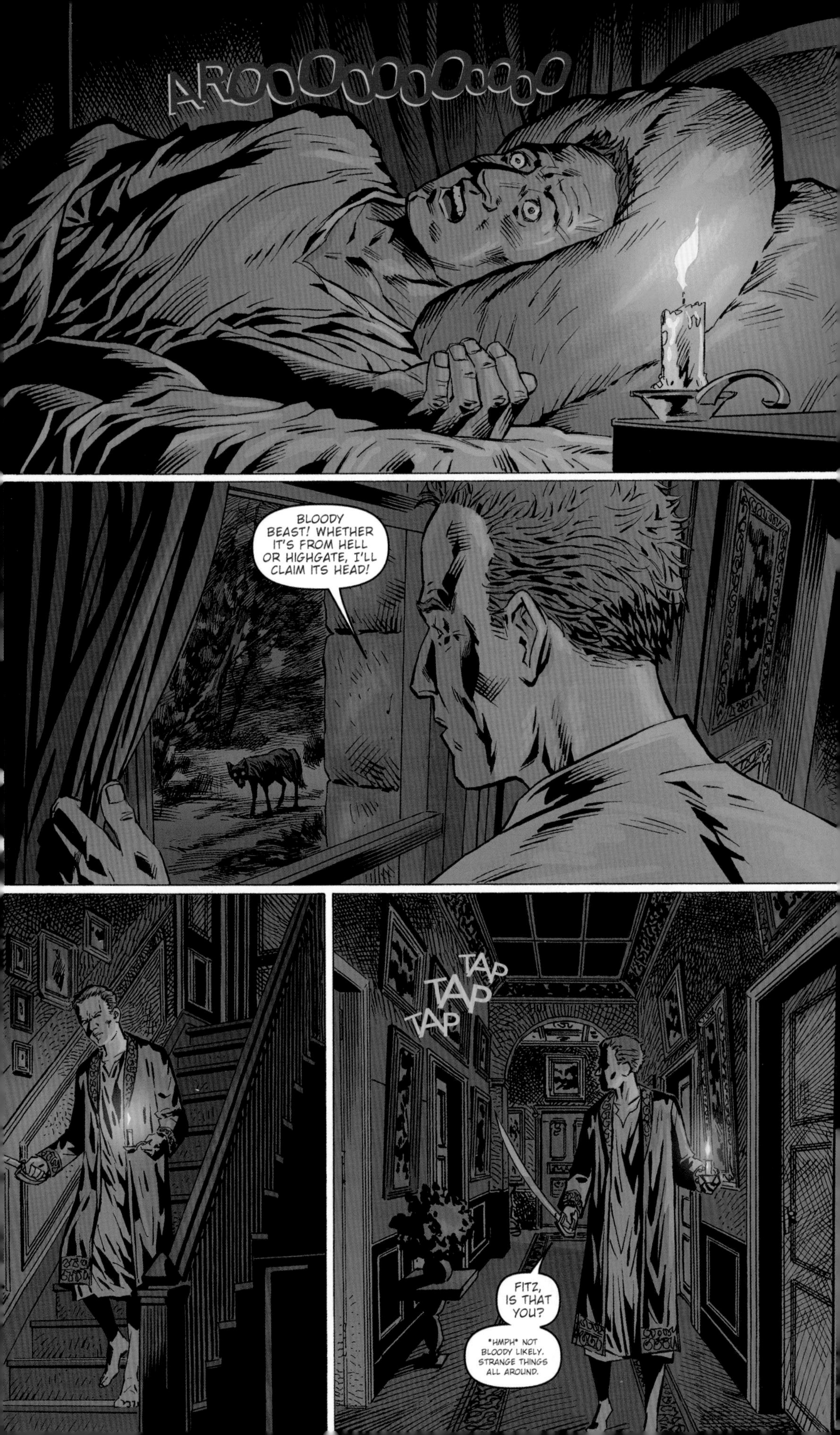
AROOOOOOOOOOoo
BLOODY BEAST! WHETHER IT'S FROM HELL OR HIGHGATE, I'LL CLAIM ITS HEAD!
TAP
TAP
TAP
FITZ, IS THAT YOU?
HMPH NOT BLOODY LIKELY. STRANGE THINGS ALL AROUND.

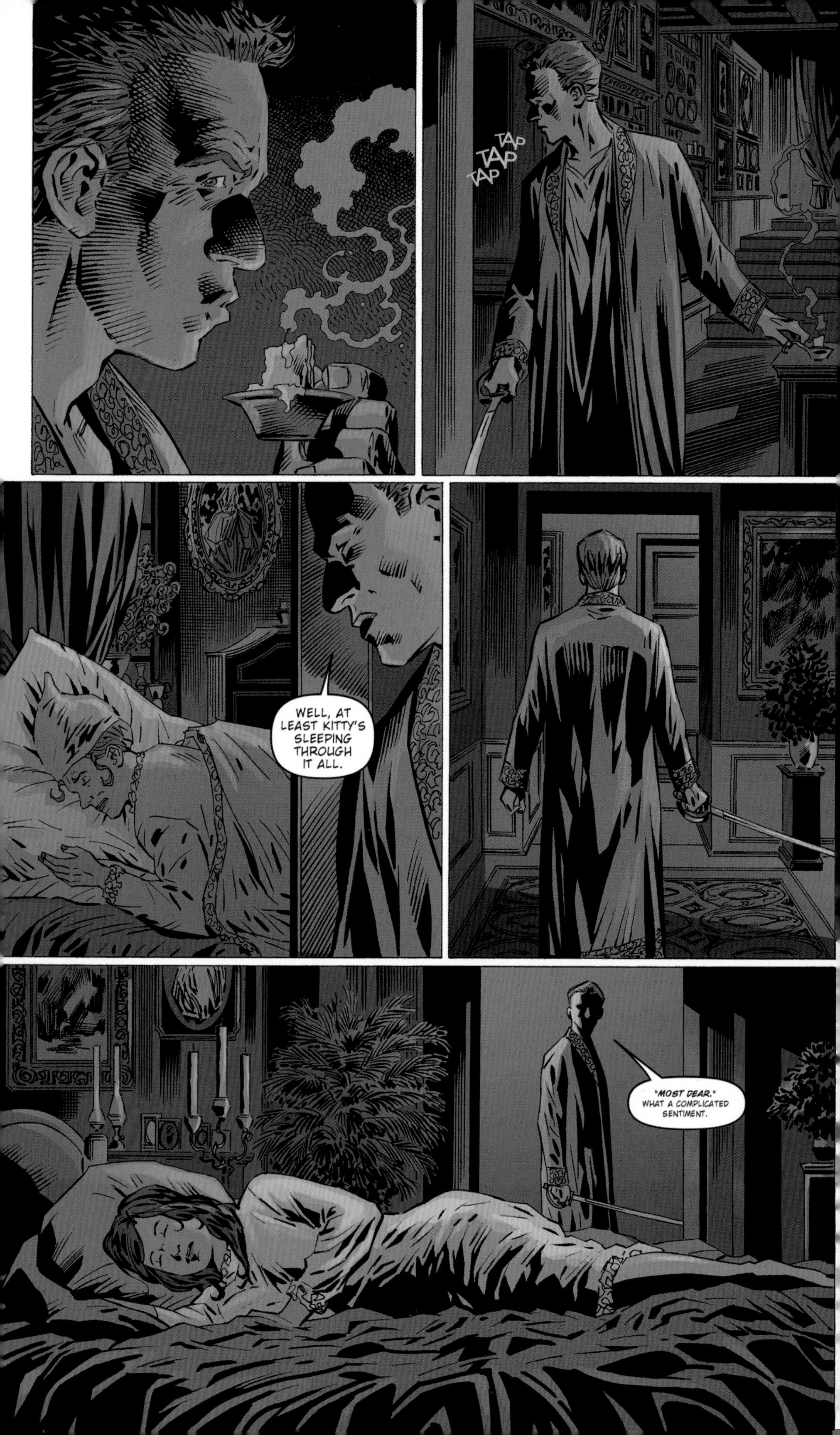
TAP TAP TAP
WELL, AT LEAST KITTY'S SLEEPING THROUGH IT ALL.
"MOST DEAR." WHAT A COMPLICATED SENTIMENT.

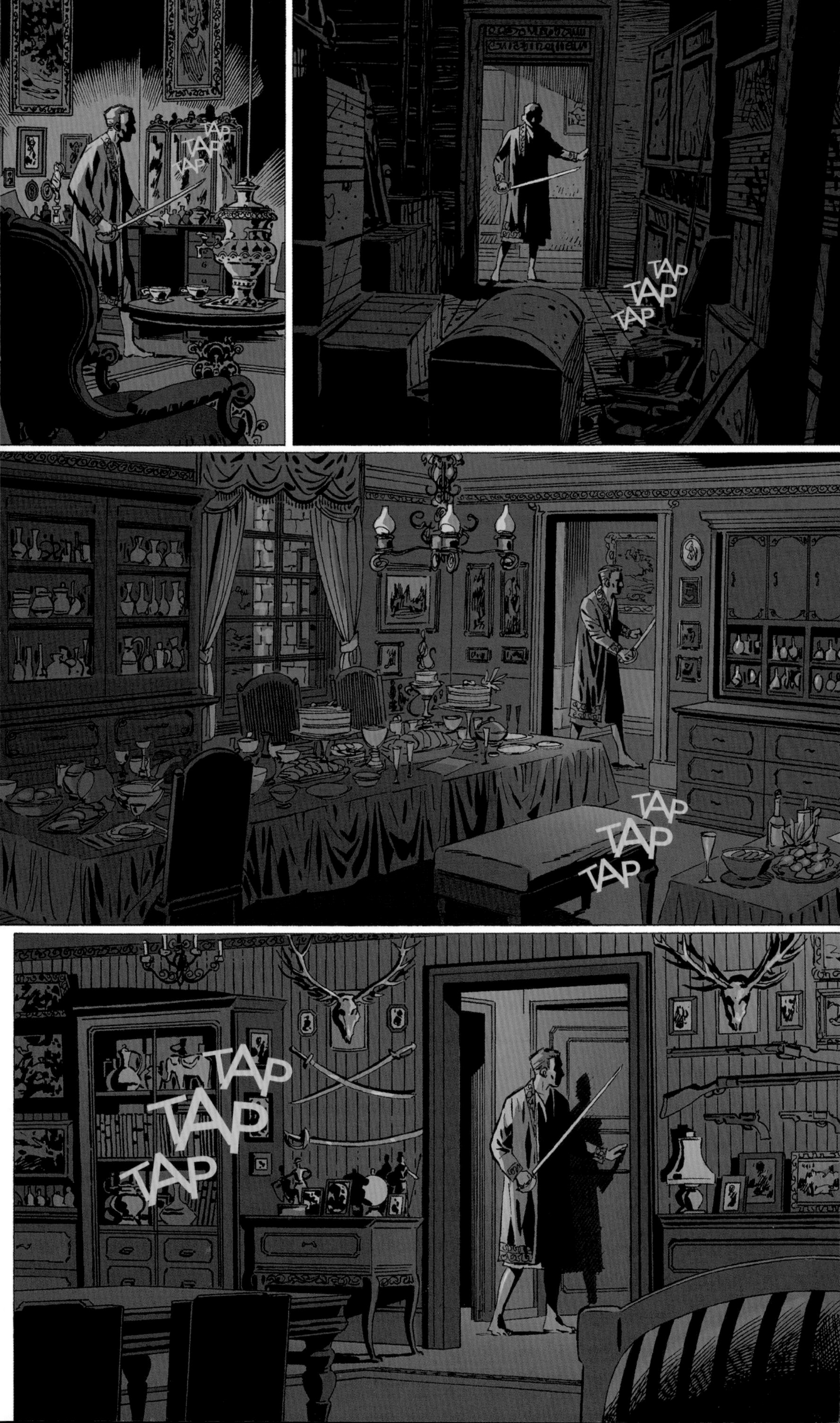
TAP
TAP
TAP
TAP
TAP
TAP
TAP
TAP
TAP
TAP
TAP
TAP

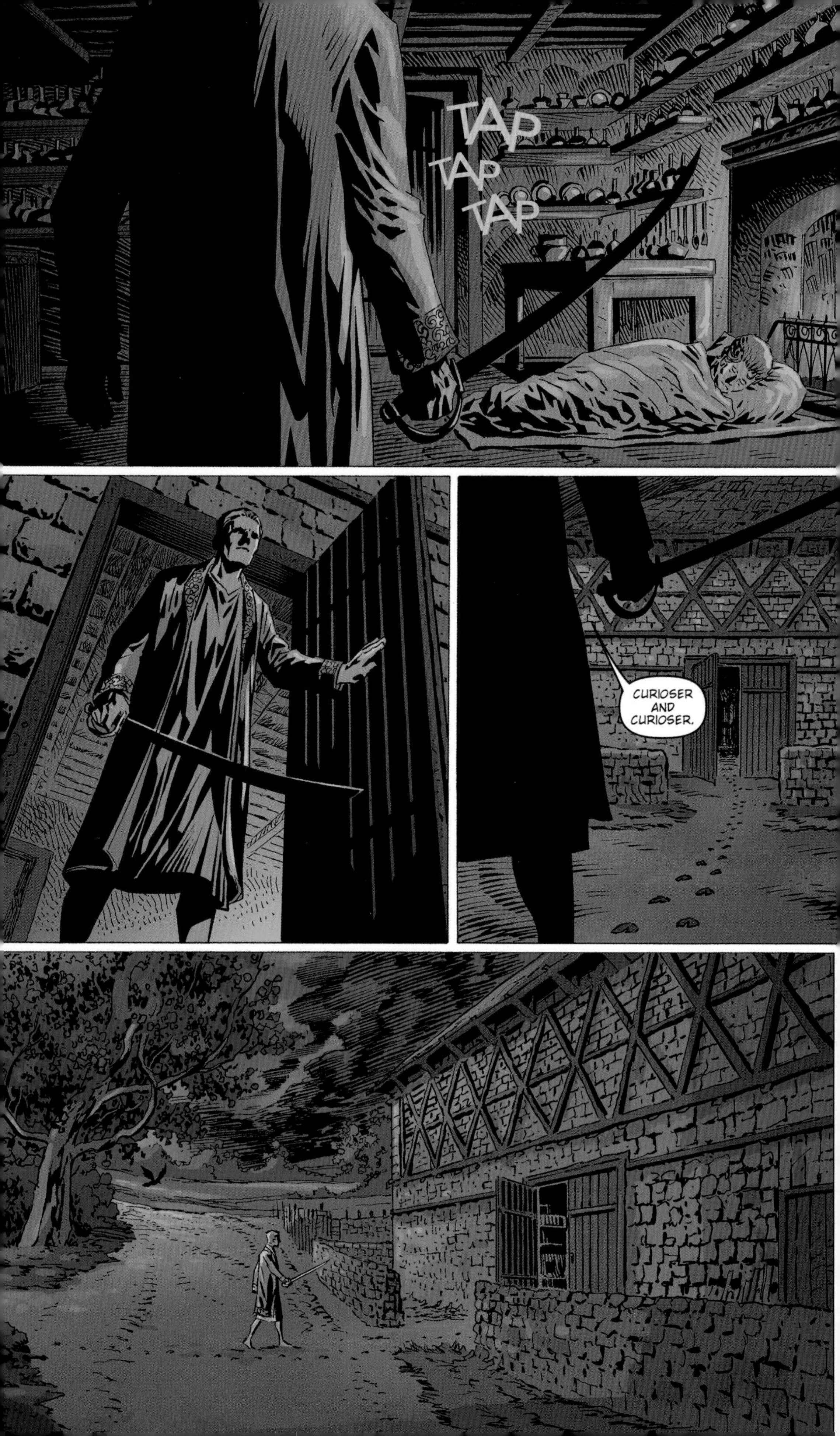
TAP
TAP
TAP
CURIOSER AND CURIOSER.

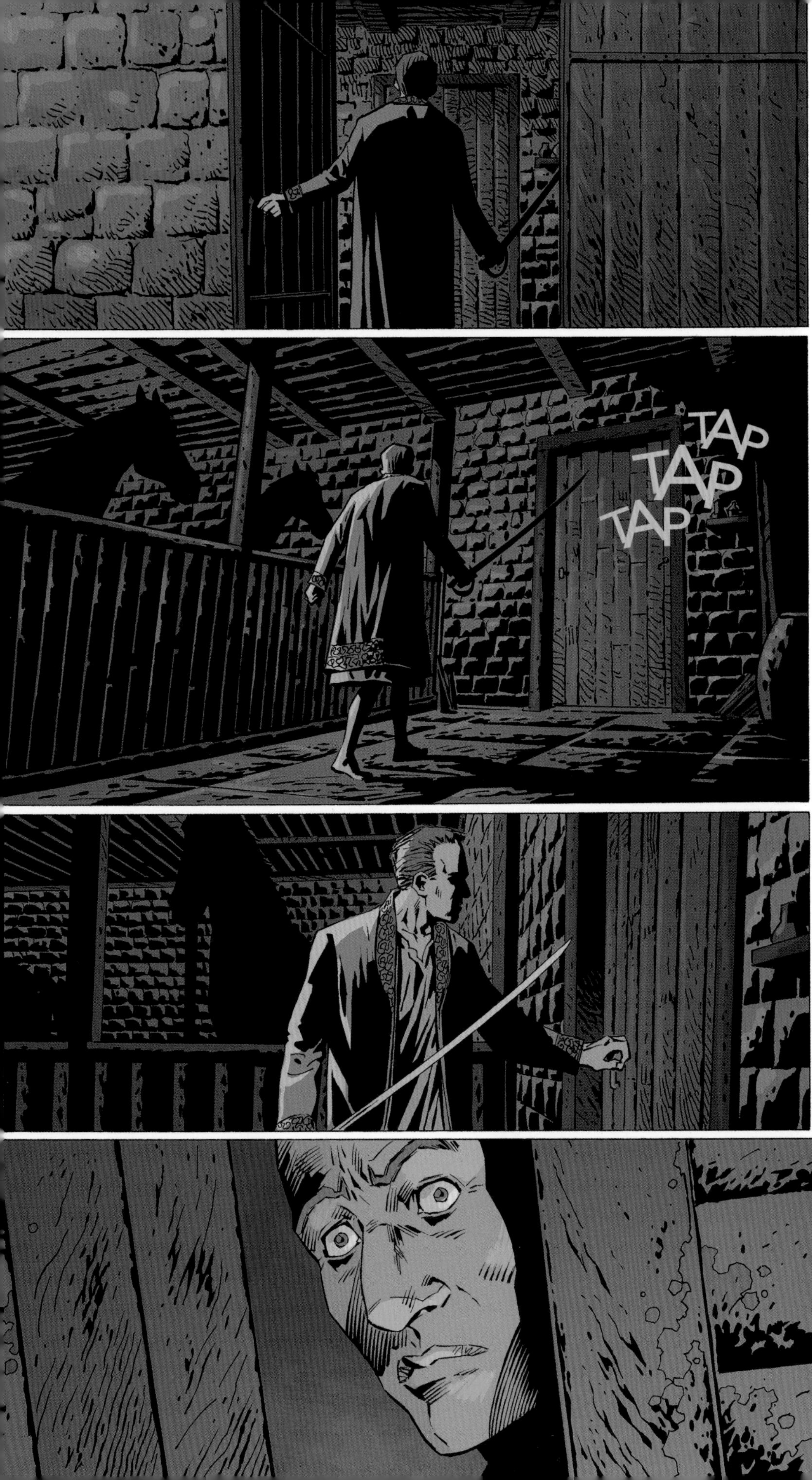
TAP
TAP
TAP

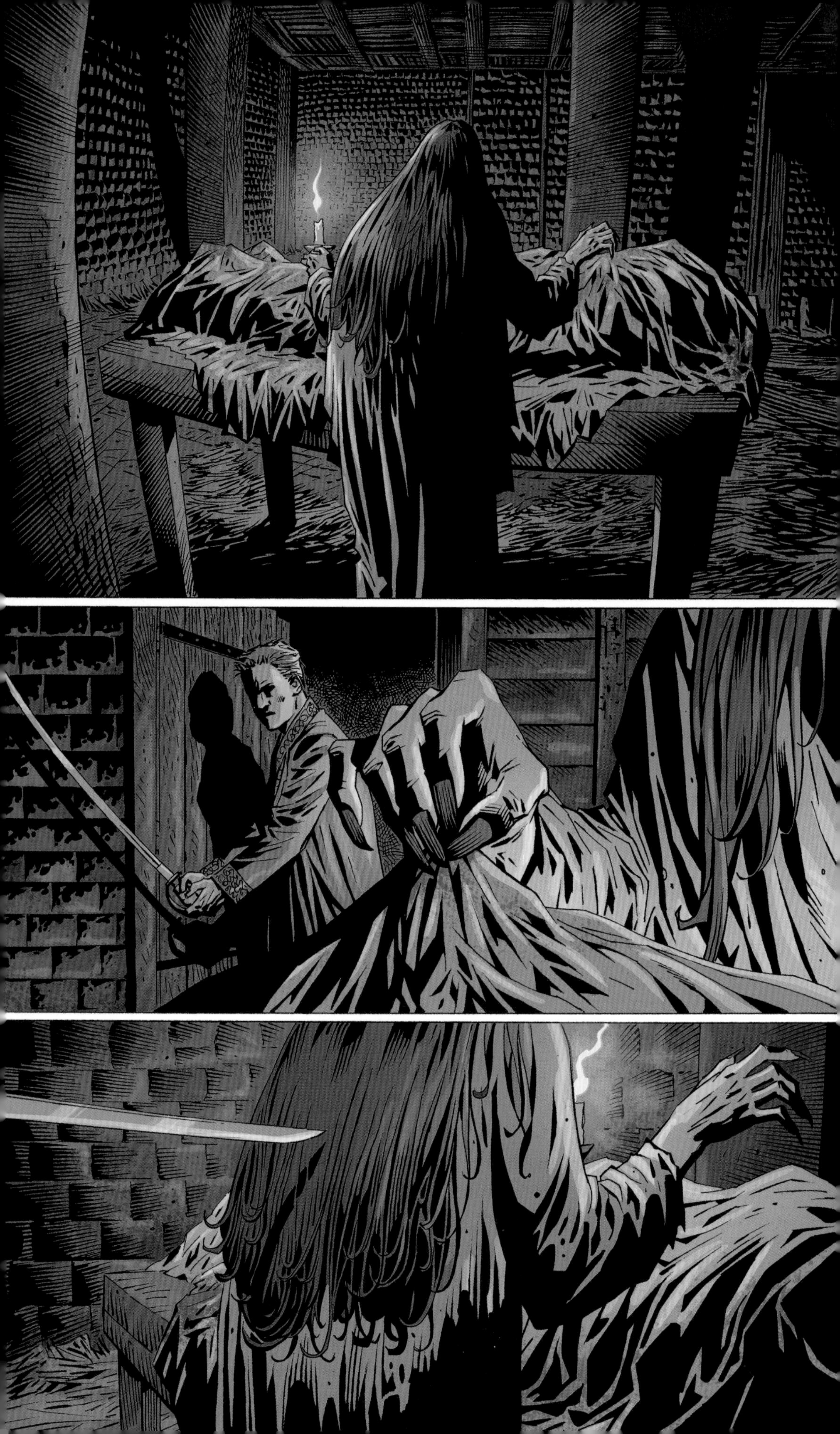

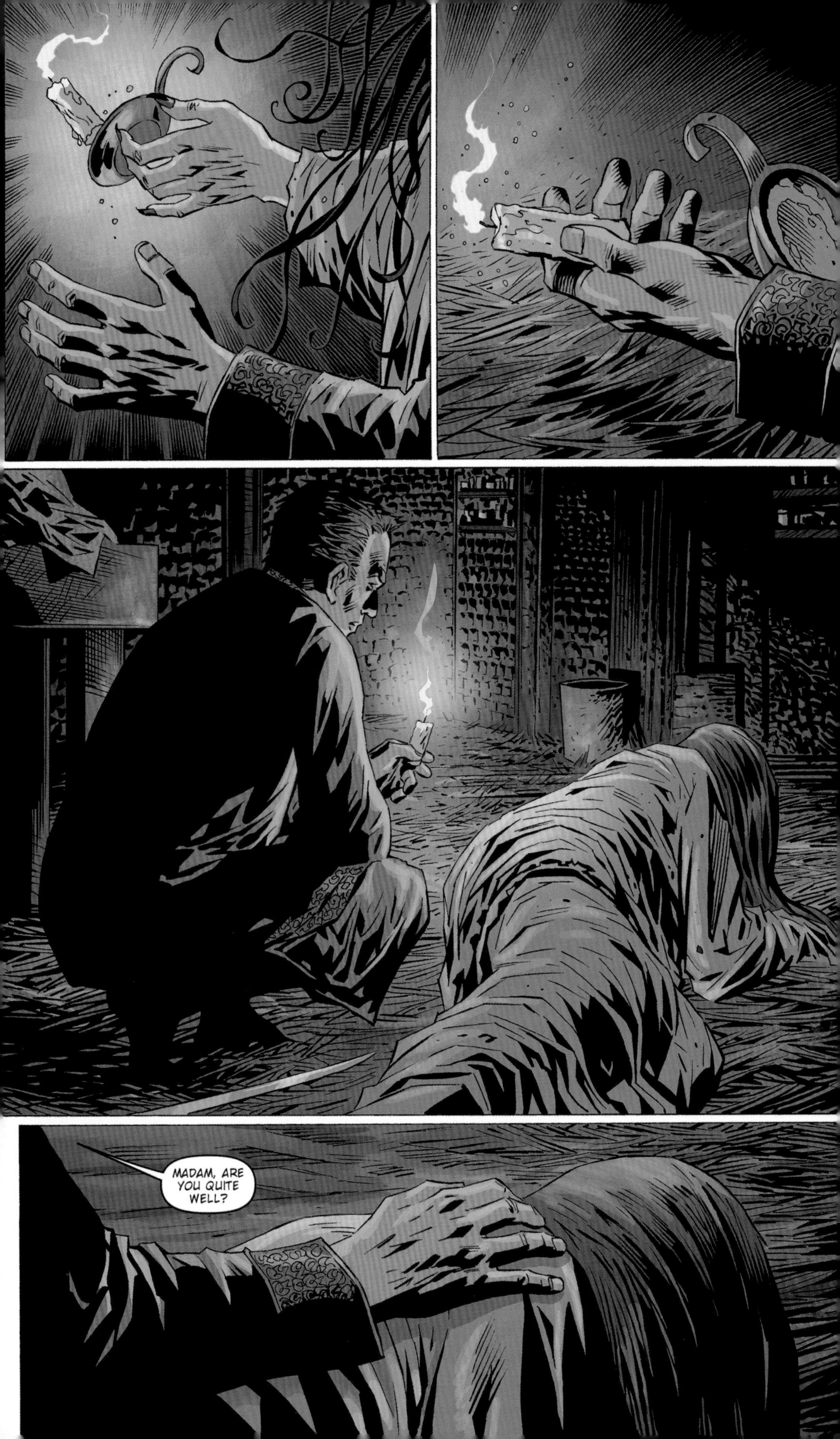
MADAM, ARE YOU QUITE WELL?

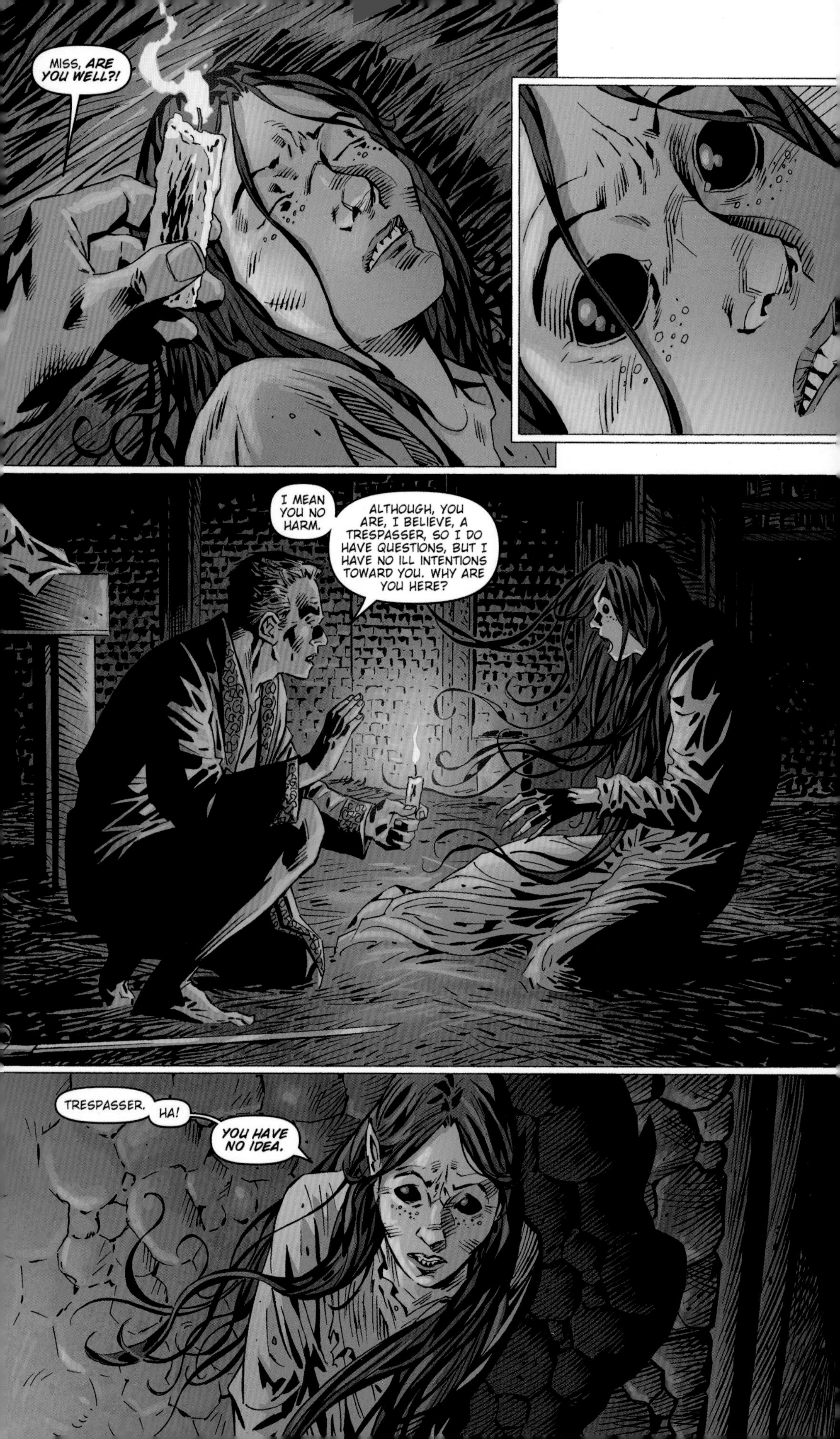
MISS, ARE YOU WELL?!
I MEAN YOU NO HARM.
ALTHOUGH, YOU ARE, I BELIEVE, A TRESPASSER, SO I DO HAVE QUESTIONS, BUT I HAVE NO ILL INTENTIONS TOWARD YOU. WHY ARE YOU HERE?
TRESPASSER.
HA!
YOU HAVE NO IDEA.

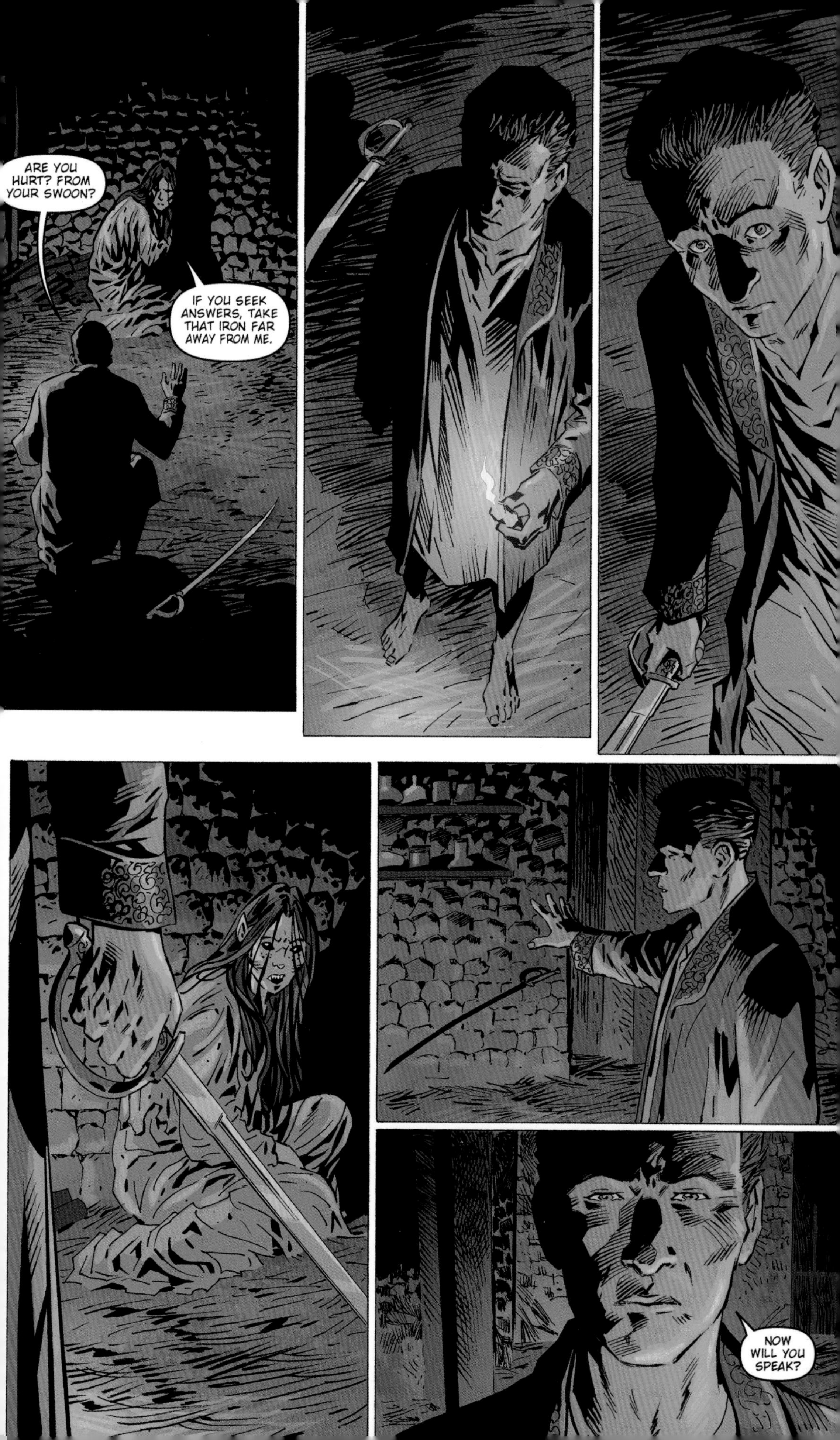
ARE YOU HURT? FROM YOUR SWOON?
IF YOU SEEK ANSWERS, TAKE THAT IRON FAR AWAY FROM ME.
NOW WILL YOU SPEAK?

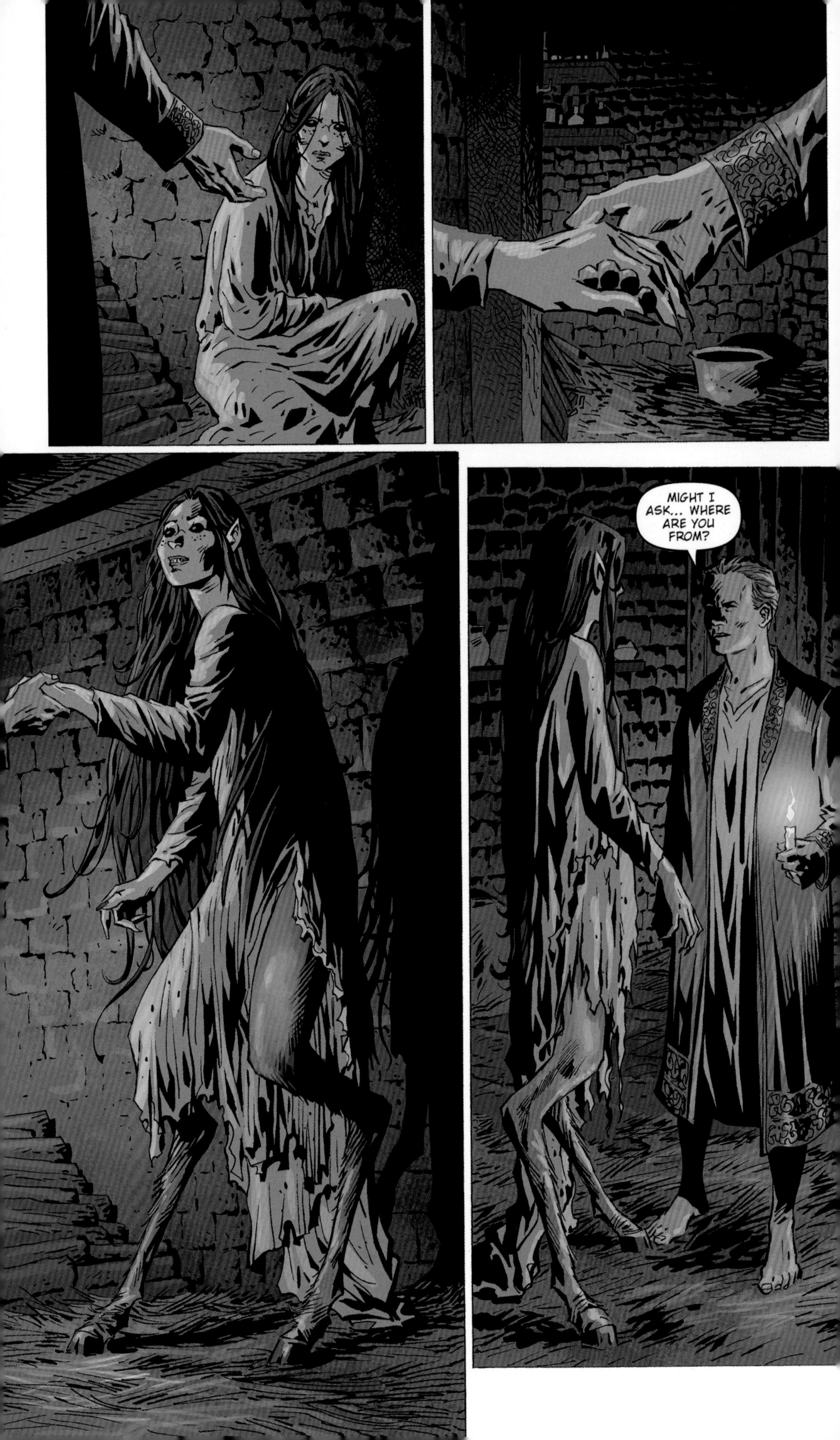
MIGHT I ASK... WHERE ARE YOU FROM?

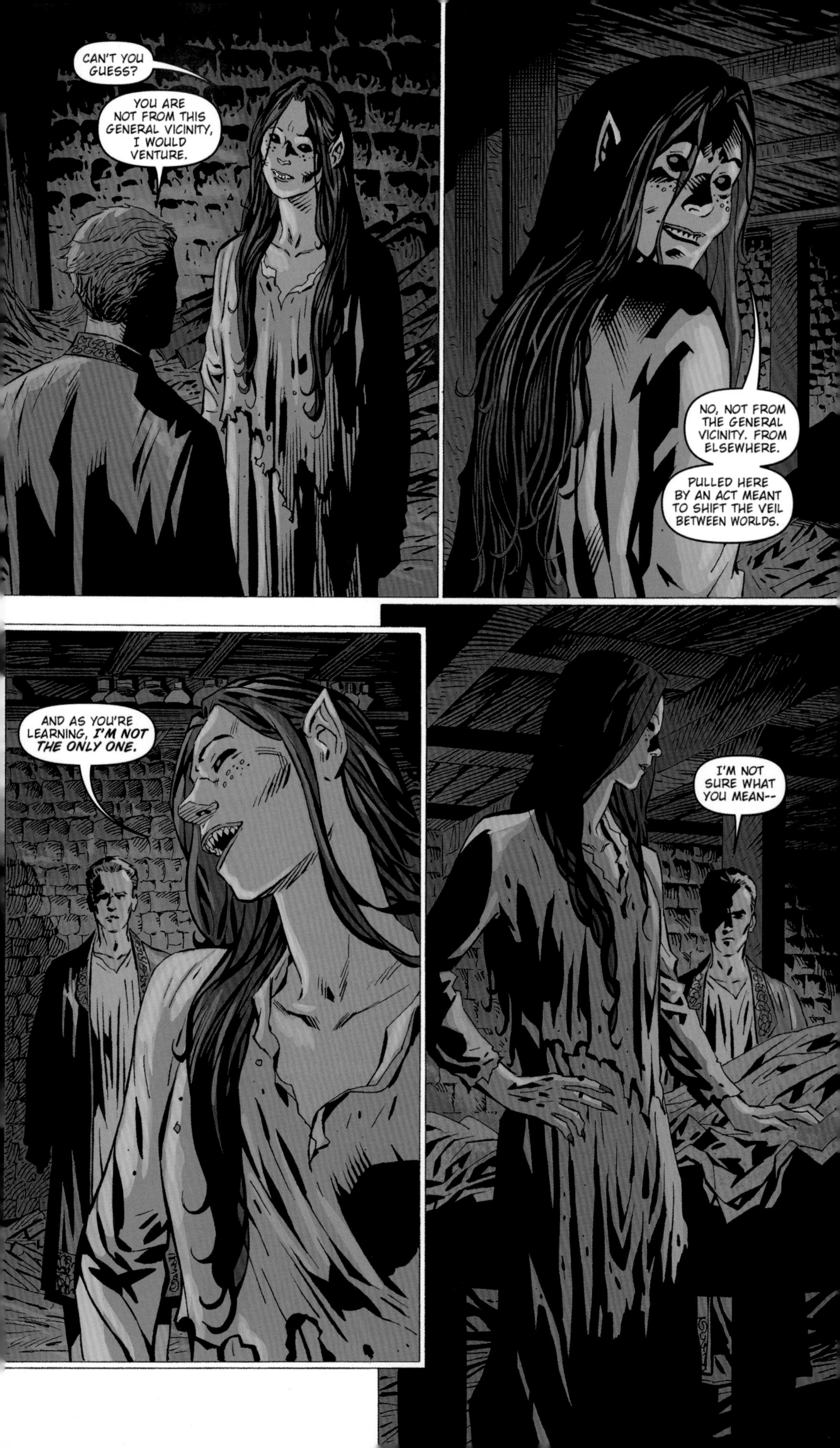
CAN'T YOU GUESS?
YOU ARE NOT FROM THIS GENERAL VICINITY, I WOULD VENTURE.
NO, NOT FROM THE GENERAL VICINITY. FROM ELSEWHERE.
PULLED HERE BY AN ACT MEANT TO SHIFT THE VEIL BETWEEN WORLDS.
AND AS YOU'RE LEARNING, ***I'M NOT THE ONLY ONE.***
I'M NOT SURE WHAT YOU MEAN--

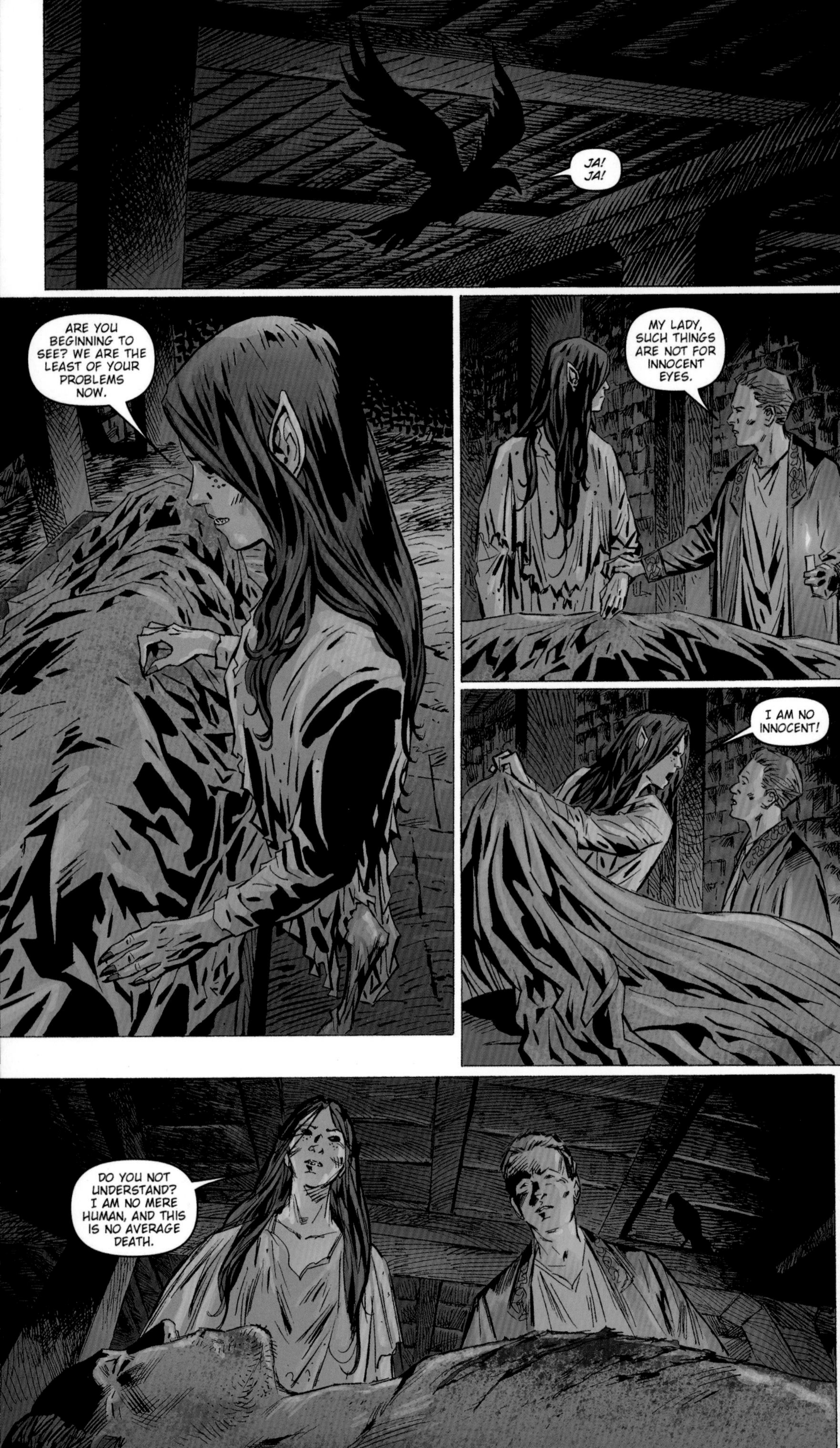
JA! JA!
ARE YOU BEGINNING TO SEE? WE ARE THE LEAST OF YOUR PROBLEMS NOW.
MY LADY, SUCH THINGS ARE NOT FOR INNOCENT EYES.
I AM NO INNOCENT!
DO YOU NOT UNDERSTAND? I AM NO MERE HUMAN, AND THIS IS NO AVERAGE DEATH.

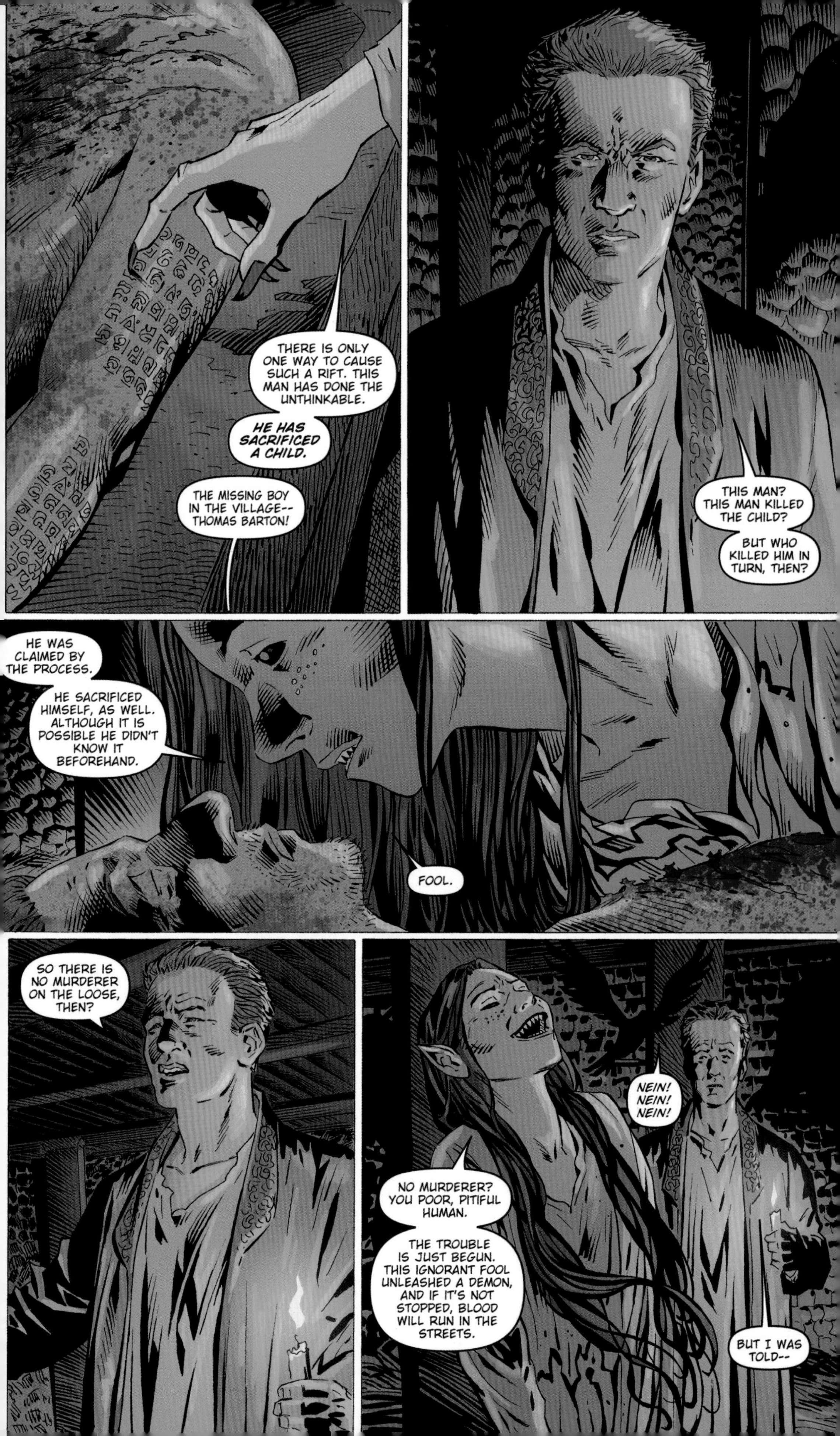
THERE IS ONLY ONE WAY TO CAUSE SUCH A RIFT. THIS MAN HAS DONE THE UNTHINKABLE.
HE HAS SACRIFICED A CHILD.
THE MISSING BOY IN THE VILLAGE--THOMAS BARTON!
THIS MAN? THIS MAN KILLED THE CHILD?
BUT WHO KILLED HIM IN TURN, THEN?
HE WAS CLAIMED BY THE PROCESS.
HE SACRIFICED HIMSELF, AS WELL. ALTHOUGH IT IS POSSIBLE HE DIDN'T KNOW IT BEFOREHAND.
FOOL.
SO THERE IS NO MURDERER ON THE LOOSE, THEN?
NEIN! NEIN! NEIN!
NO MURDERER? YOU POOR, PITIFUL HUMAN.
THE TROUBLE IS JUST BEGUN. THIS IGNORANT FOOL UNLEASHED A DEMON, AND IF IT'S NOT STOPPED, BLOOD WILL RUN IN THE STREETS.
BUT I WAS TOLD--

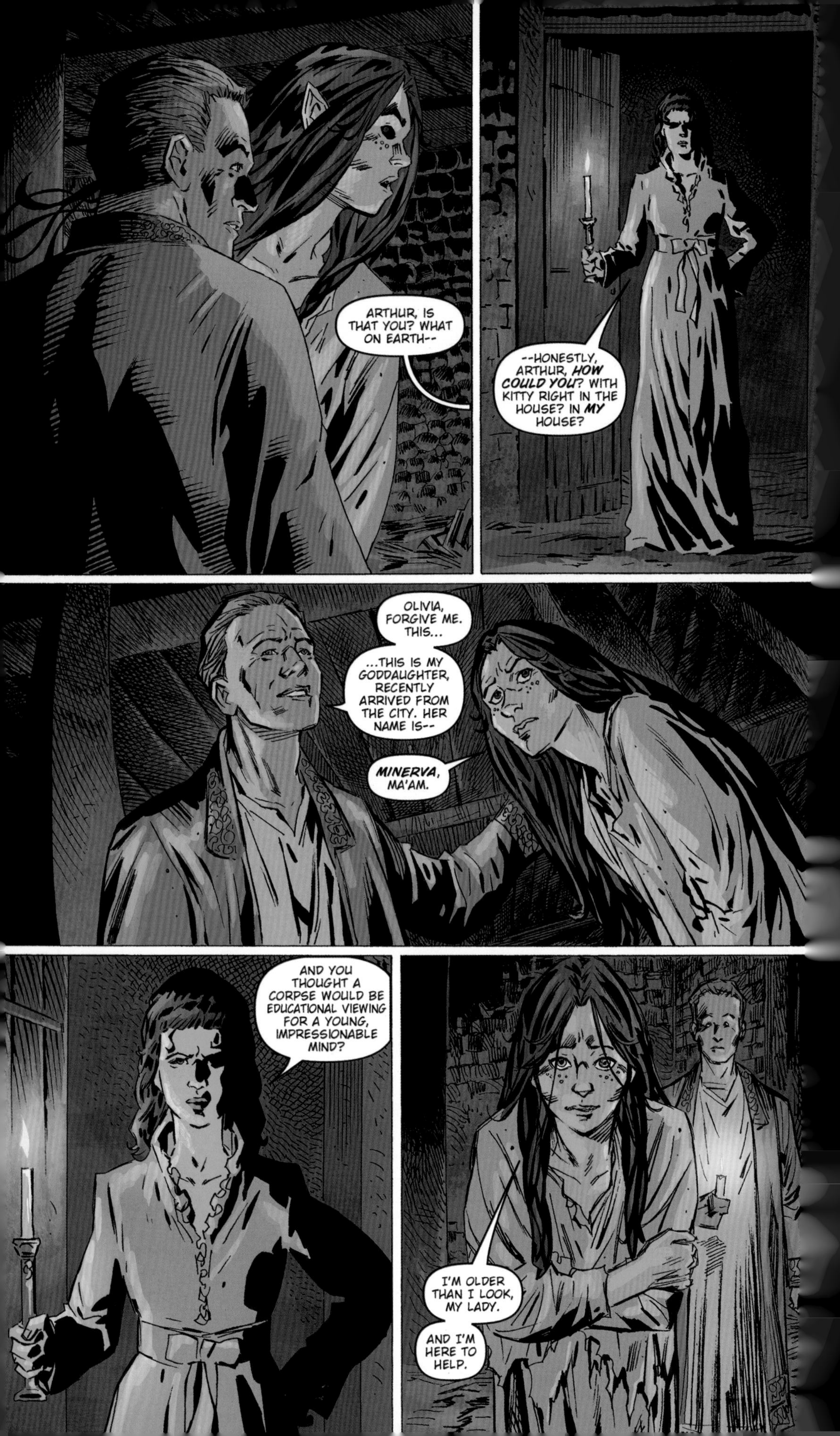
ARTHUR, IS THAT YOU? WHAT ON EARTH--
--HONESTLY, ARTHUR, HOW COULD YOU? WITH KITTY RIGHT IN THE HOUSE? IN MY HOUSE?
OLIVIA, FORGIVE ME. THIS...
...THIS IS MY GODDAUGHTER, RECENTLY ARRIVED FROM THE CITY. HER NAME IS--
MINERVA, MA'AM.
AND YOU THOUGHT A CORPSE WOULD BE EDUCATIONAL VIEWING FOR A YOUNG, IMPRESSIONABLE MIND?
I'M OLDER THAN I LOOK, MY LADY.
AND I'M HERE TO HELP.

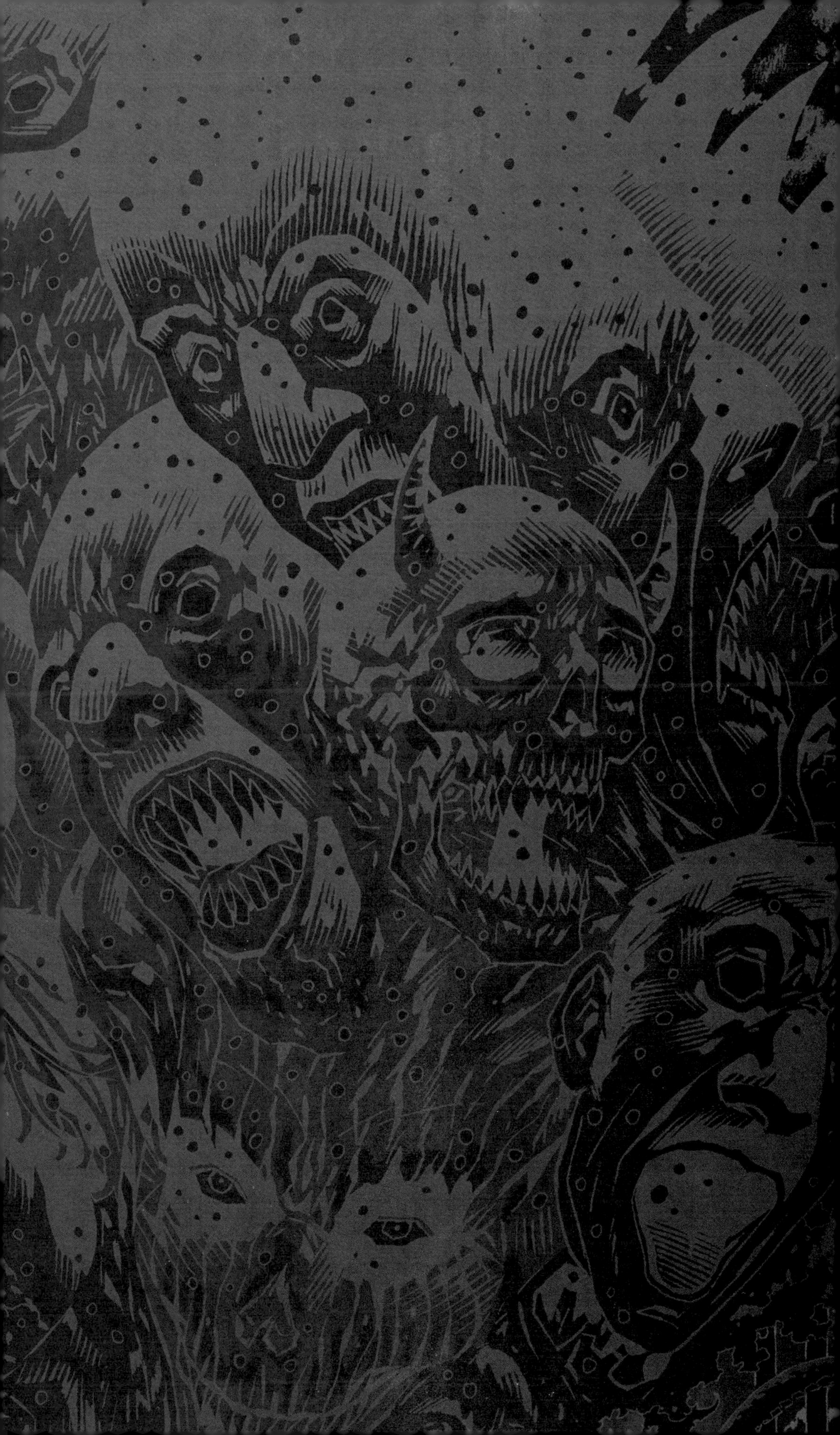

Chapter 3

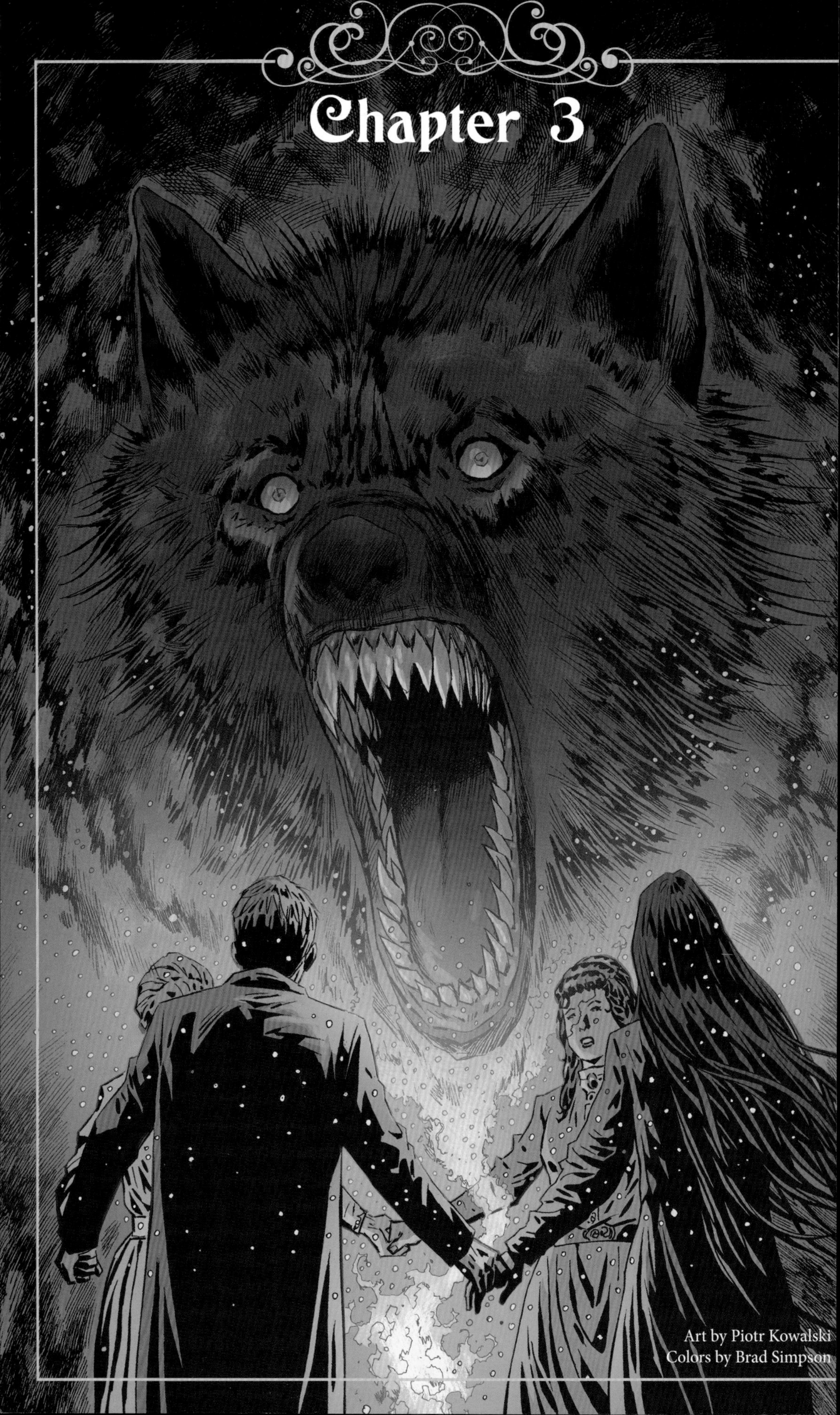

Art by Piotr Kowalski
Colors by Brad Simpson

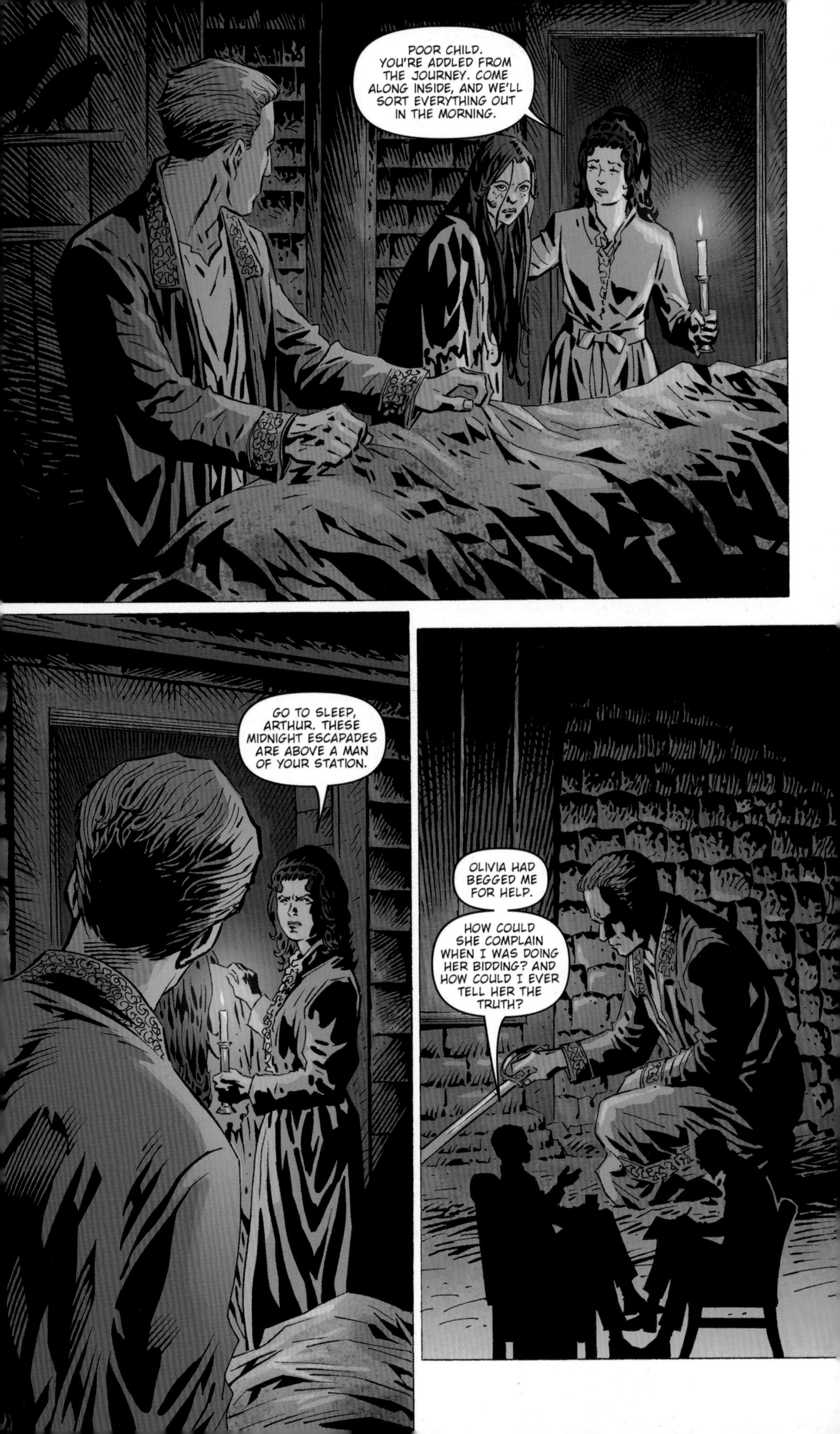
POOR CHILD. YOU'RE ADDLED FROM THE JOURNEY. COME ALONG INSIDE, AND WE'LL SORT EVERYTHING OUT IN THE MORNING.
GO TO SLEEP, ARTHUR. THESE MIDNIGHT ESCAPADES ARE ABOVE A MAN OF YOUR STATION.
OLIVIA HAD BEGGED ME FOR HELP.
HOW COULD SHE COMPLAIN WHEN I WAS DOING HER BIDDING? AND HOW COULD I EVER TELL HER THE TRUTH?

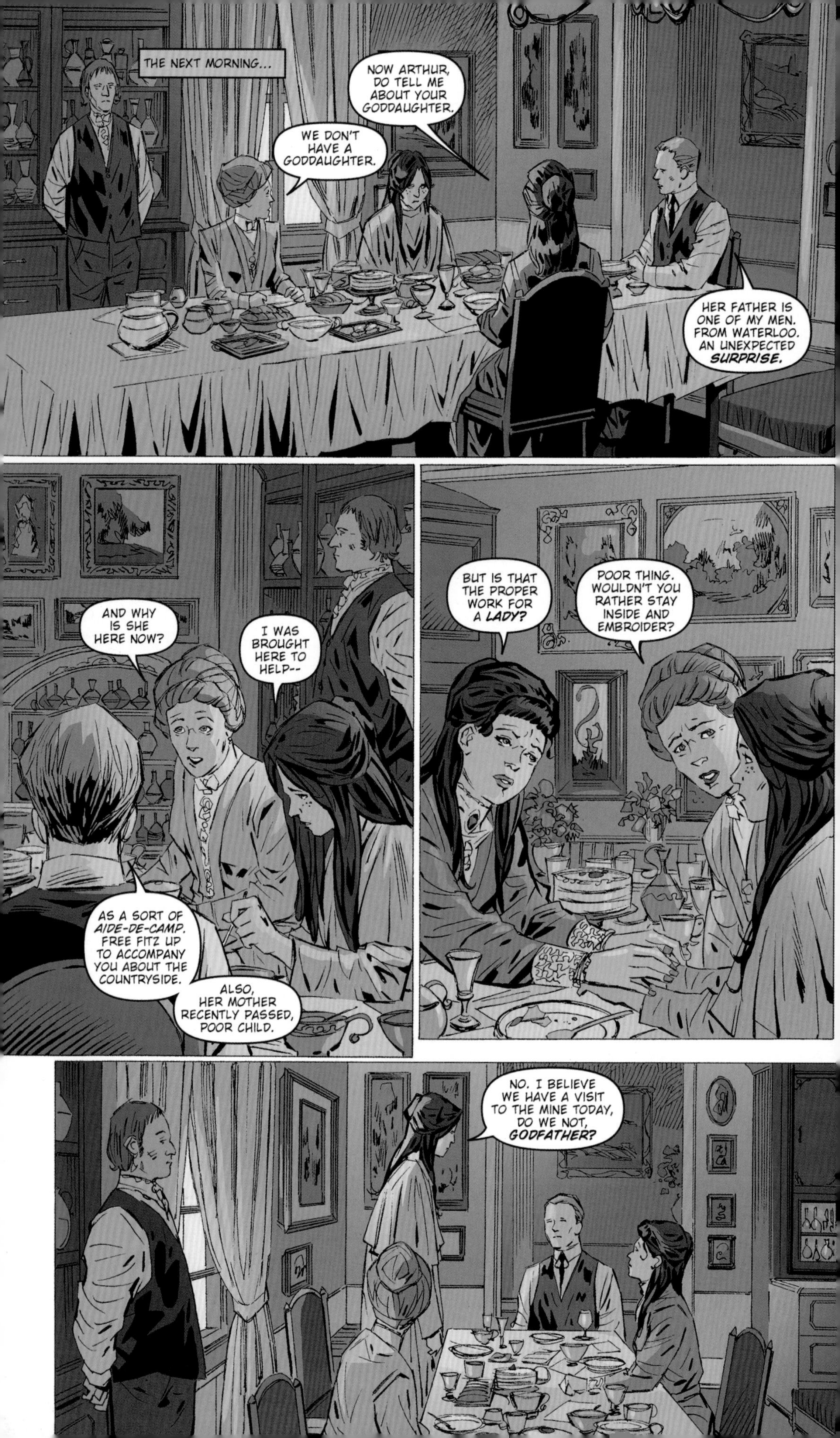
THE NEXT MORNING...
NOW ARTHUR, DO TELL ME ABOUT YOUR GODDAUGHTER.
WE DON'T HAVE A GODDAUGHTER.
HER FATHER IS ONE OF MY MEN. FROM WATERLOO. AN UNEXPECTED SURPRISE.
AND WHY IS SHE HERE NOW?
I WAS BROUGHT HERE TO HELP--
AS A SORT OF AIDE-DE-CAMP. FREE FITZ UP TO ACCOMPANY YOU ABOUT THE COUNTRYSIDE.
ALSO, HER MOTHER RECENTLY PASSED, POOR CHILD.
POOR THING. WOULDN'T YOU RATHER STAY INSIDE AND EMBROIDER?
BUT IS THAT THE PROPER WORK FOR A LADY?
NO. I BELIEVE WE HAVE A VISIT TO THE MINE TODAY, DO WE NOT, GODFATHER?

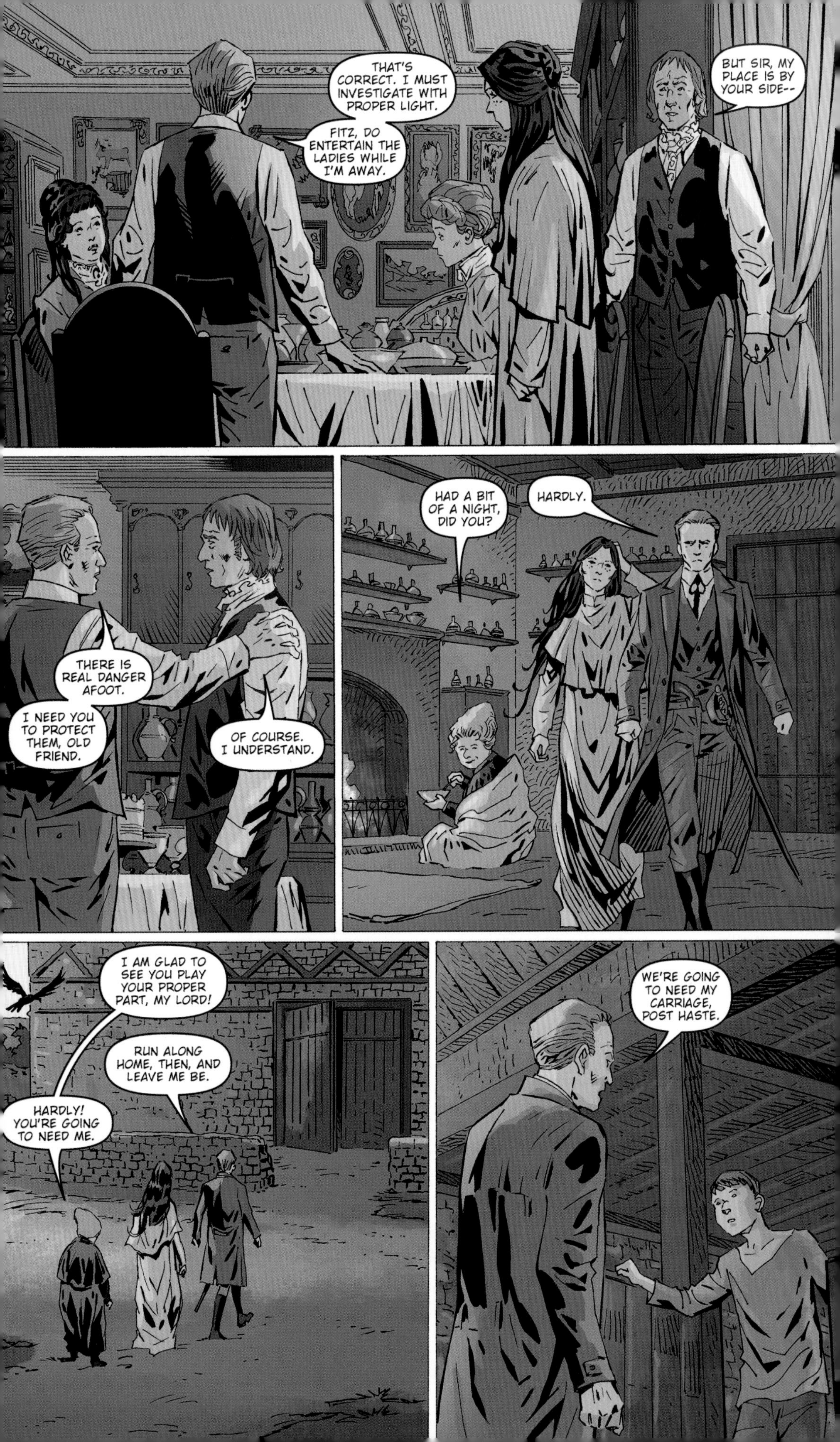
THAT'S CORRECT. I MUST INVESTIGATE WITH PROPER LIGHT.
FITZ, DO ENTERTAIN THE LADIES WHILE I'M AWAY.
BUT SIR, MY PLACE IS BY YOUR SIDE--
THERE IS REAL DANGER AFOOT.
I NEED YOU TO PROTECT THEM, OLD FRIEND.
OF COURSE. I UNDERSTAND.
HAD A BIT OF A NIGHT, DID YOU?
HARDLY.
I AM GLAD TO SEE YOU PLAY YOUR PROPER PART, MY LORD!
RUN ALONG HOME, THEN, AND LEAVE ME BE.
HARDLY! YOU'RE GOING TO NEED ME.
WE'RE GOING TO NEED MY CARRIAGE, POST HASTE.

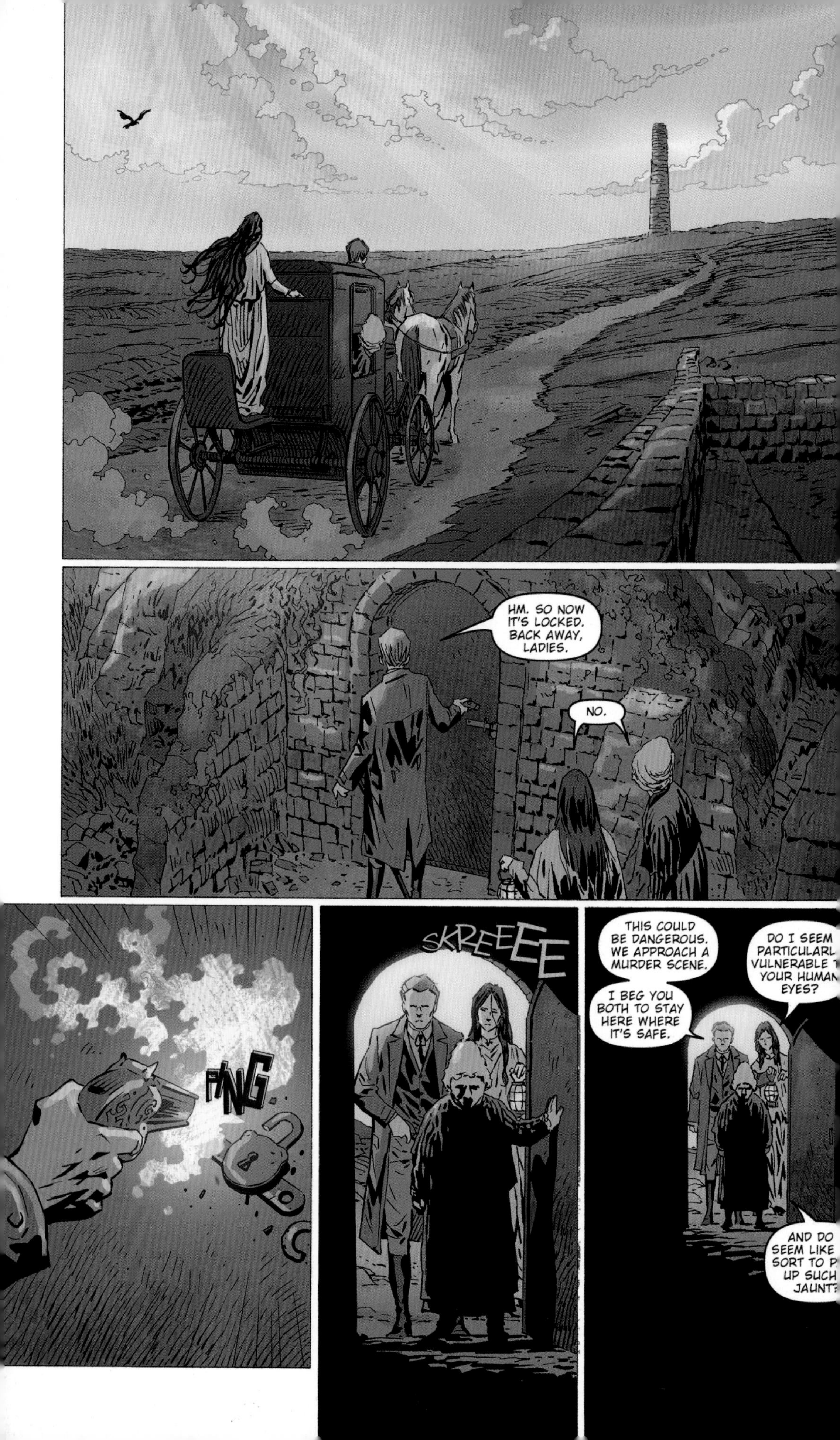
HM. SO NOW IT'S LOCKED. BACK AWAY, LADIES.
NO.
PING
SKREEEEE
THIS COULD BE DANGEROUS. WE APPROACH A MURDER SCENE.
I BEG YOU BOTH TO STAY HERE WHERE IT'S SAFE.
DO I SEEM PARTICULARL VULNERABLE T YOUR HUMAN EYES?
AND DO SEEM LIKE SORT TO P UP SUCH JAUNT?

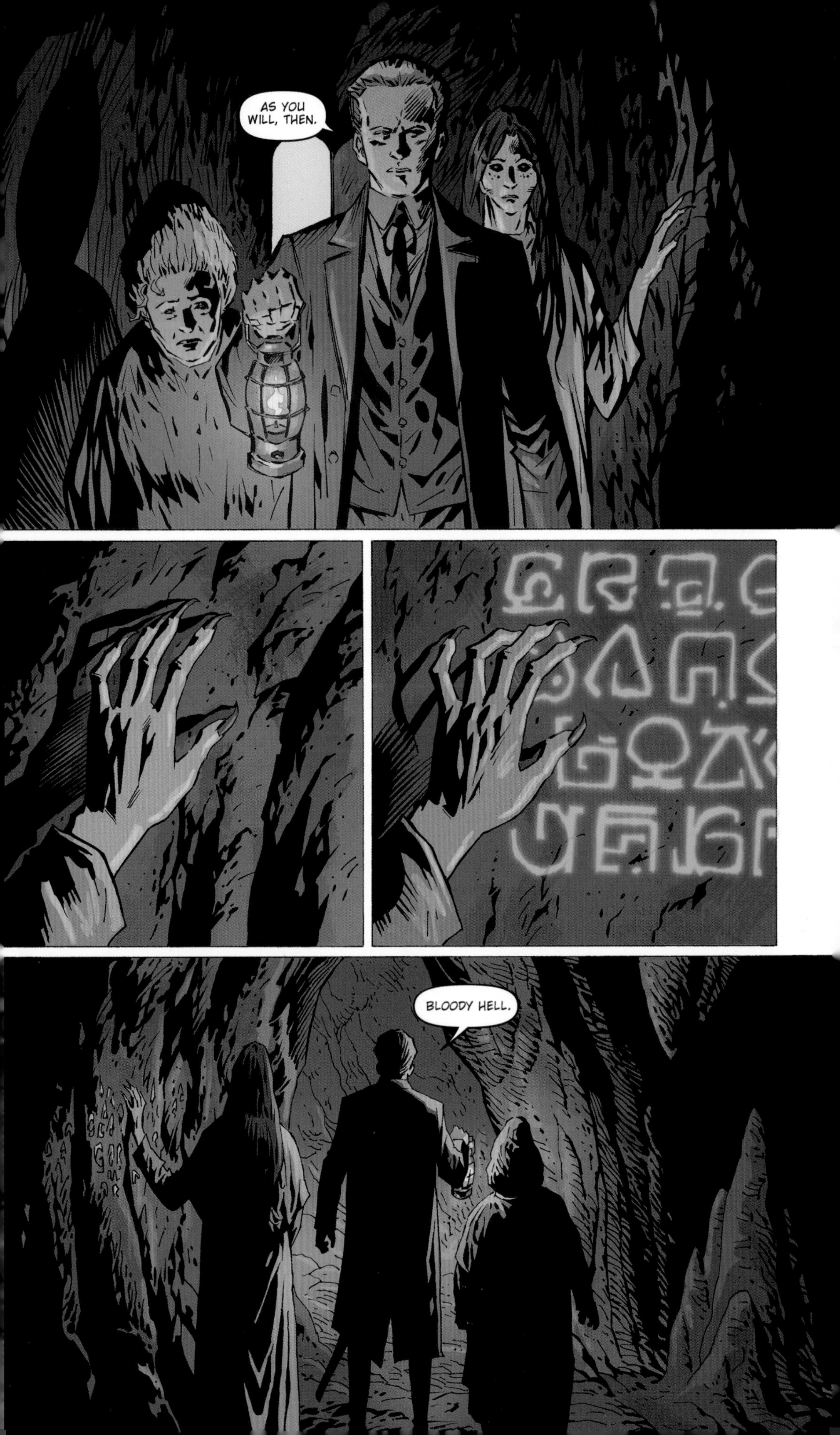
AS YOU WILL, THEN.
BLOODY HELL.

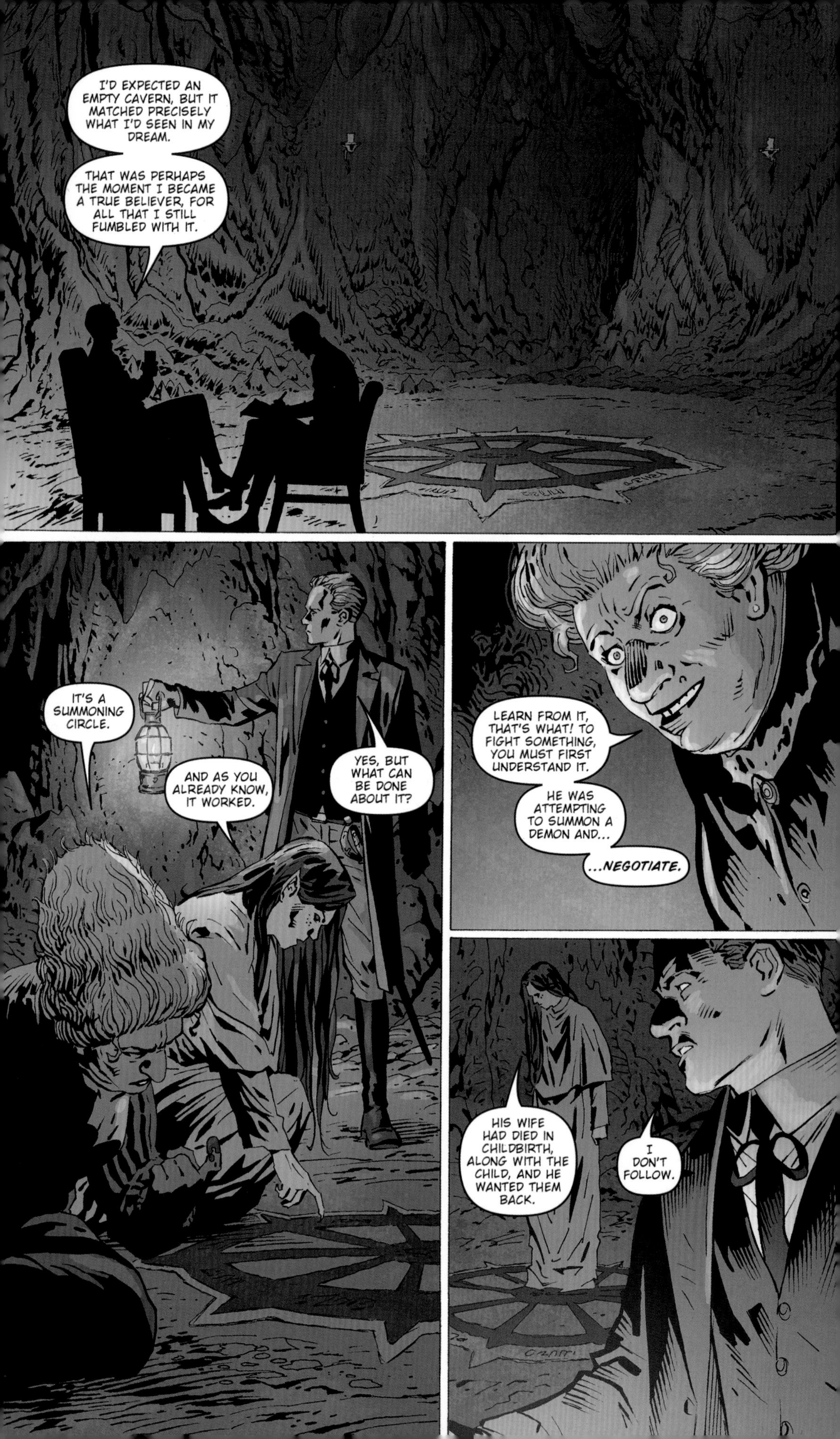
I'D EXPECTED AN EMPTY CAVERN, BUT IT MATCHED PRECISELY WHAT I'D SEEN IN MY DREAM.
THAT WAS PERHAPS THE MOMENT I BECAME A TRUE BELIEVER, FOR ALL THAT I STILL FUMBLED WITH IT.
IT'S A SUMMONING CIRCLE.
AND AS YOU ALREADY KNOW, IT WORKED.
YES, BUT WHAT CAN BE DONE ABOUT IT?
LEARN FROM IT, THAT'S WHAT! TO FIGHT SOMETHING, YOU MUST FIRST UNDERSTAND IT.
HE WAS ATTEMPTING TO SUMMON A DEMON AND...
...NEGOTIATE.
HIS WIFE HAD DIED IN CHILDBIRTH, ALONG WITH THE CHILD, AND HE WANTED THEM BACK.
I DON'T FOLLOW.

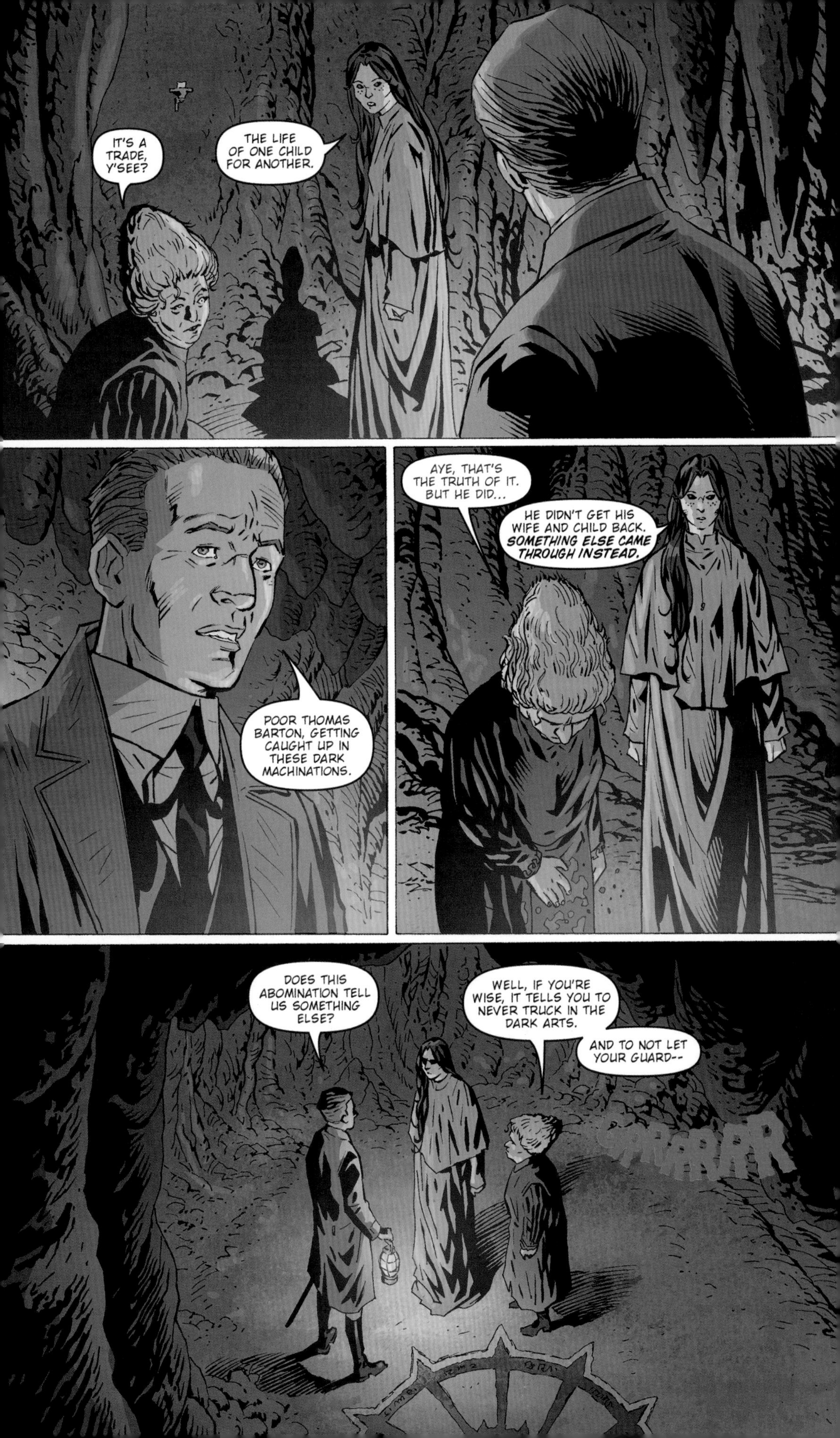
IT'S A TRADE, Y'SEE?
THE LIFE OF ONE CHILD FOR ANOTHER.
POOR THOMAS BARTON, GETTING CAUGHT UP IN THESE DARK MACHINATIONS.
AYE, THAT'S THE TRUTH OF IT. BUT HE DID...
HE DIDN'T GET HIS WIFE AND CHILD BACK. SOMETHING ELSE CAME THROUGH INSTEAD.
DOES THIS ABOMINATION TELL US SOMETHING ELSE?
WELL, IF YOU'RE WISE, IT TELLS YOU TO NEVER TRUCK IN THE DARK ARTS.
AND TO NOT LET YOUR GUARD--
GRRRRR

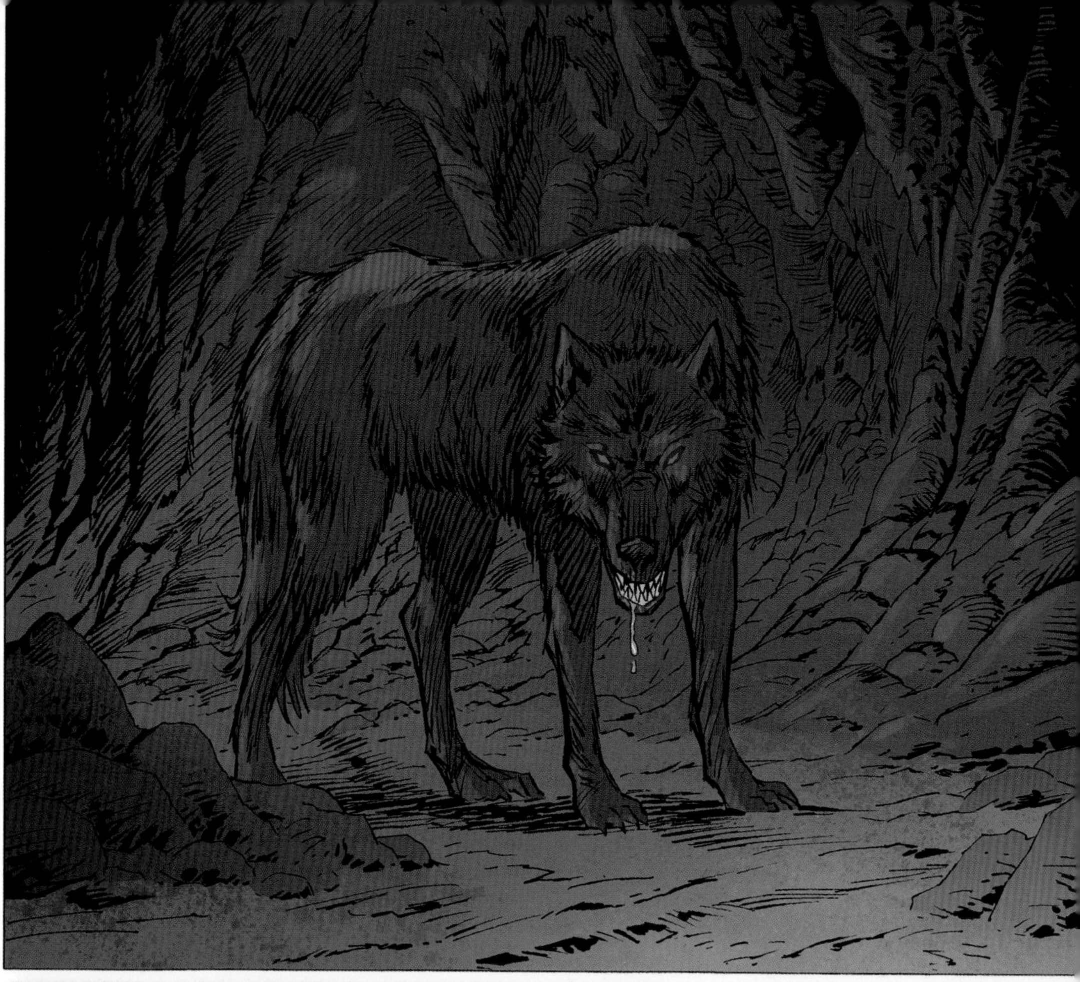

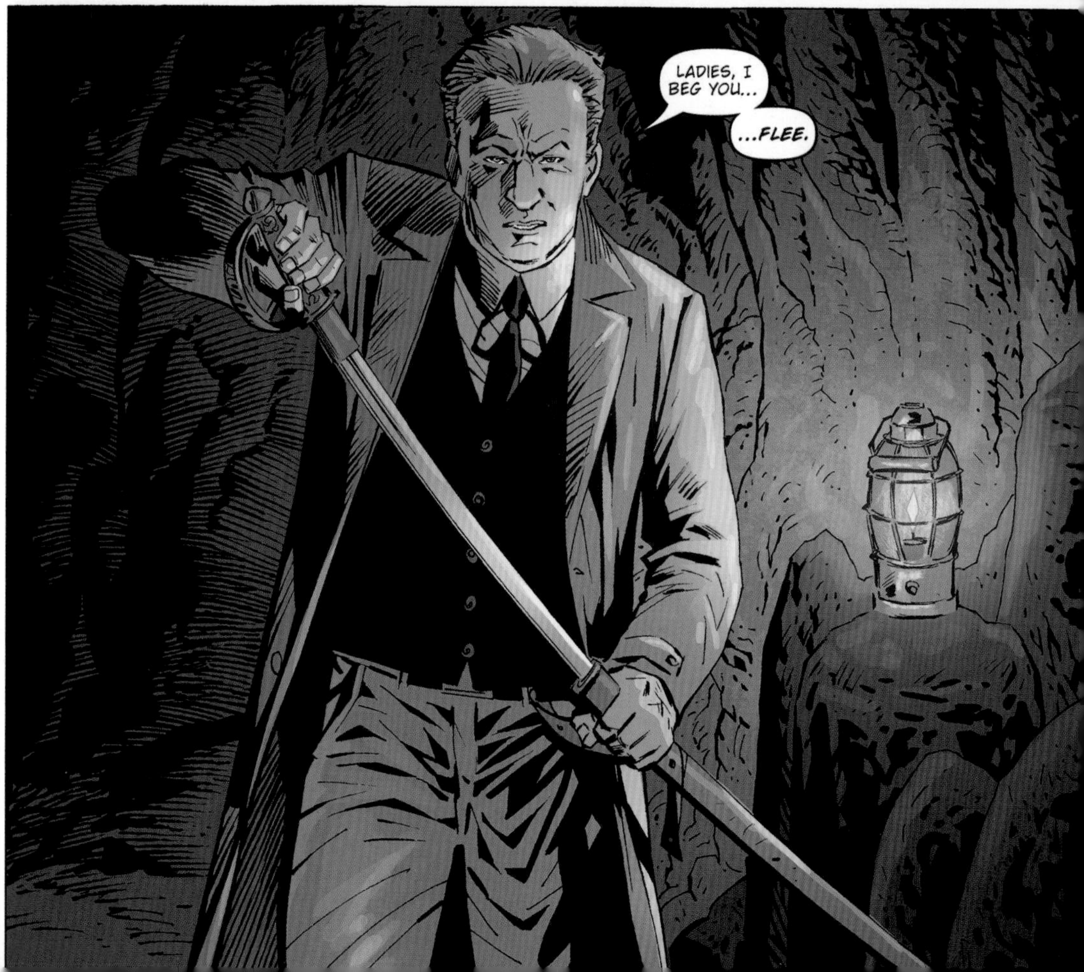
LADIES, I BEG YOU...
...FLEE.

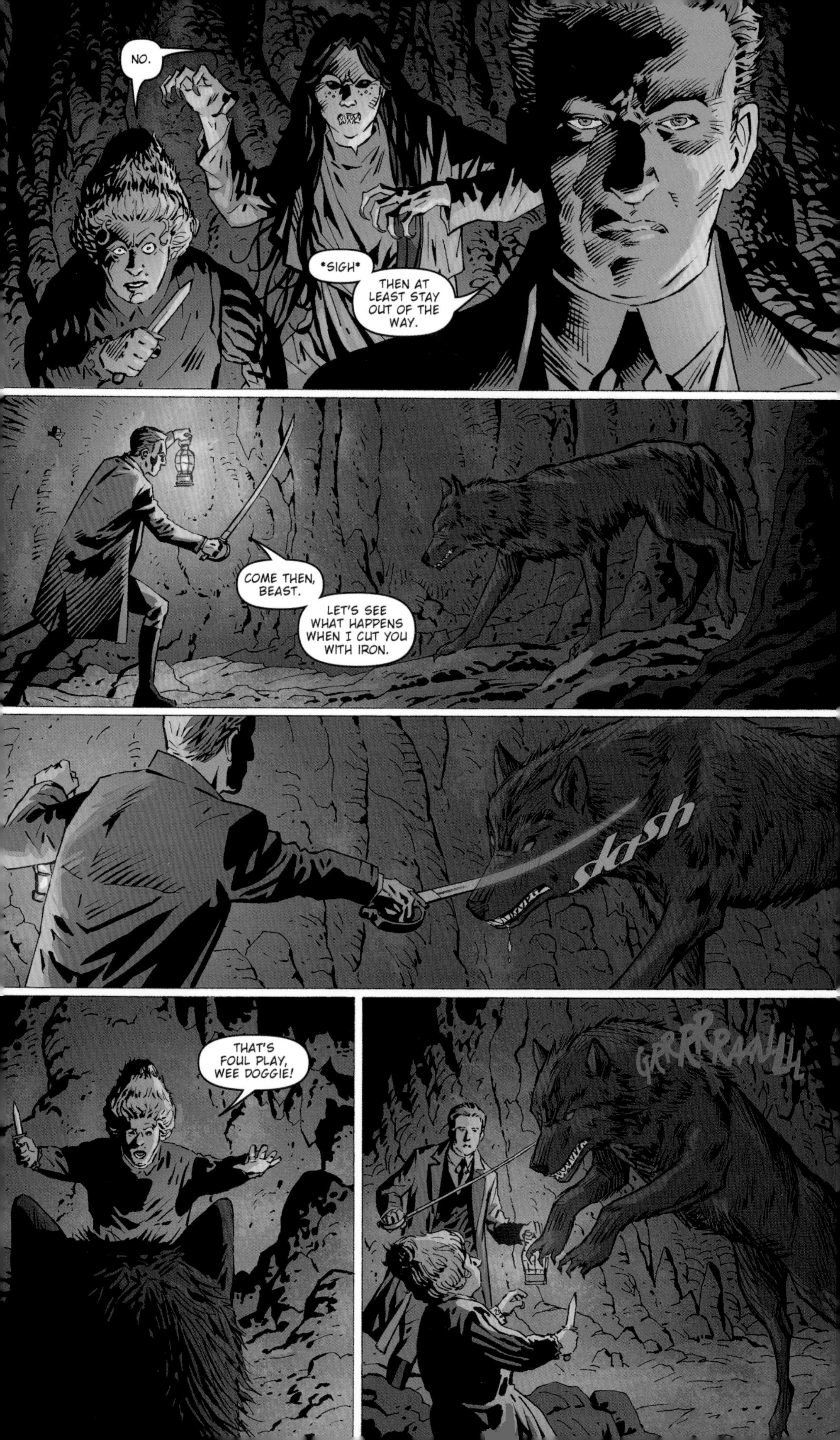
NO.
SIGH
THEN AT LEAST STAY OUT OF THE WAY.
COME THEN, BEAST.
LET'S SEE WHAT HAPPENS WHEN I CUT YOU WITH IRON.
slash
THAT'S FOUL PLAY, WEE DOGGIE!
GRRRRAWLLL

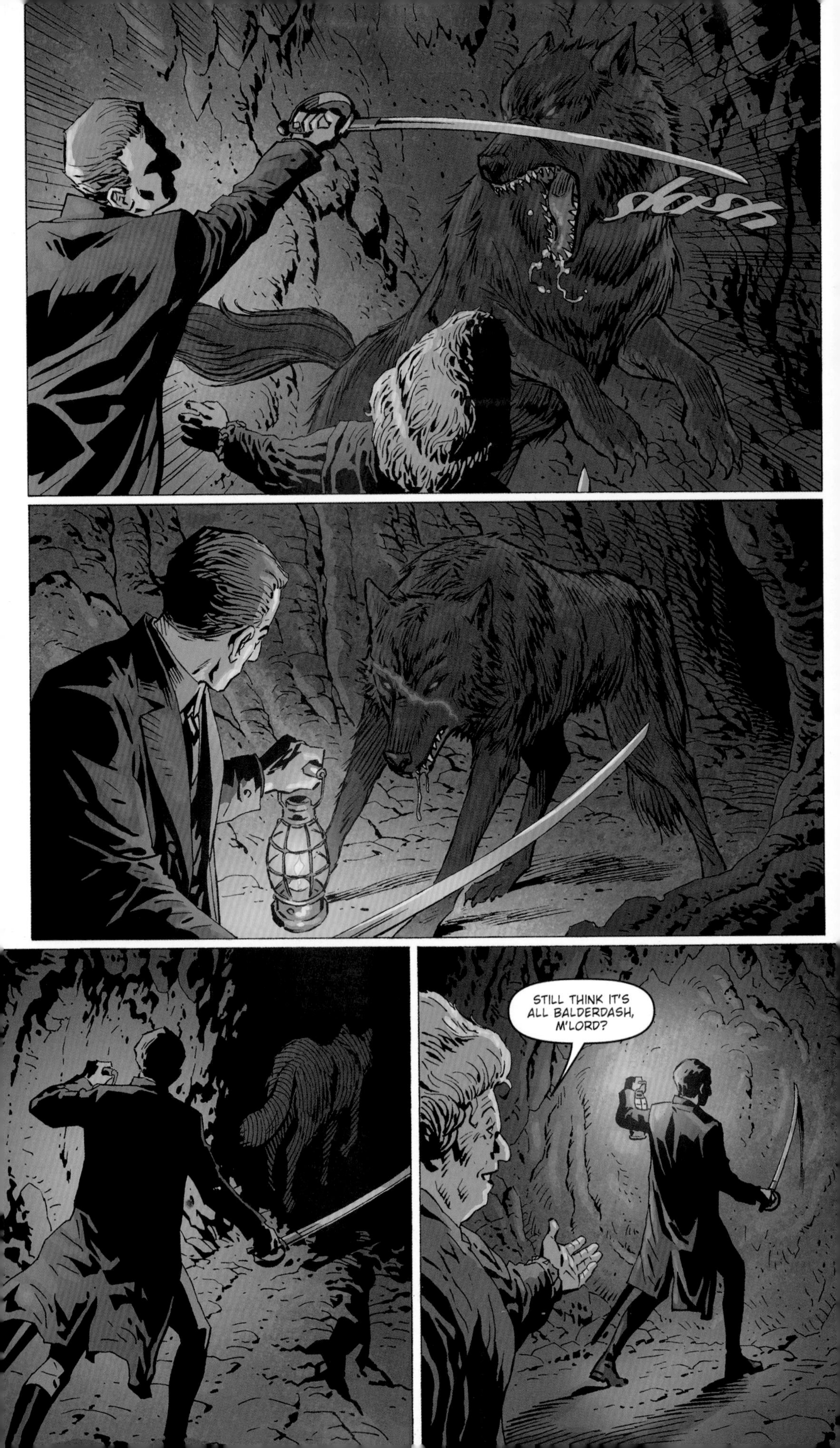

slash
STILL THINK IT'S ALL BALDERDASH, M'LORD?

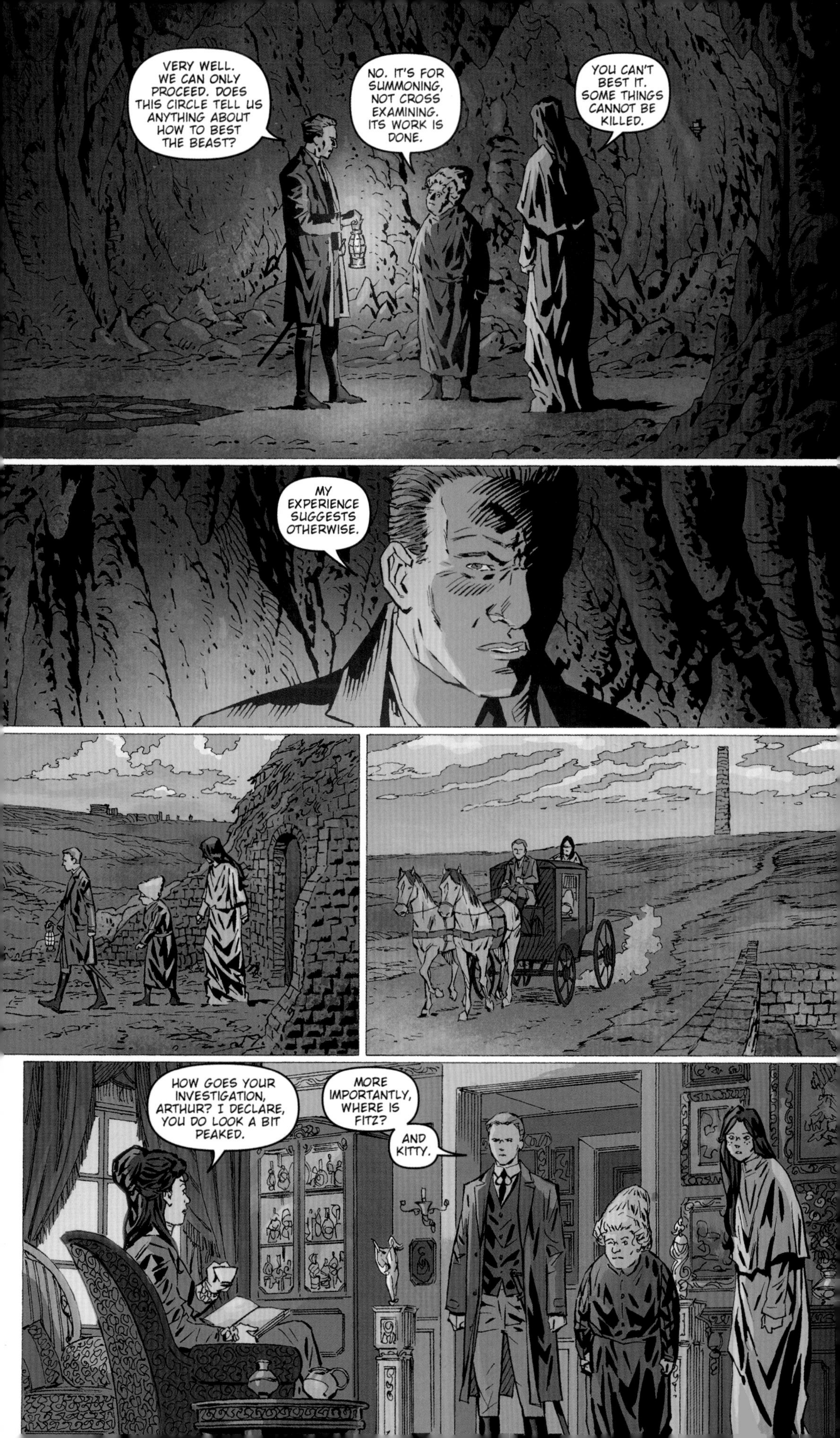
VERY WELL. WE CAN ONLY PROCEED. DOES THIS CIRCLE TELL US ANYTHING ABOUT HOW TO BEST THE BEAST?
NO. IT'S FOR SUMMONING, NOT CROSS EXAMINING. ITS WORK IS DONE.
YOU CAN'T BEST IT. SOME THINGS CANNOT BE KILLED.
MY EXPERIENCE SUGGESTS OTHERWISE.
HOW GOES YOUR INVESTIGATION, ARTHUR? I DECLARE, YOU DO LOOK A BIT PEAKED.
MORE IMPORTANTLY, WHERE IS FITZ?
AND KITTY.

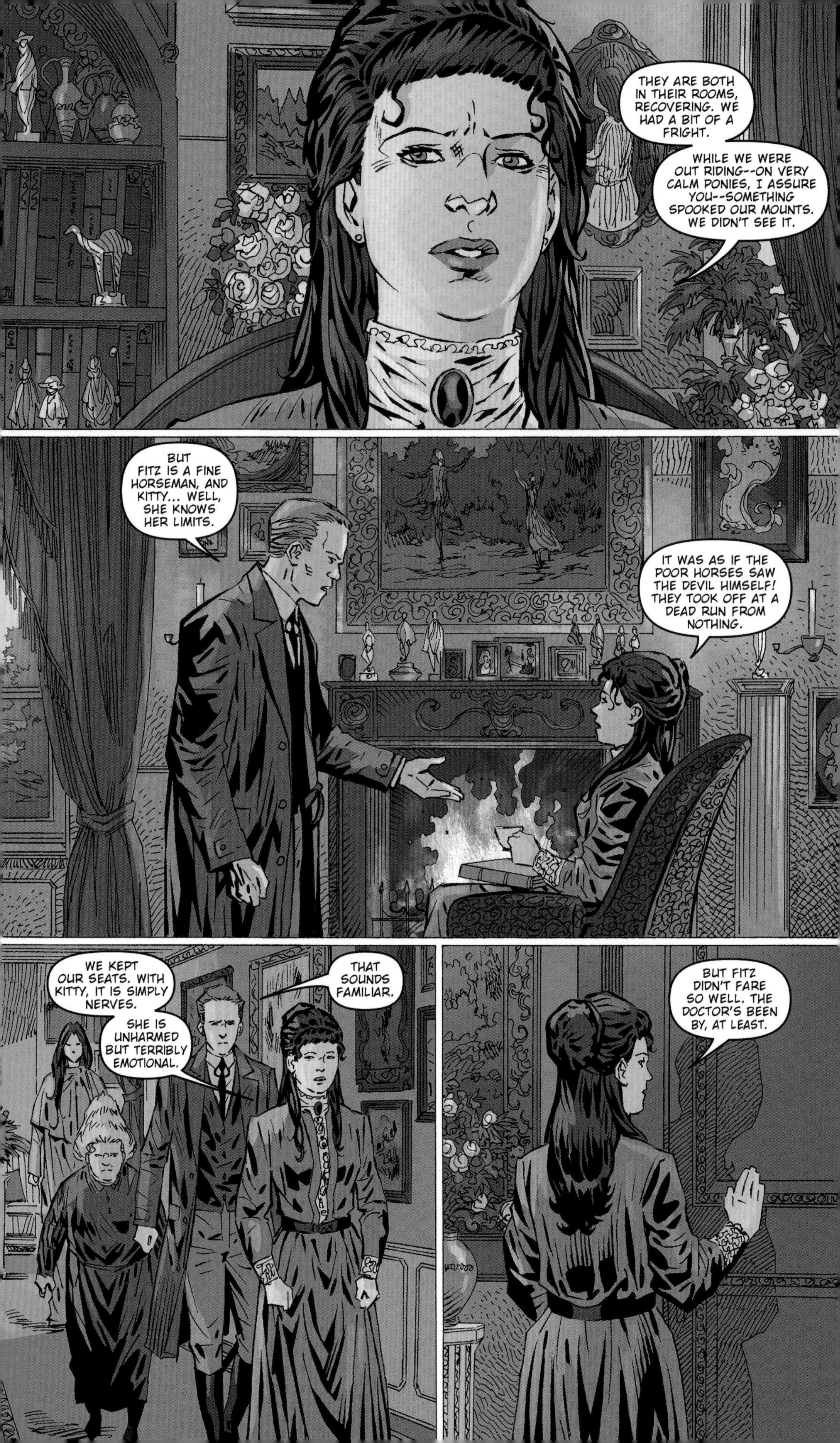
THEY ARE BOTH IN THEIR ROOMS, RECOVERING. WE HAD A BIT OF A FRIGHT.
WHILE WE WERE OUT RIDING--ON VERY CALM PONIES, I ASSURE YOU--SOMETHING SPOOKED OUR MOUNTS. WE DIDN'T SEE IT.
BUT FITZ IS A FINE HORSEMAN, AND KITTY... WELL, SHE KNOWS HER LIMITS.
IT WAS AS IF THE POOR HORSES SAW THE DEVIL HIMSELF! THEY TOOK OFF AT A DEAD RUN FROM NOTHING.
WE KEPT OUR SEATS. WITH KITTY, IT IS SIMPLY NERVES.
SHE IS UNHARMED BUT TERRIBLY EMOTIONAL.
THAT SOUNDS FAMILIAR.
BUT FITZ DIDN'T FARE SO WELL. THE DOCTOR'S BEEN BY, AT LEAST.

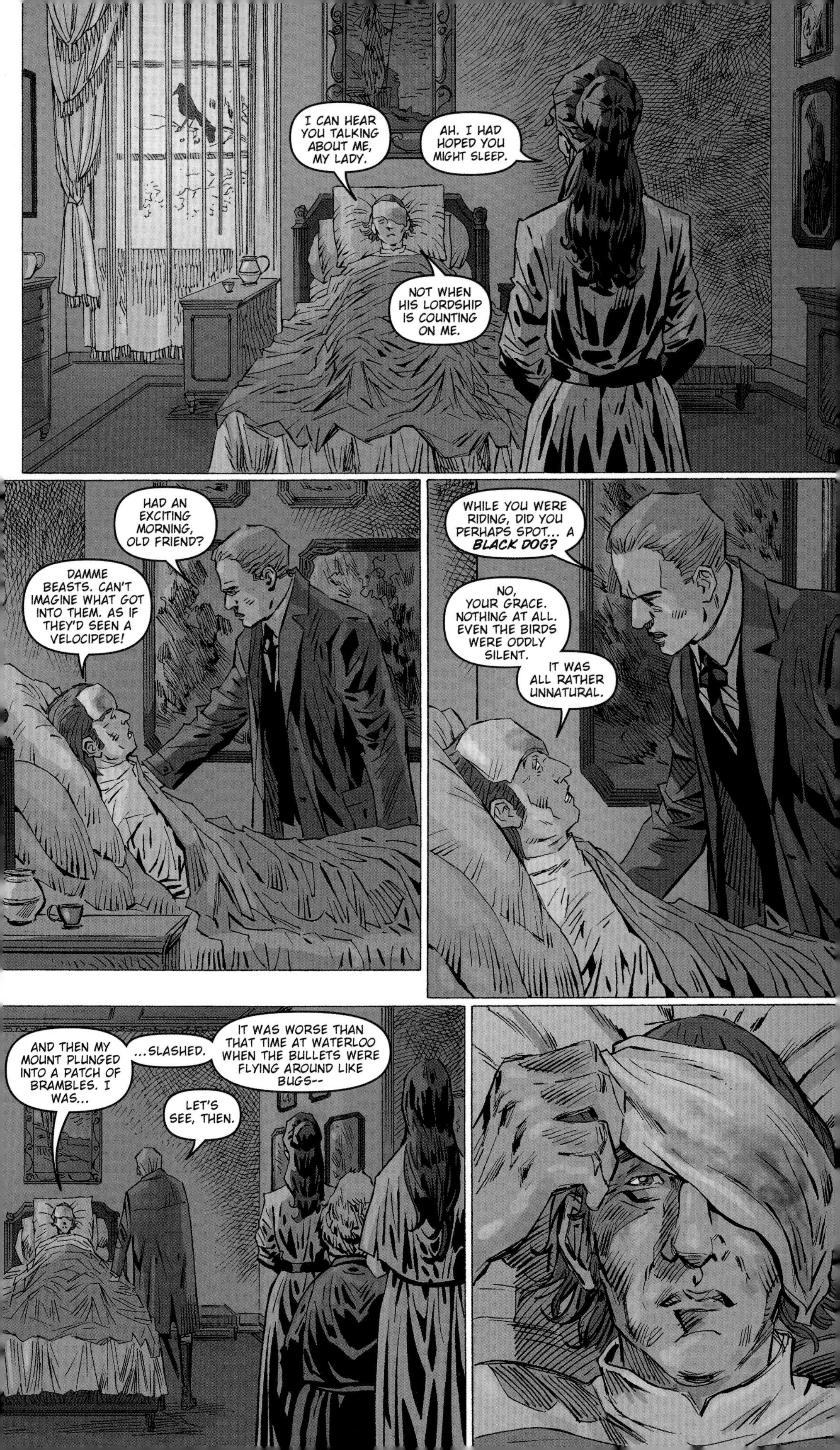
I CAN HEAR YOU TALKING ABOUT ME, MY LADY.
AH. I HAD HOPED YOU MIGHT SLEEP.
NOT WHEN HIS LORDSHIP IS COUNTING ON ME.
HAD AN EXCITING MORNING, OLD FRIEND?
DAMME BEASTS. CAN'T IMAGINE WHAT GOT INTO THEM. AS IF THEY'D SEEN A VELOCIPEDE!
WHILE YOU WERE RIDING, DID YOU PERHAPS SPOT... A *BLACK DOG?*
NO, YOUR GRACE. NOTHING AT ALL. EVEN THE BIRDS WERE ODDLY SILENT.
IT WAS ALL RATHER UNNATURAL.
AND THEN MY MOUNT PLUNGED INTO A PATCH OF BRAMBLES. I WAS...
...SLASHED.
IT WAS WORSE THAN THAT TIME AT WATERLOO WHEN THE BULLETS WERE FLYING AROUND LIKE BUGS--
LET'S SEE, THEN.

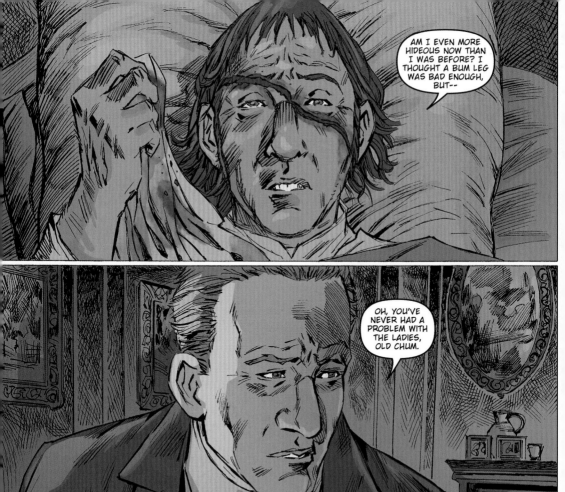

AM I EVEN MORE HIDEOUS NOW THAN I WAS BEFORE? I THOUGHT A BUM LEG WAS BAD ENOUGH, BUT--

OH, YOU'VE NEVER HAD A PROBLEM WITH THE LADIES, OLD CHUM.

GET SOME REST. I'LL KEEP OUR LADIES SAFE.

THANK YOU, YOUR GRACE. I COULDN'T SLEEP UNTIL I KNEW YOU WERE RETURNED.

GOOD MAN.

I HOPE.

THAT SLASH. SAME AS THE BEAST. THIS IS NOT A COINCIDENCE.

NEVER THOUGHT IT WAS. THERE'S ONLY ONE WAY TO GET TO THE BOTTOM OF THIS--

AND WHAT'S THAT?

A SÉANCE.

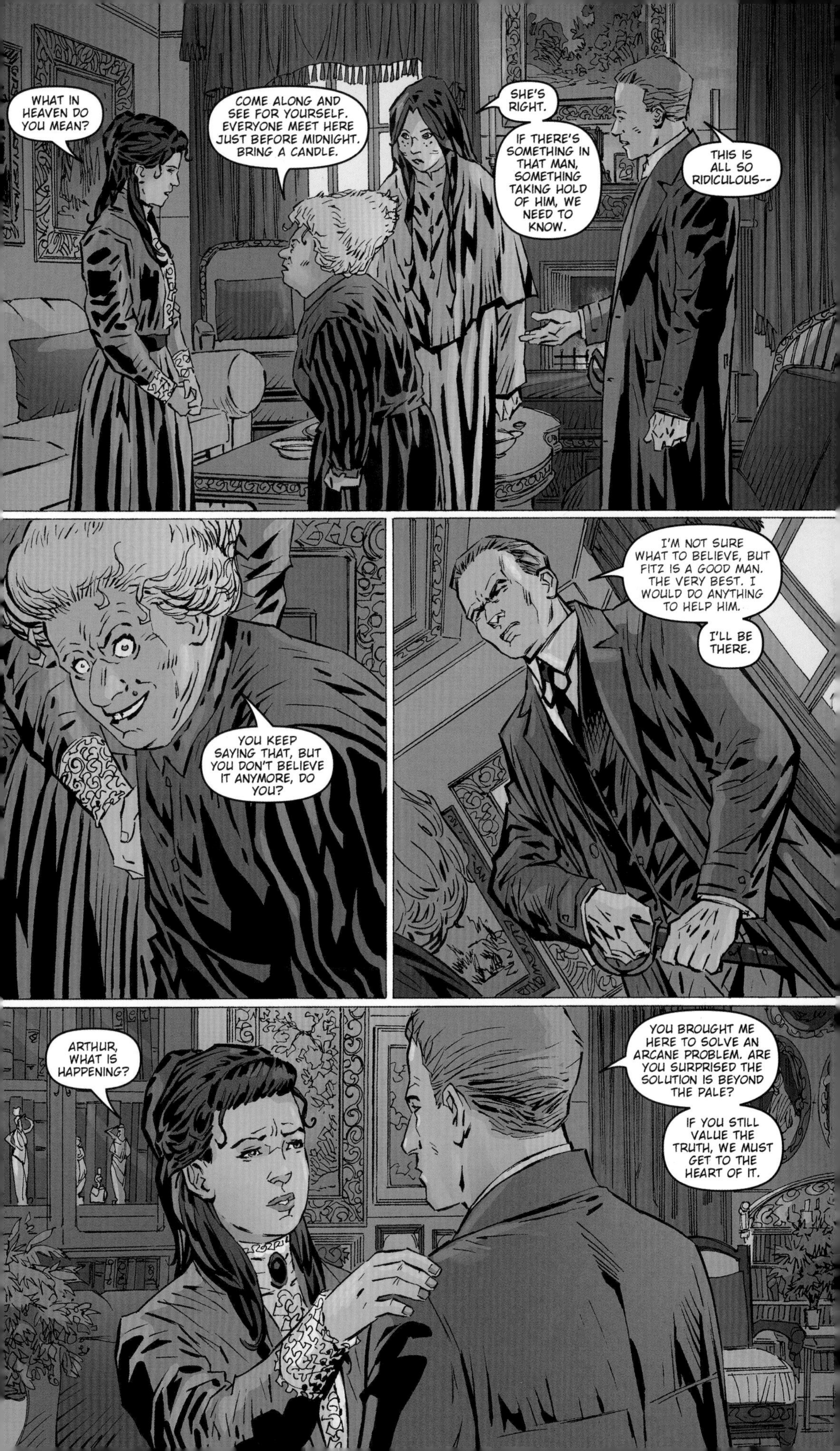
WHAT IN HEAVEN DO YOU MEAN?
COME ALONG AND SEE FOR YOURSELF. EVERYONE MEET HERE JUST BEFORE MIDNIGHT. BRING A CANDLE.
SHE'S RIGHT.
IF THERE'S SOMETHING IN THAT MAN, SOMETHING TAKING HOLD OF HIM, WE NEED TO KNOW.
THIS IS ALL SO RIDICULOUS--
YOU KEEP SAYING THAT, BUT YOU DON'T BELIEVE IT ANYMORE, DO YOU?
I'M NOT SURE WHAT TO BELIEVE, BUT FITZ IS A GOOD MAN. THE VERY BEST. I WOULD DO ANYTHING TO HELP HIM.
I'LL BE THERE.
ARTHUR, WHAT IS HAPPENING?
YOU BROUGHT ME HERE TO SOLVE AN ARCANE PROBLEM. ARE YOU SURPRISED THE SOLUTION IS BEYOND THE PALE?
IF YOU STILL VALUE THE TRUTH, WE MUST GET TO THE HEART OF IT.

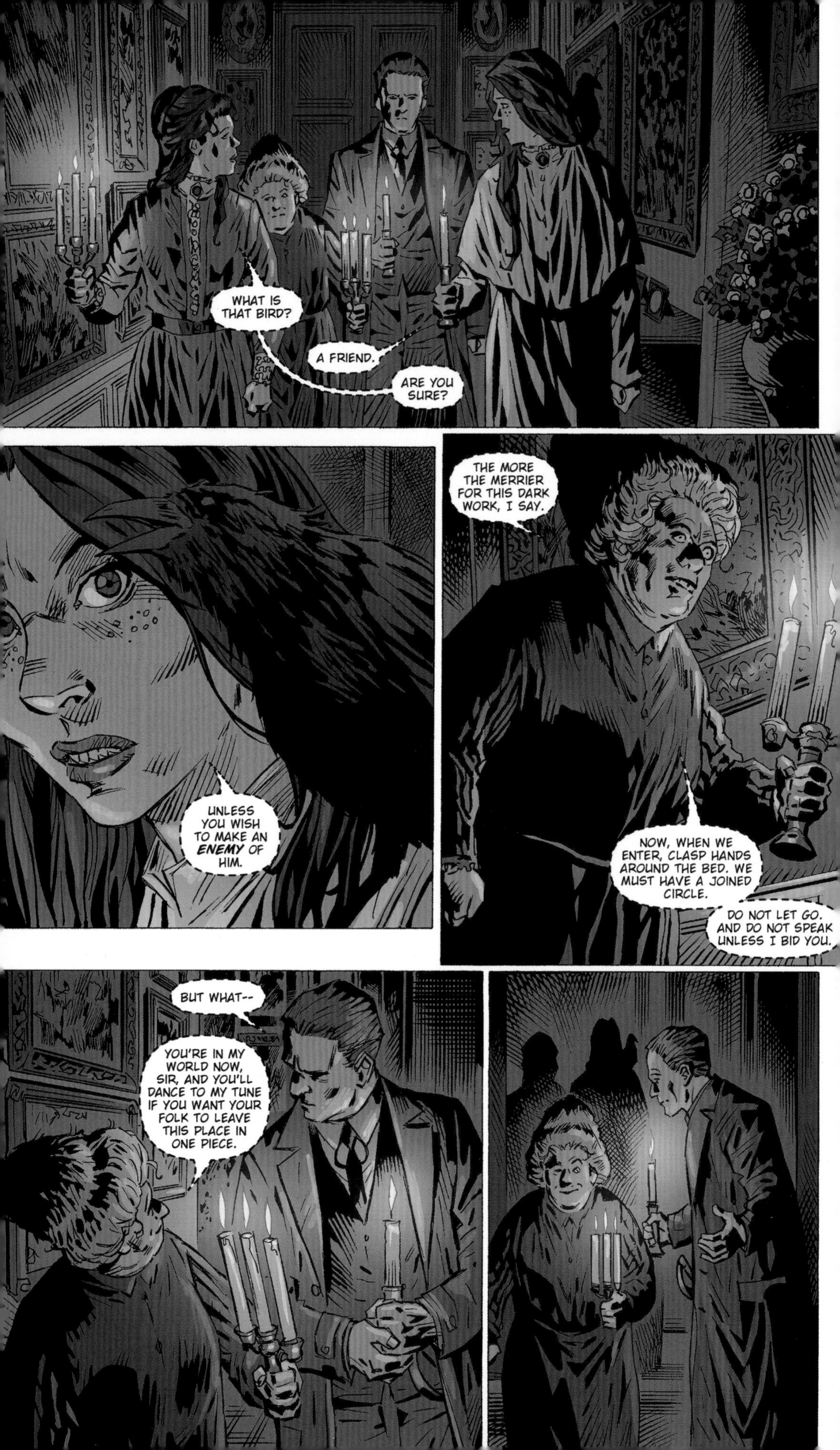
WHAT IS THAT BIRD?
A FRIEND.
ARE YOU SURE?
UNLESS YOU WISH TO MAKE AN *ENEMY* OF HIM.
THE MORE THE MERRIER FOR THIS DARK WORK, I SAY.
NOW, WHEN WE ENTER, CLASP HANDS AROUND THE BED. WE MUST HAVE A JOINED CIRCLE.
DO NOT LET GO. AND DO NOT SPEAK UNLESS I BID YOU.
BUT WHAT--
YOU'RE IN MY WORLD NOW, SIR, AND YOU'LL DANCE TO MY TUNE IF YOU WANT YOUR FOLK TO LEAVE THIS PLACE IN ONE PIECE.

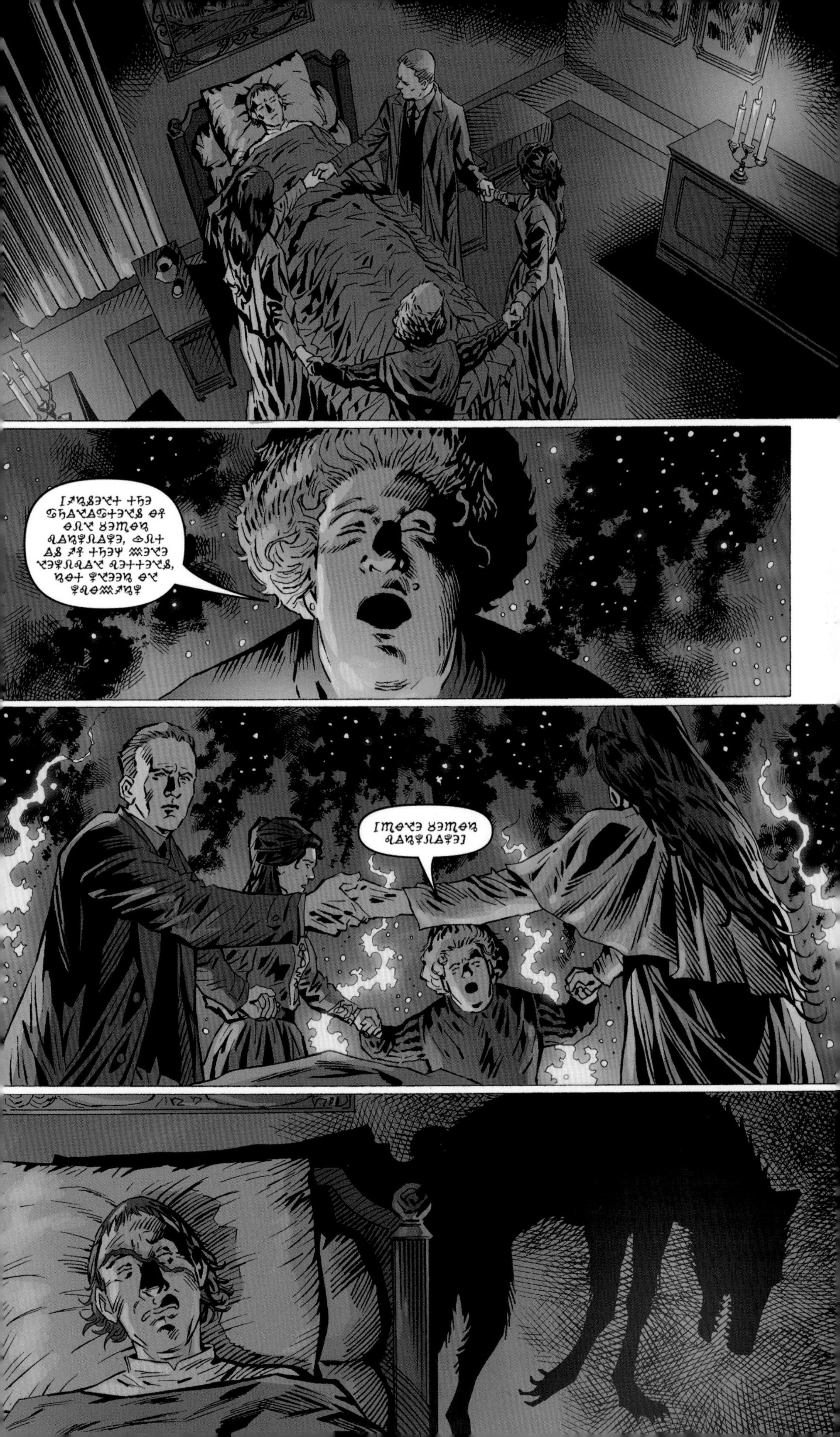

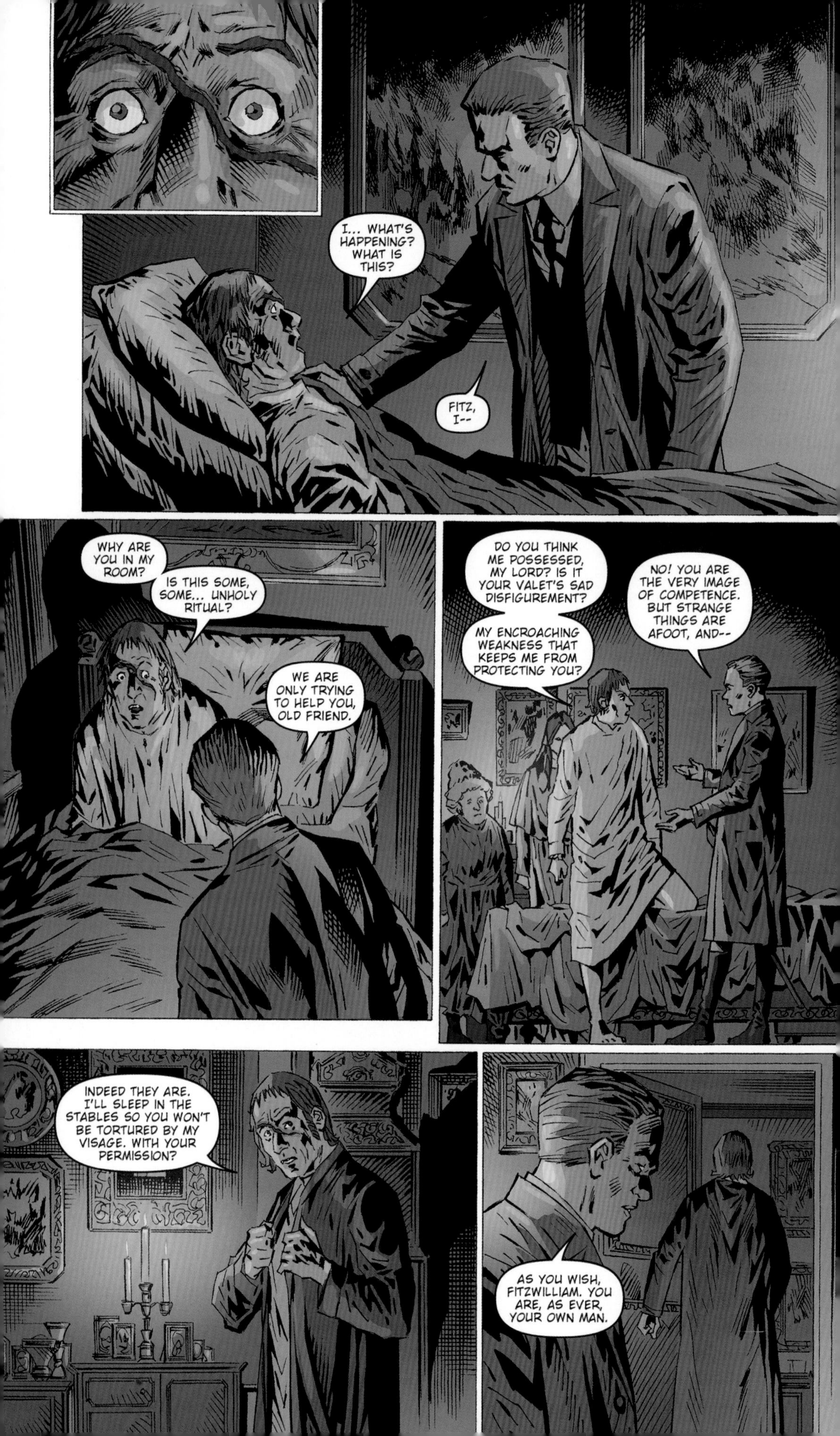
I... WHAT'S HAPPENING? WHAT IS THIS?
FITZ, I--
WHY ARE YOU IN MY ROOM?
IS THIS SOME, SOME... UNHOLY RITUAL?
WE ARE ONLY TRYING TO HELP YOU, OLD FRIEND.
DO YOU THINK ME POSSESSED, MY LORD? IS IT YOUR VALET'S SAD DISFIGUREMENT?
MY ENCROACHING WEAKNESS THAT KEEPS ME FROM PROTECTING YOU?
NO! YOU ARE THE VERY IMAGE OF COMPETENCE. BUT STRANGE THINGS ARE AFOOT, AND--
INDEED THEY ARE. I'LL SLEEP IN THE STABLES SO YOU WON'T BE TORTURED BY MY VISAGE. WITH YOUR PERMISSION?
AS YOU WISH, FITZWILLIAM. YOU ARE, AS EVER, YOUR OWN MAN.

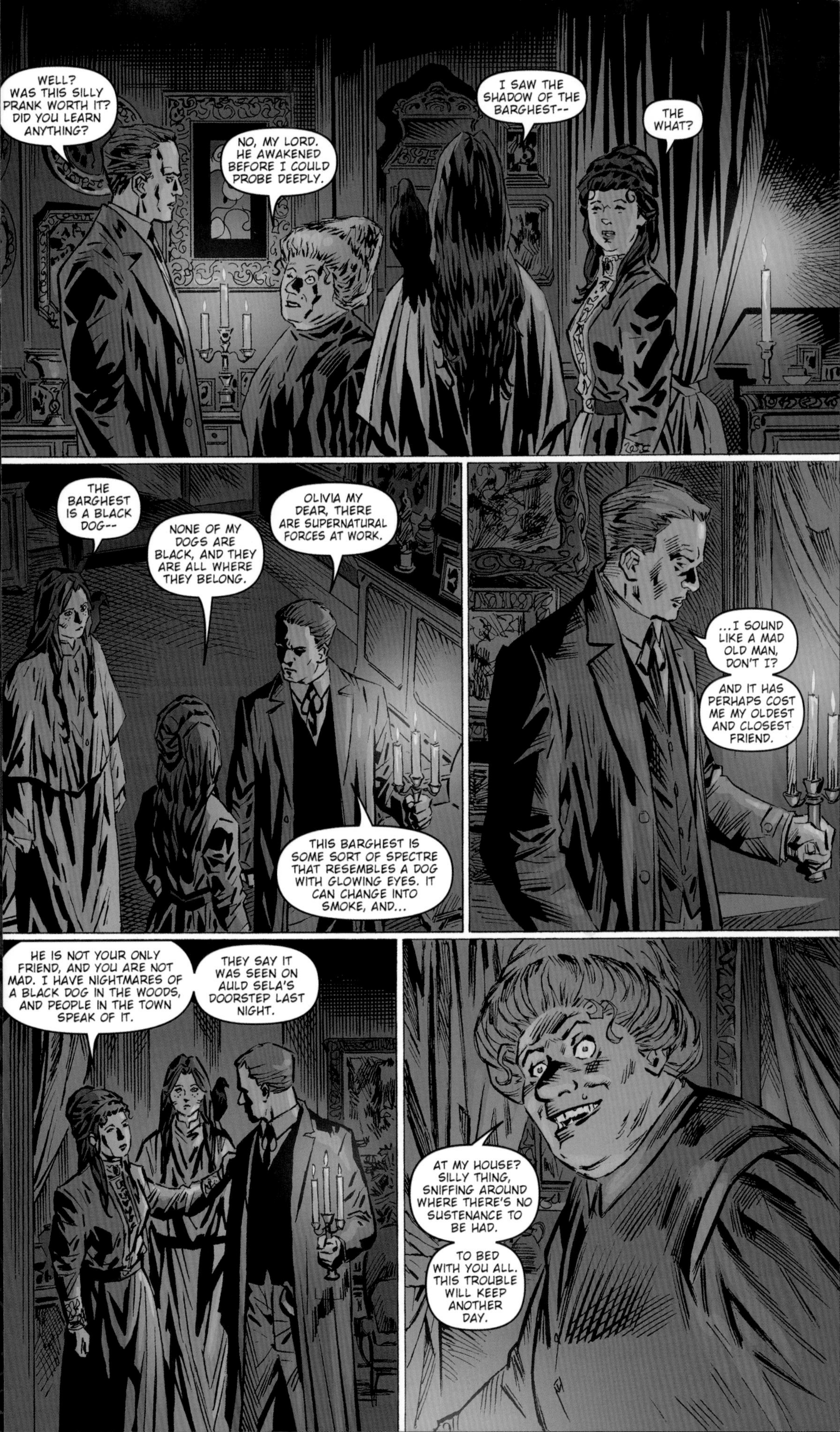
WELL? WAS THIS SILLY PRANK WORTH IT? DID YOU LEARN ANYTHING?
NO, MY LORD. HE AWAKENED BEFORE I COULD PROBE DEEPLY.
I SAW THE SHADOW OF THE BARGHEST--
THE WHAT?
THE BARGHEST IS A BLACK DOG--
NONE OF MY DOGS ARE BLACK, AND THEY ARE ALL WHERE THEY BELONG.
OLIVIA MY DEAR, THERE ARE SUPERNATURAL FORCES AT WORK.
THIS BARGHEST IS SOME SORT OF SPECTRE THAT RESEMBLES A DOG WITH GLOWING EYES. IT CAN CHANGE INTO SMOKE, AND...
...I SOUND LIKE A MAD OLD MAN, DON'T I?
AND IT HAS PERHAPS COST ME MY OLDEST AND CLOSEST FRIEND.
HE IS NOT YOUR ONLY FRIEND, AND YOU ARE NOT MAD. I HAVE NIGHTMARES OF A BLACK DOG IN THE WOODS, AND PEOPLE IN THE TOWN SPEAK OF IT.
THEY SAY IT WAS SEEN ON AULD SELA'S DOORSTEP LAST NIGHT.
AT MY HOUSE? SILLY THING, SNIFFING AROUND WHERE THERE'S NO SUSTENANCE TO BE HAD.
TO BED WITH YOU ALL. THIS TROUBLE WILL KEEP ANOTHER DAY.

Chapter 4

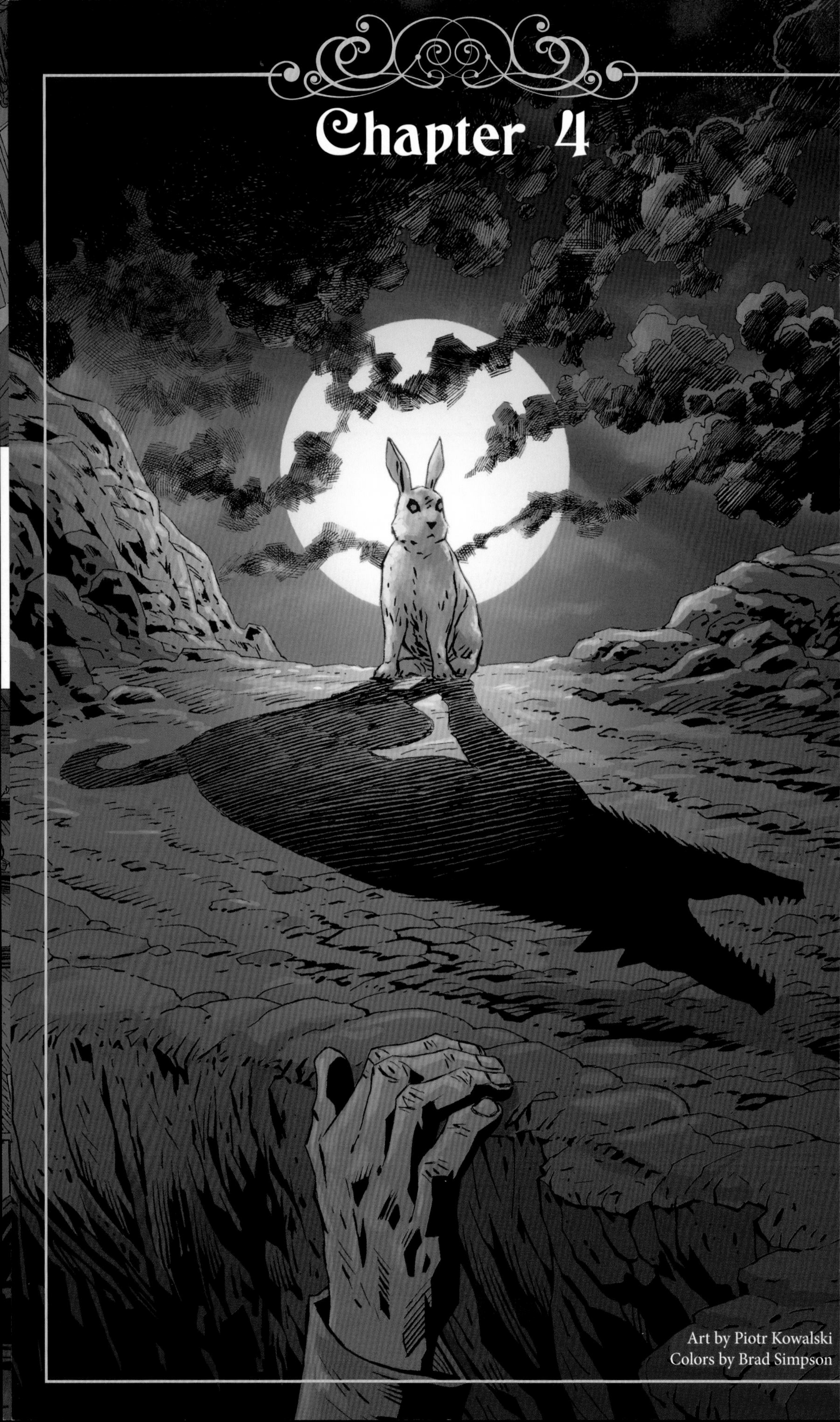
Art by Piotr Kowalski
Colors by Brad Simpson

FOR A WHILE, TIME MOVED SLOWLY, AS IT ALWAYS DOES AROUND DEATH.

WE SENT FOR THE LOCAL CONSTABULARY.

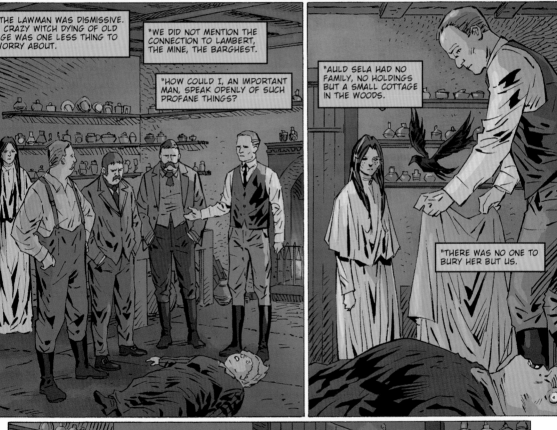

"THE LAWMAN WAS DISMISSIVE. A CRAZY WITCH DYING OF OLD AGE WAS ONE LESS THING TO WORRY ABOUT.

"WE DID NOT MENTION THE CONNECTION TO LAMBERT, THE MINE, THE BARGHEST.

"HOW COULD I, AN IMPORTANT MAN, SPEAK OPENLY OF SUCH PROFANE THINGS?

"AULD SELA HAD NO FAMILY, NO HOLDINGS BUT A SMALL COTTAGE IN THE WOODS.

"THERE WAS NO ONE TO BURY HER BUT US.

"BEFORE THAT MOMENT, I HAD BELIEVED THAT SOMETHING ODD WAS AFOOT, BUT I HADN'T REALLY *UNDERSTOOD.*

"THE WEIGHT OF A CORPSE HAS A WAY OF CHANGING ONE'S PRIORITIES..."

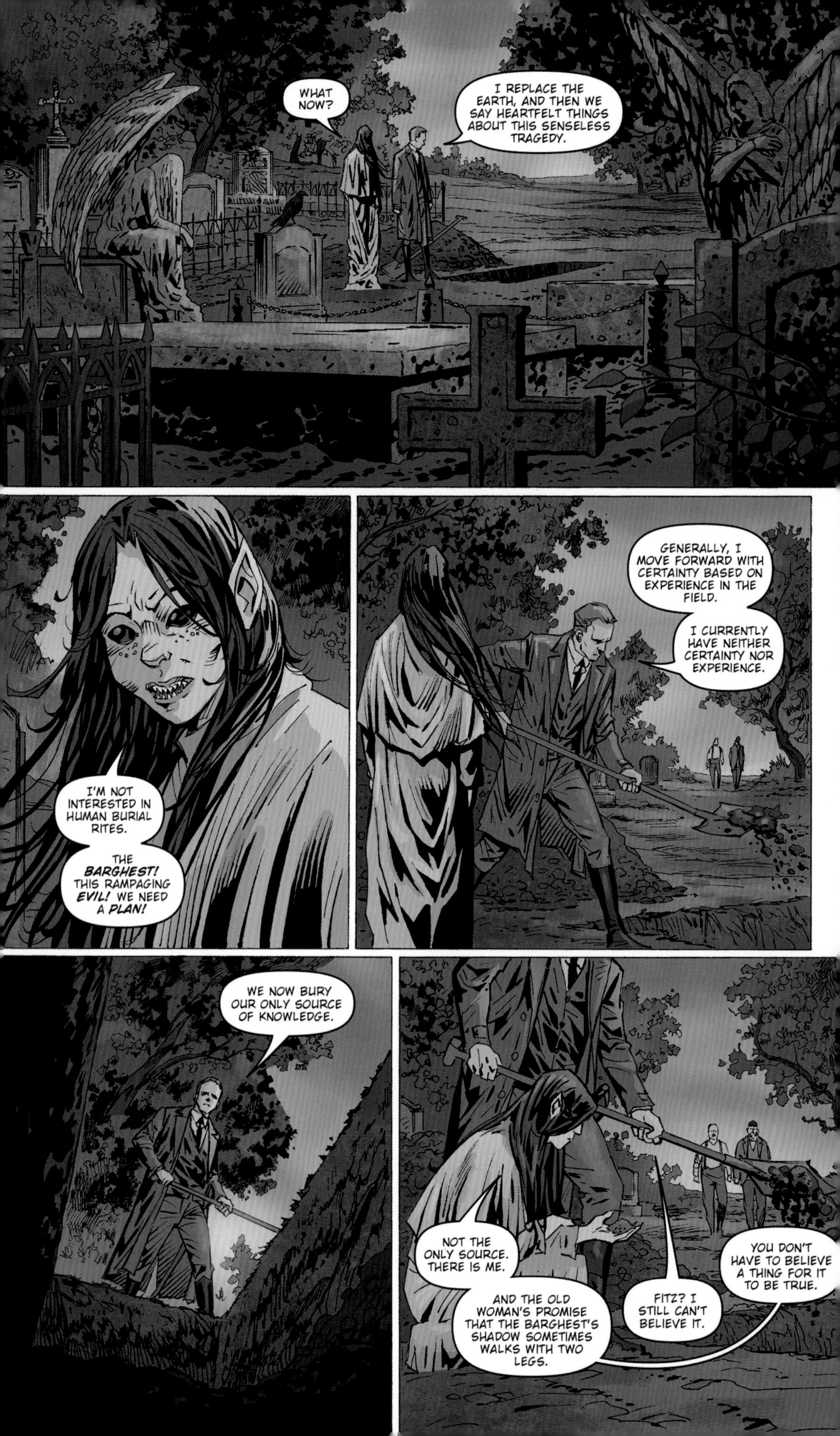

WHAT NOW?
I REPLACE THE EARTH, AND THEN WE SAY HEARTFELT THINGS ABOUT THIS SENSELESS TRAGEDY.
I'M NOT INTERESTED IN HUMAN BURIAL RITES.
THE ***BARGHEST!*** THIS RAMPAGING ***EVIL!*** WE NEED A ***PLAN!***
GENERALLY, I MOVE FORWARD WITH CERTAINTY BASED ON EXPERIENCE IN THE FIELD.
I CURRENTLY HAVE NEITHER CERTAINTY NOR EXPERIENCE.
WE NOW BURY OUR ONLY SOURCE OF KNOWLEDGE.
NOT THE ONLY SOURCE. THERE IS ME.
AND THE OLD WOMAN'S PROMISE THAT THE BARGHEST'S SHADOW SOMETIMES WALKS WITH TWO LEGS.
FITZ? I STILL CAN'T BELIEVE IT.
YOU DON'T HAVE TO BELIEVE A THING FOR IT TO BE TRUE.

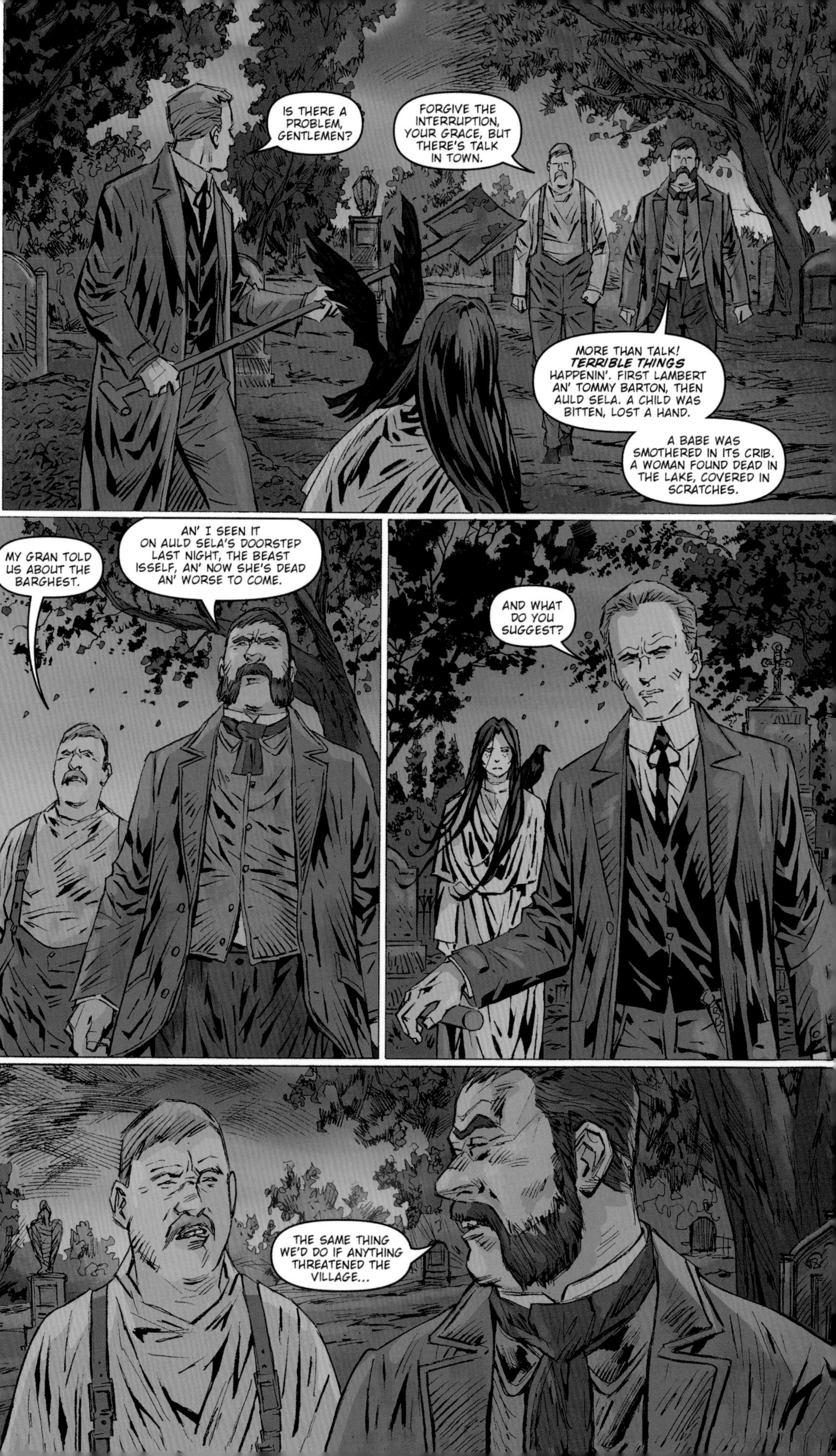
IS THERE A PROBLEM, GENTLEMEN?
FORGIVE THE INTERRUPTION, YOUR GRACE, BUT THERE'S TALK IN TOWN.
MORE THAN TALK! *TERRIBLE THINGS* HAPPENIN'. FIRST LAMBERT AN' TOMMY BARTON, THEN AULD SELA. A CHILD WAS BITTEN, LOST A HAND.
A BABE WAS SMOTHERED IN ITS CRIB. A WOMAN FOUND DEAD IN THE LAKE, COVERED IN SCRATCHES.
MY GRAN TOLD US ABOUT THE BARGHEST.
AN' I SEEN IT ON AULD SELA'S DOORSTEP LAST NIGHT, THE BEAST ISSELF, AN' NOW SHE'S DEAD AN' WORSE TO COME.
AND WHAT DO YOU SUGGEST?
THE SAME THING WE'D DO IF ANYTHING THREATENED THE VILLAGE...

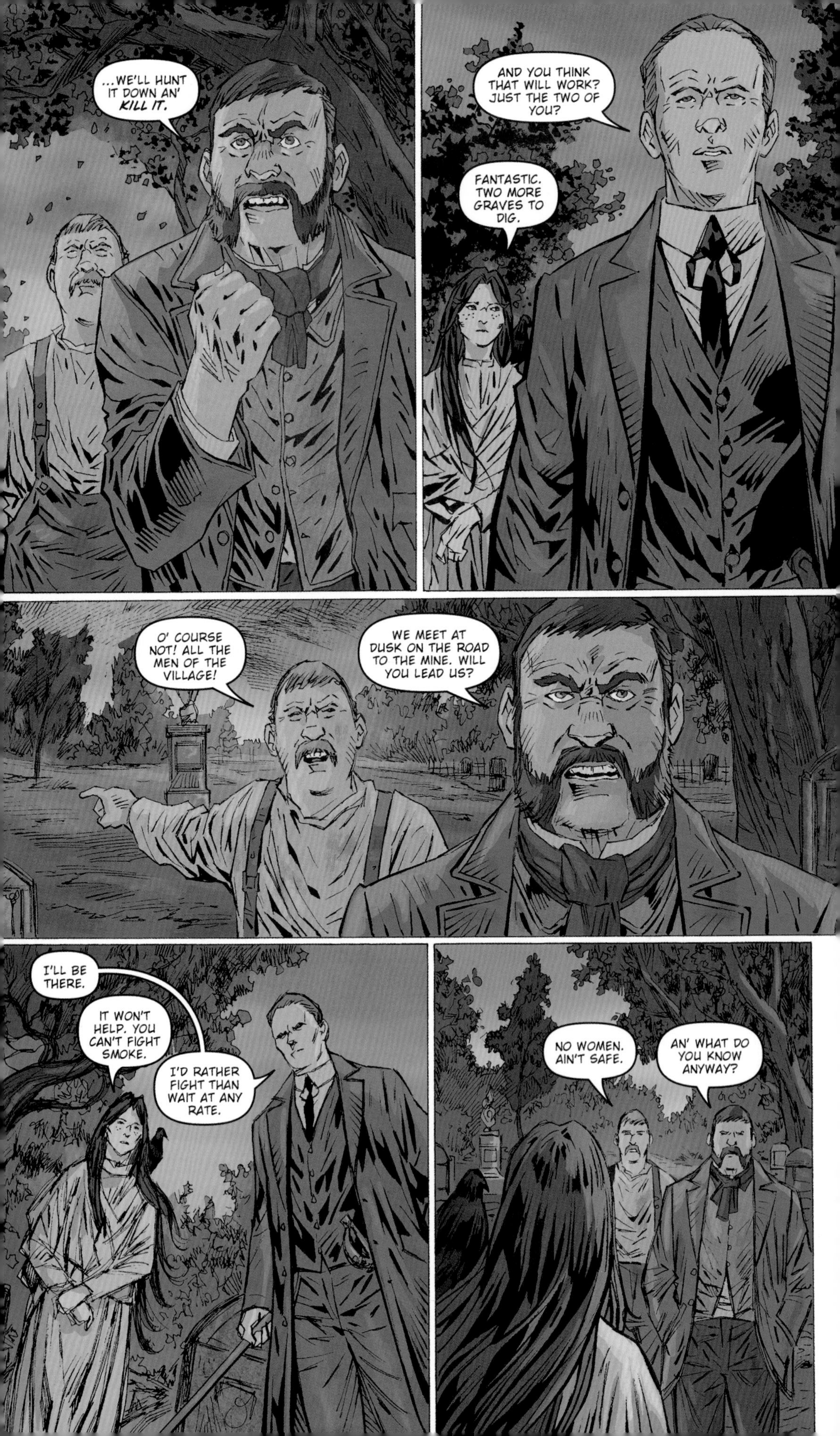
...WE'LL HUNT IT DOWN AN' KILL IT.
AND YOU THINK THAT WILL WORK? JUST THE TWO OF YOU?
FANTASTIC. TWO MORE GRAVES TO DIG.
O' COURSE NOT! ALL THE MEN OF THE VILLAGE!
WE MEET AT DUSK ON THE ROAD TO THE MINE. WILL YOU LEAD US?
I'LL BE THERE.
IT WON'T HELP. YOU CAN'T FIGHT SMOKE.
I'D RATHER FIGHT THAN WAIT AT ANY RATE.
NO WOMEN. AIN'T SAFE.
AN' WHAT DO YOU KNOW ANYWAY?

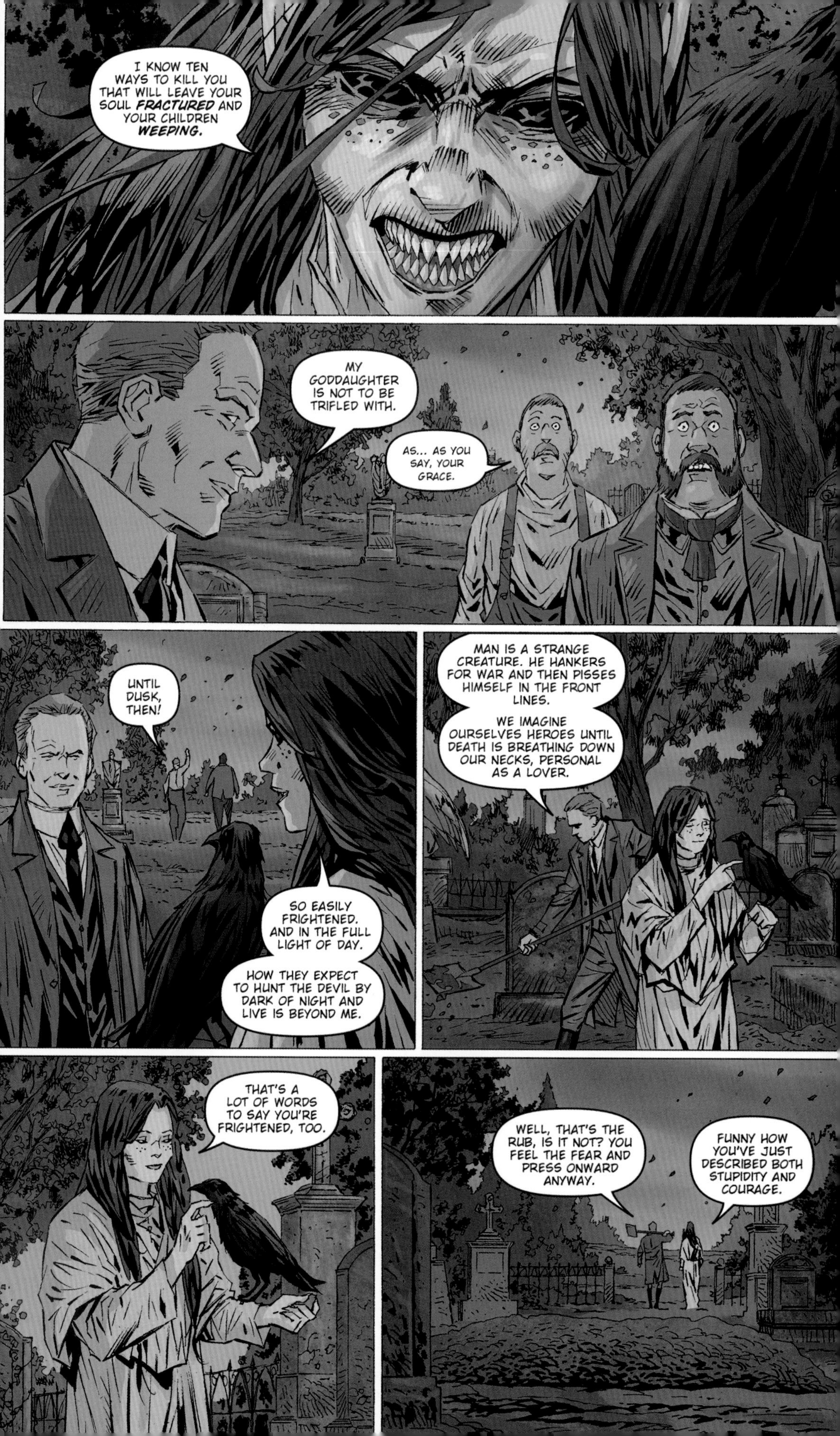
I KNOW TEN WAYS TO KILL YOU THAT WILL LEAVE YOUR SOUL **FRACTURED** AND YOUR CHILDREN **WEEPING.**
MY GODDAUGHTER IS NOT TO BE TRIFLED WITH.
AS... AS YOU SAY, YOUR GRACE.
UNTIL DUSK, THEN!
SO EASILY FRIGHTENED. AND IN THE FULL LIGHT OF DAY.
HOW THEY EXPECT TO HUNT THE DEVIL BY DARK OF NIGHT AND LIVE IS BEYOND ME.
MAN IS A STRANGE CREATURE. HE HANKERS FOR WAR AND THEN PISSES HIMSELF IN THE FRONT LINES.
WE IMAGINE OURSELVES HEROES UNTIL DEATH IS BREATHING DOWN OUR NECKS, PERSONAL AS A LOVER.
THAT'S A LOT OF WORDS TO SAY YOU'RE FRIGHTENED, TOO.
WELL, THAT'S THE RUB, IS IT NOT? YOU FEEL THE FEAR AND PRESS ONWARD ANYWAY.
FUNNY HOW YOU'VE JUST DESCRIBED BOTH STUPIDITY AND COURAGE.

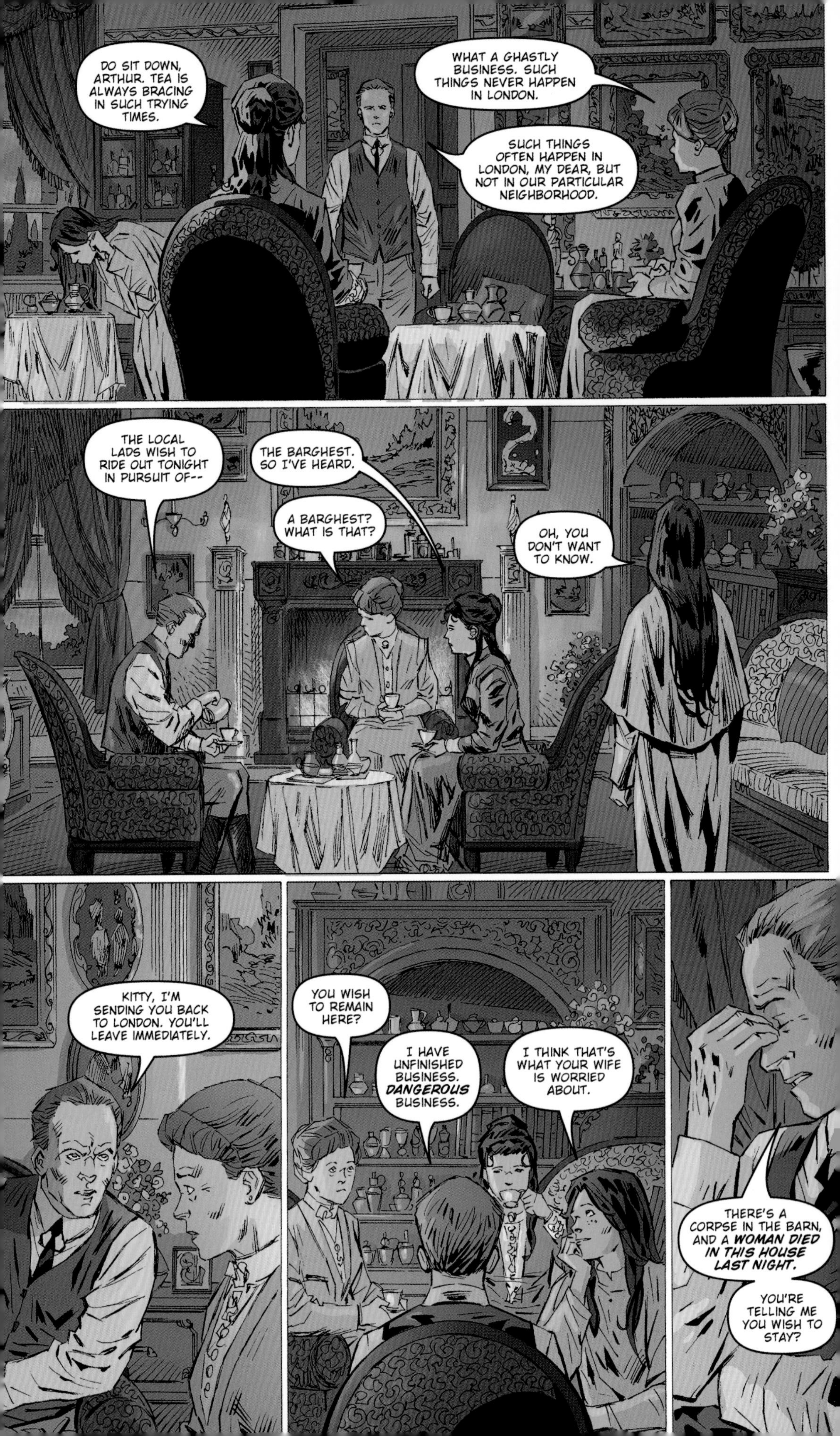
DO SIT DOWN, ARTHUR. TEA IS ALWAYS BRACING IN SUCH TRYING TIMES.
WHAT A GHASTLY BUSINESS. SUCH THINGS NEVER HAPPEN IN LONDON.
SUCH THINGS OFTEN HAPPEN IN LONDON, MY DEAR, BUT NOT IN OUR PARTICULAR NEIGHBORHOOD.
THE LOCAL LADS WISH TO RIDE OUT TONIGHT IN PURSUIT OF--
THE BARGHEST. SO I'VE HEARD.
A BARGHEST? WHAT IS THAT?
OH, YOU DON'T WANT TO KNOW.
KITTY, I'M SENDING YOU BACK TO LONDON. YOU'LL LEAVE IMMEDIATELY.
YOU WISH TO REMAIN HERE?
I HAVE UNFINISHED BUSINESS. ***DANGEROUS*** BUSINESS.
I THINK THAT'S WHAT YOUR WIFE IS WORRIED ABOUT.
THERE'S A CORPSE IN THE BARN, AND A ***WOMAN DIED IN THIS HOUSE LAST NIGHT.***
YOU'RE TELLING ME YOU WISH TO STAY?

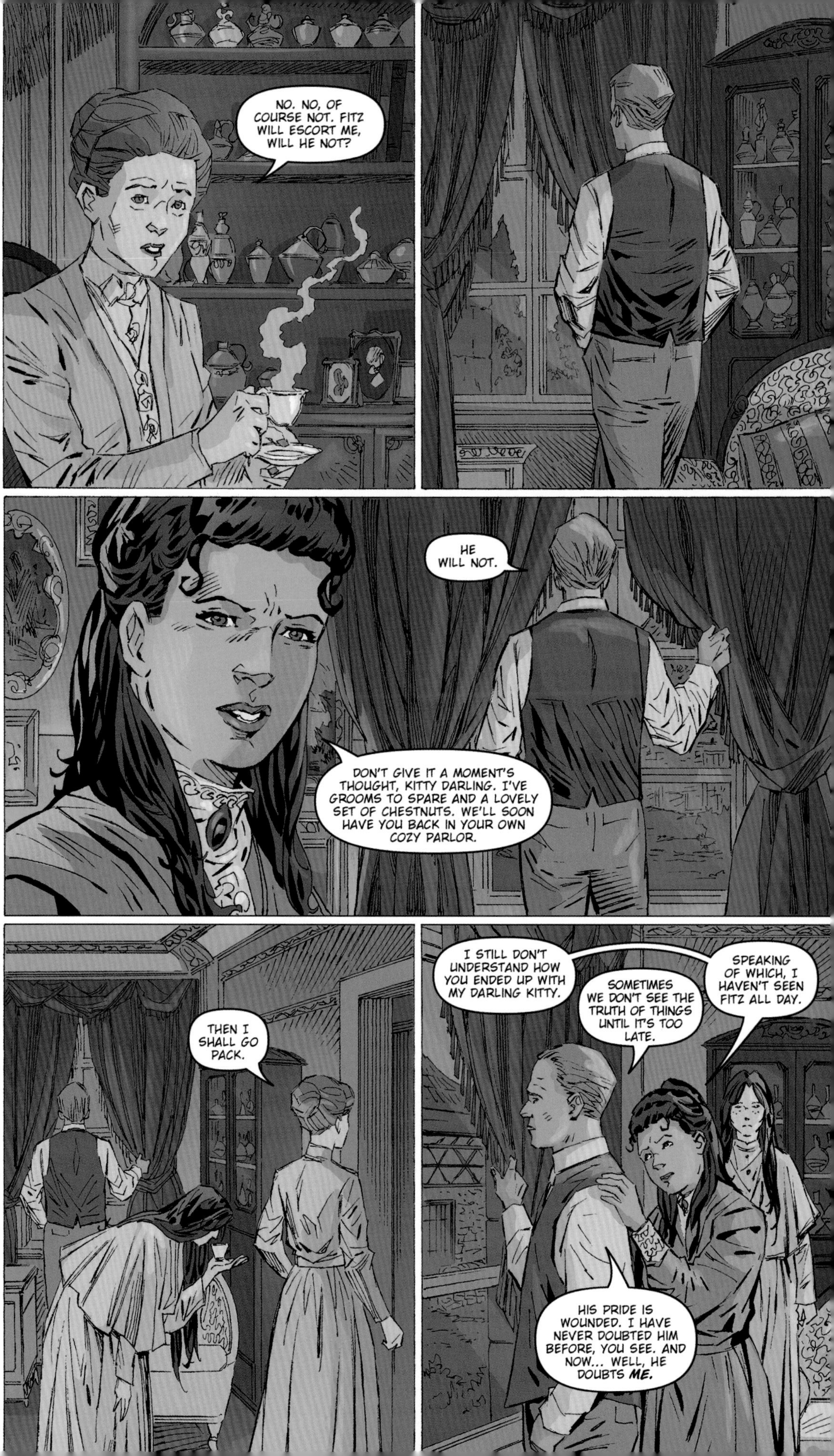
NO. NO, OF COURSE NOT. FITZ WILL ESCORT ME, WILL HE NOT?
HE WILL NOT.
DON'T GIVE IT A MOMENT'S THOUGHT, KITTY DARLING. I'VE GROOMS TO SPARE AND A LOVELY SET OF CHESTNUTS. WE'LL SOON HAVE YOU BACK IN YOUR OWN COZY PARLOR.
THEN I SHALL GO PACK.
I STILL DON'T UNDERSTAND HOW YOU ENDED UP WITH MY DARLING KITTY.
SOMETIMES WE DON'T SEE THE TRUTH OF THINGS UNTIL IT'S TOO LATE.
SPEAKING OF WHICH, I HAVEN'T SEEN FITZ ALL DAY.
HIS PRIDE IS WOUNDED. I HAVE NEVER DOUBTED HIM BEFORE, YOU SEE. AND NOW... WELL, HE DOUBTS *ME.*

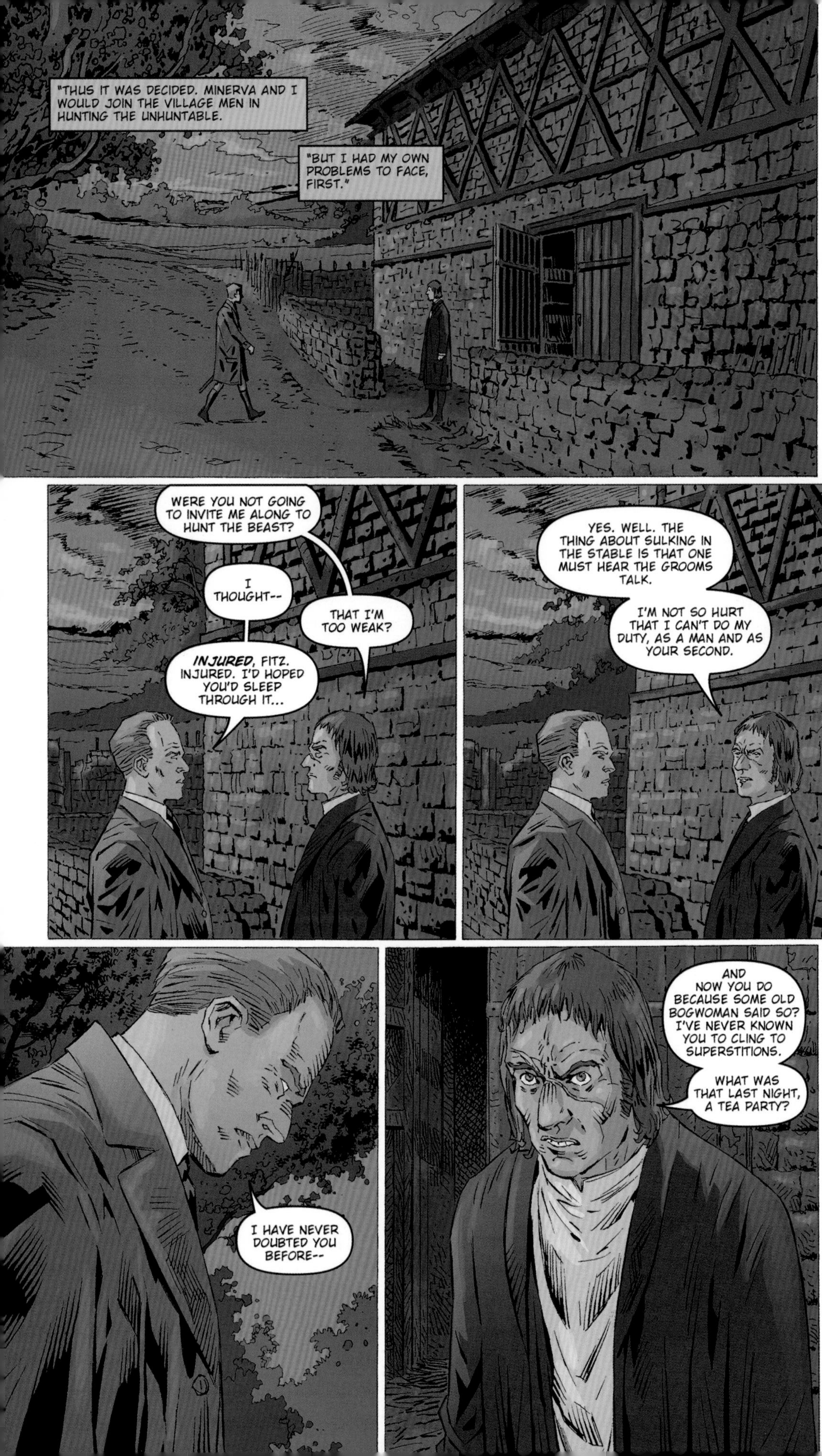
"THUS IT WAS DECIDED. MINERVA AND I WOULD JOIN THE VILLAGE MEN IN HUNTING THE UNHUNTABLE.
"BUT I HAD MY OWN PROBLEMS TO FACE, FIRST."
WERE YOU NOT GOING TO INVITE ME ALONG TO HUNT THE BEAST?
I THOUGHT--
THAT I'M TOO WEAK?
INJURED, FITZ. INJURED. I'D HOPED YOU'D SLEEP THROUGH IT...
YES. WELL. THE THING ABOUT SULKING IN THE STABLE IS THAT ONE MUST HEAR THE GROOMS TALK.
I'M NOT SO HURT THAT I CAN'T DO MY DUTY, AS A MAN AND AS YOUR SECOND.
I HAVE NEVER DOUBTED YOU BEFORE--
AND NOW YOU DO BECAUSE SOME OLD BOGWOMAN SAID SO? I'VE NEVER KNOWN YOU TO CLING TO SUPERSTITIONS.
WHAT WAS THAT LAST NIGHT, A TEA PARTY?

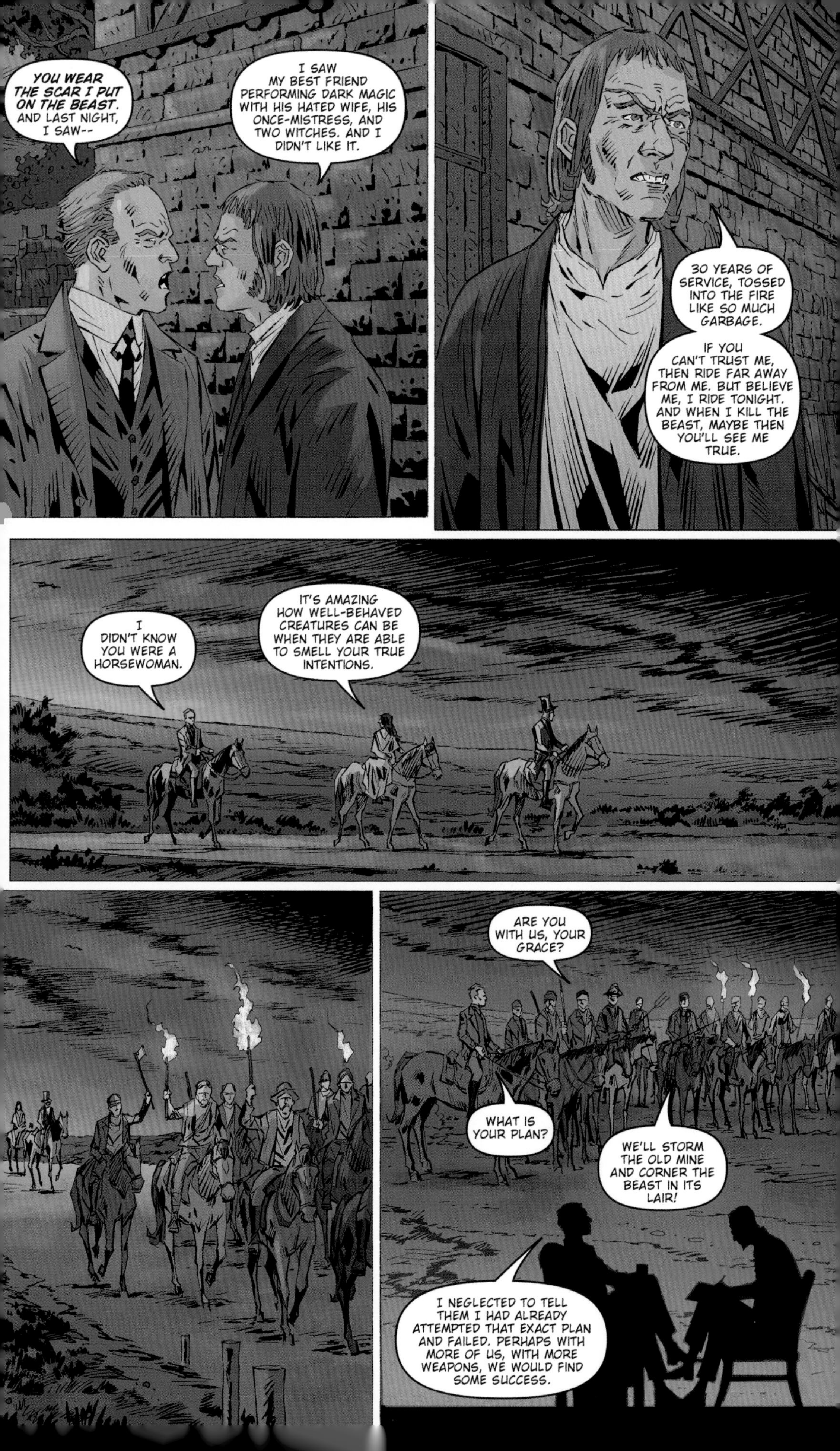
YOU WEAR THE SCAR I PUT ON THE BEAST. AND LAST NIGHT, I SAW--
I SAW MY BEST FRIEND PERFORMING DARK MAGIC WITH HIS HATED WIFE, HIS ONCE-MISTRESS, AND TWO WITCHES. AND I DIDN'T LIKE IT.
30 YEARS OF SERVICE, TOSSED INTO THE FIRE LIKE SO MUCH GARBAGE.
IF YOU CAN'T TRUST ME, THEN RIDE FAR AWAY FROM ME. BUT BELIEVE ME, I RIDE TONIGHT. AND WHEN I KILL THE BEAST, MAYBE THEN YOU'LL SEE ME TRUE.
I DIDN'T KNOW YOU WERE A HORSEWOMAN.
IT'S AMAZING HOW WELL-BEHAVED CREATURES CAN BE WHEN THEY ARE ABLE TO SMELL YOUR TRUE INTENTIONS.
ARE YOU WITH US, YOUR GRACE?
WHAT IS YOUR PLAN?
WE'LL STORM THE OLD MINE AND CORNER THE BEAST IN ITS LAIR!
I NEGLECTED TO TELL THEM I HAD ALREADY ATTEMPTED THAT EXACT PLAN AND FAILED. PERHAPS WITH MORE OF US, WITH MORE WEAPONS, WE WOULD FIND SOME SUCCESS.

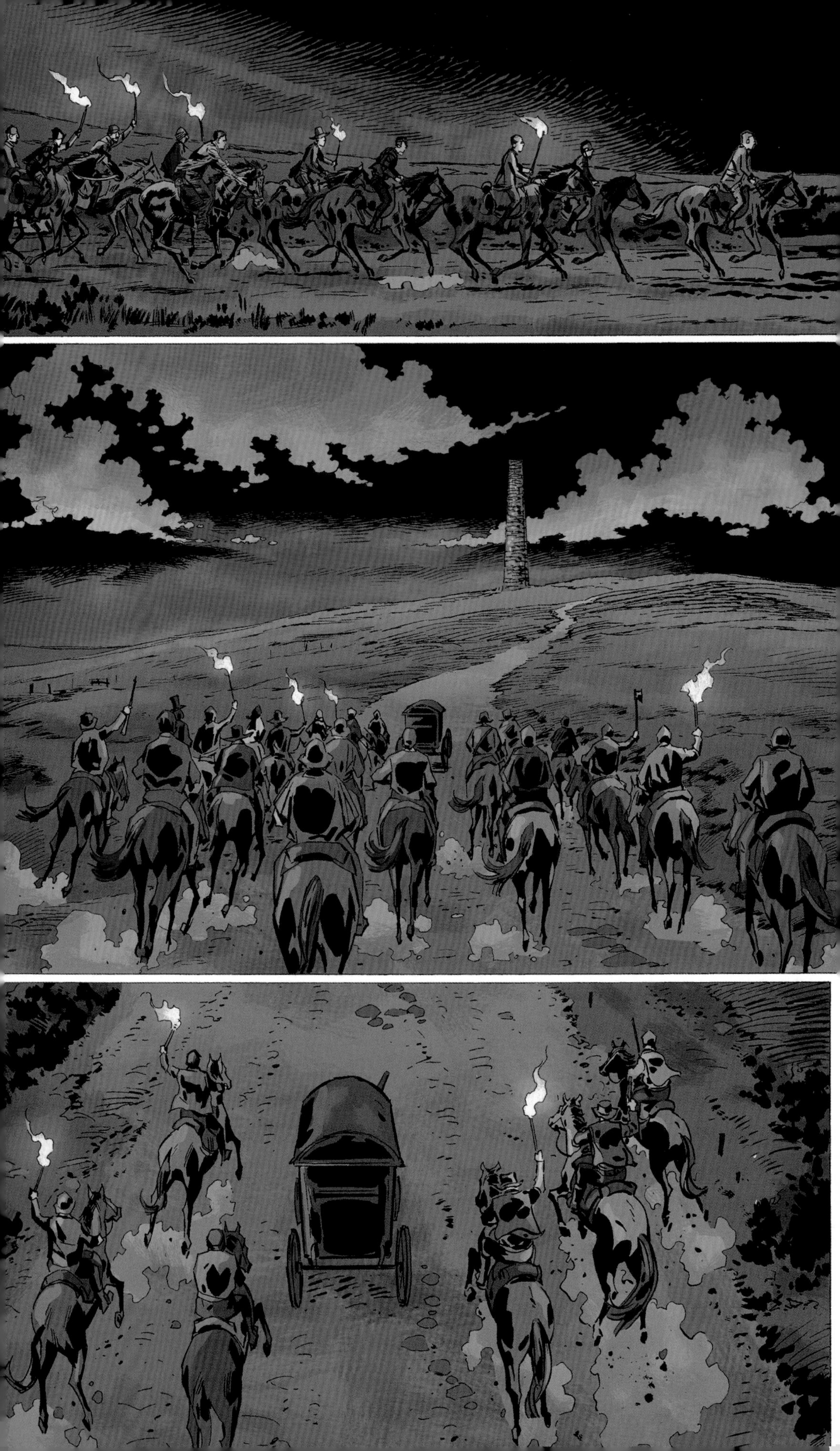

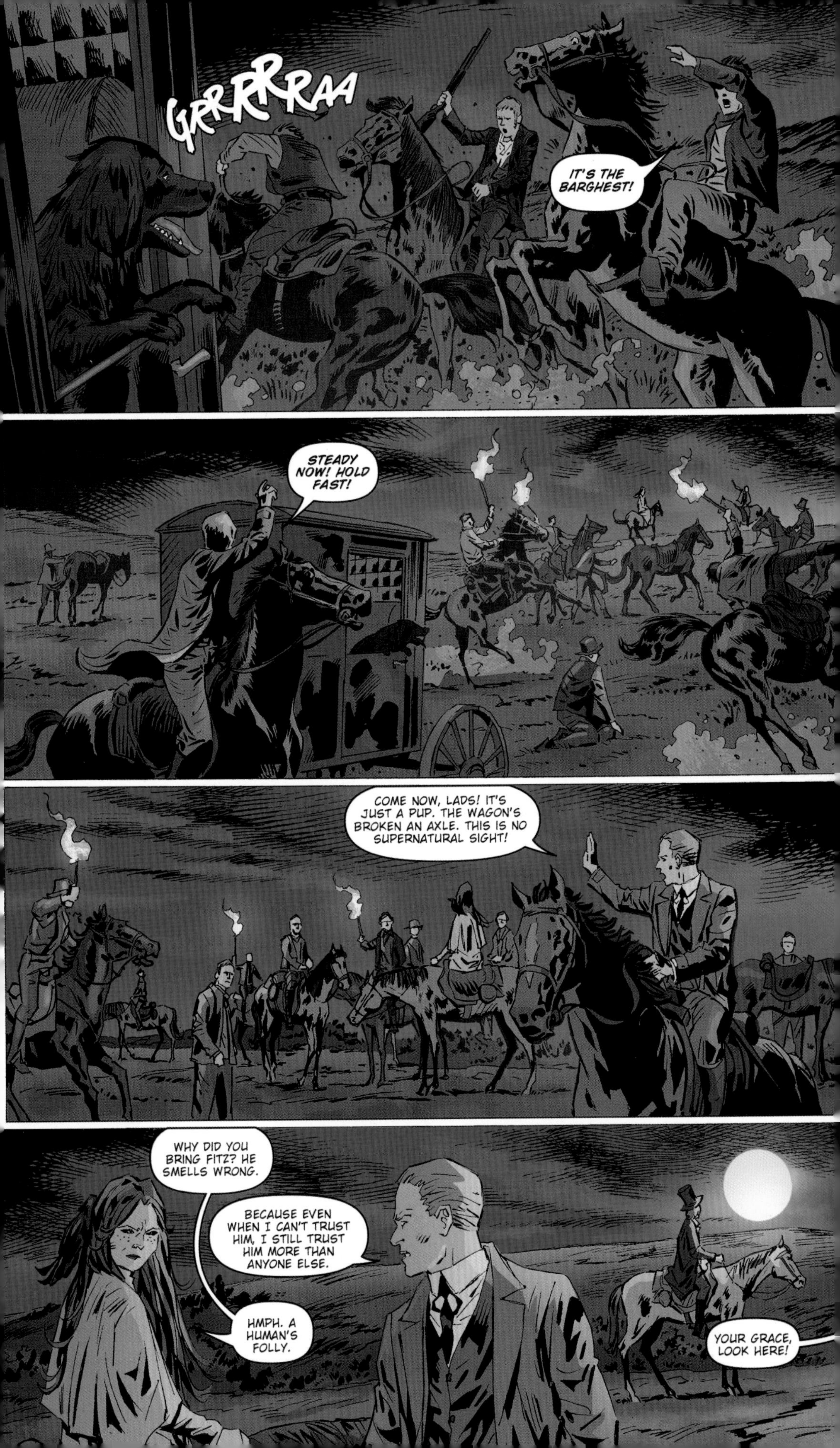
GRRRRRAA
IT'S THE BARGHEST!
STEADY NOW! HOLD FAST!
COME NOW, LADS! IT'S JUST A PUP. THE WAGON'S BROKEN AN AXLE. THIS IS NO SUPERNATURAL SIGHT!
WHY DID YOU BRING FITZ? HE SMELLS WRONG.
BECAUSE EVEN WHEN I CAN'T TRUST HIM, I STILL TRUST HIM MORE THAN ANYONE ELSE.
HMPH. A HUMAN'S FOLLY.
YOUR GRACE, LOOK HERE!

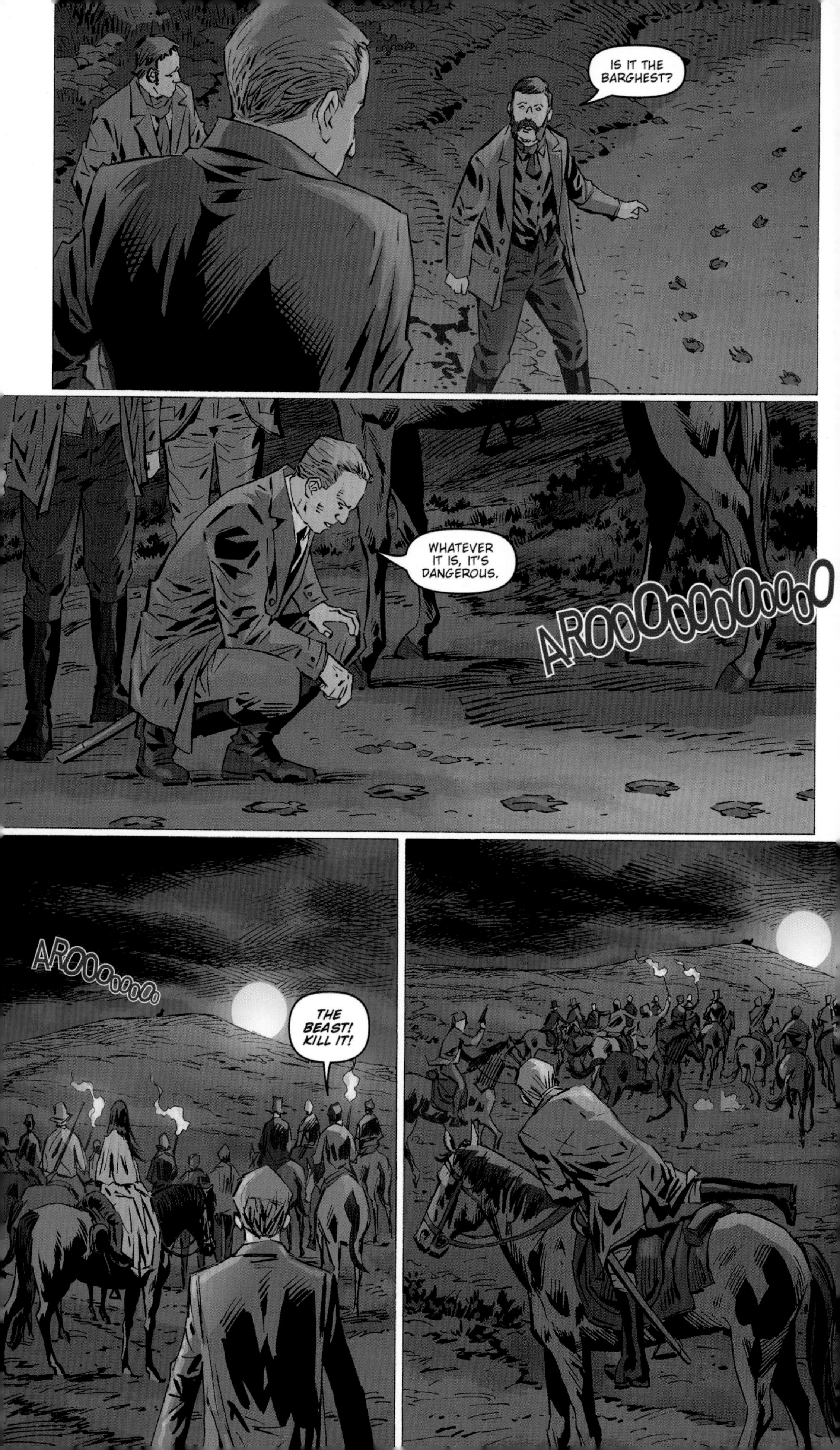
IS IT THE BARGHEST?
WHATEVER IT IS, IT'S DANGEROUS.
AROOOoooooOoooO
AROOOoooooo
THE BEAST! KILL IT!

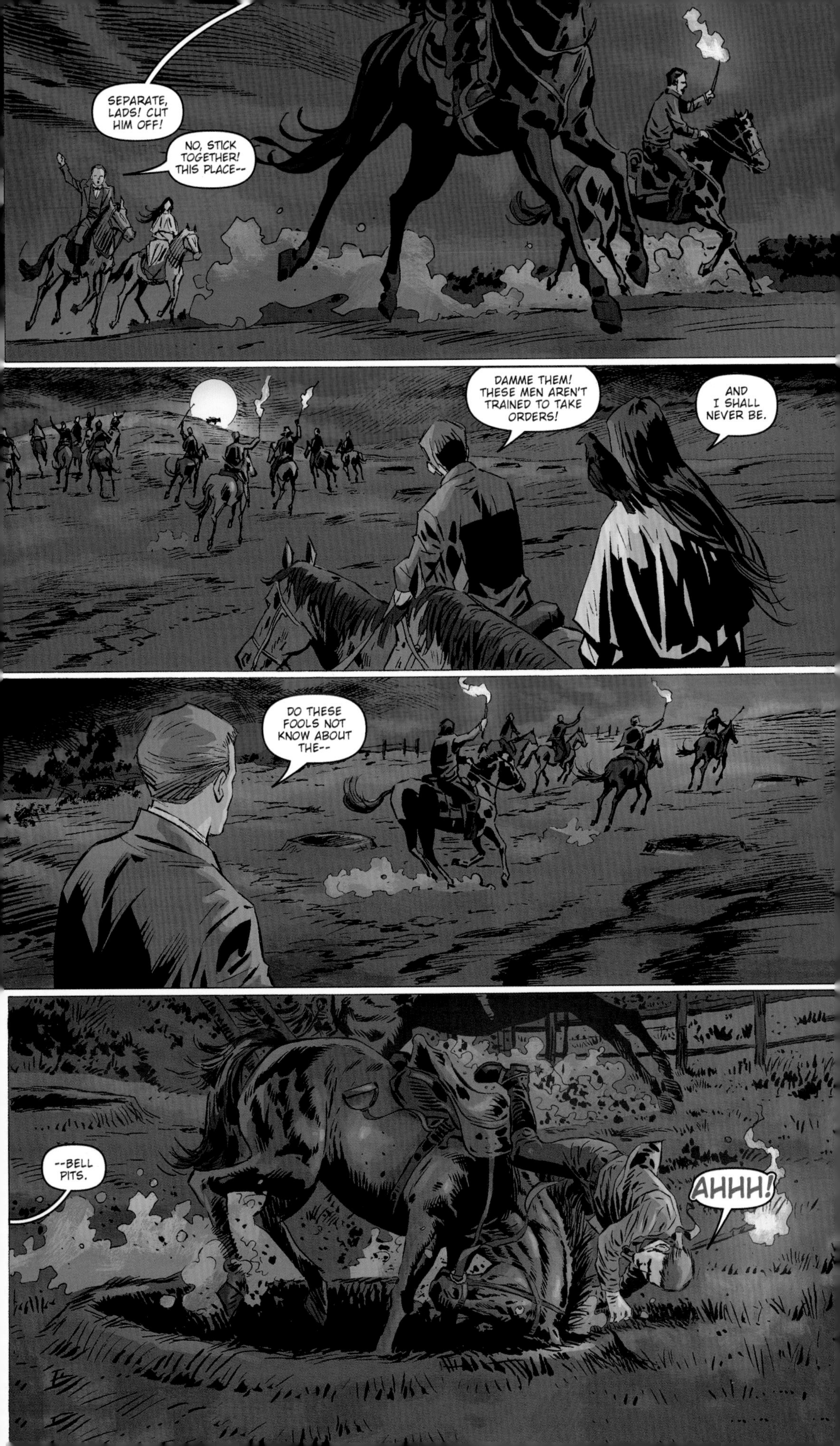
SEPARATE, LADS! CUT HIM OFF!
NO, STICK TOGETHER! THIS PLACE--
DAMME THEM! THESE MEN AREN'T TRAINED TO TAKE ORDERS!
AND I SHALL NEVER BE.
DO THESE FOOLS NOT KNOW ABOUT THE--
--BELL PITS.
AHHH!

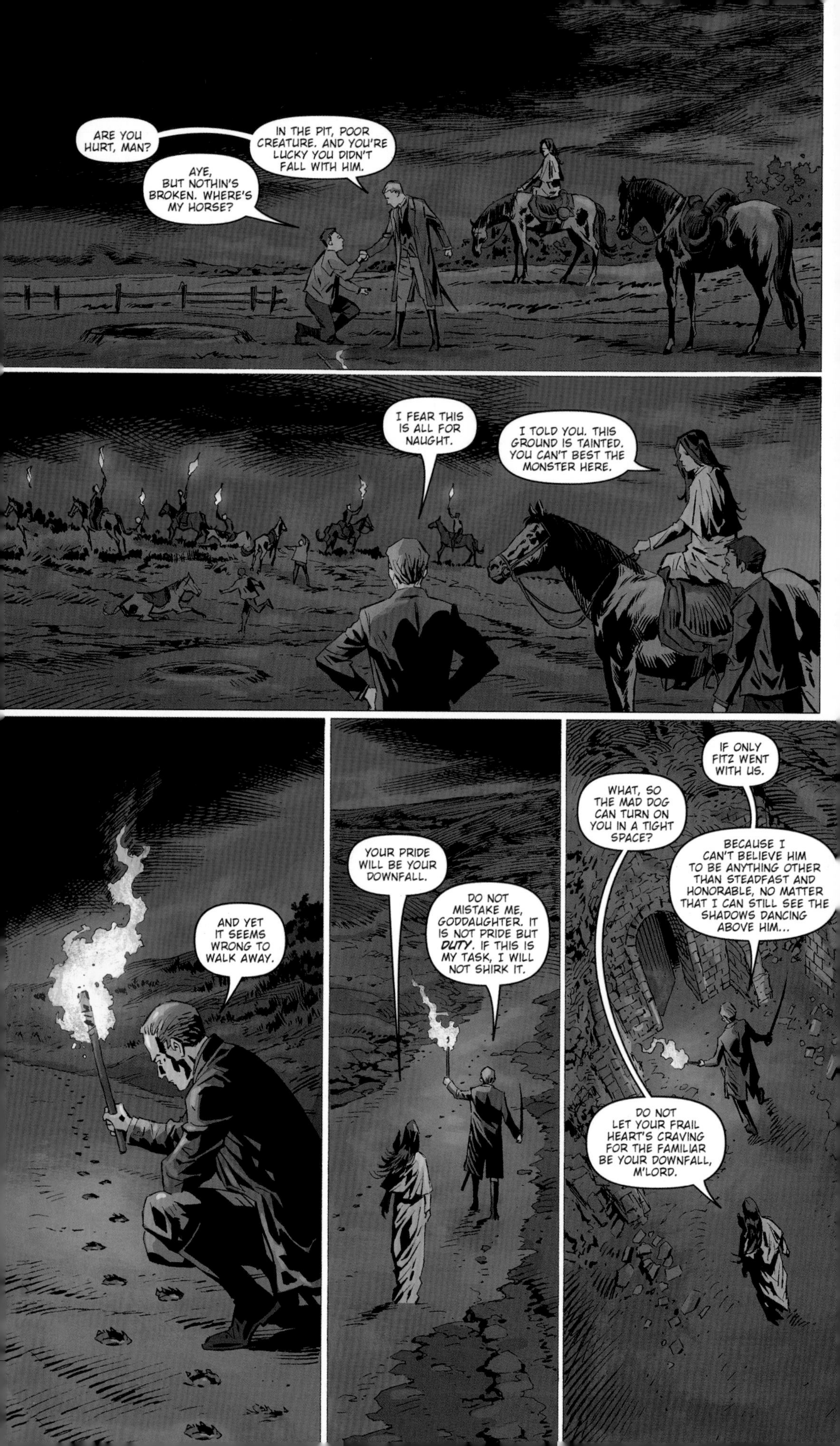
ARE YOU HURT, MAN?
AYE, BUT NOTHIN'S BROKEN. WHERE'S MY HORSE?
IN THE PIT, POOR CREATURE. AND YOU'RE LUCKY YOU DIDN'T FALL WITH HIM.
I FEAR THIS IS ALL FOR NAUGHT.
I TOLD YOU. THIS GROUND IS TAINTED. YOU CAN'T BEST THE MONSTER HERE.
AND YET IT SEEMS WRONG TO WALK AWAY.
YOUR PRIDE WILL BE YOUR DOWNFALL.
DO NOT MISTAKE ME, GODDAUGHTER. IT IS NOT PRIDE BUT DUTY. IF THIS IS MY TASK, I WILL NOT SHIRK IT.
IF ONLY FITZ WENT WITH US.
WHAT, SO THE MAD DOG CAN TURN ON YOU IN A TIGHT SPACE?
BECAUSE I CAN'T BELIEVE HIM TO BE ANYTHING OTHER THAN STEADFAST AND HONORABLE, NO MATTER THAT I CAN STILL SEE THE SHADOWS DANCING ABOVE HIM...
DO NOT LET YOUR FRAIL HEART'S CRAVING FOR THE FAMILIAR BE YOUR DOWNFALL, M'LORD.

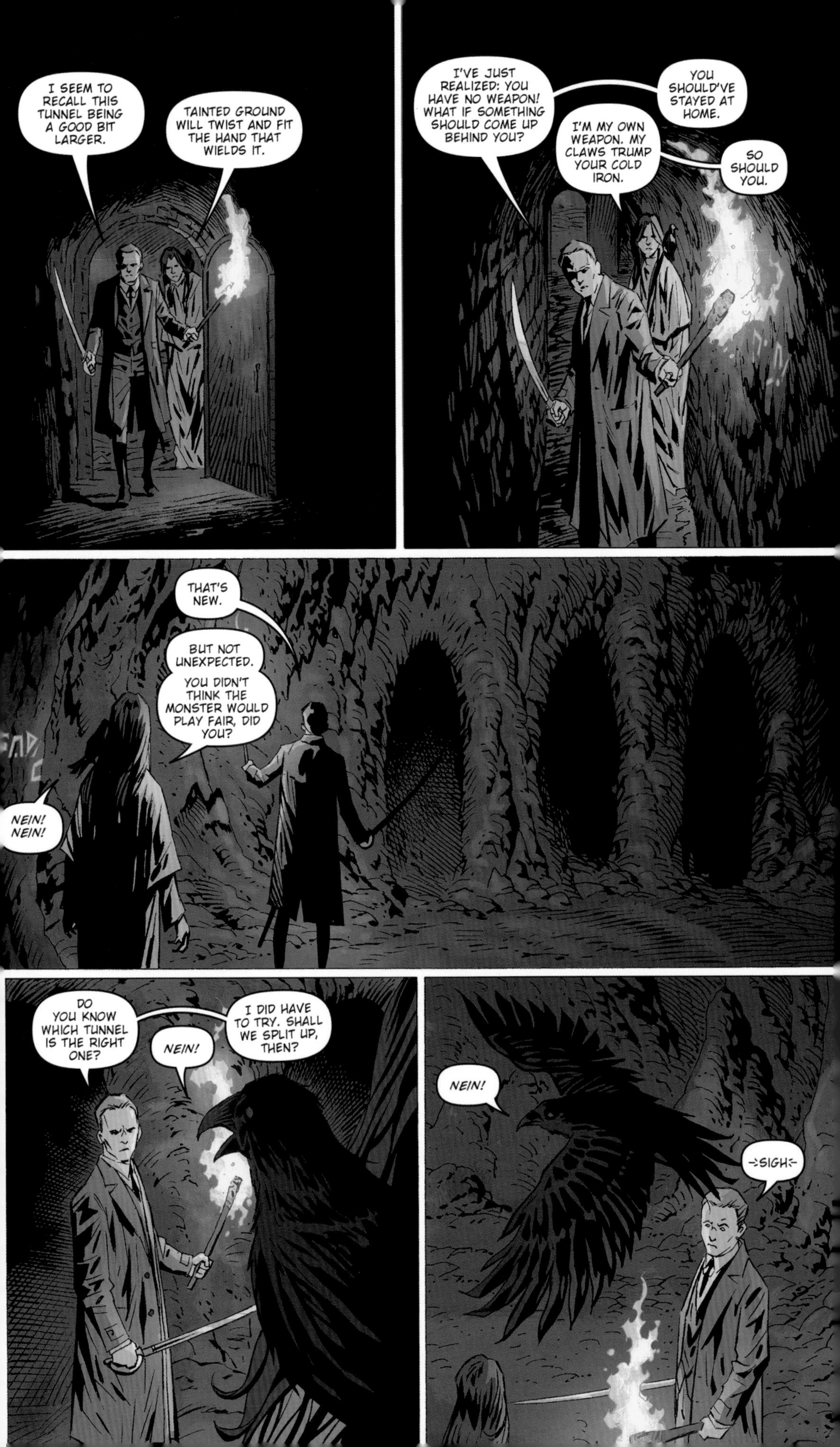
I SEEM TO RECALL THIS TUNNEL BEING A GOOD BIT LARGER.
TAINTED GROUND WILL TWIST AND FIT THE HAND THAT WIELDS IT.
I'VE JUST REALIZED: YOU HAVE NO WEAPON! WHAT IF SOMETHING SHOULD COME UP BEHIND YOU?
YOU SHOULD'VE STAYED AT HOME.
I'M MY OWN WEAPON. MY CLAWS TRUMP YOUR COLD IRON.
SO SHOULD YOU.
THAT'S NEW.
BUT NOT UNEXPECTED.
YOU DIDN'T THINK THE MONSTER WOULD PLAY FAIR, DID YOU?
NEIN! NEIN!
DO YOU KNOW WHICH TUNNEL IS THE RIGHT ONE?
NEIN!
I DID HAVE TO TRY. SHALL WE SPLIT UP, THEN?
NEIN!
SIGH

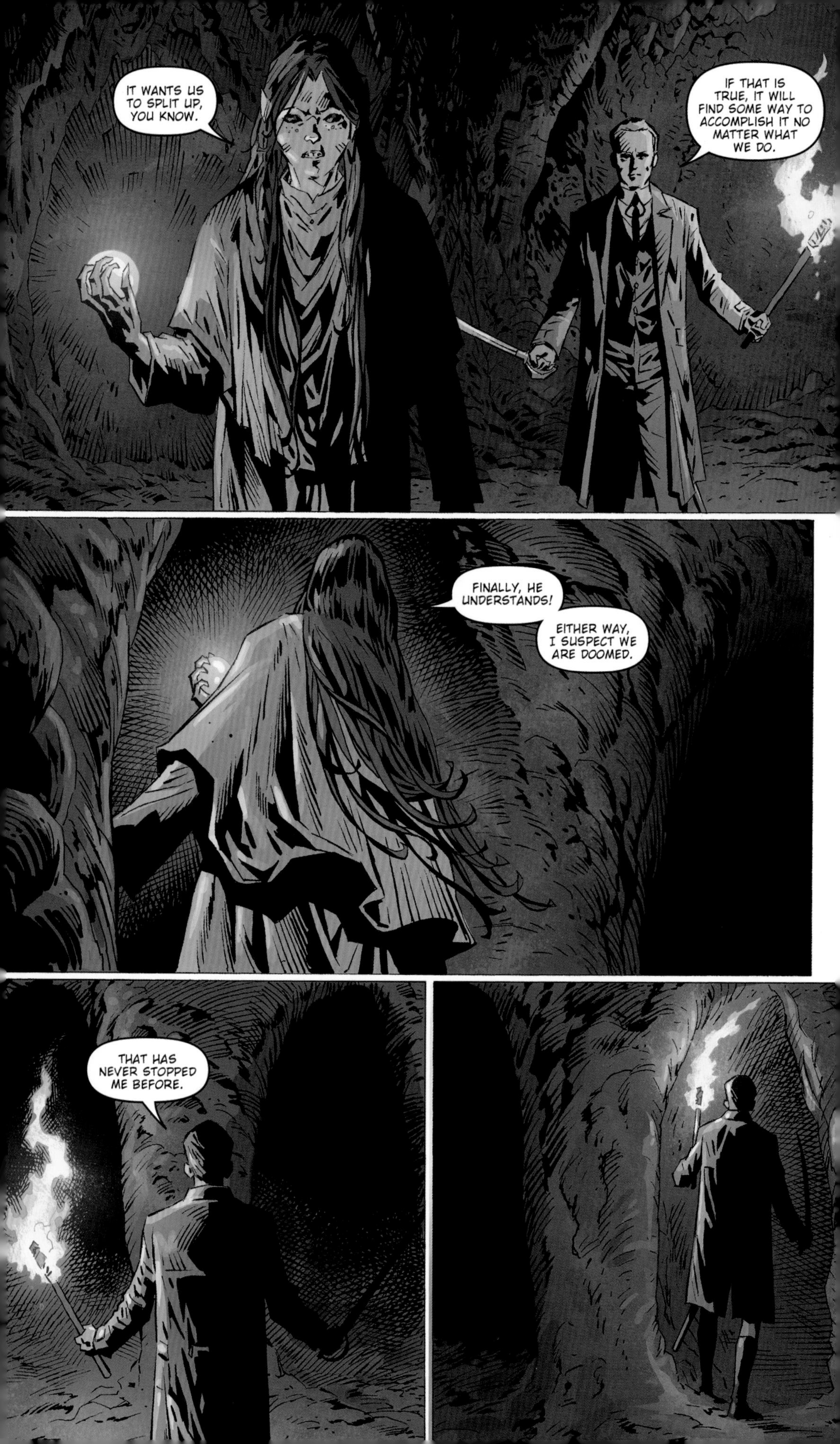
IT WANTS US TO SPLIT UP, YOU KNOW.
IF THAT IS TRUE, IT WILL FIND SOME WAY TO ACCOMPLISH IT NO MATTER WHAT WE DO.
FINALLY, HE UNDERSTANDS!
EITHER WAY, I SUSPECT WE ARE DOOMED.
THAT HAS NEVER STOPPED ME BEFORE.

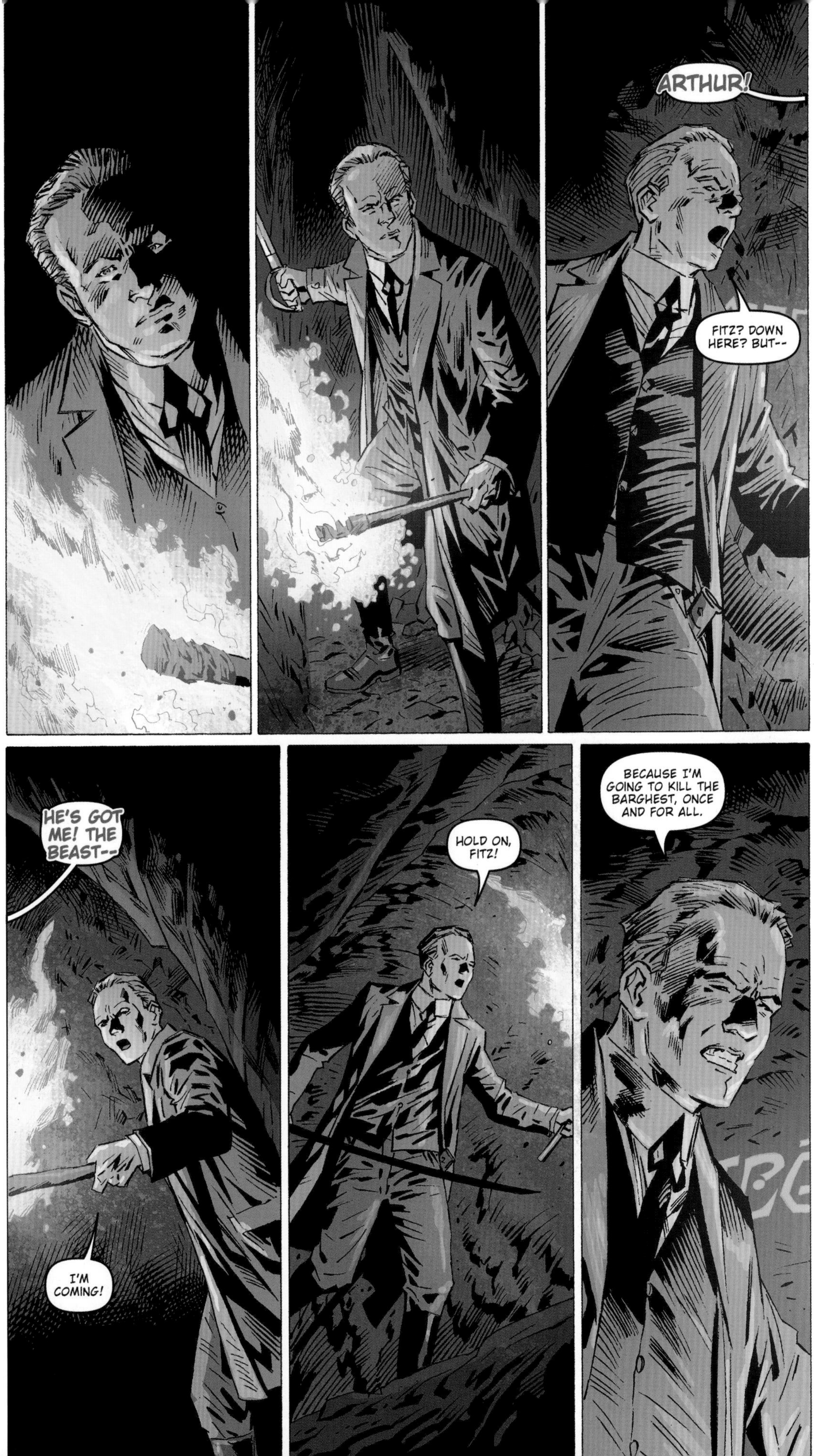
ARTHUR!
FITZ? DOWN HERE? BUT--
HE'S GOT ME! THE BEAST--
I'M COMING!
HOLD ON, FITZ!
BECAUSE I'M GOING TO KILL THE BARGHEST, ONCE AND FOR ALL.

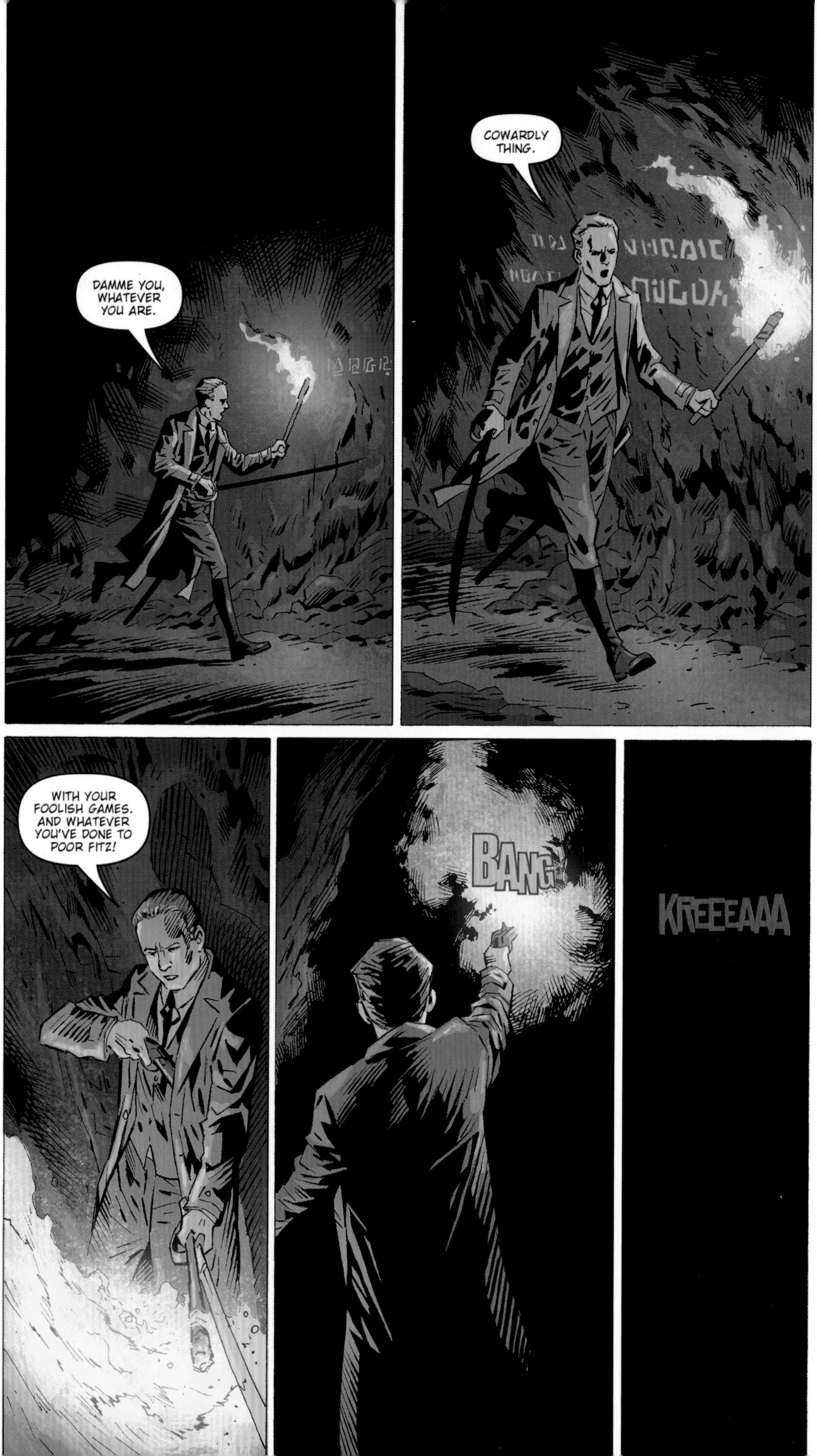
DAMME YOU, WHATEVER YOU ARE.
COWARDLY THING.
WITH YOUR FOOLISH GAMES. AND WHATEVER YOU'VE DONE TO POOR FITZ!
BANG
KREEEAAA

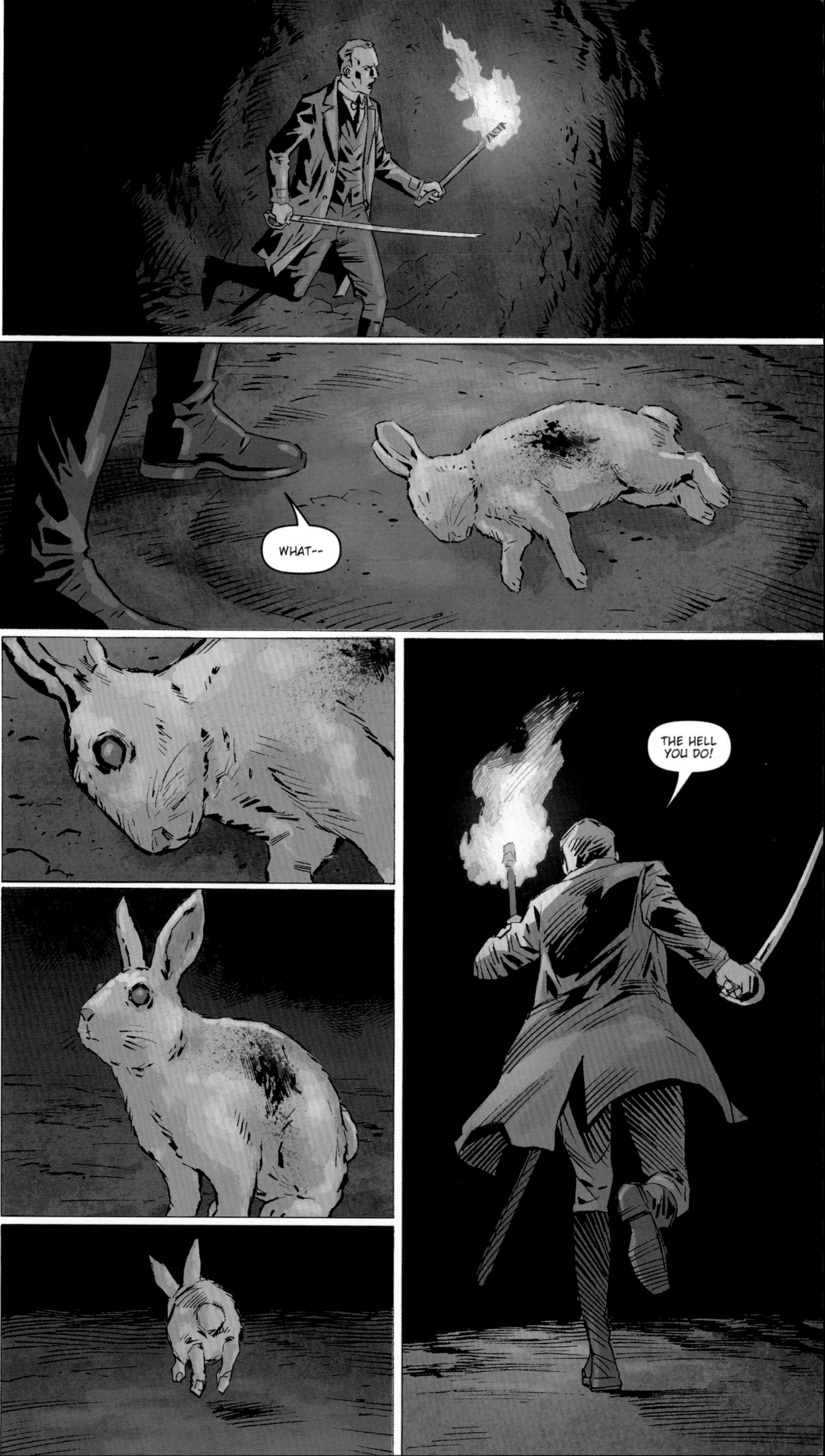
WHAT--
THE HELL YOU DO!

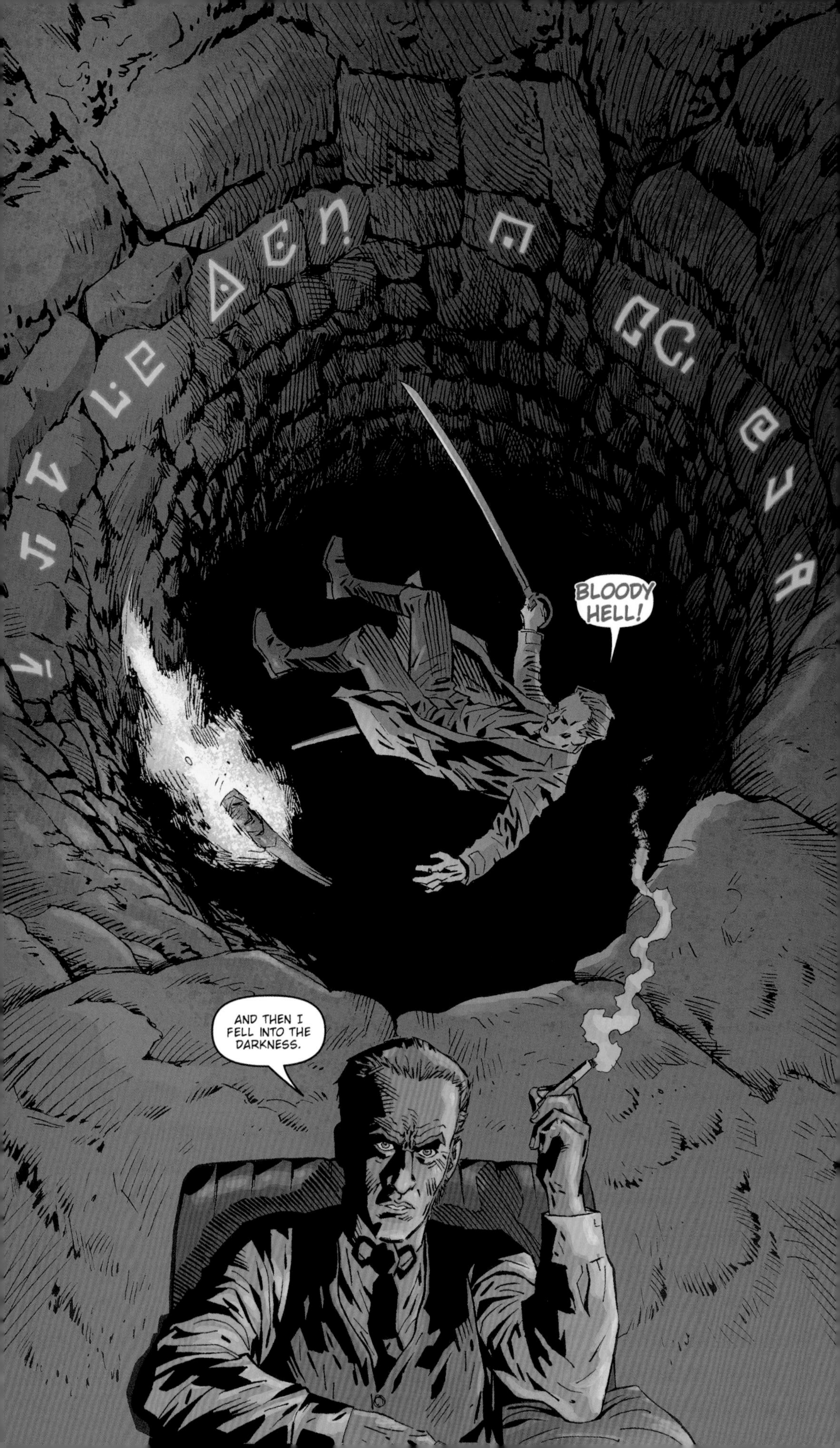
BLOODY HELL!
AND THEN I FELL INTO THE DARKNESS.

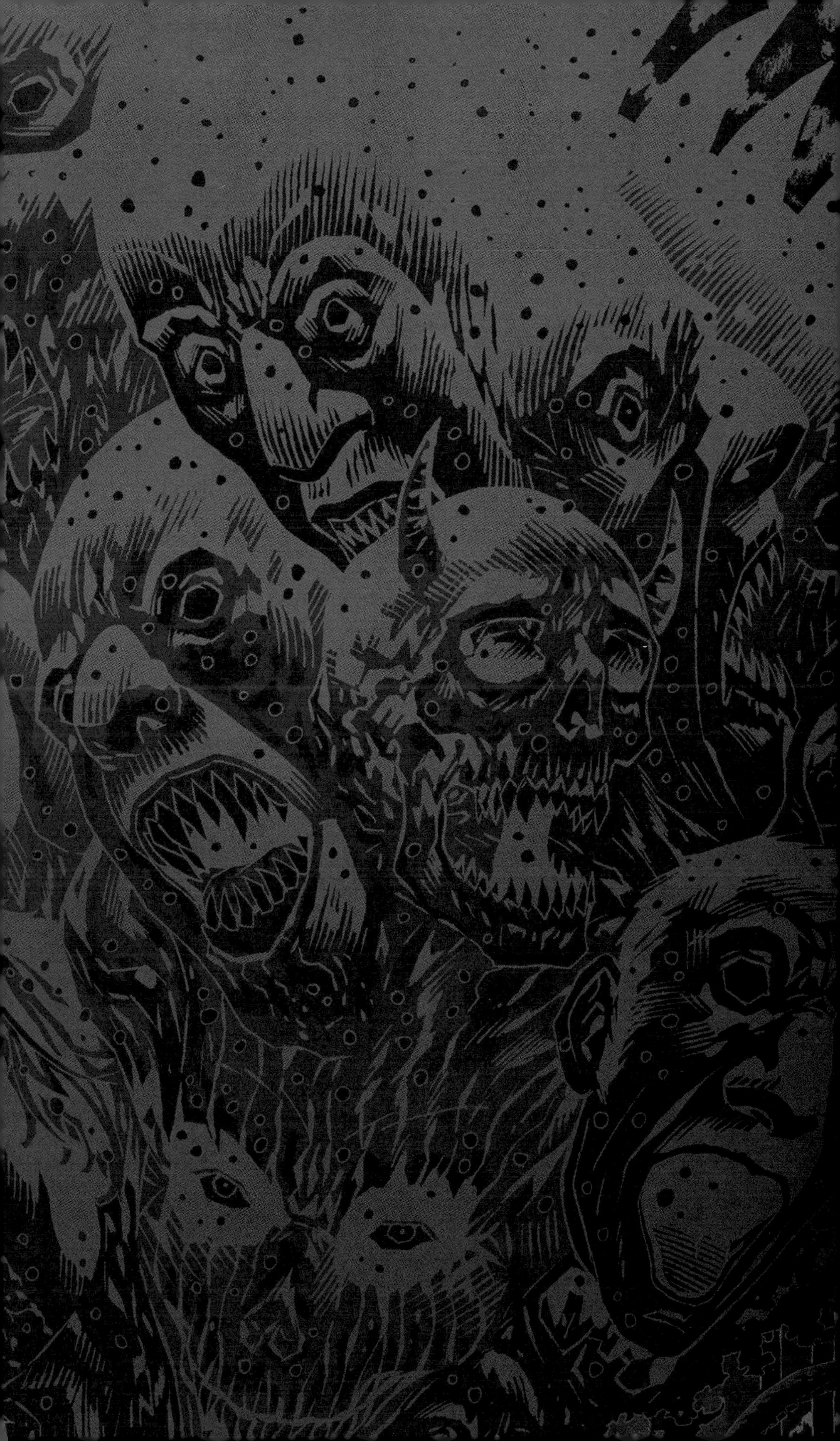

Chapter 5

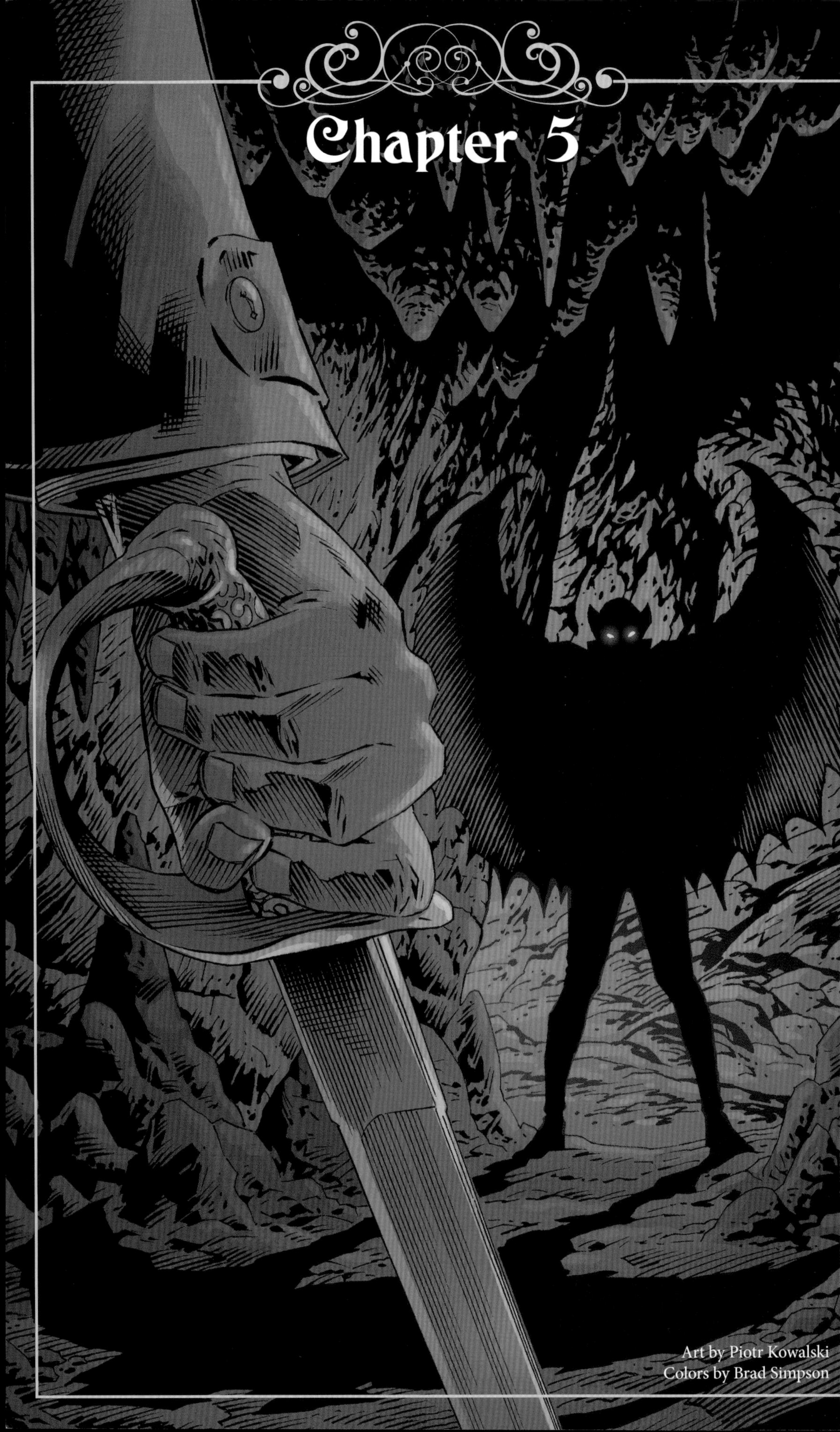

Art by Piotr Kowalski
Colors by Brad Simpson

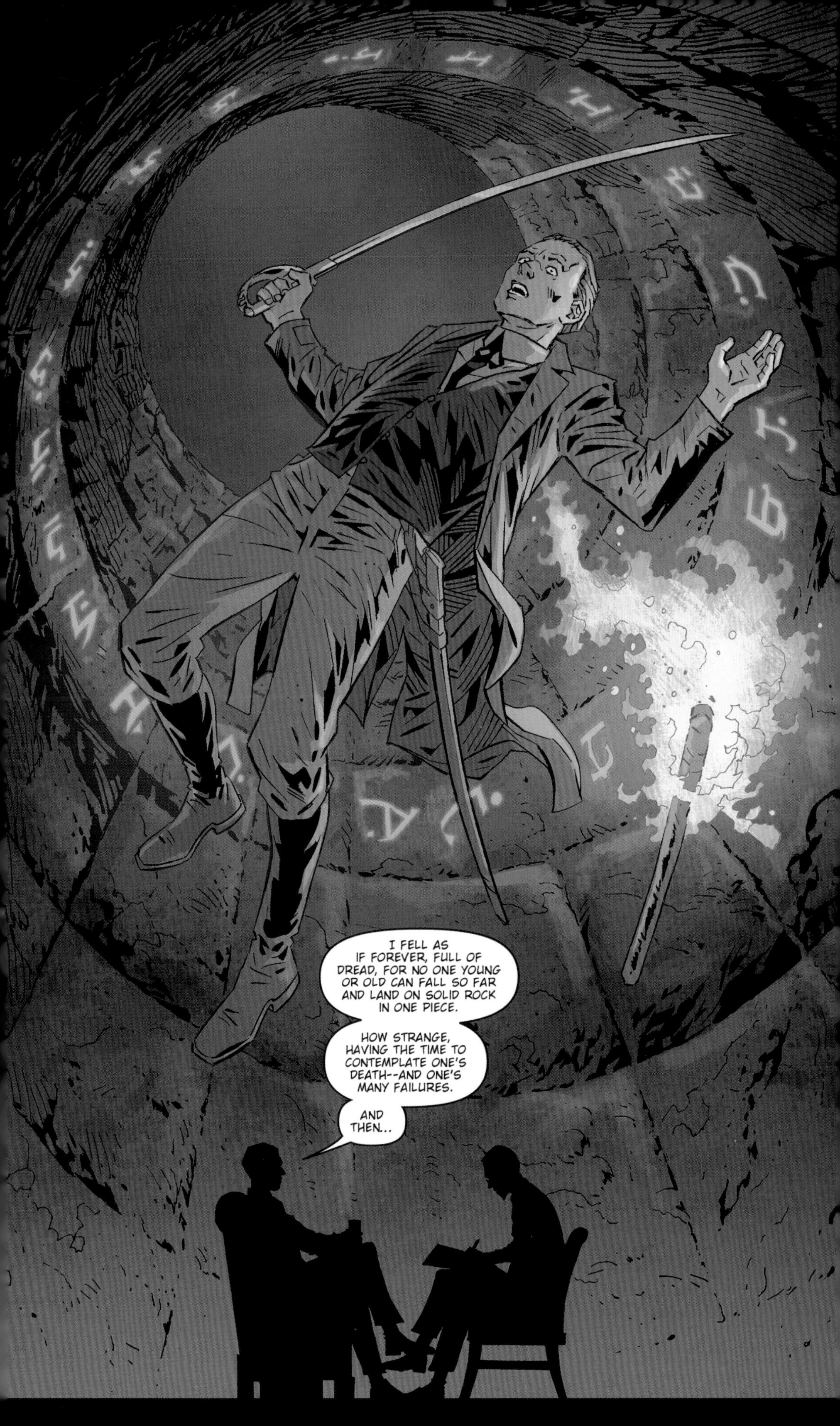
I FELL AS IF FOREVER, FULL OF DREAD, FOR NO ONE YOUNG OR OLD CAN FALL SO FAR AND LAND ON SOLID ROCK IN ONE PIECE.
HOW STRANGE, HAVING THE TIME TO CONTEMPLATE ONE'S DEATH--AND ONE'S MANY FAILURES.
AND THEN...

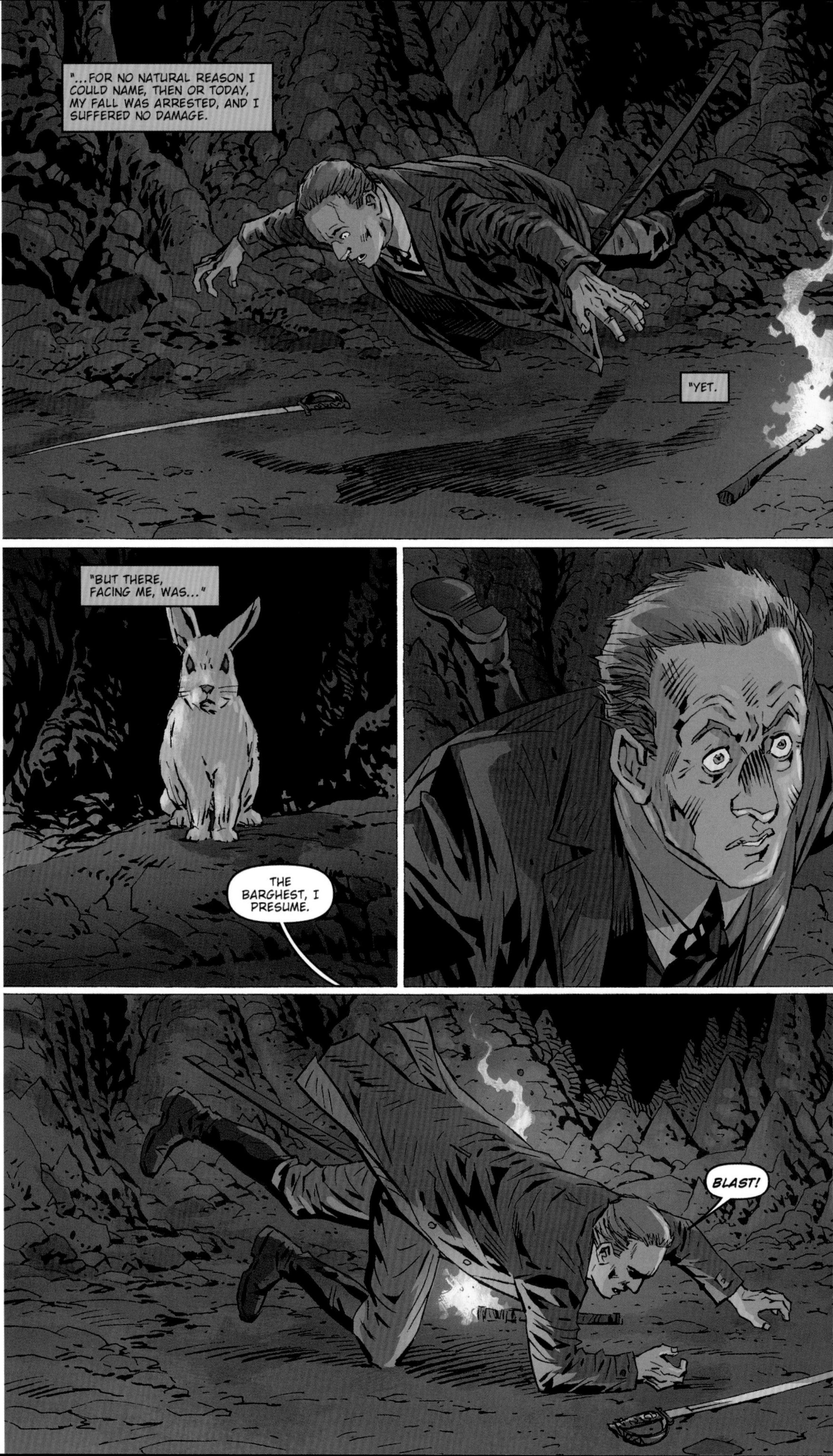
"...FOR NO NATURAL REASON I COULD NAME, THEN OR TODAY, MY FALL WAS ARRESTED, AND I SUFFERED NO DAMAGE.
"YET.
"BUT THERE, FACING ME, WAS..."
THE BARGHEST, I PRESUME.
BLAST!

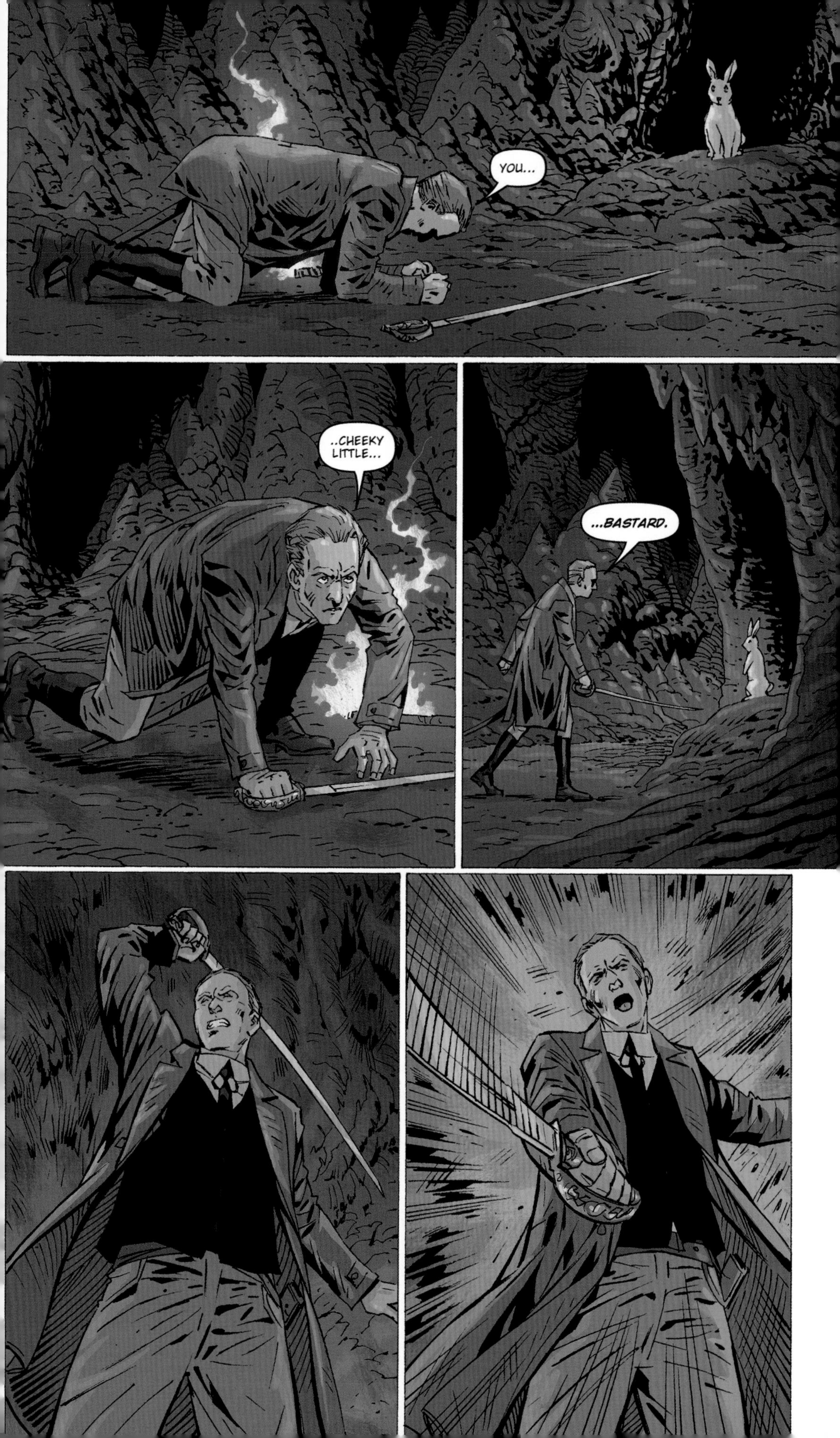
YOU...
..CHEEKY LITTLE...
...BASTARD.

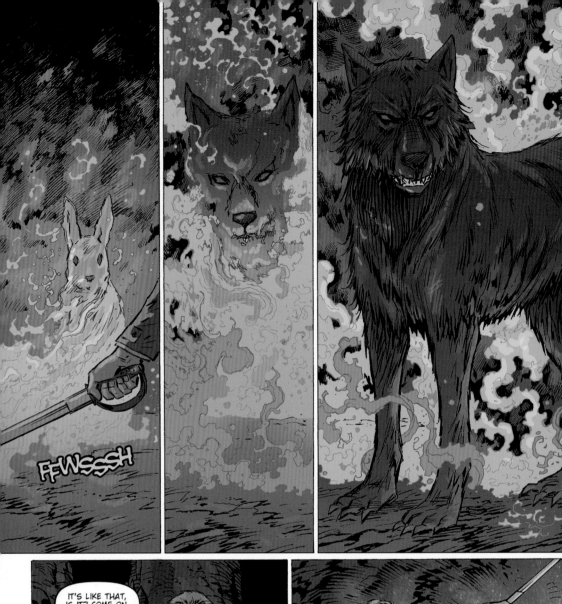

FFWSSSH

IT'S LIKE THAT, IS IT? COME ON, THEN, DOGGY--

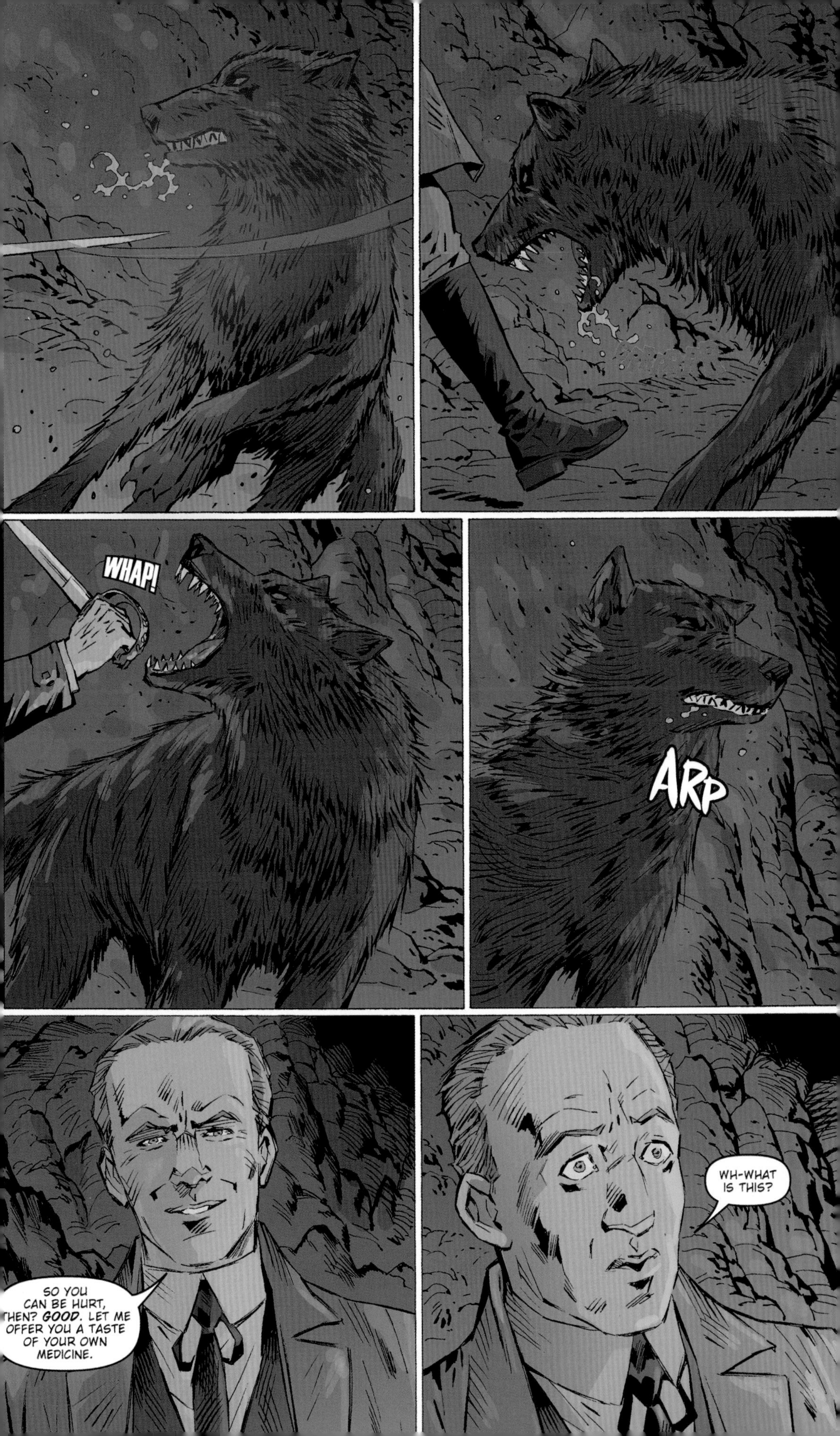
WHAP!
ARP
SO YOU CAN BE HURT, THEN? GOOD. LET ME OFFER YOU A TASTE OF YOUR OWN MEDICINE.
WH-WHAT IS THIS?

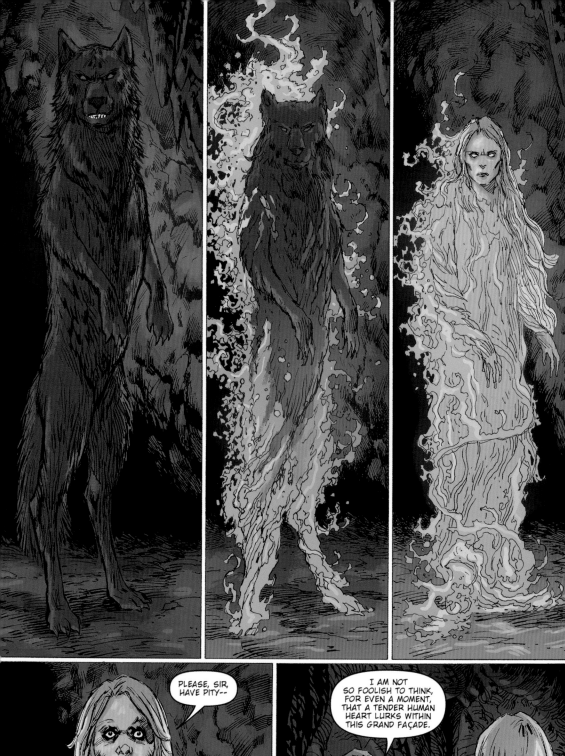

PLEASE, SIR, HAVE PITY--

I AM NOT SO FOOLISH TO THINK, FOR EVEN A MOMENT, THAT A TENDER HUMAN HEART LURKS WITHIN THIS GRAND FAÇADE.

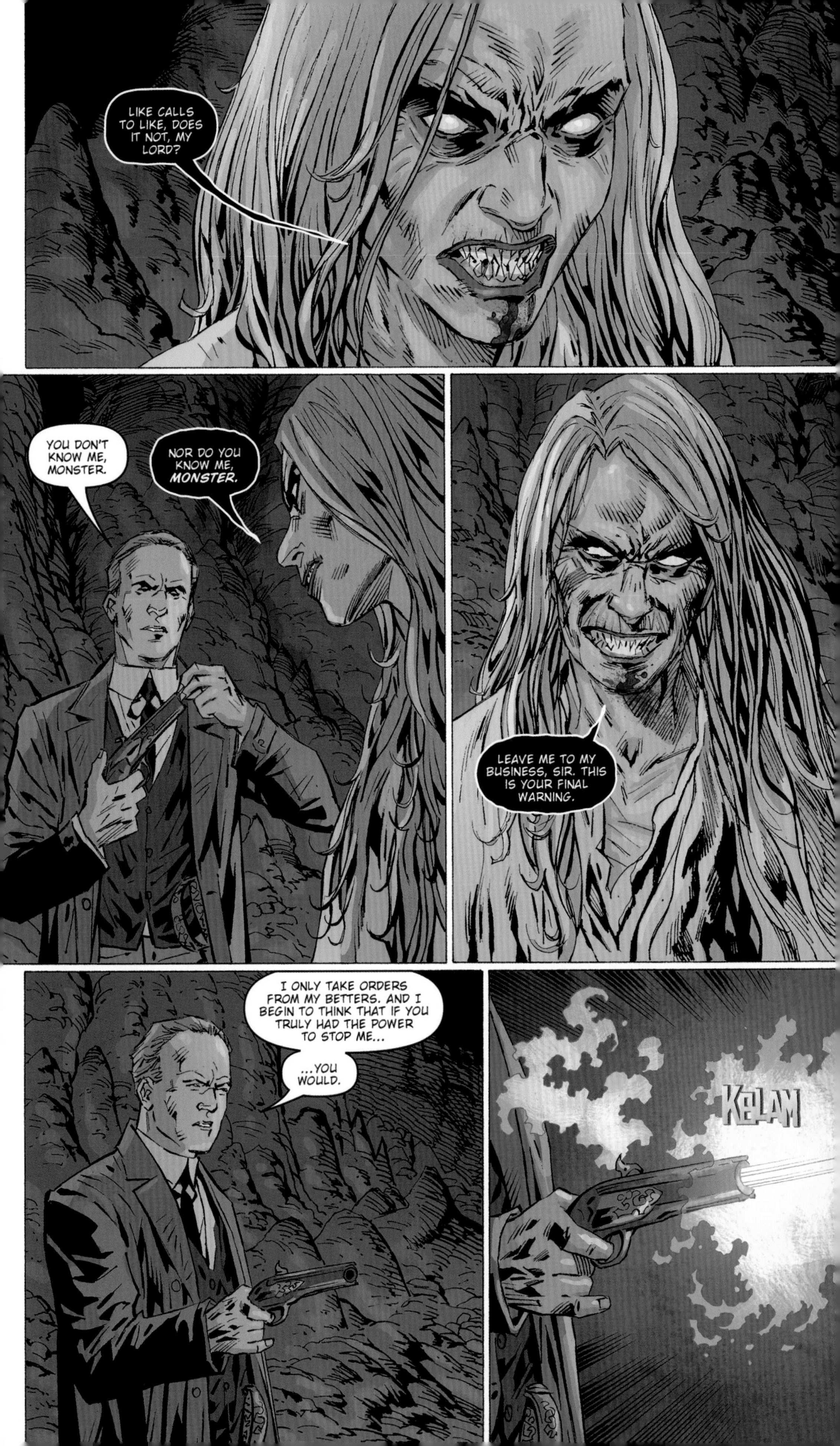
LIKE CALLS TO LIKE, DOES IT NOT, MY LORD?
YOU DON'T KNOW ME, MONSTER.
NOR DO YOU KNOW ME, *MONSTER.*
LEAVE ME TO MY BUSINESS, SIR. THIS IS YOUR FINAL WARNING.
I ONLY TAKE ORDERS FROM MY BETTERS. AND I BEGIN TO THINK THAT IF YOU TRULY HAD THE POWER TO STOP ME...
...YOU WOULD.
KBLAM

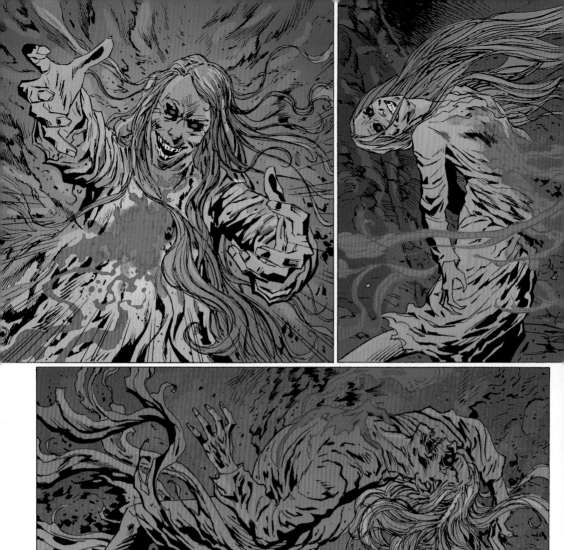

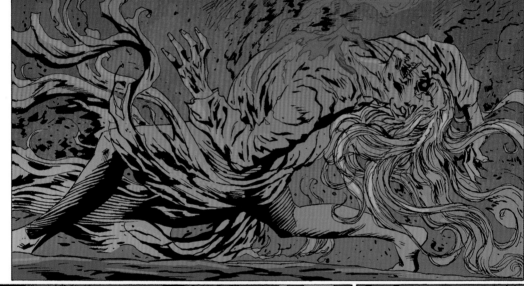

BLOOD
HELL.
IT'S--

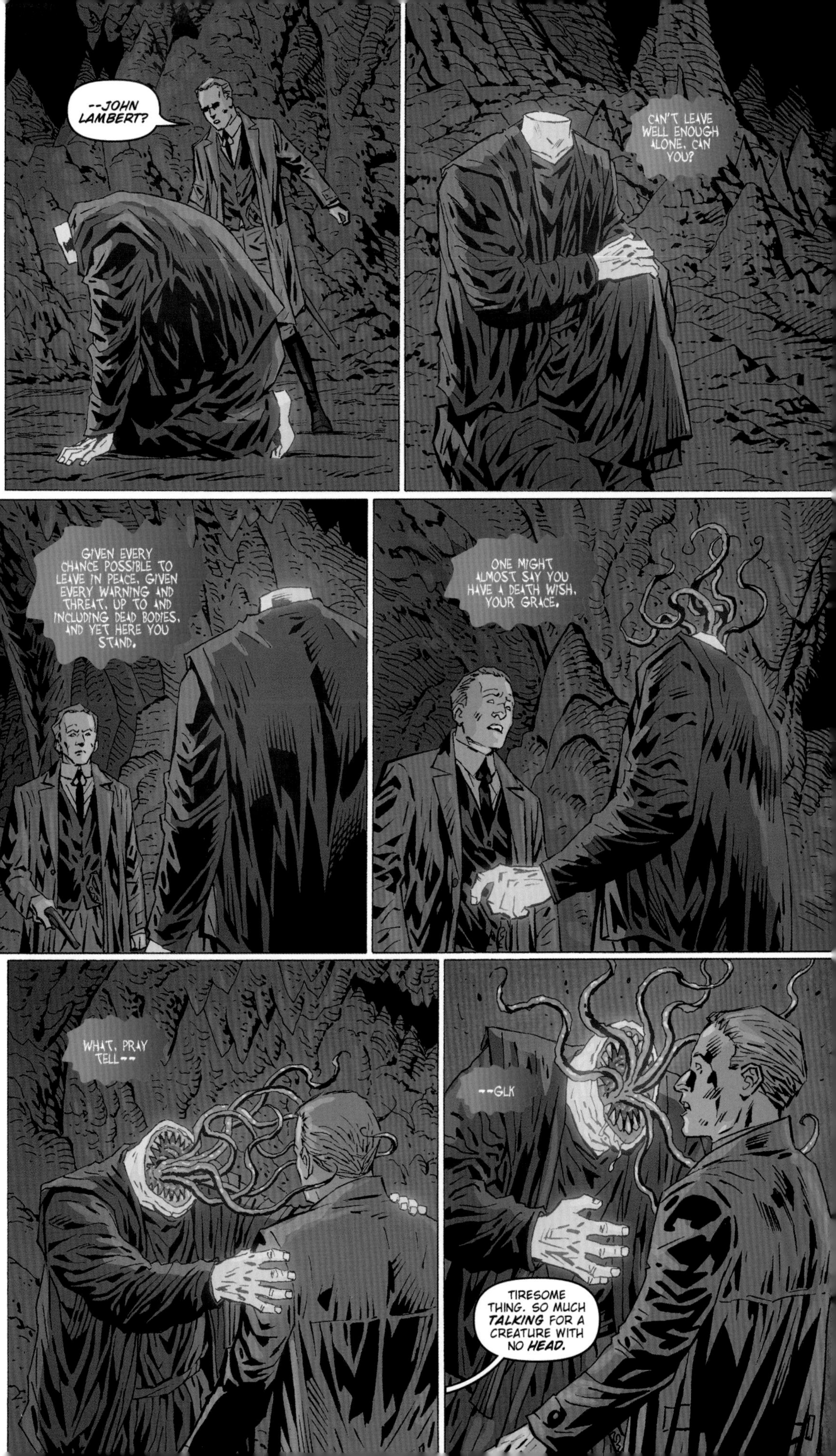

--JOHN LAMBERT?
CAN'T LEAVE WELL ENOUGH ALONE, CAN YOU?
GIVEN EVERY CHANCE POSSIBLE TO LEAVE IN PEACE, GIVEN EVERY WARNING AND THREAT, UP TO AND INCLUDING DEAD BODIES, AND YET HERE YOU STAND.
ONE MIGHT ALMOST SAY YOU HAVE A DEATH WISH, YOUR GRACE.
WHAT, PRAY TELL--
--GLK
TIRESOME THING. SO MUCH TALKING FOR A CREATURE WITH NO HEAD.

NOT THAT I BELIEVE FOR A SECOND THAT IT'S DEAD. YOU MIGHT...

...WISH TO STEP BACK. THIS COULD GET MESSY.

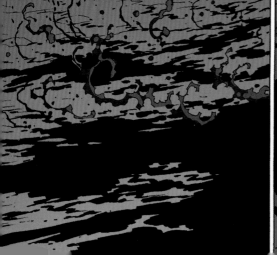

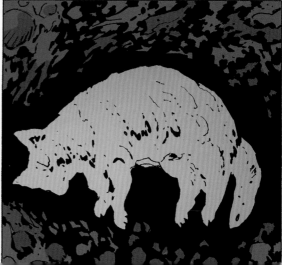

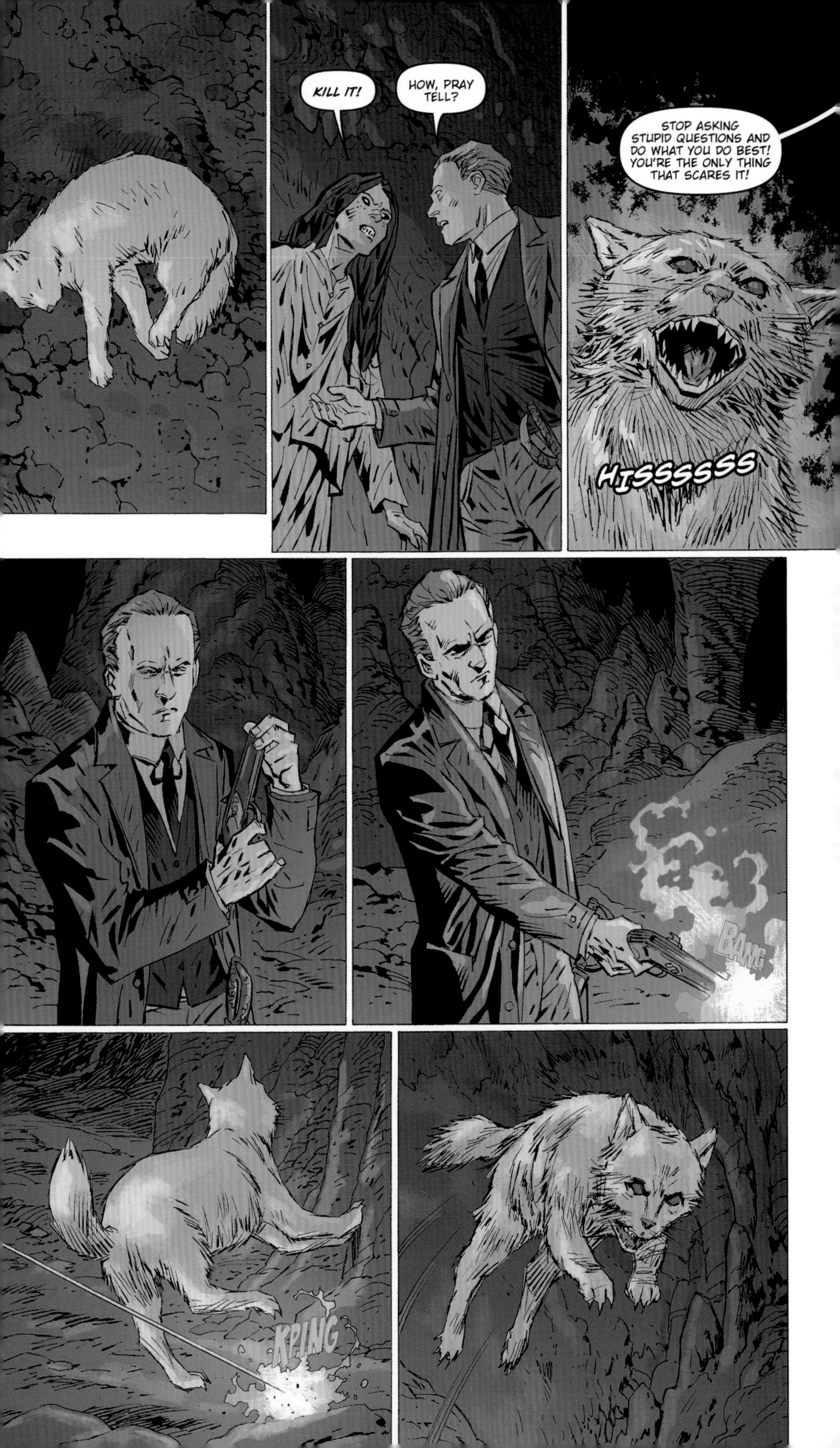
KILL IT!
HOW, PRAY TELL?
STOP ASKING STUPID QUESTIONS AND DO WHAT YOU DO BEST! YOU'RE THE ONLY THING THAT SCARES IT!
HISSSSSS
BANG
KPING

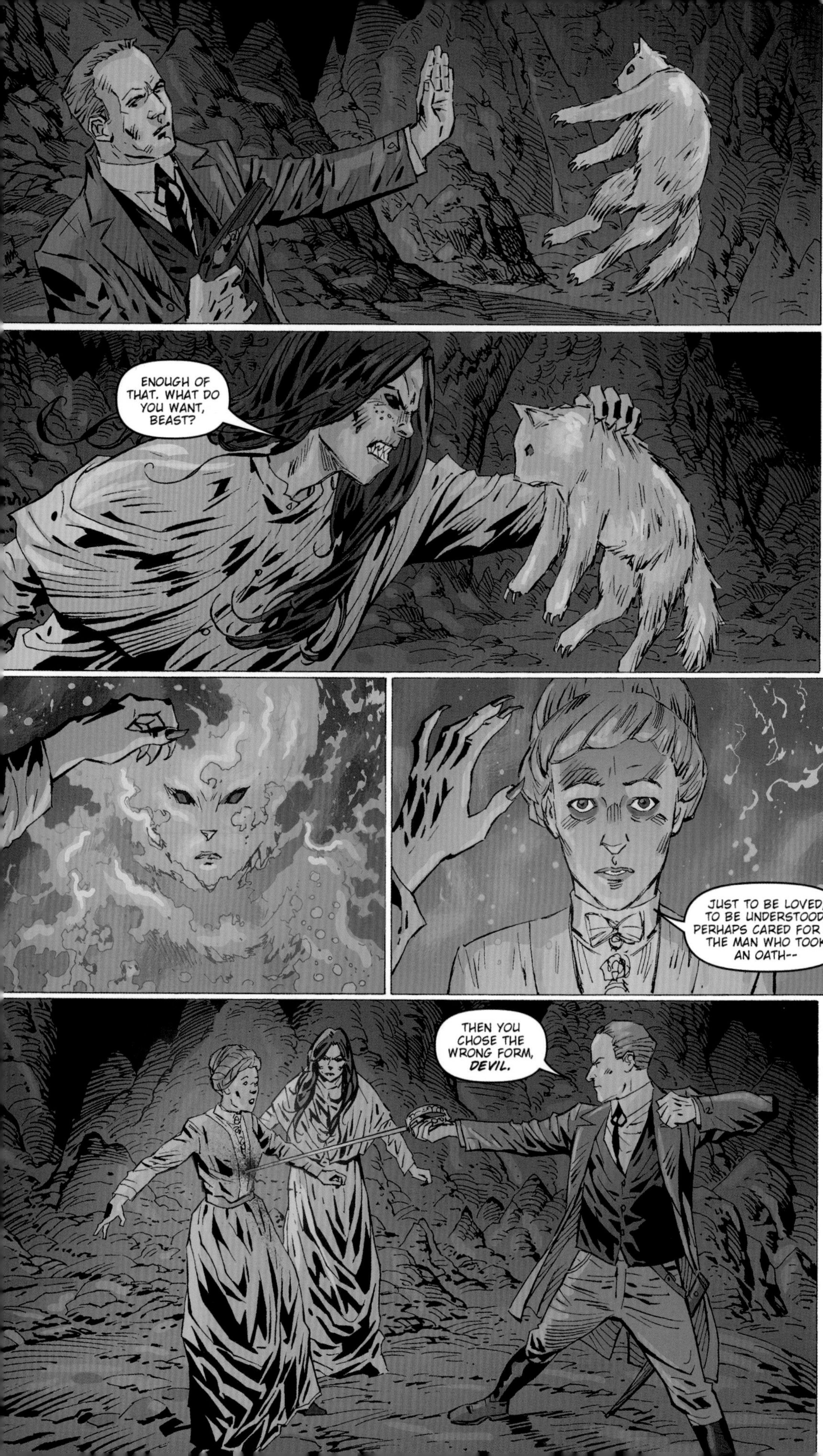
ENOUGH OF THAT. WHAT DO YOU WANT, BEAST?
JUST TO BE LOVED, TO BE UNDERSTOOD, PERHAPS CARED FOR BY THE MAN WHO TOOK AN OATH--
THEN YOU CHOSE THE WRONG FORM, DEVIL.

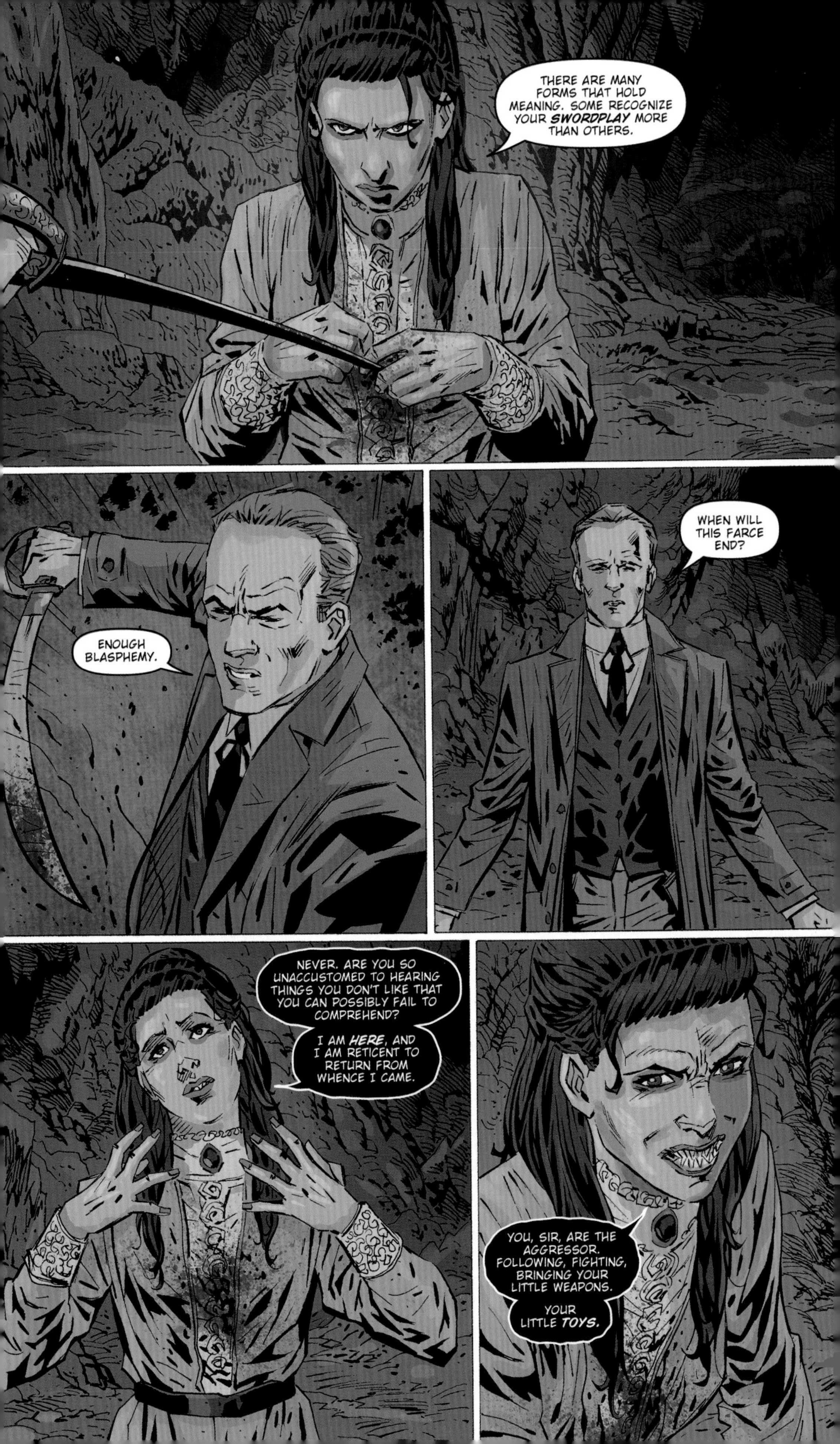
THERE ARE MANY FORMS THAT HOLD MEANING. SOME RECOGNIZE YOUR ***SWORDPLAY*** MORE THAN OTHERS.
ENOUGH BLASPHEMY.
WHEN WILL THIS FARCE END?
NEVER. ARE YOU SO UNACCUSTOMED TO HEARING THINGS YOU DON'T LIKE THAT YOU CAN POSSIBLY FAIL TO COMPREHEND?
I AM ***HERE***, AND I AM RETICENT TO RETURN FROM WHENCE I CAME.
YOU, SIR, ARE THE AGGRESSOR. FOLLOWING, FIGHTING, BRINGING YOUR LITTLE WEAPONS.
YOUR LITTLE ***TOYS.***

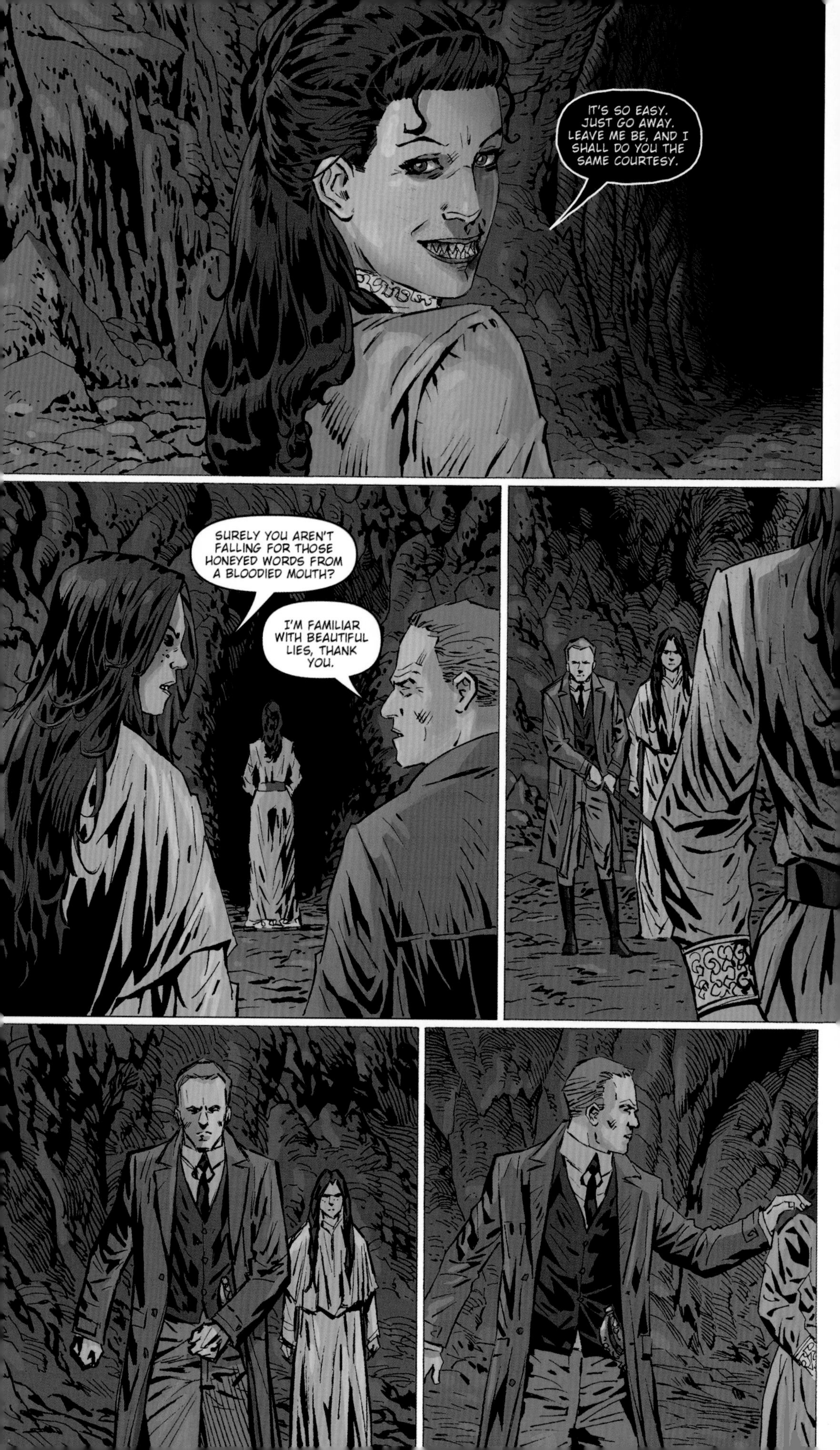
IT'S SO EASY. JUST GO AWAY. LEAVE ME BE, AND I SHALL DO YOU THE SAME COURTESY.
SURELY YOU AREN'T FALLING FOR THOSE HONEYED WORDS FROM A BLOODIED MOUTH?
I'M FAMILIAR WITH BEAUTIFUL LIES, THANK YOU.

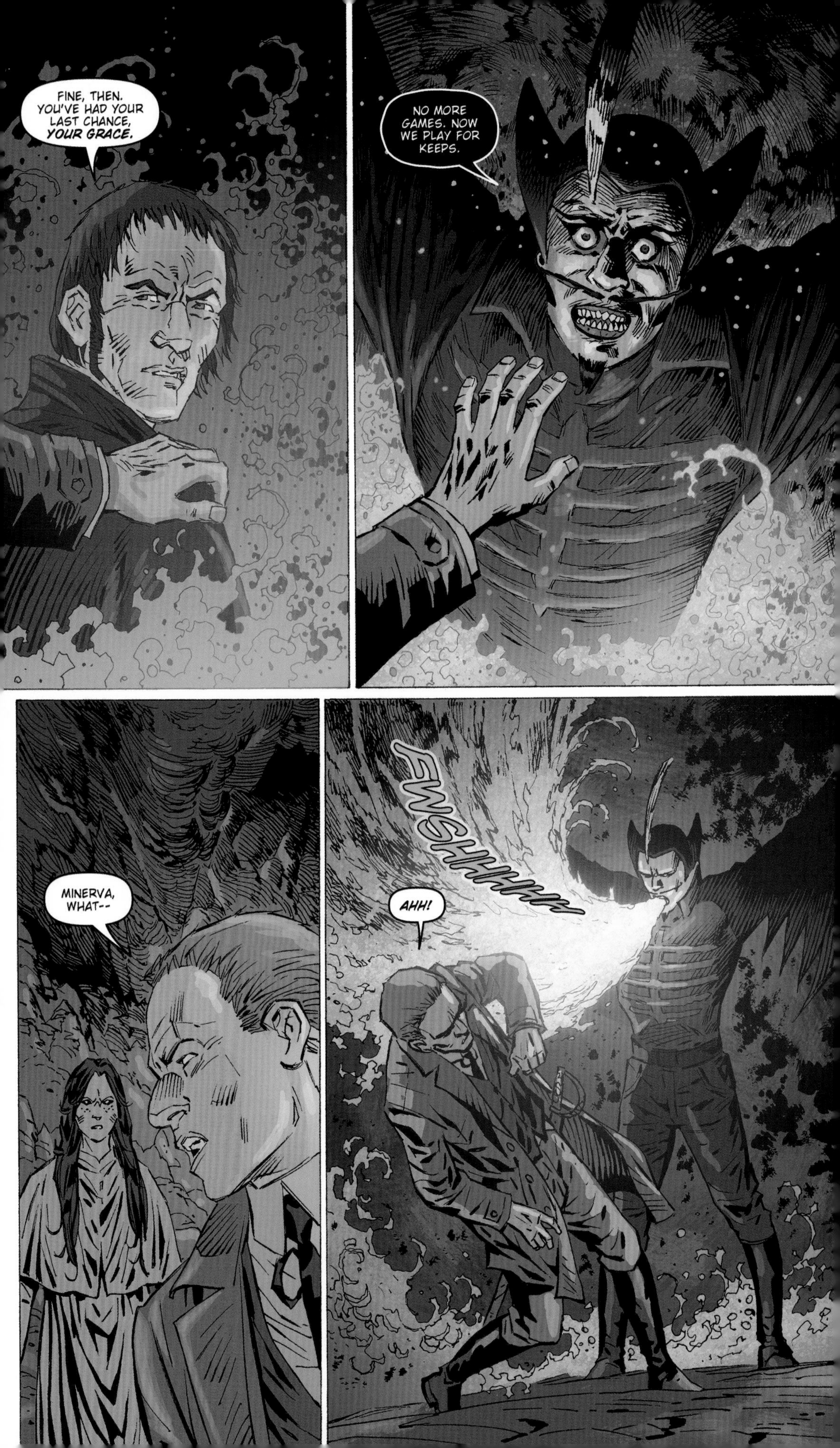
FINE, THEN. YOU'VE HAD YOUR LAST CHANCE, *YOUR GRACE.*
NO MORE GAMES. NOW WE PLAY FOR KEEPS.
MINERVA, WHAT--
FWSHHHHH
AHH!

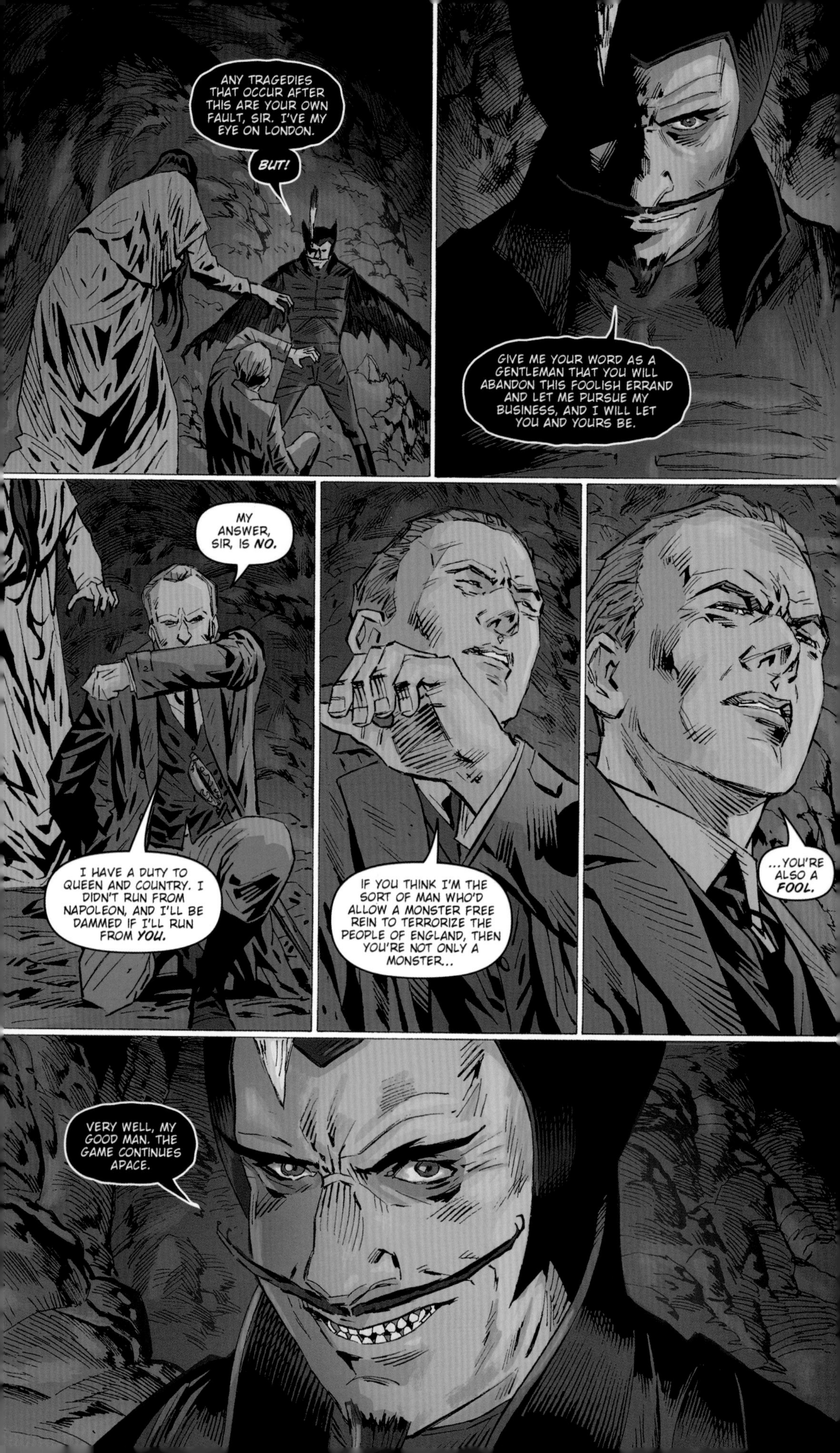
ANY TRAGEDIES THAT OCCUR AFTER THIS ARE YOUR OWN FAULT, SIR. I'VE MY EYE ON LONDON.
BUT!
GIVE ME YOUR WORD AS A GENTLEMAN THAT YOU WILL ABANDON THIS FOOLISH ERRAND AND LET ME PURSUE MY BUSINESS, AND I WILL LET YOU AND YOURS BE.
MY ANSWER, SIR, IS NO.
I HAVE A DUTY TO QUEEN AND COUNTRY. I DIDN'T RUN FROM NAPOLEON, AND I'LL BE DAMMED IF I'LL RUN FROM YOU.
IF YOU THINK I'M THE SORT OF MAN WHO'D ALLOW A MONSTER FREE REIN TO TERRORIZE THE PEOPLE OF ENGLAND, THEN YOU'RE NOT ONLY A MONSTER...
...YOU'RE ALSO A FOOL.
VERY WELL, MY GOOD MAN. THE GAME CONTINUES APACE.

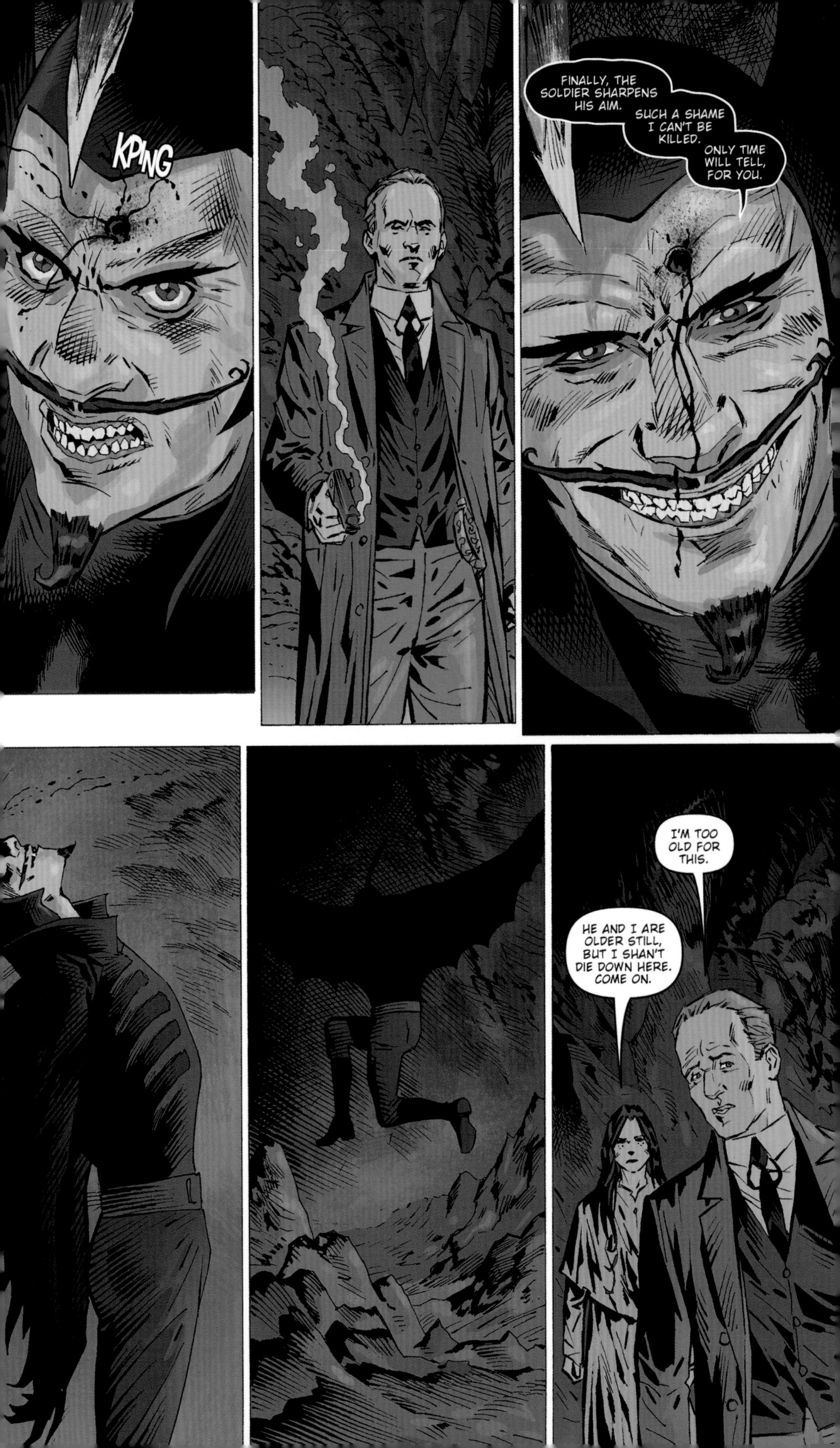
KPING
FINALLY, THE SOLDIER SHARPENS HIS AIM.
SUCH A SHAME I CAN'T BE KILLED.
ONLY TIME WILL TELL, FOR YOU.
I'M TOO OLD FOR THIS.
HE AND I ARE OLDER STILL, BUT I SHAN'T DIE DOWN HERE. COME ON.

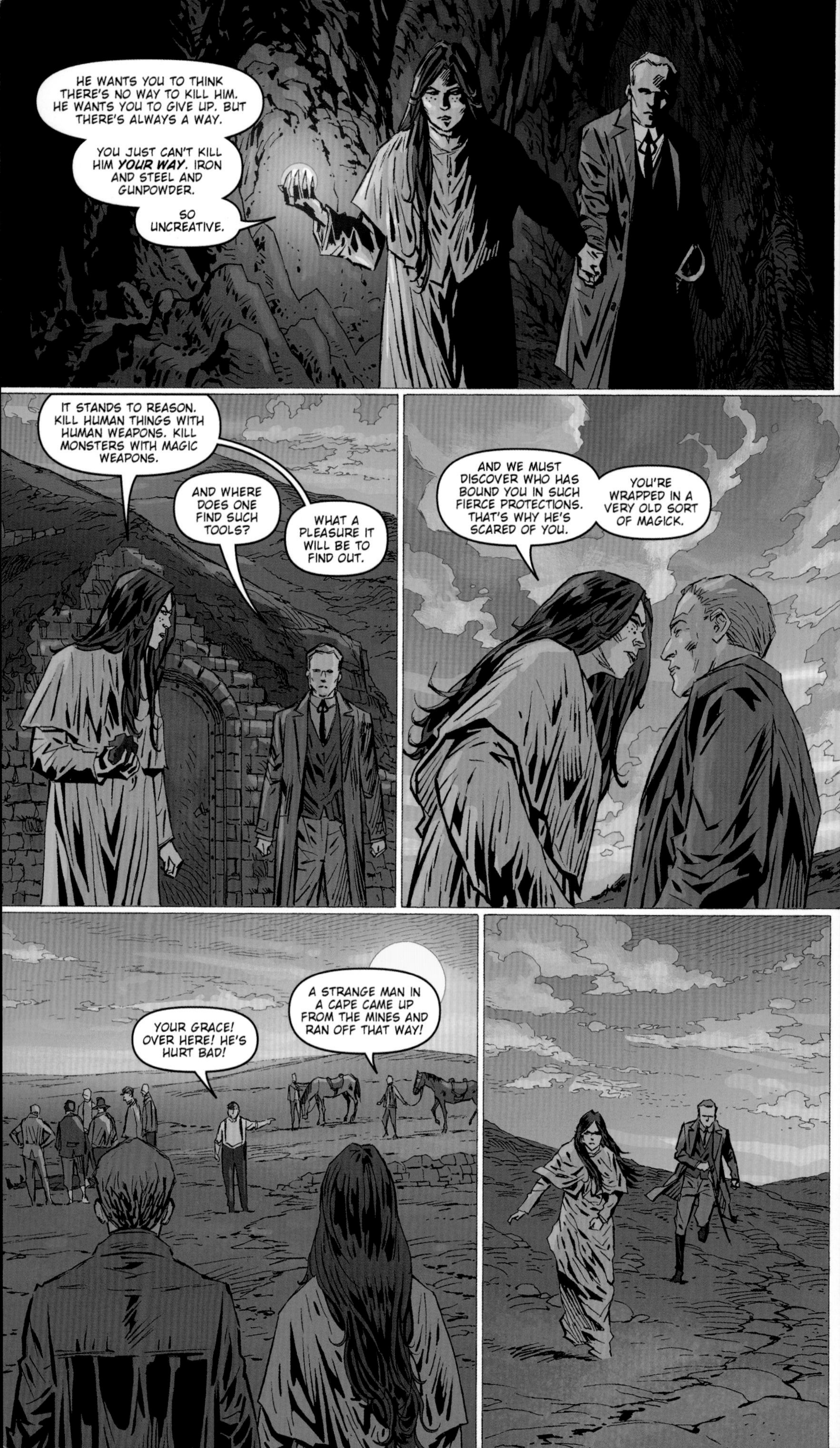
HE WANTS YOU TO THINK THERE'S NO WAY TO KILL HIM. HE WANTS YOU TO GIVE UP. BUT THERE'S ALWAYS A WAY.
YOU JUST CAN'T KILL HIM *YOUR WAY*. IRON AND STEEL AND GUNPOWDER.
SO UNCREATIVE.
IT STANDS TO REASON. KILL HUMAN THINGS WITH HUMAN WEAPONS. KILL MONSTERS WITH MAGIC WEAPONS.
AND WHERE DOES ONE FIND SUCH TOOLS?
WHAT A PLEASURE IT WILL BE TO FIND OUT.
AND WE MUST DISCOVER WHO HAS BOUND YOU IN SUCH FIERCE PROTECTIONS. THAT'S WHY HE'S SCARED OF YOU.
YOU'RE WRAPPED IN A VERY OLD SORT OF MAGICK.
YOUR GRACE! OVER HERE! HE'S HURT BAD!
A STRANGE MAN IN A CAPE CAME UP FROM THE MINES AND RAN OFF THAT WAY!

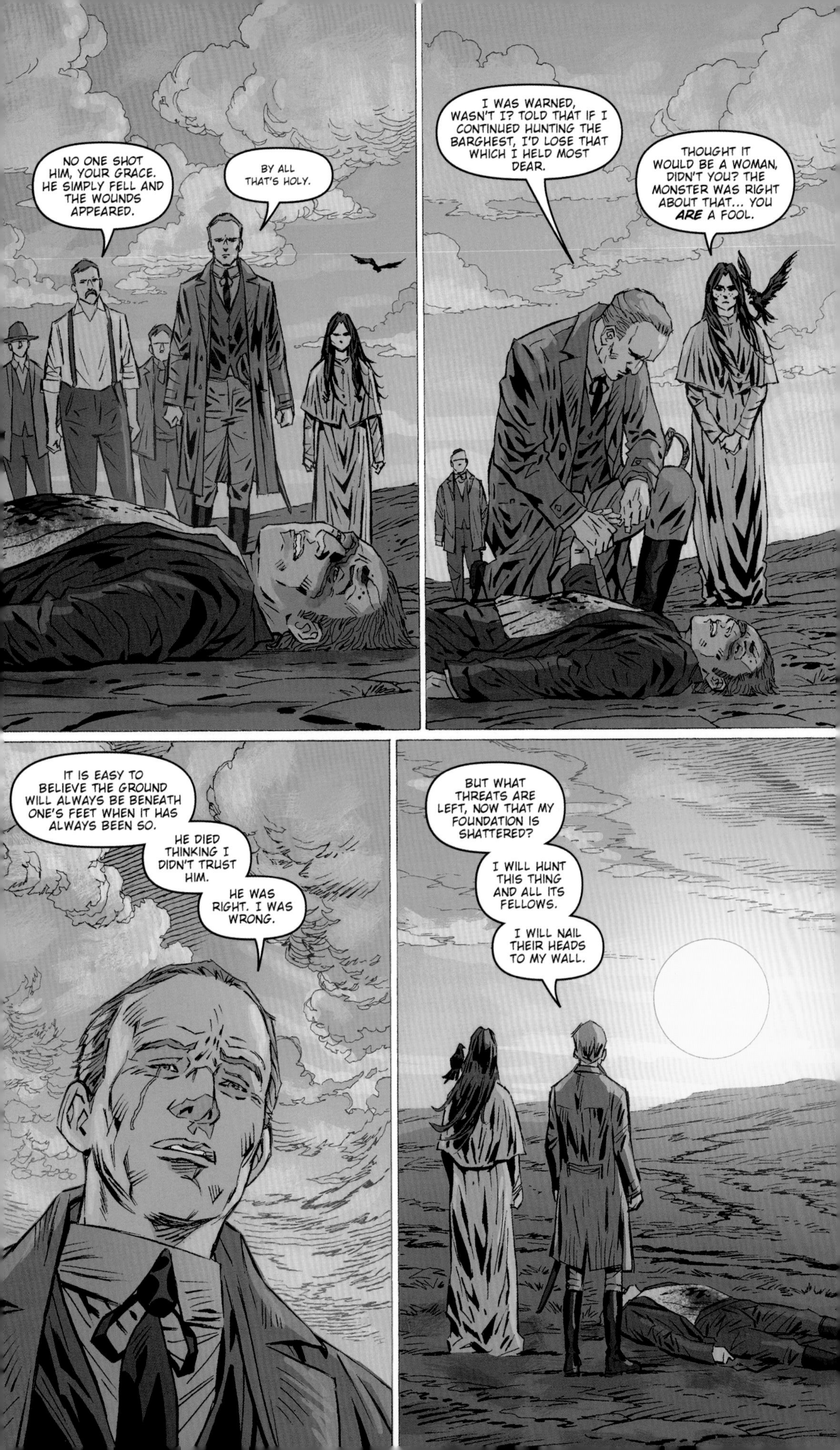
NO ONE SHOT HIM, YOUR GRACE. HE SIMPLY FELL AND THE WOUNDS APPEARED.
BY ALL THAT'S HOLY.
I WAS WARNED, WASN'T I? TOLD THAT IF I CONTINUED HUNTING THE BARGHEST, I'D LOSE THAT WHICH I HELD MOST DEAR.
THOUGHT IT WOULD BE A WOMAN, DIDN'T YOU? THE MONSTER WAS RIGHT ABOUT THAT... YOU ***ARE*** A FOOL.
IT IS EASY TO BELIEVE THE GROUND WILL ALWAYS BE BENEATH ONE'S FEET WHEN IT HAS ALWAYS BEEN SO.
HE DIED THINKING I DIDN'T TRUST HIM.
HE WAS RIGHT. I WAS WRONG.
BUT WHAT THREATS ARE LEFT, NOW THAT MY FOUNDATION IS SHATTERED?
I WILL HUNT THIS THING AND ALL ITS FELLOWS.
I WILL NAIL THEIR HEADS TO MY WALL.

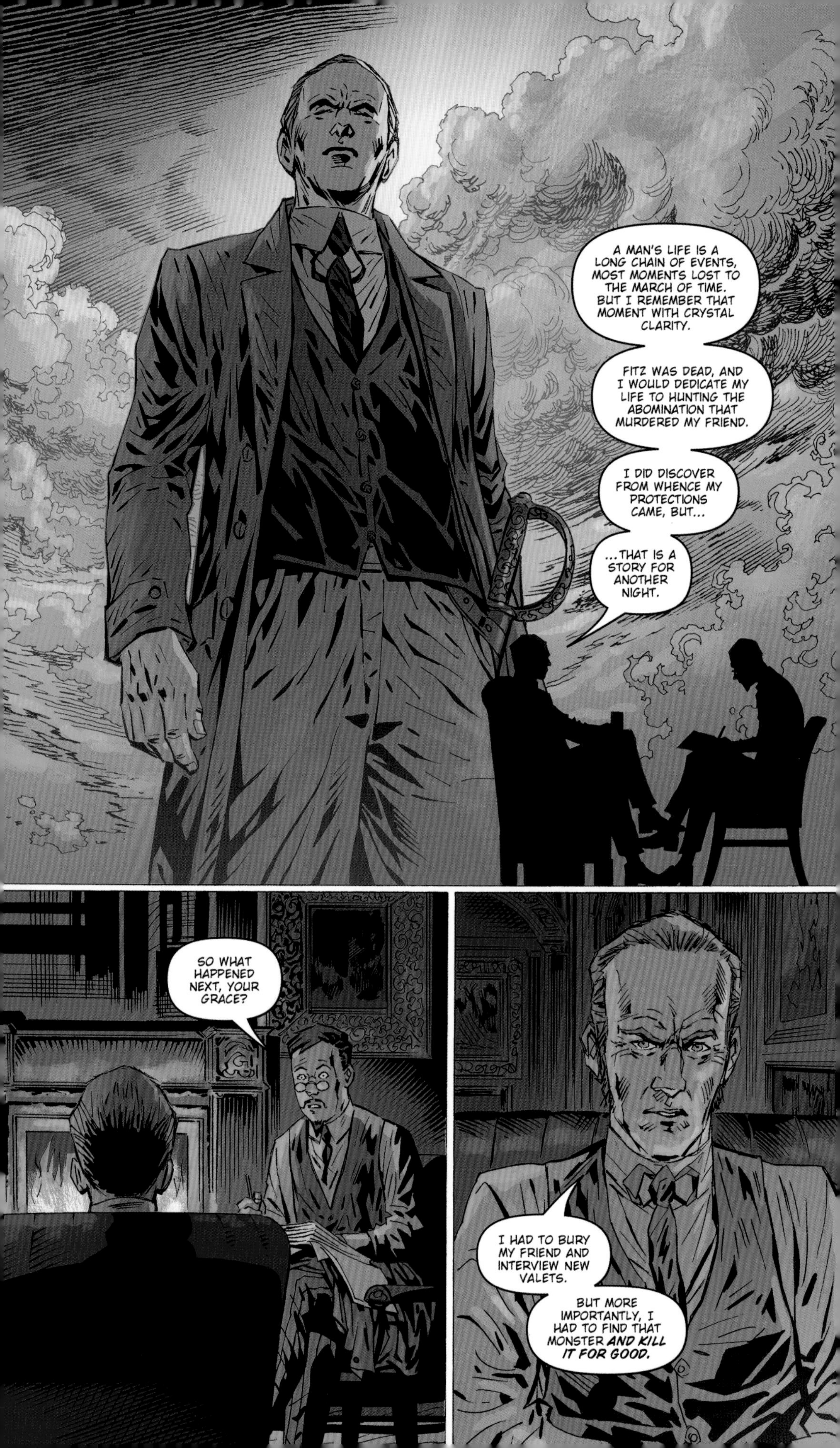
A MAN'S LIFE IS A LONG CHAIN OF EVENTS, MOST MOMENTS LOST TO THE MARCH OF TIME. BUT I REMEMBER THAT MOMENT WITH CRYSTAL CLARITY.
FITZ WAS DEAD, AND I WOULD DEDICATE MY LIFE TO HUNTING THE ABOMINATION THAT MURDERED MY FRIEND.
I DID DISCOVER FROM WHENCE MY PROTECTIONS CAME, BUT...
...THAT IS A STORY FOR ANOTHER NIGHT.
SO WHAT HAPPENED NEXT, YOUR GRACE?
I HAD TO BURY MY FRIEND AND INTERVIEW NEW VALETS.
BUT MORE IMPORTANTLY, I HAD TO FIND THAT MONSTER ***AND KILL IT FOR GOOD.***

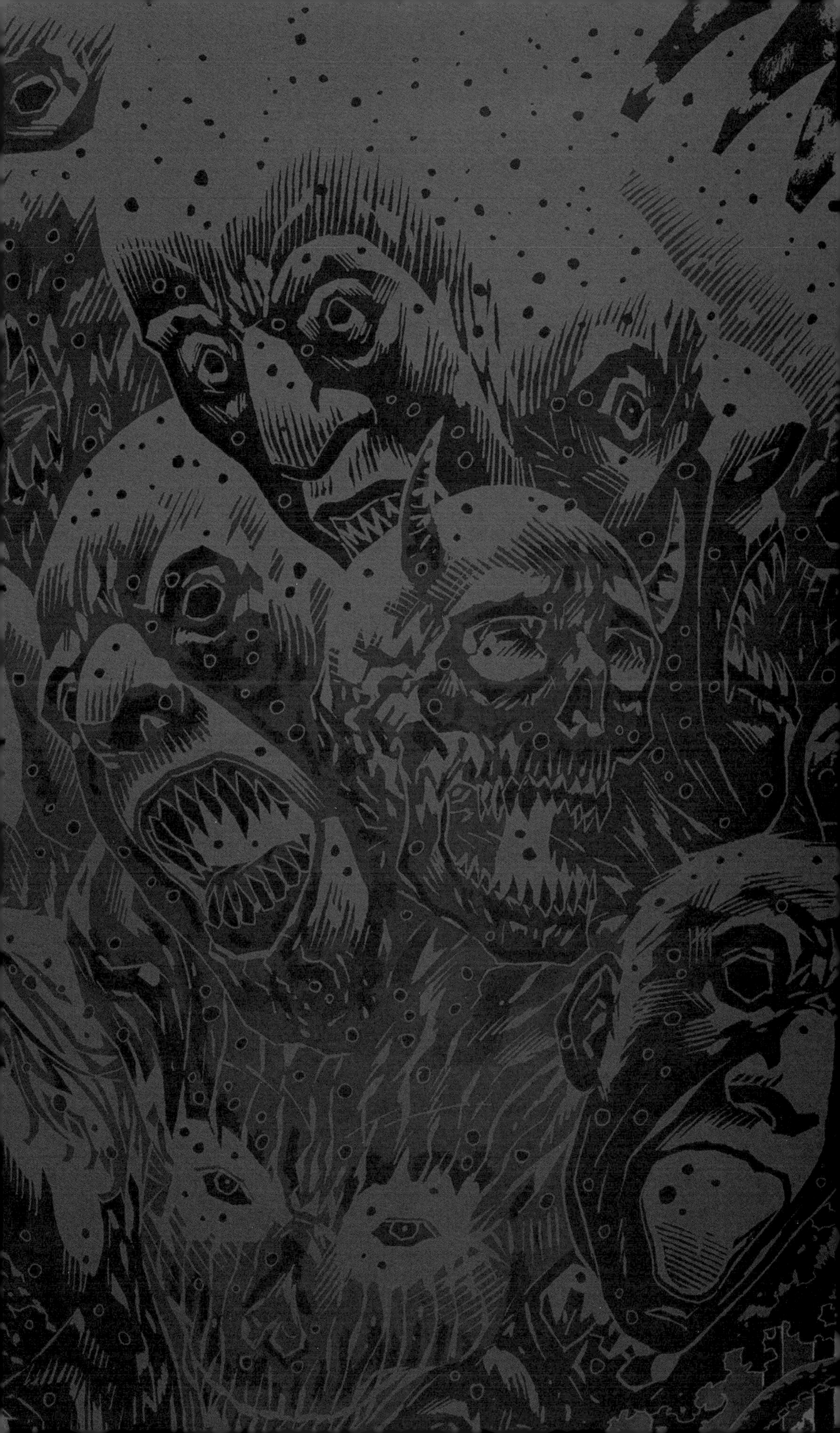

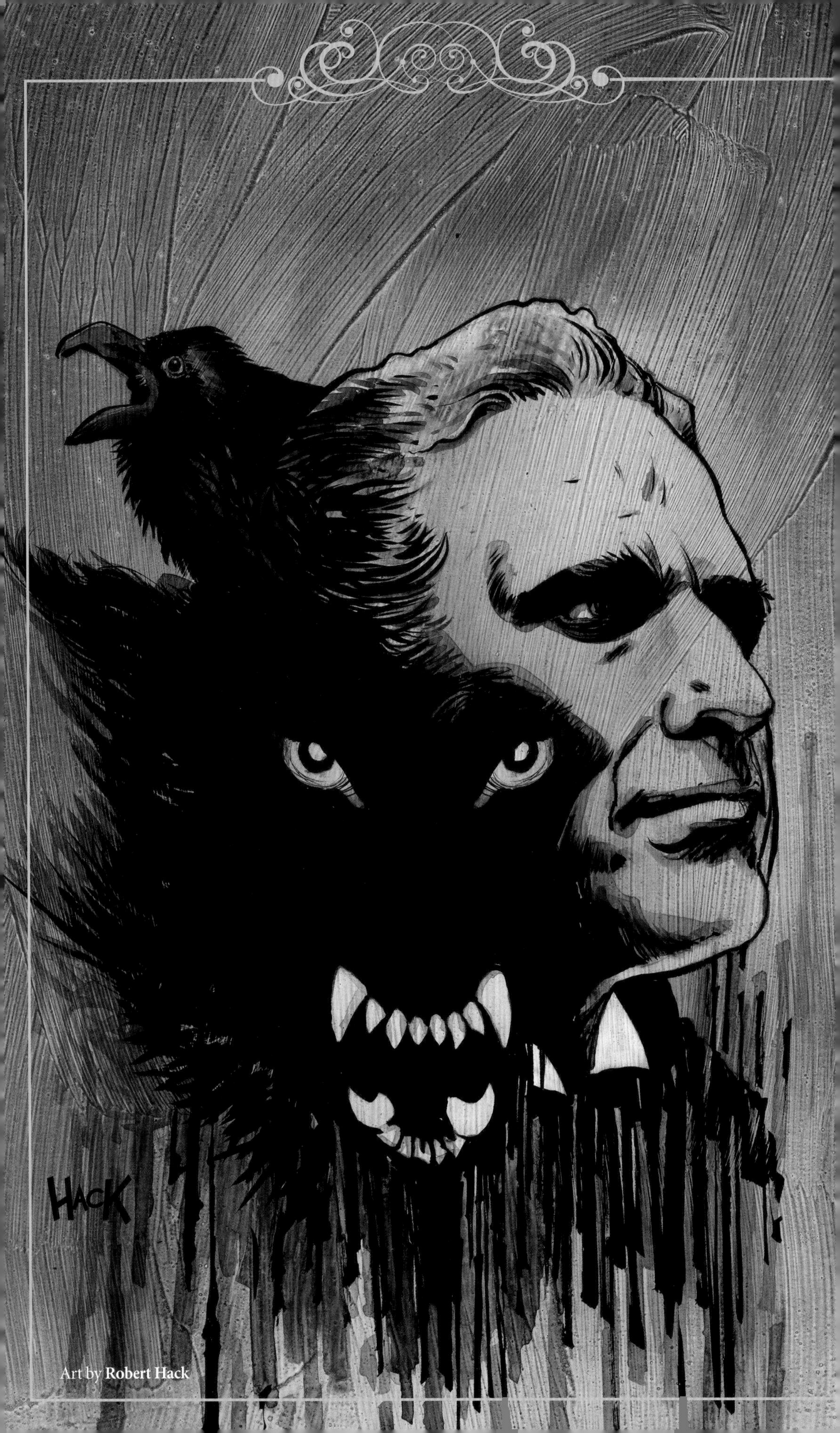
HACK
Art by Robert Hack

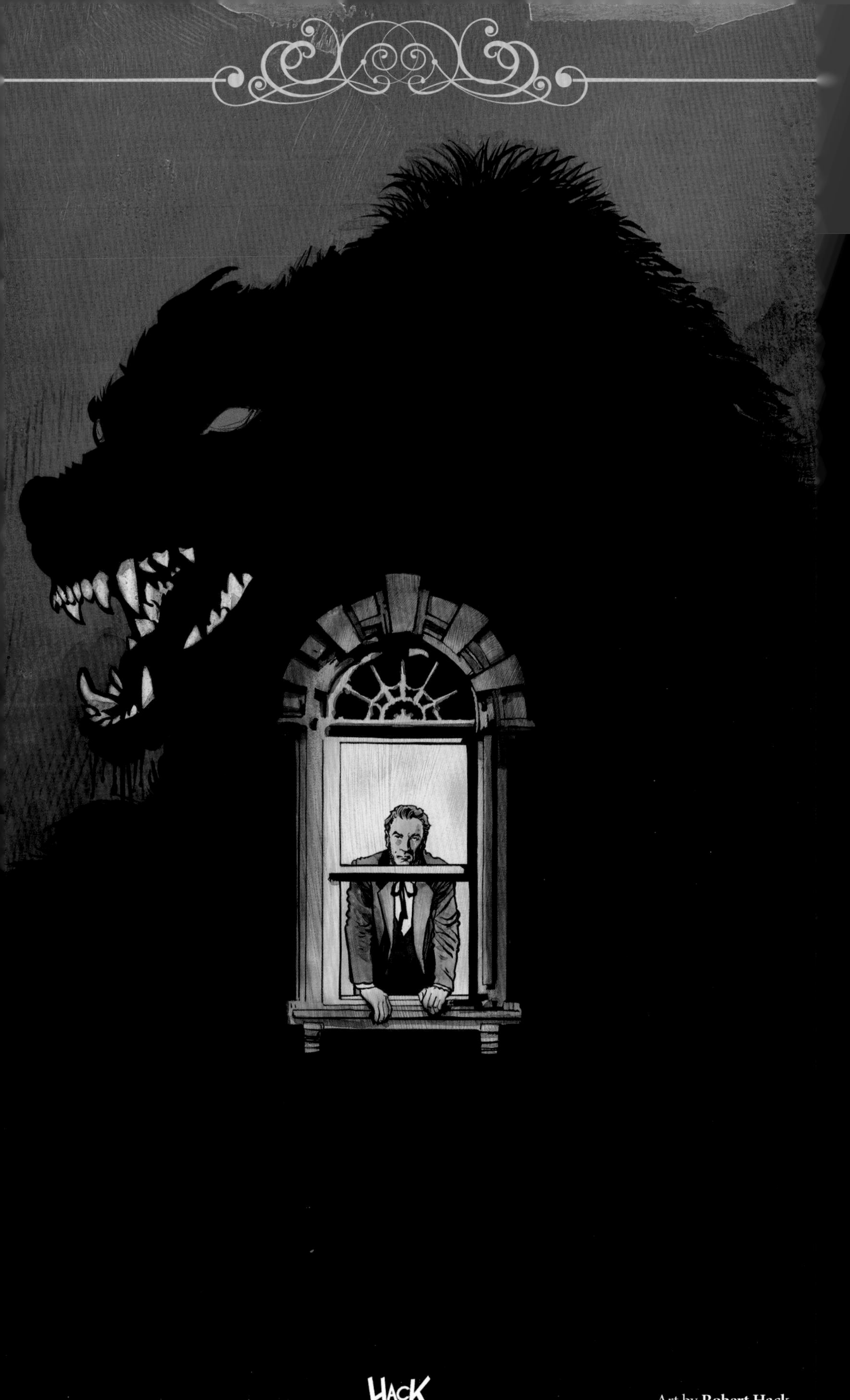
HACK

Art by **Robert Hack**

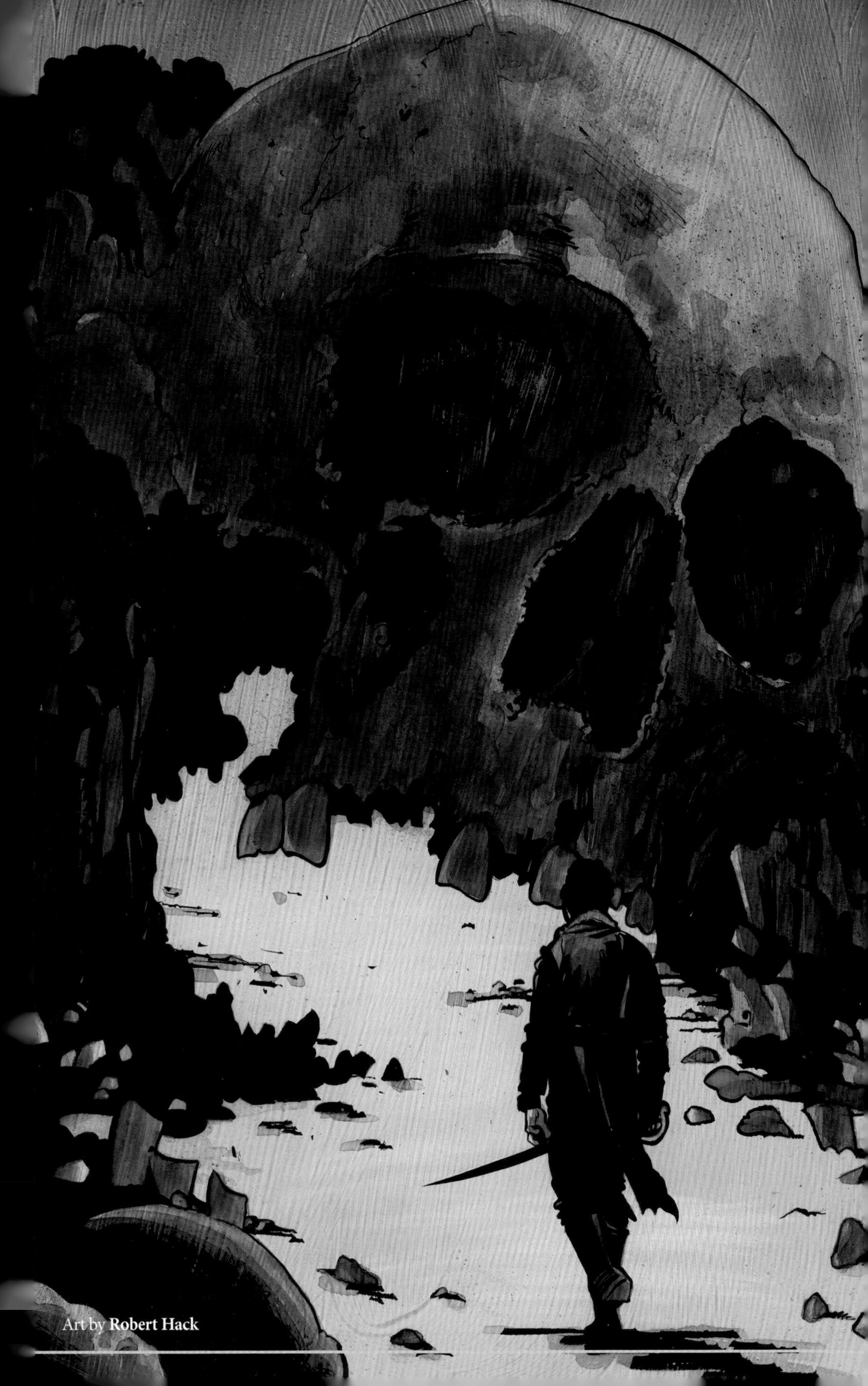

Art by Robert Hack

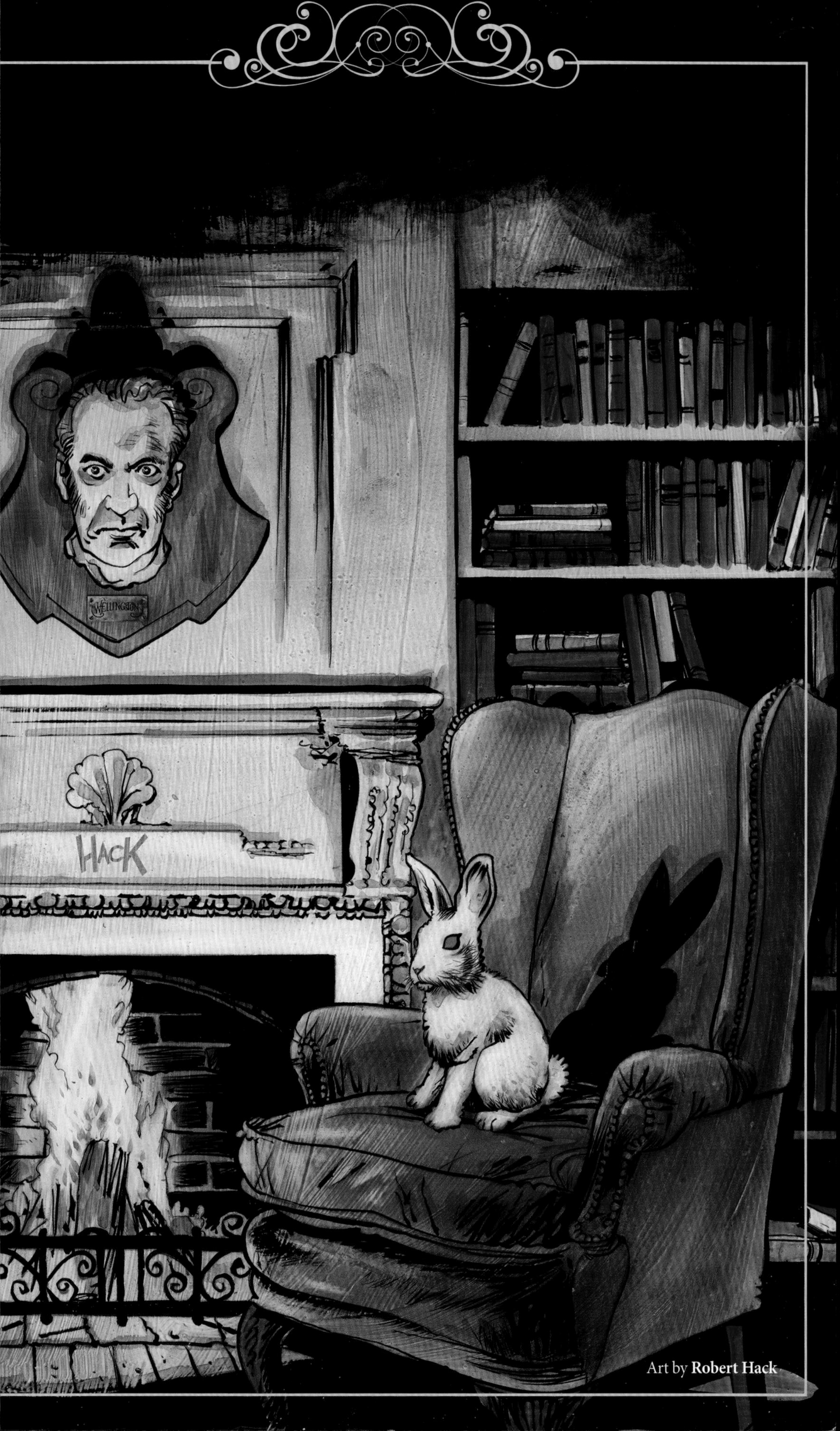
WELLINGTON
HACK

Art by **Robert Hack**

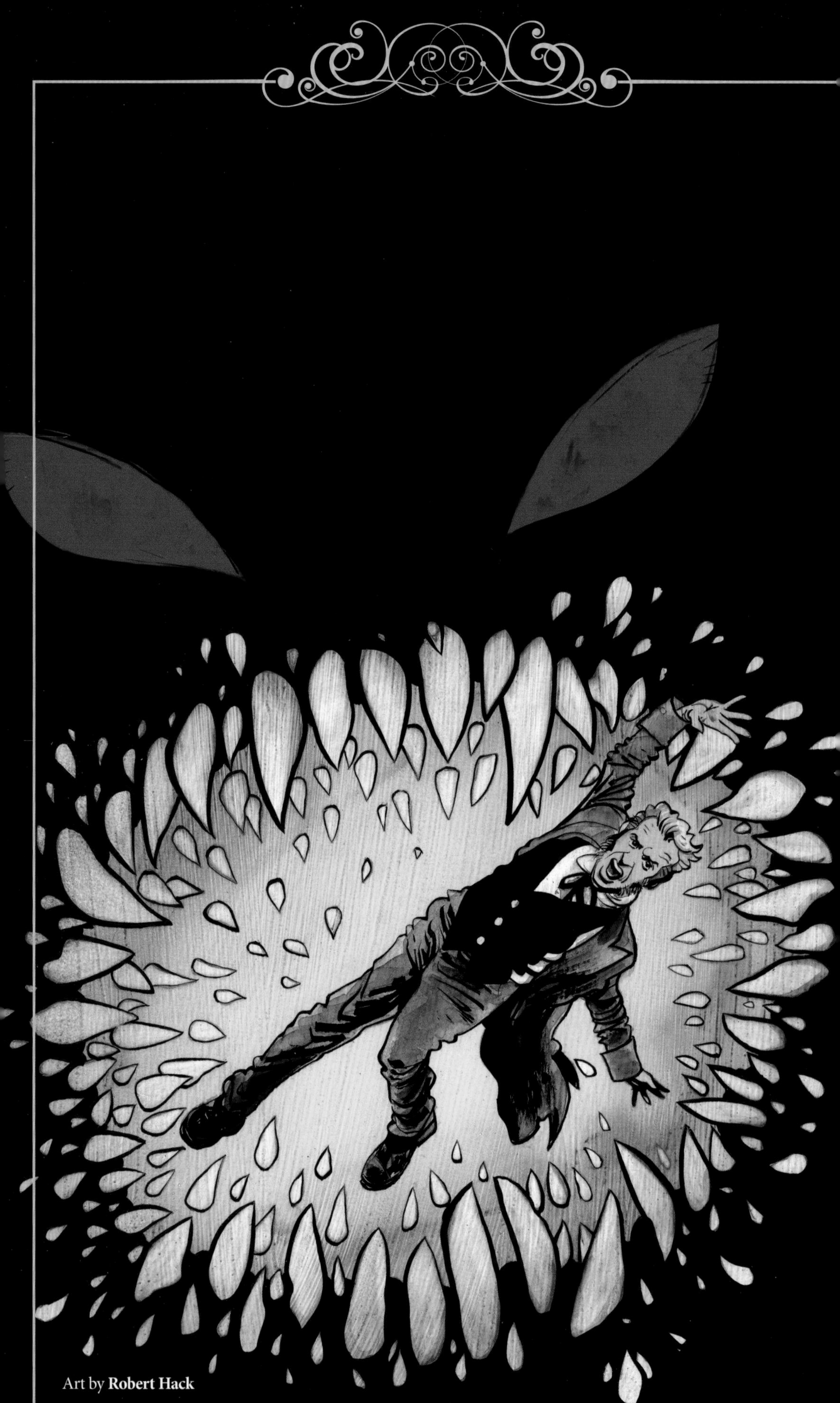

Art by **Robert Hack**

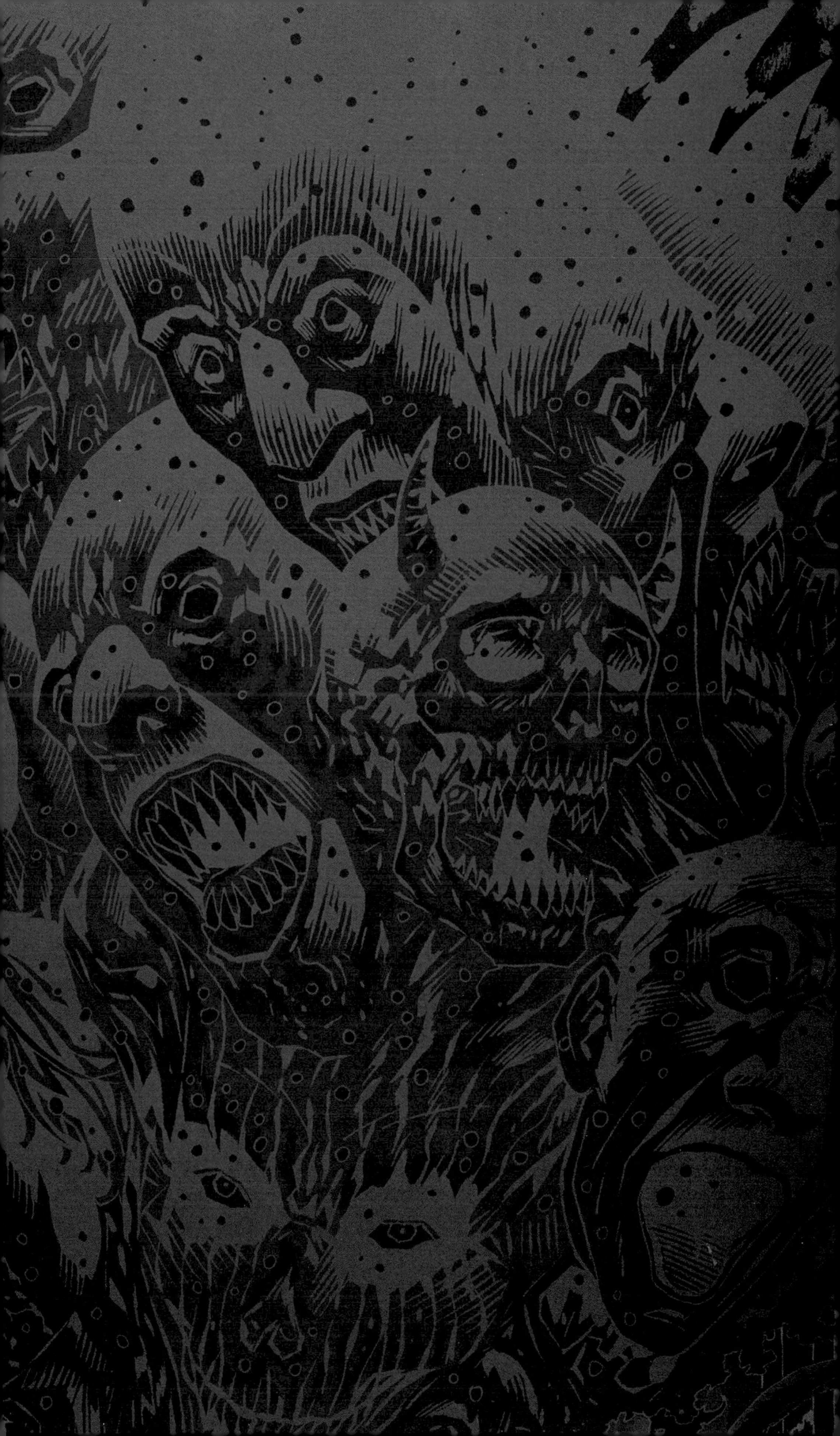

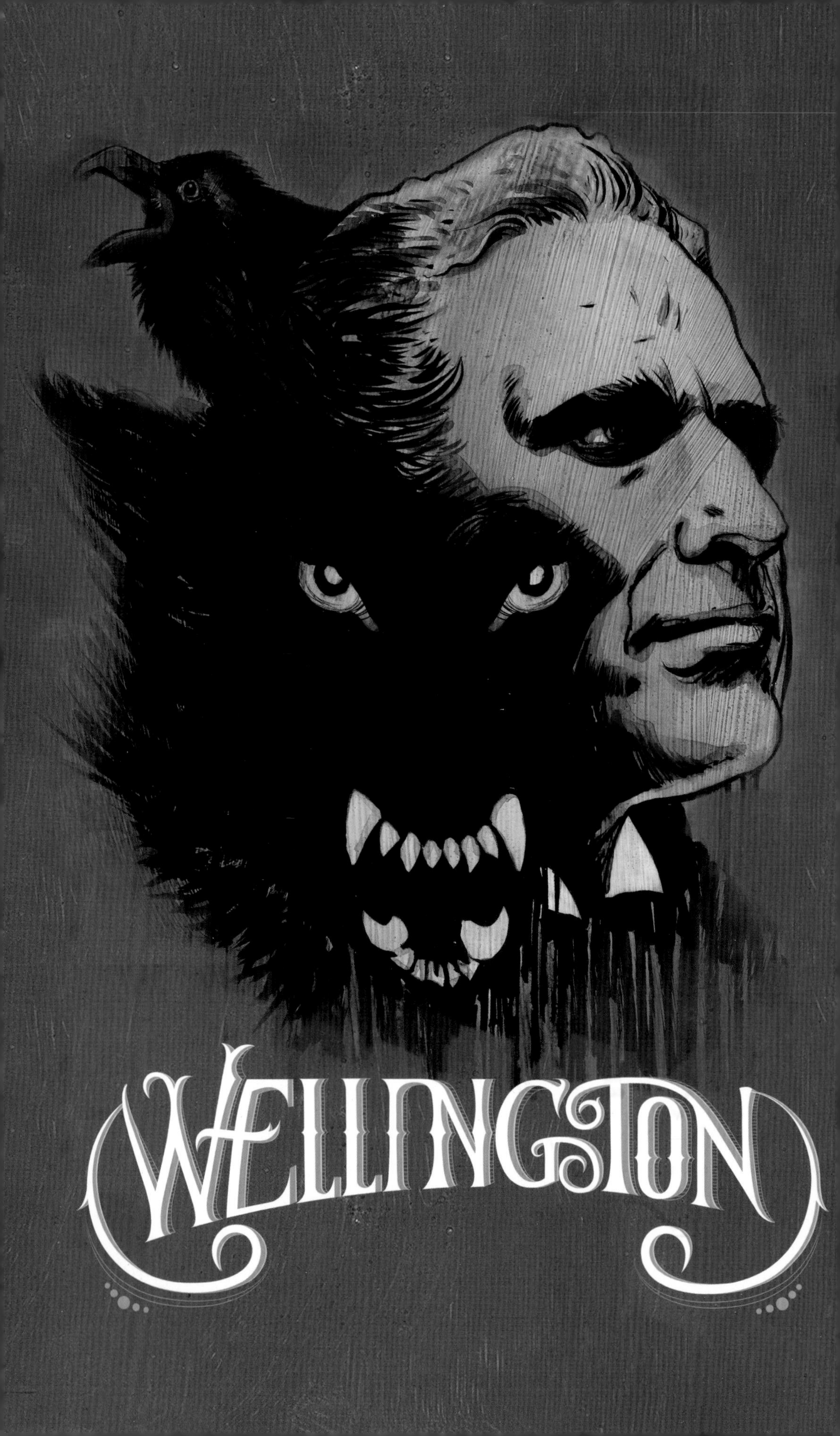
WELLINGTON